D0863533

THE QUEEN'S
NECKLACE

ANTAL SZERB

THE QUEEN'S NECKLACE

Translated from the Hungarian by
Len Rix

PUSHKIN PRESS
LONDON

First published in Hungarian as
A Királyné Nyaklánca in 1942
© Estate of Antal Szerb

English translation © Len Rix 2009

This edition first published in 2009 by

Pushkin Press
12 Chester Terrace
London NW1 4ND

ISBN 978 1 906548 08 7

Supported by the National Lottery through
Arts Council England

All rights reserved. No part of this publication may be
reproduced, stored in a retrieval system or transmitted in
any form or by any means, electronic, mechanical,
photocopying, recording or otherwise,
without prior permission in writing from
Pushkin Press

Cover: *Marie-Antoinette and her Children*
Élisabeth Vigée-Lebrun 1787
© The Bridgeman Art Library

Frontispiece: Antal Szerb
© Petőfi Literarisches Museum Budapest

Set in 10.5 on 13 Baskerville Monotype
and printed in Great Britain by TJ International Ltd
Padstow Cornwall

LOTTERY FUNDED

THE QUEEN'S
NECKLACE

The times we live in teach literary people like myself to look beyond our usual subjects and seek fresh inspiration in history.

Medieval and modern history is the history of nation states, and the first duty of the sons of those nations is to write about their own past. But there are two particular periods, the Italian Renaissance and the French Revolution, which are so universally important and seminal that they can be thought of as part of the common inheritance of the entire European race. The mood of our times has much more in common with the earthquake years in France than with the cosmic spring of Florence, and since the social class I personally belong to, the bourgeoisie, began life under the same fatal stars as the French Revolution, I am not perhaps entirely unqualified to write about it.

In fact the topic more or less chose me. It is one for which I seem to have been more or less unconsciously preparing for a great many years. More difficult was the question of genre. I could have written a scholarly study, a monograph. But the subject is a vast one, and has been so thoroughly worked over that I would have been obliged to focus on some rather minor aspect, and to deal with even the most minuscule of those would have required the sort of study I could have carried out only in those beloved haunts of my youth, the great libraries of Paris—now closed to me for the indeterminate future.

I might have written a novel, and, I must confess, that idea tempted me for some time. But I was as wary of tackling historical fiction as I would have been of setting a novel in a country I had never visited. A kind of respectful diffidence held me back from putting words they had never spoken into the mouths of once-living people, assigning feelings to them which

I could not be sure were not my own, and taking them down paths they had never trod.

And so I arrived at a genre for which at the time I had no name: I have called it a 'real history', because it eschews every kind of novelistic embellishment and amplification, and because it treats a well-known episode (from the time of Louis XVI) which historical scholarship has explored in minute detail. The very nature of the event was such that it can be seen as symbolic of the whole period, because, like an ideal work of drama, it contains within itself everything that is both quintessential and representative in the multi-faceted mass of events. Furthermore it can be treated as a viewpoint from which perspectives open out into every aspect of the age, like gazing out from one of those fountains in the grounds of Versailles from which avenues radiate, like a star, in all directions; and I have made every effort to explore those avenues.

The raw material of my narrative, the story of the necklace trial, is taken by and large from Frantz Funck-Brentano's *L'Affaire du Collier*—The Affair of the Necklace—an admirable treatise based on an exhaustive study of a vast treasury of documents. My purpose is not to shed any radically new light on the affair— Funck-Brentano's work puts any thought of that out of the question. Rather, as I have already said, I use it as a vantage point from which to take a bearing on the approaching Revolution. For this reason I do not confine myself very strictly to the story of the necklace; rather I attempt to weave into my discourse every "significant minor detail", following that unsurpassably great master Hippolyte Taine, to whom, once our youthful fascination with the history of ideas is over, we all return in our maturity. I explain the facts in as much depth as seems necessary, and as far as I understand them, but I do so in the chastening consciousness that, in the final analysis, all historical events defy explanation.

ANTAL SZERB 1942

Statement found among Antal Szerb's posthumous papers, and published on the occasion of the first printing of The Queen's Necklace.

Nothing gives me greater pleasure than to hear that some acquaintance has, to his immense surprise, read one of my books of literary history as if it were a novel. For that is exactly what I intended—to rescue the material from the layers of schoolroom dust and give it a living reality, thus moulding people's tastes by making them want to read not just best-sellers but also the great works of so-called 'literary history'. The literary historian must, first and foremost, be a propagandist, an advertising executive in the service of the eternal values. But naturally there are two sides to this. People in this country expect scholarly works to be unreadable; from which they are led, quite logically, to the erroneous conclusion that anything that is readable cannot therefore be scholarly. A great many critics have reproved the relaxed, often slightly mocking, tone of my books, insisting that I cannot possibly respect literature if I talk about it in such a cheerfully familiar way. To which I can only respond with a saying of Jules Renard: "You just don't like ironical people. They make fun of their own deepest feelings. That is like saying: 'this father cannot love his children because he plays with them'."

And now I have written a book on a historical subject. Naturally my critics will now complain that I fail to respect history. And properly speaking, they are right. I don't 'respect' it. Why should I? The past was in no way superior to the present, and what the present is like I have no need to tell you. So I may not 'respect' it, but on the other hand I do love it. Feelingly, deeply, passionately. The way I love Italy. And tea. And sleep. History is my home. Or rather, perhaps, my country of refuge. So I would say to my reader: if he absolutely insists that a writer should address him in the scholarly manner, from on high, in *ex cathedra* tones, then he should simply toss this book on the floor. My way is to speak as one human being to another, looking to find kindred spirits and good company.

The book tells the well-known story of Marie-Antoinette's necklace, or rather, it describes events leading up the French Revolution. It differs from the usual historical biography, first, in that it is not a biography at all, and secondly, and more importantly, in that I do not content myself with narrating events. I also attempt to explain them, together with their antecedents and consequences, placing them in their intellectual and spiritual contexts. In doing so, I attempt, within the framework of my tale—a tale that is both remarkably eventful and yet true to life from beginning to end—to show French society in the age of Louis XVI, along with its literature, prevailing sensibility and notable personalities, and to bring all this together in a living tableau, rich in implication, which provides a picture of the way the French Revolution came about. In terms of form, the book is somewhat experimental, and I am naturally curious to see how it will be received by the public.

Chapter One

The Necklace

IN THE DECADES LEADING UP to the Great Revolution, two German jewellers lived in Paris: Charles August Boehmer—whose name the French mispronounced as "Bo-emer"—and Paul Bassenge, whose surname reveals his family's French origins. His forebears, Huguenot refugees, had lived in Leipzig until this particular Bassenge was born, in Paris, and went on to become a partner in the firm belonging to the ageing Boehmer. Boehmer was by then very well known. During the reign of Louis XV he had purchased for himself the title of *Joaillier de la Couronne et de la Reine*—Jeweller by appointment to the Crown and the Queen.

The two men, or at least Boehmer, who plays the larger role in the main events of our story, must have been rather exceptional. They were driven by a passionate dream of greatness, and in their own field they strove for fame and immortality. With quiet diligence, over long years, they acquired a collection of the finest diamonds available on the European market; but rather than mount them in accordance with current Parisian taste, or sell them off in order to make their fortunes and, as did all the rising bourgeoisie of the day, use the money to buy the sort of landed estates that would associate them with the nobility, they took a different path. They locked the diamonds away in their shop and then, when they had amassed a vast number, set about creating a masterwork. They constructed what at the time was the most expensive item of jewellery in the world. This record-breaking treasure, the fateful diamond necklace, is the subject of our tale.

Very few people—including those who feature in our narrative—ever saw the necklace, and later we shall learn why. It never hung from anyone's neck, nor, like some sort of curse, did it bring down disaster on those who wore it. But, as with the Nibelungs' treasure in the depths of the Rhine, the short period of time it spent on earth was enough to alter the course of destiny. Diligent research carried out recently among the firm's papers has unearthed the original design, and it is perfectly clear what it was to be: not, we fear, very beautiful. It was to be so impossibly, so barbarically, huge, so like some ancient 'treasure' dug up from an age of nomadic wandering, that it was more likely to have provoked raw amazement than raptures of delight. It consisted of three chains of diamonds from which were suspended diamond medallions, the third and longest chain having several strands and ending in four diamond tassels.

The jewellers originally intended it for the Comtesse du Barry, or rather, they hoped that Louis XV would be persuaded to pay for it. But Louis died suddenly of smallpox, alone and forsaken, Du Barry went into exile at Louveciennes, and the great *sic transit* required Boehmer and Bassenge to look for a new *gloria mundi*. They offered it to the Spanish Court, but the people there took fright at the asking price.

It soon occurred to them that there was one person in the world whom fate had clearly singled out to own such a treasure—the young Queen of France, Marie-Antoinette. History tells us that the kings and queens of old were fond of jewellery, but among Marie-Antoinette's circle this fondness amounted to an ungovernable passion. She did of course have other jewellery, as did other queens. From her home in Vienna, Marie-Antoinette had brought a vast quantity of diamonds in her trousseau; then her husband's grandfather Louis XV showered her with diamonds and the pearls left by his late daughter-in-law, Marie-Josèphe of Saxony. Among these was a necklace of pearls the smallest of which was the size of an aveline (a 'tubular hazelnut', according to Sauvageot's dictionary: perhaps some American variety?). It had once been worn by Anne of Austria, and bequeathed by her to the Queens of France. Since Anne of Austria was the wife of Louis XIII, this could well be the very jewel that graced another famous neck, familiar to us all from Alexander Dumas the Elder's *The Three Musketeers*.

The Queen could hardly accuse either Louis XV or Louis XVI of meanness, but the jewellery she had received so far was still not enough to assuage her passion. Because her mother, the wise and saintly Maria Theresa, was forever scolding her in her letters and telling her that her finest jewel was her youth, she kept her purchases secret. But Boehmer knew her inclinations well. In 1774 he had sold her a pair of earrings containing six diamonds and costing 360,000 francs—also created originally with the Comtesse du Barry in mind. Boehmer had wanted 400,000 francs, but the Queen took out two of his diamonds and replaced them with a pair of her own to reduce the price, and paid off the balance in instalments.

So Boehmer could still hope that the Queen would one day purchase his record-breaking item. But in this he was doomed to disappointment. She showed herself almost willing … it was just that she found the price too high. Even for a queen, 160,000 livres was a considerable sum, especially when things were not going well for her. With France's most popular war ever in mind, the one fought against Britain over American independence, she declared: "We have more need of a warship than of any such necklace".

But the jewel remained. And, like an unwanted and badly-stored body of radioactive material, it continued to emanate a silent, unseen, and fatal influence.

Here we must pause for a minute, take a breath, and give a little thought to the wider economic background to Boehmer's enterprise. Because—this is important—creating jewellery in this way really was an enterprise. He was working not to complete a commission, as his predecessors, the great jewellers and goldsmiths of earlier centuries, had done, and as they say Benvenuto Cellini had worked, but for 'the market'. Boehmer created this piece not to supply an existing demand but to create one. Moreover, the market he was operating in was extremely high-risk in character, since the number of buyers he could count on were extremely few.

The other surprising element in this is his notion of achieving some sort of record—a dream of greatness. Greatness had for many centuries been the prerogative of the two branches of the First Estate, the Church and the Nobility. A knight might think of astounding the world by some unparalleled act of courage; a holy man might hope to rouse the sleeping conscience of his fellow men by some unprecedented and horrifying form of self-denial. In more recent centuries, a thinker or scholar might have aspired to some work that would dwarf all previous efforts in his field. But the bourgeois, the merchant, the mere manufacturer? Even if he did amass a fortune, he would never have done so with the intention of achieving some sort of record, since there would always be those who had even more than he did. But nor was Boehmer simply trying to create a masterpiece, like his predecessors working in the ancient guilds. He wanted to set a new standard not in terms of his craft but as a entrepreneur—to create an item of jewellery not more beautiful but simply more expensive than any other. In his own way, he was a pioneer. And he suffered the pioneer's usual fate.

We know of course that capitalism existed long before Boehmer, but his behaviour was an early example of the peculiar Anglo-American version of it that came to the fore in the second half of the nineteenth century. In his day, it must have been rare indeed.

This also makes him an excellent illustration of the idea that the *Ancien Régime*, the age of Louis XV and XVI, is not divided by some vast chasm from what came after the Revolution. Tocqueville, the great political thinker of the last century, tells us that, "In 1789 the French made the most thoroughgoing attempt of any people to ensure that their history would be divided into two distinct parts, with a deep gulf dividing what had been from what was to be." But their more critical and objective successors could no longer take that claim at face value. Tocqueville saw, and for fifty years scholars have been very largely in agreement with him, that the Revolution did not create something new out of nothing. Rather, it was the sudden, almost miraculous ripening of everything that had been sprouting and budding for quite some time, and which would perhaps have come to fruition, only more slowly, had the Revolution never happened.

Which is what makes Boehmer's enterprise so remarkable. It shows that the ur-capitalist mentality, with its drive for growth at any price, and its quest for unprecedented wealth, was already in place by the eighteenth century, creating upheaval and overturning whole worlds just as much then as it did later. It was not, as opponents of the Revolution insist, simply the result of institutions brought into being by that event.

There are other implications too. It is unlikely to have occurred to a jeweller to create a product of absolutely unprecedented size in a climate of national economic gloom. Such an ambition bears witness to the financial self-confidence of an entire generation, or indeed the whole country. It confirms that the Ancien Régime was witness to a strong economic upsurge. Tocqueville was the first to suggest as much, but it was only at the start of the twentieth century that two non-French scholars, the Russian Ardasev and the German Adalbert Wahl, working independently of each other, confirmed his insight using statistically-based scholarly methods.

The boom had already begun under Louis XV, was briefly halted by the Seven Years War, then gathered pace again under Louis XVI. The number of iron mines and furnaces grew. Previously France had bought the iron needed for its manufactures from England and Germany; now it produced its own, in the steelworks of Alsace, Lorraine, Nantes and above all Amboise. There were huge advances in the textile industry, especially in wool-weaving, while Sèvres porcelain, Gobelin tapestries, St Gobain glass, Baccarat crystal and faience ware from Rouen and Nevers supplied the world. The Machine had begun its triumphal progress. Marseilles became one of the world's leading ports. Following the Peace Treaties of Versailles, a trade agreement was made with Britain in 1786 which proved favourable to France's agriculture but rather less so to her commerce and manufacturing. Nonetheless, the country remained the second richest in the world after England. (In the aftermath of the Revolution, it was not until 1835 that trade returned to its level of 1787.) Perhaps we might also mention, as another sign of this accelerating heartbeat, that the stock market had grown to such proportions during the reign of Louis XVI that in 1783 Mirabeau felt obliged to deliver his thundering proclamation against it.

When Louis XVI ascended to the throne, symptoms of wealth were evident on every side. They found exactly the sort of expression you would expect from his reign. The towering coiffures worn by the ladies gave symbolic representation to the general feeling: at the coronation of Louis XVI their heads were as heavily laden as the wheat fields in the countryside.

And the deranged economic situation in the kingdom, the credit deficit that sparked off the Revolution? Well, yes. But that financial crisis involved the Royal Treasury, not the country at large, and certainly not the people. It was a matter of the King's—that is, the State Treasury's, expenditure exceeding its income. The position could have been helped in one of two ways: either by reducing outgoings or increasing revenues. The private tragedy of the monarchy, it could be said, was that given the situation they were in at the time they could not, for purely internal reasons, hope to achieve either. But the relative affluence or poverty of the country as a whole was not the issue.

The general upswing under Louis XVI can be observed not just in the economic arena but also in foreign politics. After the pointless and in some ways disreputable military campaigns of his two predecessors, France, guided by the gentle King and his outstanding Foreign Minister Vergennes, now pursued a sensible policy of peace. Louis resisted the military adventures into which his restless ally Joseph II (Marie-Antoinette's brother, who we know as our own 'hatted king') tried repeatedly to draw him. He involved himself in only one war, against England, over American independence. That war was reasonably painless, with minimal loss of French blood, and long periods of fluctuating fortunes during which the English would occupy French colonies and the French would occupy English ones, until at last, in 1781, the combined American and French armies achieved their decisive victory at Yorktown. In 1782 Lafayette, the French hero of the American war, returned home to be crowned with laurel in the Opera House. On 3rd September 1783 the Versailles Peace Treaty was signed (and what a fateful second such treaty was to follow it!). The French were not much pleased by its conciliatory terms, but were nonetheless delighted that they had erased the blot inflicted on their *gloire* during the Seven Years War.

But it was above all in the world of ideas that this all-embracing upsurge could be felt. In 1780, Tocqueville tells us, the French lost the feeling that their country was in decline, and it is precisely at this moment that we see the emergence of the belief in human perfectibility, the notion that in time both man and the world could become ever better and better—in short, the idea of Progress. The signs were everywhere: flying boats soaring into the skies—Montgolfier with his hot-air balloon and Charles suspended beneath one filled with hydrogen; some, like Pilâtre de Rozier, plunging into *La Manche* and drowning; others, like Blanchard, flying over it and planting the French flag on the English side. New machines were being invented, new medicines discovered. Under Buffon's canny eye the immense age of the planet was coming to light. Since the excavations at Pompeii the glories of the ancient world had come to enjoy a new renaissance, and people were starting to have a true understanding both of how it felt to be alive in those days, and of the classical cult of beauty: *magnus ab integro saeculorum nascitur ordo*—A whole new order is being born out of the fullness of time.

No, in no way could it be said that this was an age of decadence, the morbidly-beautiful autumn of an old and dying regime. Historical periods cannot be likened to decades: each carries the seeds of the next. Everyone knows Talleyrand's famous observation: "No one who has not lived under the Ancien Régime can know the full sweetness of life." Familiarity with that sweetness was of course confined to those of privileged birth, and they were rather few in number. Even so, for everyone else the France of Louis XVI can hardly have been hell, though at the height of its raging turmoil they came close enough to it.

At the end of the eighteenth century France was 'in training'. Spengler uses this sporting term for those nations capable of shaping both their own history and that of the wider world. France was in training, limbering up for the great Rationalist miracle that no one saw coming—the Revolution. The purpose of this history is to explore the secret workings of that process of unconscious preparation.

Chapter Two

The Comtesse

HAVING NOW INTRODUCED OUR SUBJECT, that is, our subject with a capital *S*—the fateful Nibelung Treasure—we should now, as in the old films, present the actors centre stage. These portraits, and the histories behind them, will claim a fair amount of space, but that is only natural insofar as our tragedy—or comedy—is one of character, as our school textbooks conceive of the form: if we placed such and such a person in a given situation on stage, each would be bound to behave in such and such a way, their fates following from their characters. By simply stating what sort of people we are dealing with we shall have told you half our story.

Our heroine, or rather, one of our heroines, the Comtesse de la Motte, began her career at a rather humble level. When she first appears on our stage, she is eight years old and a beggar. Prior to that, she had tended geese, but reluctantly.

The Marquise de Boulainvilliers, accompanied by her husband, was on her way by coach to their estate at Passy, which at that time was not a suburb of Paris but a separate little village, some way from the capital, where Parisians took their holidays. The carriage was going very slowly. A little girl, holding an even smaller child in her arms, ran towards the coach and began to beg, in the following remarkable terms:

"In God's sacred name I implore you, spare a few coppers for two little orphans who carry the royal blood of Valois."

Something about her appearance, it seems, lent a mysterious emphasis to her words. Despite her husband's protests, the Marquise halted the chaise. The little girl had already launched into her strange tale. Her Ladyship heard her out, and declared that if what she was saying could be proved, she would give her a home and be a second mother to her.

She duly pursued the matter, making enquiries among the local people, especially the parish priest to whose flock the little mendicants belonged. In the entire story of the necklace, says Stefan Zweig, the strangest thing is that even its least credible details turn out to be rooted in fact. The priest confirmed, with incontrovertible evidence, that the little girl's story was true. The royal blood of Valois did indeed run in their veins.

They were descended in a direct line on their father's side from Henri II (the son of François I, The Great) who ruled from 1547 to 1559. Their great-great-grandfather, Henri de Saint-Rémy, was the offspring of Henri's liaison with Nicole de Savigny; Henri acknowledged his son and declared him legitimate. In terms of blood, they stood perhaps even closer to the throne of St Louis than the ruling Bourbons. Their coat of arms consisted of two bundles of sticks on a field argent, beneath three lilies, the illustrious lilies of Valois. "The little beggar-girl was familiar with the crest, and indeed it was the only thing, in her terrible abandonment, that she did know," declares Funck-Brentano. "And when she spoke in such astonishing detail about it, or about her ancestor the royal bastard born to Nicole de Savigny, her little body, bowed as it was with oppression, became erect, proud and defiant."

And with good reason. The blood of Valois in one's veins— what a fatal inheritance, and what a cursed Nibelung treasure! Perhaps the most fundamental and interesting scholarly debate of our century is whether a person's character and fate are determined before or after birth: by inheritance or environment; by 'genes' or behaviourism; by those mysterious little bodies which are passed on from one's ancestors to one's descendants, or by the 'conditioned reflexes' acquired in childhood, instinctive modes of behaviour, which repeat themselves in response to certain conditions.

Probably both camps are right, or rather, neither is. Inheritance must play some role in shaping human character, as must habits learnt in childhood, and besides the question of personality is highly complicated, and too complex to explain with reference to either of those factors alone or even as the product of the two working together. So perhaps we should not give excessive credence to the notion that the little beggar girl Jeanne inherited much of her nature from the Valois kings. With so many intermarriages down the generations, a proportion of somewhat less-than-aristocratic blood would also have flowed in her veins. A perfectly sufficient explanation of the way her character was shaped lies, as we have seen, in her childhood and her social situation when she became aware of the fact that she was a descendant of the house of Valois: her ancestry did indeed exercise a decisive influence on her fate, not through the mysterious workings of heredity but simply through her consciousness of it.

Nonetheless we might allow ourselves to play with the idea for a moment. They say miraculous throwbacks do occur …

The house of Valois ruled France from 1328 to 1589, throughout the Hundred Years War, the Renaissance and the centuries of barbarism. It was on their account that Joan of Arc was burnt at Rouen; it was they who forged a unified kingdom from a France hitherto divided into feudal estates; their proud armies fought in the Italy of Leonardo and Michelangelo; and it was they who ordered the St Bartholomew's Day massacre. They included lunatics like Charles VI, bloody tyrants like Louis XI, and fiery-spirited Bohemian grandees like François I. They were a great and appalling family, famous hunters, with history resounding in every step they took. So why not see in this proud Jeanne, with her kittenish ferocity, her wildcat defiance and needle-sharp teeth, a spirit harking back to its forebears? Or again, in the story that is about to unfold (essentially a war between two women) why not see it moreover as two ancestral enemies still at each others' throats—two families which, as the 'neighbouring houses' of Habsburg and Valois, shaped all Europe, and whose mutual hatred was passed on to later generations?

The Saint-Rémy family had lived for generations on their estate at Fontette, near Bar-sur-Aube, in the north-eastern part of France. They lived as becomes the sons of princes when not actually on the throne: they farmed and hunted, did the odd bit of poaching, and from time to time discreetly exercised the royal craft of coining. They certainly had need of the last, but, it seems, did not put it to very much use. Jeanne's father, Jacques de Saint-Rémy, Baron de Luz and de Valois, was thoroughly impoverished. He no longer lived in the manor—its roof had fallen in and it was visibly crumbling—but in the farmhouse. He mixed with the peasantry, and married his village sweetheart, who became Jeanne's mother. The woman finally bankrupted him, and when he fell ill she threw him out. He ended his miserable life in the Hôtel Dieu hospital in Paris. She then took up with a soldier; and now the fate of little Jeanne, who had been born in 1756, really took a turn for the worse. She was sent out to beg, and her foster father vented on her all the rage he felt against his own unbearable existence.

It was at this point that, in 1763, the Marquise de Boulainvilliers took little Jeanne into her home, together with her baby sister, who died of smallpox shortly afterwards. Jeanne was raised in a girl's boarding school up to the age of fourteen, after which her patroness placed her with a Parisian dressmaker.

During the years when rococo was in fashion, such establishments ranked among the most celebrated places in Europe, just as they are in our day, perhaps even more so. One of the most striking features of Paris at the time was the number of dressmakers' workshops and couturiers. Louis-Sébastien Mercier, to whom we shall frequently refer, compiled a wonderful inventory of the city in 1781, thus inaugurating that delightful genre, which has become popular only in our time, of books about cities. In his study he devotes a lengthy chapter to the seamstresses:

"They sit in their shops, side by side in rows, in full view from the street windows. They sew pompons, little accessories, the elegant insignia that fashion summons into being and then promptly replaces. You are free to stare in at them, and they are equally free to stare back at you.

"Chained to their workbenches, needle in hand, the girls are forever glancing out into the street. No passer-by can avoid their eye. There is an army of men queuing up to bestow their admiring stares, and a fierce struggle is waged for the place nearest the window.

"The girls are thrilled by the looks directed at then, and each imagines that every man is in love with her. The large number of passers-by simply adds to the variety, increases the glamour and inspires further curiosity. This is what makes their professional bondage tolerable, the combined pleasures of seeing and being seen. But one has to arrange things so that the prettiest girl is always seated nearest the window.

"Every morning they set forth in large numbers, with their baskets of pompons, to call on great ladies at their dressing tables. Their task is to adorn the brows of their rivals in beauty; they must keep their secret sexual jealousies to themselves and behave in a professional manner while titivating the good looks of those who treat them with contemptuous indifference. Sometimes the shop girl is so very pretty that the proud brow of her wealthy patroness pales to insignificance beside her. The beau is instantly unfaithful; his eyes are on the watch only for the fresh little mouth and ruddy face in the corner of the mirror … but she of course has neither footmen nor family.

"Quite a few of these girls will make it in one bound into an English carriage. A month ago she was a mere shop girl; now when she arrives with her wares her head is held high, her face a picture of triumph, while her former supervisor and 'dear, dear colleagues' turn green with envy.

"There are some establishments where the tone is strict and the girls are all very respectful, but even the proprietress finds this astonishing, and recounts the fact to everyone as if it were some sort of universal miracle. It is as if she has a wager that one day she will be able to say, 'There is in Paris one fashion house where every girl is a virgin, and it's all due to my strength of character and vigilance.'"

In a word, we can surmise that Jeanne learnt a great deal more in the shop than she would have at the girls' boarding school where she resided until the age of fourteen.

She learnt a lot, but she was not happy. She had the sort of nature that is never satisfied. There was a burning, mordant restlessness in her, and she could never settle to anything. Such was her nature she would probably have been dissatisfied whatever her circumstances—but how fiercely that inborn dissatisfaction was exacerbated by consciousness of her royal origins! From time to time the Marquise would take her back so that she could keep an eye on her, but in the great house Jeanne felt reduced to the level of a servant, and her sense of painful humiliation simply grew. She remained duly respectful towards her patroness until her Valois ancestry was formally recognised in 1776 and the King granted her a civil-list pension of 800 livres. Then she summoned her one surviving younger sister, Marie-Anne, and together they entered the convent at Longchamps, where only the daughters of the aristocracy were admitted as pupils.

Jeanne was twenty-one, and her restlessness was steadily increasing. No matter what happened, she could not erase the memory of her childhood: she would always be the Valois heir who had begged in the dust of the highway; the *déclassée*: an enemy of the entire social order.

"My indomitable pride I was given by nature," she wrote, "and Mme de Boulainvilliers's charity simply exacerbated it. Oh God, why was I born of Valois blood? Fatal name, you exposed my soul to savage pride! You are the cause of these tears; it is because of you that I am so unhappy."

This sort of person always possesses a certain insinuating eloquence: especially when they are parading their sorrows.

She did not remain long in the convent. She felt not the slightest calling to become a nun, and one fine day she and her sister made their escape. The word went round Bar-sur-Aube that two duchesses had come to recover their ancestral lands and had taken rooms at the very cheapest hotel. A Mme Surmont, wife of the Master of the Law Court and the lynchpin of local society, decided it was her duty to take them—two young ladies in distress, no doubt pursued by mysterious enemies—into her home. Since both were clad in the meanest of attire, she immediately lent each of them one of her own dresses, much to the amusement of the young people present, since the good lady was extremely large. By the next day they had been completely retailored to make a perfect fit. The Master's wife was somewhat taken aback, but she slowly became used to the fact that Jeanne was now mistress of the house. The two girls came for a week and stayed for a year. That year, the lady said later, was the most painful of her entire life.

It was here that Jeanne met Marc-Antoine-Nicolas de la Motte. He was a young nobleman, an officer with the *gendarme* regiment stationed at nearby Lunéville, where his father, a Knight of the Order of St Louis, had also once served. The local aristocracy in Bar were keen on amateur dramatics, as was the whole world at that time. La Motte was considered a great theatrical talent, and there can be no doubt that Jeanne really was one. They were often in the same play. "They recited and rehearsed together," comments Funck-Brentano, in his benevolent elderly manner, "to the point where it became urgently necessary to marry." They were united on 6th June 1780.

The Master's wife finally took the opportunity to throw Jeanne out, and after a period of wandering the young couple settled in Lunéville. Twins were born, but they died soon after, and it seems that, for reasons of economy, Jeanne returned for a while to the convent. Otherwise the couple lived on credit and from La Motte's shady dealings. At around this time he began to call himself Comte.

There is nothing particularly to be said about this gentleman, and no need to describe him in detail. He was one of those suave and thoroughly loathsome characters, those shameless and craven pimps that everyone who goes to France has met by the thousand—a type long established in that country, it seems. He hated work, loved women, was extremely ugly, but thought himself so extraordinarily handsome that every so often some woman or other actually believed him.

In September 1781 the young couple learnt that Jeanne's patroness the Marquise de Boulainvilliers was staying at Saverne Castle as the guest of Cardinal Rohan. The mysterious inner voice that directed all Jeanne's talents spoke again—they packed up and removed to Saverne.

Jeanne was now twenty-five. Her hair was naturally curled and chestnut brown, her eyes blue and expressive, her mouth equally so, if a little on the large side. Her smile was enchanting. As Beugnot, speaking from experience, put it, it "spoke to the heart". Her bosom was considered by contemporaries to be rather underdeveloped. Her main attractions, it seems, were her voice and her conversation. "Nature gave her the dangerous gift of eloquence," said one of the leading actors in the necklace trial, who added: "—eminently suitable for discussing those matters of civil law and ethics of whose existence Mme de la Motte, in all her innocence and eternal naturalness, had not the slightest suspicion."

Chapter Three

The Grand Seigneur

THE GREAT HISTORIANS OF ANTIQUITY, in particular Livy, would always introduce their account of some major event by detailing the signs and auguries that foretold it. This was partly a religious requirement, since they did after all believe in these things, but it was also, it seems, a device to elevate the tone of the writing. The enlightened modern reader is unlikely to subscribe to any such superstition—we naturally do not ourselves—but everything is after all interconnected, and since the ancients were wise men notwithstanding we might just mention one or two such omens.

Goethe, who spent the most titanic years of his youth in Strasbourg, was there when the fourteen-year-old Marie-Antoinette arrived on her way to Paris. Strasbourg, an island on the Rhine, the then border between France and the Holy Roman Empire, was neutral territory, and here the Dauphine (wife of the Dauphin, the heir to the French throne and the equivalent of the Prince of Wales) was presented to the French. Her marriage had taken place in the Church of the Augustine Friars in Vienna, by proxy, her brother Prince Ferdinand standing in for the absent bridegroom.

On the island they had built a grand pavilion. A few days before the official reception Goethe bribed the custodians and went along with some friends to see the rooms and admire the Gobelin tapestries. Most of the company were delighted, especially with some hangings inspired by Raphael cartoons. But the work dominating the main room filled Goethe with unspeakable horror. It depicted a mythological scene, the story of Jason, Medea and Creusa. "To the left of the throne," Goethe writes in *Dichtung und Wahrheit*, "the young bride is seen writhing in the extremity of an agonising death. To the right, Jason stands shuddering, his foot planted on the prostrate bodies of his murdered children, while the Fury (Medea) ascends to the skies in her dragon-drawn carriage …

"'What on earth,' I cried out, entirely forgetting there were others present. 'What utter thoughtlessness is this? How could anyone set this most appalling of all examples of a wedding before the eyes of a young queen, the moment she sets foot in the country? Did none of those French builders, decorators and upholsterers understand that images carry meanings; that they influence our minds and feelings, that they leave profound impressions and arouse ominous presentiments? Not one of them, it seems.'" Goethe's companions reassured him that no one but he would think of such things.

"The young lady was beautiful, aristocratic, as radiant as she was imposing. I have retained a vivid memory of her face ever since," he continues, in the courtly manner of his later years. "Everyone had a good view of her in her glass coach, sharing little confidences with her female attendants, as if making a joke about the huge procession streaming ahead of her." Perhaps even then she gave the impression that she found people amusing.

Goethe goes on to mention that this first ill omen was quickly followed by an even more horrific one. When the Dauphine arrived at Versailles a firework display was arranged in her honour in Paris. Fire broke out, the streets were blocked, and the crowd was prevented from escaping. People were crushed underfoot, leaving thirty-three dead and hundreds more injured.

However he fails to mention the third omen, the strangest of all. The day after she passed through the door of Strasbourg Cathedral, the Bishop appointed his coadjutor, who then celebrated the mass. This was Prince Louis de Rohan, who would later cause her more distress than anyone else in the world.

Even in those aristocratic centuries, the Rohans ranked among the most aristocratic families of France. They enjoyed the status of foreign princes, coming, together with the Ducs de Lorraine, immediately after the royal family. Their proud motto was: *Roi ne puis, prince ne desire, Rohan suis*—"I can never be king, I have no desire to be a prince: I am a Rohan." One Rohan duchess, Chamfort relates, when asked when she was expecting a family event, replied: "I flatter myself I shall have the honour within a fortnight." The honour, that is, of bringing a Rohan into the world.

Characteristically, not a single member of this family was ever a statesman or general, or sufficiently distinguished in any other field to justify such overweening pride. In this they were very much as one thinks of the grandees of the Ancien Régime: they "did nothing but be born—and given a choice they would not have taken the trouble to do that", as Figaro remarks.

The odd thing is that the details of their origin survived at all, against a background of wandering populations and prolific mythmaking. They claimed descent from the rulers of Brittany—their ancestor Guéthénoc, youngest son of the Duc de Bretagne, became the Vicomte de Porhoët in 1021. The family had used the name Rohan ever since 1100. Even so, Brittany remained a small, half-savage domain in the back of beyond until Anna, the last little 'clog-wearing Duchess', married Charles VIII of France, taking the entire peninsula with her as dowry. This marks the entry of the Rohans into France.

The Protestant branch of the family, the Rohan-Gies, produced some stubborn and brave men of conscience during the wars of religion, but the line died out in 1540. In the eighteenth century two major branches remained, the Rohan-Guéménées and the Rohan-Soubises. The latter's best-known son was the Maréchal de Soubise, a courtier who was made a general through the influence of Mme de Pompadour, despite his complete lack of talent. It was he who, together with an Austrian duke, achieved the remarkable feat of leading an army of 60,000 to defeat against 20,000 soldiers of Frederick the Great at Rossbach, the decisive battle of the Seven Years War.

The other branch, Rohan-Guéménée, is noted chiefly for the fact that despite annual revenues of astronomical proportions, its representatives went bankrupt in 1781, in debt to the tune of thirty-three million livres, taking countless lesser folk down with them, simple Breton sailors who had put their money with them in the expectation of life annuities. The Guéménées, finding what was left of their fortune insufficient to maintain their lifestyle, were forced to give up their courtly status and pretensions. Their bankruptcy contributed significantly to the general loss of respect for the aristocracy.

The Strasbourg bishopric was part of the family inheritance, so to speak. Half-a-century before the grand entry of Marie-Antoinette, another Rohan had received a foreign princess at the cathedral door. This was Maria Leszczynska, who became the unhappy wife of Louis XV.

Duc Louis de Rohan was born in 1734. In 1760 he was appointed coadjutor to his uncle the Bishop of Strasbourg, and simultaneously made Bishop of Canopus in Egypt *in partibus infidelium*—the honorary prelate of a diocese that had been in the hands of pagans for well over a thousand years. The top echelons of the Church had always included persons of the highest social rank, but by the seventeenth century the aristocratic families associated with the French Court had appropriated the sees of bishops and archbishops exclusively for themselves. Not only was Rohan's uncle a bishop, his cousin Ferdinand de Rohan was Archbishop of Cambrai, and the ducal La Rochefoucauld family alone filled three episcopal sees: Rouen, Beauvais and Saintes. The Court aristocracy, like the princes of the Church, made few adjustments to their personal lives or outward manner of living—one of the reasons why the French Church was so weak in the eighteenth century. The gulf between its upper ranks and the poorly-endowed lower clergy was every bit as great as that between the aristocracy and the nation at large. At a critical moment in the early days of the Revolution representatives of the lower ranks of the clergy aligned themselves with the citizenry, an act that had decisive consequences.

Louis de Rohan was not just a dignitary of the church. Since 1761 he had also been a member of the Académie Française, counting among the 'Immortals'. Of its thirty-eight members in 1789 (two places were vacant) there were seven nobles and five senior churchmen—an aristocratic age indeed. Earlier, under Louis XIV, France's bishops and academicians had been almost entirely of bourgeois origin. The final years of the Ancien Régime were by far the most aristocrat-dominated.

What sort of man was this Duc Louis de Rohan? According to his contemporaries he was extremely refined and well-mannered, a witty companion, and a fine speaker—by no means a disgrace to the Academy. He was both chivalrous and genuinely good-hearted, and his followers noted countless touching acts of charity carried out behind the scenes: a true son of the times, a man of feeling, as indeed was his royal master, Louis XVI.

But these facts tell us almost nothing, and the surviving portraits of the man add little more. They show the refined but somewhat expressionless features of the frail, rather spoilt, offspring of elderly parents: the face of a man almost impossible to describe. The sort of man of whom you might say: had he not been born a prince he would be indistinguishable from anyone else. But that judgement would be superficial. Rohan was a true-born prince—his Rohan qualities were as integral to his being as any inherited predisposition to disease of the organs. They determined his character and his fate as surely as tuberculosis or neurasthenia.

If we wish to understand him, our point of departure must be not his personal traits but his social position.

Rohan was a *grand seigneur*, in the heyday of his type—a time when to be one implied not merely differentness but a way of life based on aristocratic rule, at a time when the whole of Europe, so to speak, existed to sustain the lofty status of his class.

Western culture was essentially aristocratic. From its birth at the end of the eleventh century down to the French Revolution its aim had been for a small number of the chosen to attain the dream of the beautiful life; a life as pure, ordered and wonderful as a work of art from the hand of a genius, and no less independent of the mundane world and the vicissitudes of fortune. Such a culture finds its most complete expression in the royal court, the idealised life-that-transcends-life. This ideal was served by chivalry, ceremony and protocol, and its underlying aims by art and poetry.

But this is all rather general. The precise nature of Rohan's status and condition as a *grand seigneur* can be better demonstrated by some biographical and statistical facts.

There was a general feeling in Marie-Antoinette's France that he would not long remain a mere coadjutor. His two extremely influential aunts, Mme de Guéménée and Mme de Marsan, Royal Governess to the young princes (the term 'governess' not to be understood in the modern sense), supported by Mme du Barry and the government minister the Duc d'Aiguillon (who owed his position to her favour), persuaded the ageing Louis XV to send him as ambassador to Vienna. Since France and Austria were at the time allies, loyal if mutually suspicious, the roles of French envoy to Vienna and of his Austrian counterpart to Versailles were the most important diplomatic postings in Europe. The Austrian representative, Comte Mercy-Argenteau, was among the most eminent people in Paris. His influence was that of a minister. He was counsellor to the young Marie-Antoinette and his mistress was the most celebrated beauty of the opera. And what he was in Paris, Rohan aspired to become in Vienna, a city second only to the French capital in its *savoir-vivre*, its sense of life as a work of art.

Now for some more personal information. Rohan took with him to Vienna (omitting, for the sake of brevity, a truly astonishing quantity of material goods): fifty stallions, and accompanying personnel; six cadets from the most aristocratic families of Alsace and Brittany; their instructor in the handling of weapons, and their Latin tutor; two noblemen in his own service, '*pour les honneurs de la chambre*', one of them a knight of Malta, the other a captain of horse; six valets, a maître d'hôtel, a head of household, two liveried attendants, four couriers (their costumes costing 4,000 livres each), to 'glitter in the sunlight, as in a fairy tale'; twelve footmen; two 'Swiss guards', the leaner of them to command the inner door, the other, who was extremely plump, to man the gate; six musicians, to play during meals; a steward, a treasurer, four embassy officials of high social rank; the Jesuit Abbé Georgel as secretary to the legation, and four under-secretaries to assist him. All these persons were fitted out in fairy-tale splendour, and of course maintained and salaried by Rohan himself.

They arrived in Vienna, and soon filled the imperial city with awe. Everyone talked about them, the women in tones of rapture. It was hardly surprising. Rohan arranged vast hunts. His masked balls were spectacular. At Baden he lavishly entertained almost the whole of Lower Austria. Between a hundred and a hundred-and-fifty nobles attended his banquets, which, dispensing with the usual diplomatic practice, were served not at a single long table but at several smaller ones so that everyone might feel at ease. Dinner was followed by cards, a musical concert, dancing and flirting in the miraculous rooms of the Lichtenstein Palace and its garden, which was of course illuminated—just as it would have been at Versailles.

That was one side of the coin. The other was that Rohan had no money—neither he, nor either of the two branches of his family. He is reported to have had royal permission to raise one million livres against his estates, but that did not last very long. He was unable to pay his people regularly, and they in response abused their extra-territorial diplomatic immunity and devoted their time, very successfully, to smuggling. They did this with such typically French openness that Maria Theresa, though reluctant to offend the Court at Versailles, withdrew the privilege of immunity from the entire legation. That at any rate is the story according to Mme Campan, Marie-Antoinette's *première femme de chambre* (hardly 'chambermaid': she was as much a chambermaid as the Duchesse de Marsan was a governess). Her famous *Memoirs*, written around 1820, are our single most important source, as they are for everyone who writes about Marie-Antoinette and her times. However Mme Campan was writing specifically to rescue the memory of her mistress, and her portrait of Rohan is accordingly painted in the darkest of hues.

The crucial fact that Rohan had no money remains indisputable, as will be made clear in the story of the necklace. But how could he possibly not have money? His income from the bishopric at Strasbourg and his various abbotships alone brought him 60,000 livres per annum, on paper: in reality, more like 400,000 livres. The value of the livre at that time Funck-Brentano puts at about ten francs; that is, pre-war francs, worth a third of a Hungarian pengő in peacetime.

While we are considering Rohan as a typical representative of his social class, it might be interesting to add a few further details about his income, to compare him with others of his rank. They are taken from Funck-Brentano's *L'Ancien Régime*—

"M de Sartine, Chief of Police, was given 200,000 livres (that is two million francs) to pay off a portion of his debts. The Keeper of the Seal Lamoignon received a small gift of 200,000 livres—modest indeed, when his successor Miromesnil accepted 600,000 livres (six million francs) towards 'furnishing his house'. The Duc d'Aiguillon was awarded 500,000 (five million francs) in compensation when he left the ministry in 1774. The widow of the Maréchal de Muy, the Minister for War, had an annual pension of 30,000 livres, and when the Comte de St Germain gave up his position of Secretary of State for War he took an annual pension of 40,000 livres and 155,000 in compensation. (Multiply all these last figures by ten!)

"Marie-Antoinette once gave the Duc de Polignac 1,200,000 livres, and the Duc de Salm 500,000. Calonne, during his years in charge of the Treasury, paid out fifty-six million livres to the older of the King's two brothers, the Duc de Provence, and twenty-five million to the younger, the Comte d'Artois. *C'est à hurler!*" ('It makes one want to cry aloud!'—not my words, but those of the elderly Funck-Brentano, that most conservative-minded of men.) At any one time the Duc de Condé had twelve million livres to hand, and an annual income of 600,000 (six million francs).

These facts also appear in Taine's *L'Ancien Régime*, unsur-prisingly perhaps, since he appears to be Funck-Brentano's source. Both writers provide a mass of other similar examples.

You have to cry out, or rather, the facts themselves cry out to Heaven. What was this? What strange madness had seized the hearts of the French kings, that they should hand out such legendary sums (very rarely asking for anything in return) simply as a reward for the possession of noble ancestry? It was of course not madness, but an inescapable consequence of the historical situation. In the Middle Ages France, like other European states, had been controlled by the feudal aristocracy. For some centuries its kings had been struggling to centralise power, that is to say, to prise it from the grip of the great barons and arrogate it to themselves. As is well known, this goal was finally achieved by Louis XIV when, in no sense boastfully, he remarked, '*L'état c'est moi*'. The rural feudal nobility had been transformed into one based at the Court. The barons could no longer reside on their estates but were required to remain near the King, who kept an eagle eye on any absences and punished them by the withdrawal of his favour. From this point on the people were plundered not by the barons but by the King's *intendants* and the *fermiers généraux*, and the money now went to the royal coffers. That was why it had become necessary to bail out the nobility: with annuities, gifts, offices at Court commanding unheard-of salaries, and positions in the church and army. Later, perhaps, the need for all this fell away: all autonomous power had been leached out of the barons and they were no longer capable of mounting any sort of rebellion against the King (but nor could they provide him with support, one major reason why the Revolution triumphed so swiftly). By then, simple necessity dictated that they remain loyal to him. But by the time of Louis XVI, this once rational and necessary system of 'reimbursement' had come to seem a straightforward abuse, a pointless and unjustified luxury that quite rightly drew censure from the workers and provoked revolutionary anger in the people.

The next question is, what did they do with such vast sums of money? It is difficult for us now to believe they could spend so much. A modern American millionaire would struggle to do so. But American millionaires and other people with huge amounts of money are not grands seigneurs. The owner of a vast fortune achieved through economic activity will even in his wildest moments retain some degree of business sense, and preserve some sort of method even in his madness. But the old French grandees were never, in their most sober moments, thinking economists, and had no idea of system or method. Just where money went in the age of Louis XVI we shall seek to explain by means of a few extracts from the work by Taine mentioned earlier.

"The lady-in-waiting to Louis XV's daughters, the three little old ladies known as the *Mesdames*, burned candles to the value of 215,068 francs, and the Queen 157,109 francs. In Versailles they still point out the street, once filled with little shops, where the royal footmen would come and feed the entire town on desserts left over from the King's table. According to the official estimate, the King himself consumed 2,190 francs worth of almond tea and lemonade. The 'round-the-clock' consommé kept for Madame Royale, the two-year-old daughter of Louis XVI and Marie-Antoinette, cost 5,201 livres a year." While Marie-Antoinette was still the Dauphine, the *femmes de chambre* ran up a bill against her account for "four pairs of shoes per week, three spindles of thread per day to stitch their hairdressing gowns, and two reels of ribbon to adorn the baskets in which her gloves and fans were kept." (The rules forbade that one should simply hand them to her: they had to be presented in a basket.)

Naturally, tradespeople were never paid on time. When Turgot was Finance Minister the King ran a debt of some 800,000 livres with his wine-merchants, and 3,500,000 with his caterers. (Multiply these figures by ten, advises Funck-Brentano.)

Next come figures which confirm that the nobility did not lag far behind the Court in the scale of their debts and general spending. "On one occasion the Maréchal de Soubise (Rohan's relation) entertained the King at his country mansion for dinner and the night. The bill came to 200,000 livres. Mme de Matignon allowed herself 24,000 livres a year for a new coiffure every day. Cardinal Rohan owned a needle-lace silk chasuble valued at over 100,000 livres; his saucepans were made of solid silver. And nothing could have been more natural, when you consider the way they thought about money at the time. To economise, to set money aside, was like turning a flowing stream into a useless, foul-smelling swamp. Better to throw the stuff out of the window. Which is precisely what the Maréchal de Richelieu did, when his grandson sent back the bulging purse he had been given because he 'couldn't think what to do with it'. So out it went—to the great good fortune the street-sweeper who picked it up. Had the man not happened to be passing by the money would have ended up in the river.

"Mme de B," Taine continues, "once intimated to the Prince de Conti that she would like a portrait of her canary as a miniature set on a ring. The Prince volunteered his services. The lady accepted, but stipulated that the miniature should be kept quite simple, with no accompanying diamonds. She was indeed given a simple gold ring, but the picture was set not under glass but under a finely-cut sheet of diamond. She sent the diamond back, whereupon the Prince ground it to dust which he scattered over the letter she had written. The cost of this little heap of powder was between four and five thousand livres (raising questions about the tone and content of the letter). The highest gallantry often combined with the most extravagant generosity, and the more fashionable the gentleman, the weaker his understanding of money."

However, the sheer size of these sums does give cause for wonder.

First and foremost: it could well be that Funck-Brentano's principle of multiplying by ten is wrong. The money can hardly have been worth that much. To establish its value in today's terms is not easy. Funck-Brentano seems not to have taken into account its actual purchasing power, or he would have found that the livre would have bought a great deal less than ten pre-war francs. Here are one or two facts which struck us in our reading around the subject.

During the exceptionally cold winter of 1784 the Comédie Française offered a special evening performance for the poor (it was the premier of La Harpe's *Coriolan*) where the takings amounted to 10,330 livres. In today's Budapest Playhouse, with approximately the same seating capacity, a full house would bring in around 7,000 pengős.

Or again, we know what Marie-Antoinette paid for some of the hats she bought from the celebrated Mlle Bertin. They cost her forty-eight, seventy-two, ninety and (possibly) 280 livres. In pre-war Paris the price of a woman's hat ranged from thirty to 1200 francs. Even the most expensive of those royal purchases hardly justifies the ten-times rule. Further examples: Louis XVI, as I shall mention later, kept a precise record of his petty cash expenditure. From his notes we learn that he paid twelve livres for one hundred apricots for preserving; three livres for six pounds of cherries and two baskets of strawberries; one livre and ten sols for collecting wood and, for one pound of pepper (much more expensive then than here in peacetime), four livres. On the basis of these figures it seems reasonable to conclude that the purchasing power of the livre was very roughly that of today's Hungarian pengő.

The figures may diminish our sense of the scale of the sums involved, but they are still monstrous. One wonders how it was possible to pay out such amounts in the coinage of the day. Ever since the collapse of the system introduced by John Law at the start of the century the French had been extremely wary of paper money. In 1776 they set up the Caisse d'Escompte to issue banknotes, and those notes were generally preferred to the not always reliable coinage. But in our particular period only very small numbers of banknotes were issued, and by 1783 there were no more than forty million livres' worth in circulation.

And that gives rise to another little puzzle: whether the aristocracy really did always get their hands on their supposed income. We have seen that Louis XVI owed huge sums to his caterers and wine merchants, so it is possible that the Treasury itself was in debt, and the reason why Rohan and his peers found themselves in permanent financial difficulty was that their stipends were purely nominal, or were received only in part.

Despite all this, they must still have had access to vast sums, which brings us to the third question: where did it all come from? We have seen the size of the bills presented to the King and his nobles, both by their suppliers and by those who billed them in the name of those suppliers, for almond-tea, lemonade or whatever. They suggest a very cosy relationship between two social groups: on the one hand, the tradespeople and merchants supplying the Court and the aristocracy, and on the other, the *intendants* (financial administrators for the Court and nobility) with their army of clerks and assistants, together with the many different orders of flunkey.

As regards this last group, we find some interesting notes in our treasured guide to the old city, Louis-Sébastien Mercier's *Tableau de Paris*: "The principal footman of a high-ranking man at this time would enjoy an annual income of 40,000 livres, and he too would have a footman, who in turn had one of his own. This lowest functionary's task was to brush Monseigneur's coat and straighten his wig. The head footman would take the wig from the last of four hands in line, and had merely to arrange it on the head in which reposed the great questions of state. This momentous task being duly accomplished, it became his turn to be dressed by his men. He would order them about in a loud voice, scolding them fiercely: he was expecting visitors, he would explain loftily, as he ordered them to make his carriage ready. The footman's footman did not have a carriage, but that too suited him perfectly well … The principal footman's possessions included an engraved gold watch, lace apparel, diamond buckles and a little vendor of fashionable goods as his mistress.

"This pointless and purely ostentatious army of servants was viewed in Paris as a most dangerous form of corruption, and as their numbers grew ever larger it seemed only too frighteningly obvious that they would one day bring a major disaster down on society." In the backyards and basements, a new social class was coming into existence—Figaro's class. Intelligent, affluent and sharp-tongued, they had seen the aristocracy from close up, with no real experience of what lay behind the facade: they knew only one side, the weaker. As Hegel reminds us, no man is a hero to his valet.

On the other hand, the luxury enjoyed by the nobility enriched the citizenry both directly and indirectly. The money might drain away through the hands of the privileged, but it came to rest in the reservoirs of the bourgeoisie, and increased the general prosperity we spoke of earlier—which, paradoxically, was itself one of the most important reasons behind the changing times.

But to return to Vienna. The city had its own *grands seigneurs*, but the scale of Rohan's magnificence astonished and enchanted everyone, and no one, it seems, was troubled by those financial concerns that, from the distance of a century-and-a-half, are so obviously disquieting. Rohan charmed everyone, even the cynically superior Emperor Joseph II and his wise and canny chancellor Kaunitz. He charmed everyone, with one exception—the one person who mattered—Maria Theresa.

Maria Theresa probably disliked him simply because everyone else was charmed, and here we can see just how blind Rohan could be. The Empress did not take kindly to a foreigner overshadowing her royal household in pomp and splendour—something the Habsburgs had quite understandably never liked. Their censor had even suppressed József Katona's opera *Bánk Bán* on the grounds that it cast aspersions on the imperial house. And how could the Episcopal Coadjutor, accustomed as he was to French ways of doing things, understand how deeply his manner of life—so often unworthy of his position—might offend her religious sensibilities? No doubt the Empress saw him as the embodiment of the French frivolity and immorality that so alienated her. But perhaps, in the end, it wasn't Rohan himself that she loathed so much as the people behind him, the vast entourage from whom she wished to protect her people.

She did all she could to have him recalled. She saw him as the ambassador to her Court not only of France but of the Powers of Darkness. She mobilised her envoy to Versailles, Mercy-Argenteau, and she mobilised her daughter, the Dauphine.

This constant call to action from her mother was one of the causes of Marie-Antoinette's tragedy. The Empress regarded her daughter as a diplomatic instrument comparable to d'Argenteau, an attitude inherited by her son, Joseph II. But as far as Marie-Antoinette was concerned, her mother was the closest to her of all living creatures, and she sought to obey her in every way possible. For all her sagacity, the Empress did not know, or did not want to see, that despite the present alliance between her country and France the ancient enmity between the French and Germans was a far more deeply rooted affair; nor could she imagine that the same person could be at the same time a good Frenchwoman and a good German. As she wrote to her daughter: "Be a good German—it's the best way of being a good Frenchwoman." In short, she sacrificed her daughter to her political ambitions.

Not every child smothered with love by a mother who makes herself indispensable continues to feel strongly bound by that love. But we do sometimes see examples of the reverse— children who remain permanently tied to mothers who want to dominate them for ever. Maria Theresa did not exactly swamp her children with maternal affection—she would not have known how to. Like all Habsburg rulers, she sacrificed every moment to her implacable sense of duty. The Habsburgs ruled the way a born writer writes, and a born painter paints— in the middle of the night, waking between two dreams. For centuries they had had little time for tenderness. Their style was the direct opposite of the idle and voluptuous Bourbons', with whom Marie-Antoinette, the most delicate flower of the Habsburg forest, was now entangled.

Of course we might think otherwise when we gaze on Maria Theresa's imposing baroque tomb in the Capuchin cemetery in Vienna. The Empress sits enthroned amidst her offspring, the multitudinous little princes, like some ancient fertility goddess, a Magna Mater, the very symbol of motherhood. But her actual practice is revealed in the words of Marie-Antoinette, as recorded by that gifted writer, her *première femme de chambre* (not, we repeat, 'chambermaid'!), Mme Campan: "Whenever she heard that some foreigner of note (*un étranger de marque*) had arrived, the Empress would surround herself with her family, sit the little ones at table and create a tableau to suggest that she was bringing them up herself." It was certainly not the case.

So it might well have been from a sense of duty that Marie-Antoinette adopted her mother's stance of intense hostility towards Rohan. She had met him only once, in Strasbourg. It is possible she took a dislike to the rising young churchman even then. Carlyle may well be right: "Perhaps even then, her fair young soul read, all unconsciously, an incoherent *Roué*-ism, bottomless mud-volcano-ism, from which she by instinct rather recoiled."

Carlyle was the second person, after Goethe, to give literary expression to the necklace trial, in his famous essay *The Age of Romance*, written from the necessary historical distance at the beginning of the last century. In what follows we shall be frequently quoting his highly compressed, savagely ironic and eloquent phrases. In the lines transcribed above he employs the term *'roué'*. The word is still in use today, but it first became current in Rohan's time. Originally it signified the sort of man who ended up being broken on the wheel; then, once it became fashionable, someone who simply deserved such a fate. But it was not just the word that came into vogue: so did the behaviour. A great many people aspired to the name. Mercier has some important remarks on the subject, if our reader would care to hear them:

"'What is an *'aimable roué'*?' a foreigner who thinks he understands French might ask. He is the sort of man of the world who has neither virtues nor principles, but gives his vices a veneer of charm and dignifies them by means of his agreeable wit … If the foreigner is then surprised that such an expression should take root in our language, he will find that gallows humour has a long history in our common parlance. Thirty years ago an abbé was hanged for a banking fraud. The miserable fellow hesitated at the foot of the ladder leading up to the scaffold. 'Come, come, M Abbé,' said the hangman, 'don't be such a *bébé*.' Another time, a drunk came out of a pub in the Place de la Grêve, just as they began an execution. The man on the wheel started bellowing, cursing and swearing in his agony. The drunk raised his head towards the scaffold, took offence at what was being said, and called out: 'There's no need for rudeness, even if they are breaking you on a wheel.' This quip was much admired in aristocratic circles."

So far as the two Queens were concerned, Rohan's chances were ruined for ever by the indiscretion of Mme du Barry. At the time Prussia and Russia had just carved Poland up between them. Maria Theresa, while strongly condemning their actions, could do nothing about them and demanded a share for Austria. Rohan, who had a justified reputation among his contemporaries as a wit, took the occasion to write to the Duc d'Aiguillon: "Maria Theresa holds a handkerchief in one hand to wipe away her tears, and a sword in the other, hoping to becoming the third partner in the spoils." D'Aiguillon sent the letter to Du Barry, who took great delight in reading it aloud to her guests over dinner, and they were quick to repeat the contents to Marie-Antoinette the following day.

But while the blundering ambassador slandered Vienna in Versailles, he took every opportunity to slander Versailles in Vienna. Stories that he was spreading about Marie-Antoinette reached Maria Theresa's ear. Her maternal heart was so aggrieved that she sent Baron Neni to find out what truth there was in them, and the Baron established that Rohan's source was baseless chatter emanating from the Du Barry-Marsan-Guéménée clique, who so despised the young Queen.

So it was perfectly understandable that Marie-Antoinette too should do everything in her power to have the doubly indiscreet ambassador brought home. But Rohan was protected by his powerful aunts, and while Louis XV was alive, and Mme du Barry remained who she was, it was impossible to remove him.

In April 1774 Louis XV contracted smallpox. Du Barry took herself off to Rueil, and only his daughters remained at his bedside. The Court continued at Versailles, waiting impatiently for the candle burning in his window to signal that his appalling death struggles were over, so they could then leave the infected Palace and withdraw to Choisy. Finally, on 10th May 1774, the flame was extinguished.

The King's corpse lay there, slowly breaking open. It was already half-decayed, and a hideous stench was pouring from it. The Duc de Villequier, *Premier Gentilhomme de la Chambre*, called on the surgeon, Andouillé, to carry out his traditional office and apply balsam to the body. Andouillé knew that it would inevitably mean catching the infection himself, and replied: "Very good; but it is your duty, Your Excellency, to hold the head while I do it." Villequier dispensed with the embalming.

"The Dauphin was with the Dauphine," records Mme Campan. "They were awaiting news of Louis's death together. A dreadful noise, *absolument* like thunder, was heard in the outer apartment above them. It was the crowd of courtiers who were deserting the dead sovereign's antechamber, to come and do homage to the new power of Louis XVI. This extraordinary tumult informed Marie-Antoinette and her husband that they were called to the throne; and, by a spontaneous movement, which deeply affected those around them, they threw themselves on their knees; both, pouring forth a flood of tears, exclaimed: "O God, guide us and protect us. We are too young to reign."

Thus Marie-Antoinette ascended the French throne. That same year Rohan was recalled from Vienna.

His departure was not very dignified. Maria Theresa refused to receive him before he left. Rohan sent his friends a portrait of himself engraved on a thin layer of ivory, and such was his popularity that it was much copied onto rings and encircled with pearls and diamonds. Even Chancellor Kaunitz wore one, to the Empress' intense annoyance.

He was replaced as ambassador to Vienna by Baron Breteuil. Rohan could not forgive the man for succeeding him, and Breteuil was even less forgiving of the hostile treatment he received. When the time came, his loathing would be fatal for Rohan.

Still greater discomfiture awaited the ex-envoy in France. The King received him coldly; the Queen refused even to see him. She simply sent word that he should forward the letter he had brought her from Maria Theresa. Rohan was in disgrace.

In the Ancien Régime, to be disgraced was not necessarily fatal in a material sense. There was no chance of his starving to death. In fact, during his time in this supposed wilderness he achieved one enviable distinction. In 1777 the post of *Grand Aumônier*—Grand Almoner—which had long been promised him, fell vacant. The incumbent would be the King's chaplain, the head of his household clergy, and by that token the highest dignitary in the Court. The King was naturally reluctant to let him have it, and Marie-Antoinette protested vehemently. But once again the powerful aunts prevailed—fairy godmothers indeed!—and Rohan was appointed. From then on, the Queen refused to speak to him.

Then Rohan's uncle died, and he became Bishop of Strasbourg. It was the richest diocese in France. Next, through the intervention of King Stanislas Poniatowski of Poland, he was made a cardinal. He was now a truly imperial prince, the Comte d'Alsace and Abbé de Saint-Vaast (where his stipend of 300,000 livres exceeded even that from Strasbourg), *Proviseur* of the Sorbonne, *Supérieur Général* of the Royal Hospice of the Quinze-Vingts, and a Commander of the Order of the Holy Spirit. And all the while, the Queen refused to speak to him.

You, dear reader, would surely, in such circumstances, believe yourself hopelessly lost to her favour; and you would console yourself that its loss was of no material significance, since retaining it was so difficult in practice. But that, my dear reader, is because you are thinking in practical terms—in francs, pengős and honorary titles, and you fail to imagine just what the loss of royal favour would mean to a person of that time. It is an old cliché, but we must spell it out—the King's favour was the ray of sunlight that gave life to his courtiers, and without it they withered. The King's favour was the very air, and without it they could not breathe. The King's favour was the metaphysics through which a courtier was admitted to matters eternal, and without it life was as meaningless as that of a true believer who has lost his God. The loss of favour had broken greater hearts than Rohan's—think of Racine!

Rohan mobilised everyone and everything. In 1777 Joseph II came to France, and tried to bring his sister round to the cause. The intervention was not a success. Marie-Antoinette heard her brother out coldly, and exasperated him by her non-stop hectoring tone: 'I am prepared to take advice from my mother,' she seemed to say, 'but to my brother I shall speak my mind.' The only two men she was ready to listen to were the Comte Mercy-Argenteau and her old tutor, the Abbé Vermond. She was too mindful of the Empress' advice ever to let Rohan worm his way into her favour.

"Men have, indeed, been driven from Court; and borne it, according to ability," says Carlyle. "A Choiseul, in these very years, retired Parthian-like, with a smile or scowl, and drew half the Court-host with him. Our Wolsey, though once an *ego et rex meus,* could journey, it is said, without strait-waistcoat, to his monastery, and there, telling beads, look forward to a still longer journey. The melodious, too soft-strung Racine, when his King turned his back on him, emitted one meek wail, and submissively—died. But the case of Coadjutor de Rohan differed from all those. No loyalty was in him that he should die; no self-help, that he should live; no faith, that he should tell beads." Rohan lived on, to put it in poetical terms, like a winter tree waiting for some fairy-tale spring.

For Rohan—and this really comes as a surprise—was ambitious. Rank and fortune were not enough. He yearned for power. This is particularly surprising because he was clearly not the sort of person for whom power is his natural element, who finds his greatest happiness in determining the fate of others. Had he been that sort of person he would have put his time in Vienna to far better use, and in his role as bishop he would have made his subordinates feel the weight of his authority. But there is no evidence that he did anything of the sort.

What then was the source of this burning ambition? We all live out our lives in terms of roles—or aspire to do so. At the simplest level, this role-play takes an elementary form: a woman might smile and do her hair in the manner of her favourite actress, and even strive to assume her supposed mental attributes. A man will take on the persona of distinguished physician, the self-sacrificing paterfamilias, the charming bohemian or some other traditional part. On a higher level, nobler and more complicated souls are tempted by the nobler and more complicated roles offered by history and literature—the Muse, the Martyr, the Poète Maudit, the Great Statesman (like Széchenyi) or Voice of the Revolution (like Petőfi). The phantom that hovered so teasingly over Rohan's consciousness was the gloriously visible one of the all-powerful Cardinal—Wolsey, Richelieu, Mazarin and Fleury. But here the pampered *grand seigneur*, with his tendency to corpulence, was quite out of his depth. Richelieu was a gaunt ascetic, who out of his dreams forged himself a character of bone and steel. Working with his secretary Baron Planta—a Swiss Protestant, no less—he laboured away at his great plans to make his country a happier place, and only when his guests had finally gone to bed, as dawn approached and he had a few brief hours to himself, did he allow himself to dream of 'taking power'.

To the 'taking' of such power, Rohan felt in his more optimistic moments, there was only one obstacle: the Queen's anger. The King he probably considered a *quantité négligeable*, as he usually was. It was not the King's favourite but the Queen's who exercised power. For a child of the age of Pompadour and Du Barry the notion of a favourite carried essentially erotic implications. In France, the real ruler was the person who ruled the Queen's heart. And why should that not be him, Rohan, the *Belle Eminence*, as his followers called him? Mazarin, with far less manly appeal and *grand-seigneurial* charm, had once ruled his queen, Anne of Austria, and through her, France.

But a person who falls under the spell of erotic dreams does not remain immune to their power for long. Rohan had dreamt for so many years that the Queen was in love with him that he ended up falling desperately in love with her himself. In this he showed some taste, especially when we consider who he was, and who the Queen was, and we can forget the shades of Mazarin and the other great cardinals. Marie-Antoinette was both young and one of the most beautiful women in France. Rohan, however, was approaching fifty, and in those days, as we all know, people aged more rapidly and died younger: the average life expectancy in France was twenty-eight years and nine months. Perhaps Rohan was seized by *Torschlusspanik*, the sexual passion bordering on madness that is triggered by approaching old age.

And here is something else. The varieties of sexual attraction can be analysed in terms of sociological type. There are some people who can love only those of lower standing than themselves—gentlemen of birth who pursue female servants, and ladies of rank who adore coachmen. There are those whose passions are strictly confined to members of their own stratum, and those who can love only those from a bracket higher than their own—people in whose minds sex and ambition are inseparably fused. These are the main groups, and most of us fall into one of them or another. And if Rohan was indeed one of those who could only love their superiors, then there was just one woman of higher rank than himself—the Queen. He was like the very tall man whose fate is to be attracted only by women taller than himself. In Rohan's adoration of the Queen there may well have been a similar element of fatal compulsion.

Neither contemporary sources nor later historians like Funck-Brentano raise the question of Rohan's actual feelings for her. But there is one piece of information well known to scholars that supports my theory, psychologically improbable as it might seem. Mme Campan records the following story, which makes very little sense unless we assume that Rohan was indeed in love with her.

In the summer of 1782 Archduke Paul Petrovics, the son of Catherine the Great who became Paul I of Russia and later went mad, came to Paris with his wife. They travelled incognito, as the Count and Countess North—a poetic name indeed. The Queen gave a banquet in their honour at Trianon, and the park was illuminated. Rohan bribed the concierge (a 'janitor' in the sense that Mme Campan was a 'chambermaid'? Indeed not, but a genuine concierge) to let him into the park, claiming he wanted to see the lights after the Queen had left for Versailles. So he hid himself in the porter's lodge. But he failed to keep his promise to go out only after the Queen's departure, and when the man's attention was distracted he slipped out into the park. He was 'in disguise', but that consisted only of a greatcoat beneath which his purple stockings were clearly visible. Once in the park, he stood, thus strangely attired, and with a 'face of mystery', as Mme Campan writes, peering out, from two separate locations, at the royal family and their train of attendants. Marie-Antoinette was deeply shocked and wanted to sack the porter the next day, but Mme Campan successfully intervened on his behalf.

What was His Eminence hoping for in the park? Was it to reveal himself in the confident expectation that her heart would melt when she saw him? Rohan was not that stupid: he had a paunch, he was no longer young, and the ludicrous disguise would hardly have advanced his cause. The only possible explanation is that he desperately wanted to see the Queen, and that was why he had gone there.

But whatever the case, there is no doubt that he was driven by the desire, verging on compulsion, to diffuse the Queen's anger and win her favour. This is the second such *idée fixe* in the story, according to Carlyle, the first being Boehmer's with his necklace. And when two such obsessions come together, a force comes into being that could destroy a nation. All that is needed is for them to combine with a third.

And that was how Jeanne de la Motte found Rohan when she met him at Saverne, the Bishop of Strasbourg's country seat. The old manor house had burnt down in 1779, but Rohan had rebuilt it in fashionable pomp and splendour and fitted it out, again in the taste of the time, with collections of natural history and art, and splendid libraries. The number of his guests had not diminished since his days in Vienna. He lived like a prince. They came in such numbers, from all over Germany and France, and even from the Court at Versailles, that often there was no room for them all in the mansion, despite its seven hundred awaiting beds. "There was no noblewoman of such good family that she did not dream of Saverne," wrote a contemporary. "The hunts were especially magnificent." Six hundred peasants drove the game into the gentlemen's guns, with the women following on horseback or in carriages. At one o'clock the entire party assembled for luncheon, in a marquee erected in some picturesque spot on the banks of a stream. So that the pleasure should be shared by everyone, there were even tables waiting on the lawn for the peasantry: it was Rohan's wish that every one of them should have a pound of meat, two pounds of bread and half a bottle of wine. At Saverne they certainly enjoyed to the full what Talleyrand calls 'the sweetness of life'.

It was to this fairy-tale castle that Jeanne de la Motte, dissatisfied and inwardly eaten up as ever, came with her husband. Her great patron Mme de Boulainvilliers introduced her to the Cardinal and commended her to his favour. She told him her story while he listened in rapt silence—which is hardly surprising, given the details that might have come from a novel. The unvarnished realities of a defenceless life, the bitter taste of poverty, would have been particularly fascinating to a man whose own days had been passed in the most cushioned elevation, and to whom the woes of ordinary life were comprehensible only as some sort of exotic and compelling tale. And Jeanne knew supremely well how to present her tale with steadily mounting effect. On a number of occasions her later writings reveal—it is quite noticeable—that she had practised extensively and this was the form she finally evolved. One can imagine her using her spare moments to rehearse it over and over again, honing it down to one particular version with its ever-increasing drama.

So Rohan listened, and believed everything. He usually believed what people told him. Two days before his arrest, Cagliostro persuaded him that he would be dining with Henry IV, though he would not actually see his illustrious guest. If one were writing a play on the subject one would have to ignore everything else and focus on this trait alone, because in the entire drama of the necklace it is the most significant. He showed the most extraordinary, indeed unbelievable, gullibility. The most problematic aspect of the whole affair, Funck-Brentano tells us, was the degree of credulity we are required to attribute to him. It is the most improbable feature in the whole improbable story—but it is undeniable.

The most obvious explanation for it, other than some character trait of unknown origin, can once again lie only in his social position. How would anyone born into the purple, and destined to become a cardinal, get to know people, the circumstances of their lives—and the sheer nastiness circumstances can provoke in them? Any other nobleman, busying himself with affairs of state or military matters, would have rapidly discovered what people are really like. But Rohan was a man of the Church, and he took no interest in his diocese. People showed him only their better side and revealed only the noblest of their motives to him. And Rohan was himself a thoroughly benevolent man. Where would he possibly learn about the sheer malice of ordinary people? He was as innocent as a king—as his own King, Louis XVI.

To this social conditioning was added another determinism, that of blood—which, again, and most remarkably, not one of the great historians of the necklace affair considers worth a mention. Rohan was a Celt. His family origins were Breton. True, by this time several hundred years had passed since they had left Brittany, but there must have been constant intermarrying with the Breton nobility, and there is always the possibility of genetic regression. The Celts, as we know, are a fantastical and superstitious people. Matthew Arnold, the great

English essayist of the last century, writing in his study of Celtic literature, tells us they lived "in a state of permanent rebellion against the tyranny of facts". In the Arthurian Cycle, which lasted from the time of the Middle Ages through to Tennyson and Wagner, and had such a seminal influence on European poetry, it was the old kings of the Irish and the Highland Scots who could produce the greatest giants, the tiniest dwarves, and the most magical fairylands. By the eighteenth century the Highlanders had added many other proudly distinctive gifts, including second sight, by which they could see the souls of those who had just died. Dr Samuel Johnson, the leading light of eighteenth-century English literature, made a special journey to Scotland to enquire into it. Until very recently, all four Celtic peoples—the Irish, Welsh, Highland Scots and Bretons—inhabited a world that verged on the theocratic. They consulted their priests in almost everything and looked to their magical powers for instruction in even the most mundane of matters.

Thus Rohan too, with the blind faith inherited from his Breton ancestors, turned for guidance to the great magus with whom fate had linked him—Cagliostro.

Chapter Four

The Magician

FIRST OF ALL, we should apologise for Cagliostro's presence in the case, like that of Pontius Pilate in the Creed. His innocence was established beyond doubt in the course of the trial. Nonetheless close attention must be paid to this mysterious personage. His contemporaries always believed that he was implicated in the necklace affair, and that is how he is remembered. Mention Cagliostro and people immediately think of the necklace; mention the necklace, and they think of Cagliostro. The truth of such legends often runs deeper than the facts of history. He is one of the main characters in the story not so much in terms of those facts but by reason of its nature. By understanding that, and what it represents, we can truly understand the significance of the whole story and its place in world history.

The source materials relating to his life are many and unreliable. They are many because he exercised the imaginations of his contemporaries and they in consequence wrote a great deal about him; and unreliable because the eighteenth century—which has been called the century of women—adored and cultivated malicious gossip to an extent one now finds astonishing. For all that the period witnessed the development of a generally more critical attitude among people, it also welcomed and enjoyed scandal and rumour unquestioningly, so long as it was sufficiently spiteful and amusing.

Thus the material presents us with two directly contrasting images of the man. The overwhelming majority of extant writings vie with one another in their efforts to blacken him, gleefully portraying a wily trickster—a charlatan, quack and bogus prophet. But in his own writings, and in comments made by his followers, he appears as a genuine prophet and worker of miracles.

The file is by no means closed. The nineteenth century was generally hostile towards his adherents. In 1904 Henri d'Almeras's *Cagliostro* amassed a pile of painstaking evidence to show him as one of the greatest frauds of all time, and yet a swindler who, for all his little peccadilloes, remains entirely sympathetic. D'Almeras characterises him, most aptly, as the Figaro of alchemists.

A more recent work is Dr Marc Haven's *Cagliostro, le maître inconnu*, which assembles even more evidence to argue the reverse, rehabilitating the man and claiming him to be, as his followers had always maintained, the great master of arcane lore. But Haven is himself an occultist, and his intention is quite clearly to use Cagliostro to defend the honour of occult learning in general. And in any case it remains true that those contemporaries who wrote about Cagliostro were often even greater scoundrels than he was.

So it is understandable that two flatly contradictory versions of his early life have come down to us—his own, and the one put together by his many enemies. Perhaps we should begin by paying this unusual character the courtesy of hearing his own account first. The story can be found in the memoir written in 1786 by his defending counsel M Thilorier, just after the necklace trial.

His origins and name, he informs us, he never knew, but he believed he had been born on the island of Malta. He spent his childhood years in Medina, where he was known as Acharat, under the protection of the great mufti Salahym. He had four people to attend to his needs: one white footman, two black footmen and his wise teacher Altotas. While he was still very young Altotas remarked on his exceptional capacity for learning. As a child he was taught the secrets of botany and medicine, acquired several oriental languages and fathomed the mysteries of the Egyptian pyramids. Meanwhile Altotas informed him that his parents had been Christians of noble birth.

At the age of twelve he and his teacher left Medina and went to Mecca. There, they were clad in rich attire and presented to the Sharif. "When I caught sight of the Prince," he tells us, "I was filled with inexpressible perturbation, and my eyes filled with the sweetest of tears, and I noticed that he too could barely restrain his own." He remained in Mecca for three years, spending every day with the Sharif, who at last bestowed on him a look of the most profound tenderness and emotion. It was what was called at the time 'blood speaking to blood'. It made Cagliostro feel he should regard the noble Sharif as his father, even though that contradicted what Altotas had told him.

Not long afterwards came the painful moment of separation. Acharat and his supposed father fell into each other's arms. "God be with you, unhappy child of nature!" pronounced the Sharif, as tears poured from his eyes.

The young man and his teacher now went to Egypt, where the priests took them into places not permitted to the ordinary traveller; then they sailed on to the island of Rhodes, and finally Malta. Here the most surprising transformation awaited him. The wise Altotas removed his Muslim garb and revealed himself to be not only a Christian but one of the knights. From this point onwards Acharat called himself Count Cagliostro, and was received as a guest at the palace of Pinto d'Alfonseca, Grand Master of the Order.

Then, sadly, Altotas died. With his dying breath he whispered these words: "My son, always remember to fear the Lord and love your fellow man. Soon enough, you will know that all I have taught you is true."

Despite repeated requests from the Grand Master, Cagliostro did not join the Order but continued on his way, to devote his life to medical studies. He toured the islands of the Archipelago before reaching Rome in 1770, where he married a high-born young lady, Serafina Feliciani.

All this is Cagliostro's own account. The alternative version is contained, in its fullest form, in the *Compendio della vita e delle gesta di Giuseppe Balsamo*, which appeared in 1791. It was written by a cleric, in the form of notes recorded by the Inquisition. Its author clearly seeks to condemn Freemasonry in the person of Cagliostro, so it too is not completely reliable, but at all events it sounds rather more probable that his own version.

According to it, the man's real name was Giuseppe Balsamo. He was born into a lower middle-class family in Palermo on 8th June 1743. His mother had an uncle called Cagliostro, the name he later adopted.

The author of the *Compendio*, like some of his contemporaries, asserts that Cagliostro was of Jewish origin, at least on his father's side. The many extant portraits do nothing to dispel the idea; but of course, we might on the same principle declare that the face has a distinctly Italian look. Goethe, who took an intense interest in the whole necklace affair and wrote a play about it because he felt that it summed up the spirit of the age, actually called on Cagliostro's relations while in Palermo and was given a warm welcome. Goethe does not mention their being Jewish, but it is true that he spoke only to the mother, sister and sister's children, and no one from the supposedly Jewish side.

There seems to be no doubt that Cagliostro was born and brought up in Palermo. Sicily was of course a wonderful environment for an aspiring trickster. It was home to Europe's most credulous, superstitious and miracle-loving people—a people, moreover, not overly devoted to work. At a very early age Cagliostro developed his inclination to live not by his own efforts but on the credulity of his fellow men—on what was in fact a by-product of their religious faith.

According to the scribe, he began his career at an early age. He ran away from the monastery at Caltagirone where he had been entered, and where he had acquired some of the basics of medicine. There followed a long series of escapades: he swindled, beat up the local policeman and robbed his own family. Among the more successful of these youthful adventures was the episode of the buried treasure. He persuaded a jeweller called either Murano or Marano that he knew of a cave in which there was hidden booty. But, as usual, it was guarded by devils. These would have first to be appeased by the recitation of arcane scripts, and by leaving two hundred ounces of gold at the cave's entrance.

One night the two men made their way to the site. The jeweller set the gold down, and Cagliostro began to declaim in Italian and Latin, but mainly in Arabic. But some error must have crept into the text, because it had precisely the opposite effect from the one intended. Four black devils rushed out of the cave and beat Marano thoroughly, until he ran off home, howling all the way. Marano tried to sue, but Cagliostro had found it prudent to make a rapid departure from the city of his birth.

Now, apparently, he really did travel through the Levant, and indeed in the company of someone called Altotas. He even went to Malta, where Pinto d'Alfonseca, the Grand Master of the knightly Order, did actually take him in, so that Cagliostro could assist him with his alchemical experiments. Either he inserted these real names and facts into his otherwise fanciful autobiography, or some of them were added by the scribe.

From Malta he went to Rome, and there he did in fact marry. The lady concerned was Lorenza (not Serafina) Feliciani, who was not exactly of noble birth but the daughter of a simple foundry worker. Where the many sources do agree is that she was extremely beautiful, with her girlish charm and blue-eyed allure. Casanova wrote about her in his memoirs in tones of the greatest rapture—which may not mean much in itself, since he used the same language about all the ladies (the secret of all Don Juans being to find all women pleasing)—but in this case there are other, less flamboyant, expert witnesses. However Cagliostro is not ranked among the experts. Men did fall in love with her at a distance, but in the eighteenth century love was not a particularly romantic business, but somewhat detached. The sort of people who rhapsodised about her had never seen her. Two of them actually fought a duel over whether the dimple was on the left or the right side of the face.

When, later on, the lovely Lorenza was incarcerated in the Bastille during the necklace trial, her lawyer, Maître Polverit, described her to the court as an "angel in human form, sent down to earth to share and sweeten the days of her wonder-working husband; a woman so lovely that her beauty had no equal; and yet, for all that, she is a model of gentleness and obedience, submitting to her fate because she could not conceive of any other way to bear it. Her radiant nature, and her perfection above all other mere mortals, hold out a symbol which we can worship but not understand. And this angel, so incapable of sinning, is now held under lock and key. It is a cruel absurdity, and one that must be put right forthwith. What can a being of this nature have to do with the business of a law court?" And the Paris Parlement took one look at her and set her free.

Lorenza accompanied her husband on his escapades and in his rather unusual daily life, loyally and sometimes not so loyally, like the sort of favourite charm you might keep in your pocket to ward off bad luck. She was always the angel-doll, untouched by life because she simply didn't understand what it was all about. Perhaps that explains her huge success in French society, where the women understood it only too well.

Malicious minds knew of course that as soon as things started to go badly for Cagliostro he would put her on the market. According to some, he had the generosity of her 'patrons' to thank for his subsequent, undoubtedly huge, fortune. In her numerous statements to the court Lorenza regularly mentions some gentleman or other approaching her with less than honourable intentions, while she, generally, defends her innocence and honour. Generally, we insist, because there was an occasion when she moved in with a lawyer called Duplessis, who maintained the two of them for a while until he became bored with the whole business and had Cagliostro locked up as a fraudster. She then gave evidence against her own husband, denouncing him as work-shy and a *coquin*, and was detained at his request in the St Pelágia prison. But she later withdrew her allegation, and he withdrew his, she got out of prison, and they loved one another just as much as before.

One story says that she turned one of her suitors away on the grounds that she couldn't possibly betray her husband because he could make himself invisible and be present in more than one place at a time.

He certainly pops up in a great many places, whether passing himself off as a soldier in the Prussian army or as earning his living as a draughtsman and stage designer. He travelled to Madrid, made a pilgrimage to Santiago de Compostela, then returned to Palermo, where the jeweller Marano took him to court, but a powerful local prince (Lorenza's admirer) beat up the prosecution lawyer and put an end to the case. Finally, in 1777, he turns up in London once again—and here the true story begins. If we can believe his detractors, he had up to this point been a mere petty swindler—an underworld figure, an insignificant member of the social underclass. But his wanderings had shaped his character. He had matured, gained much useful experience, and come to the point where, as Almeras puts it, he still lived by throwing dust in people's eyes, but its quality was now very much finer.

The great change began on 12th April 1777, when Cagliostro and his wife were admitted to the Hope Lodge of Freemasons in London, whose members were mostly French and Italian craftsmen and manufacturers. It became the Archimedes point from which Cagliostro would move the world.

When, dear reader, you hear what follows about the Order of Freemasons, think of it as quite unconnected with whatever else you know (or believe you know) about the organisation.

Do not think of it now in terms of its links with the liberal-democratic powers, and whether those powers were the cause of past, present and future wars. In the eighteenth century the movement stood for something very different from what it later became. To support this argument we need only mention that most authorities are convinced that French Freemasonry had a strongly Catholic character from the outset. This meant that, by its rules, no atheist could be admitted to its ranks; and indeed, for all their supposed tolerance, no French lodge in the period admitted a single Jew. A later charge against the organisation is that it prepared the way for the Revolution. Quite how far that is true is difficult to determine, but what is beyond question is that the Revolution put a temporary stop to the working of the lodges.

Freemasons are pleased to trace the history of the 'Royal Art' back to the earliest biblical times. James Anderson, the first historian of the movement, claimed in a work published in 1723 that, "During their wanderings in the wilderness, Moses, in his capacity of Grand Master, would often assemble the Israelites in a regular lodge which they all attended." King Solomon was also a Grand Master, since he built the temple, and so too, for reasons which are rather less clear, was Nebuchadnezzar.

Other writers trace the origins of the movement back to the Knights Templar, and others again to the mysterious and, properly speaking, non-existent Rosicrucian fraternity of the seventeenth century. Less fanciful observers settle for English precursors of the lodges in the medieval stonemason corporations, or guilds. That suggestion has the ring of probability, but even it cannot be proved. The theory is that at some point in the seventeenth century the stonemasons, by now rather isolated and very much in decline, admitted (in full accordance with their basic constitution) members of the gentry and upper middle class who wished to exchange views and opinions of the world in a secure atmosphere under the protection of the guild. These would be people who were disenchanted with religious wars, thus entrenching the principles of tolerance and open-ended inquiry into ideas that were ahead of their time. The records of some of these lodges go back a very long way. Those of Edinburgh Mary's Number One, for example, claim to date from 1599.

The movement finally emerges from this twilight of myth and conjecture in 1717, when, on St John's day (St John being their patron saint), the first English Grand Lodge was founded, absorbing most of the other English lodges that were still active. Its French counterparts had come into being a few years earlier.

It is difficult to be very sure what these first lodges actually did, and on what sort of ideological basis they existed. What is sure is that dinners had a prominent place on their agendas, often with the Grand Master as presiding host. By this time he probably considered the lodge as his own property, effectively a component of his business or factory, and no doubt this further softened the general ethos towards one of 'enlightened' Epicureanism.

The history of the French lodges in the eighteenth century is rather more troubled. In 1737 the authorities began persecuting them, and in the following year Clement XII issued a Papal Bull excommunicating their members. But neither the religious or secular authorities took this very seriously.

In 1737 a Scottish nobleman called Ramsay reformed the French lodges and founded the so-called Scottish Order, creating a great many more ranks than the original three, the better to reward members' loyalty. In this celebrated re-foundation the ethical principles of Freemasonry are more clearly manifest. Ramsay wrote to his brethren about four ideals: first, philanthropy, the love of one's fellow man, regardless of nationality or religious denomination, thus giving an element of universal brotherhood to the organisation; second, moral purity (a homosexual, for example, could not be admitted until he changed his ways and affirmed that he would pay appropriate respect to the 'fair sex'); third, absolute secrecy; and finally, love of the fine arts. Among these he included academic scholarship, and held out certain universal disciplines as the most ideal: his hope was that the Order would undertake something like the project which, a few years later, became the *Grande encyclopédie*.

In 1738 the French Freemasons elected a member of the royal family, Louis de Bourbon-Condé, Duc de Clermont, as their Grand Master. Clermont fulfilled his duties with the usual Bourbon insouciance, deputing a dancing master, Lacorne, in his place. Lacorne's rather dubious character alienated the more serious elements in the membership, and this led to rifts and divisions that lasted for decades. To counterbalance this they instituted the Grand Orient. Its Grand Master, the Duc de Chartres, finally reunited the warring lodges after Clermont's death in 1771. This Duc de Chartres was none other than Philippe-Égalité, the future revolutionary Duc d'Orléans, who, though a Grand Master and supporter of the Revolution, did not himself escape the guillotine, but whose descendants became the ruling (junior Bourbon) House of Orléans.

What were the Freemasons doing when not at war with one another, and what did their work consist of? They organised meetings, initiated new members, progressed up the ranks via elaborate ceremonies, dined, performed charitable deeds, and practised philanthropy. It was an intensely theatrical age—as early as 1754 the appearance of the actor Manelli in a new *opera buffa* had led to such heated conflict between the devotees of French and Italian music that the Parisian Jansenists and ultramontanes set aside their mutual hostility that had been threatening a religious civil war. In such a climate, when everything was played out in the full glare of publicity, and the arrival of a new theatre company could put a temporary stop to revolutionary activity, the Freemasons no doubt took a charitable view of all varieties of theatrical genre.

In 1782 a market vegetable stall-holder called Mme Menthe was disinherited by her wealthy sister. Despite this she then gave a home to this wicked sibling's illegitimate son, even though she already had ten children of her own. Shortly afterwards she gave birth to her nineteenth child (eight having died young), and to mark the occasion the Sincerity Lodge arranged a grand surprise for her. "The meeting," wrote a contemporary, "took place with more than one hundred and forty illustrious members, of both sexes, present. After the usual ceremonies, the curtain rose and there on the stage, seated on a throne, was the worthy Mme Menthe, surrounded by her ten children, and, at her feet, the child she had so magnanimously taken in. The entire family (so deserving of compassion!) had been fitted out with new clothes at the Lodge's expense. The presiding Marquis, in a speech that was as harrowing as it was eloquent, explained the meaning of the striking tableau before our eyes. At the most moving point in his address, the Comtesse X placed a citizen's crown on the lady's head, the Marquise Y held out a purse to her containing a considerable sum of money, and the Comtesse Z profferred a trousseau for the infant so newly brought into the world. The child that Mme Menthe had taken in was then adopted by the Lodge, who undertook to raise it and take every care of it."

The brothers Goncourt mention a letter written to the Princesse de Lamballe by Marie-Antoinette, in which she states: "I read with great interest what was happening in the Freemasonry lodges you took charge of at the start of the year. I see that all they do apart from their charitable works is sing pretty songs. But by working for the release of prisoners and finding homes for young women your lodges are following in our own footsteps—which will certainly not stop us doing the same for the girls in our care or finding homes for the children on our list."

But the real attraction of Freemasonry in this period lay in its secrecy. Members were bound to that absolutely. Most of the time those secrets, involving special symbols, practices and so forth, would have had no significance whatsoever: mystique was practised for its own sake. Of course, people have always loved secrets—they still do. But in eighteenth-century France, when life was lived in permanent public view, when non-stop gossip ensured that everyone knew everyone else's business and the whole country was one great, malicious family, privacy held an especially powerful attraction. The favoured Court style, rococo, with its exquisite, tiny interiors, was an art of intimacy; and the rest of the nation also lived in confined spaces. The idea of a shut door was unknown. In such an age, the concept of a closed and secret meeting fulfilled an important spiritual need.

Everyone—especially the very young and the adolescent—adores a secret. Youth is a time of secret writing, secret languages, secret symbols daubed on walls. Some secrets are to be shared only between boys, never with women, not even mothers (especially, Freudians would say, not with mothers). Within young male groups, by some atavistic process, some ancient primitive impulse rises out of the deep layer that Jung calls the collective unconscious, a race-memory of the male-bonding and male-only societies of primitive peoples. In ancient times, and even today in rural parts of Africa and New Guinea, pubescent youths are initiated into manhood in harsh tests involving cruel rites. Thereafter they become independent of their families and live with other youths in all-male compounds, where women are admitted only on very special occasions. The juveniles form a separate little social group in defiant opposition to the adults, and leave these closed communities only to establish families of their own. It is from these all-male societies that the great negro outlaw gangs are formed, such as the Leopard People of Liberia, who hold entire countries in terror.

The higher civilisations were founded on the family unit, thus abolishing these exclusive pre-adult and adult male-only societies. But they could not root out the innate tendency which still sometimes surfaces, the eternal impulse of the man to turn his back on women and the family, return to his boyhood-self and join some all-male group in a great, daring, heroic and pointless adventure. The same primal impulse gave rise to the knightly orders, whose initiation ceremonies are a vestige of the old puberty rites. And initiation was the central feature of the Freemasons' ceremonies too, because the movement was, at base, another such all-male society, much tamed, of course, and gentrified. This, after the element of secrecy, must have been its second most important attraction.

The secretiveness of the Freemasons tempted certain individuals to set up imitation lodges for the sort of people who wanted to be part of a secret society but were deterred by their own frivolous natures from the more serious, or morally daunting, purposes of the real ones. Thus we find the Mopsli Order (in Austria) whose initiation rites required the new member to kiss a dog of that breed, not on the mouth but at the opposite end. However, when the intrepid candidate bent over to approach his task, a pleasant surprise awaited him: the dog was made of silk and velvet. In the Tappo Order in Italy (the name means 'cork' or 'plug') would-be knights and ladies were required to kiss the Grand Master in a similar place, only to discover that it wasn't actually the Grand Master, etc etc. Members of the French Ordre de la Félicité would set out on a journey to the Blessed Isles carrying Freemason-style emblems. For these fellowships, as with the Fendeurs Charbonniers and the Nymphes de la Rose, the purposes were purely erotic, involving secret orgies … if indeed these societies did exist, and were not simply an invention of the gossiping tendency of the age.

Goethe, as we have already mentioned, was so fascinated by the case of the Queen's necklace that he wrote a play about it, *Der Gross-Kophta*. In it he writes: "*Der Menschen lieben die Dämmerung mehr als den hellen Tag, und eben in der Dämmerung erscheinen die Gespenster*"—Men prefer twilight to the full glare of day, and it is in the twilight that the ghosts show themselves. In the mysterious darkness that the lodges exploited to satisfy people's eternal longing for secrets, the ghosts were not slow to appear. Eighteenth-century Freemasonry became the home of occultism. For more mystical souls, the secrets that existed merely for their own sake, the noble aspirations and symbols, were not enough. They held meetings separately from the lodges to seek out the real mysteries, those of nature itself, and the supernatural. In other words, to pursue alchemy and spiritualism.

Thus eighteenth-century Freemasonry became associated with Satanism, black magic and even the conjuration of devils. The Grand Master, Philippe-Égalité himself, personally believed in the black arts and, if we can trust the retrospective memoirs of the Marquise de Créquy, even invoked Satan, who appeared in the form of a naked man, very pale, with black eyes and a scar across his left temple (apparently the result of a lightning strike), pronounced the ominous words: "*Victoire et malheur! Victoire et malheur!*"—Victory and disaster!—and vanished into thin air.

The various strands of eighteenth-century occultism all converge in the person of the great seer Emanuel Swedenborg. It was he who gave form and direction to the mystical aspirations of the time, and his considerable influence is with us still. There are sects in America today whose beliefs derive from his teachings.

Emanuel Swedenborg (1688-1772) was a natural scientist and engineer in his younger days, who went on to become an important person in his native Sweden, was ennobled, and was elected to membership of most of the learned societies in Europe. In 1745, he was dining in a private room in his favourite restaurant in London. When he finished, a kind of fog filled the room and hideous creatures appeared, writhing on the floor. The fog dispersed, and in a corner of the room he saw a man bathed in light. The man commanded him, in ringing tones: "Do not eat so much!" and vanished. Swedenborg went home, but the man reappeared the next day, dressed in purple, and informed him that he was God.

From that point onwards, Swedenborg was a prophet. He gave up all his official positions in order to live for and by his revelations. In his books he writes (at incredible length) about his supernatural experiences as dictated to him by spirits.

What most surprises the modern reader about his visions is the easy, natural, phlegmatic way he moves among scenes of the other world. As he records the location of the heavenly cities, the variety of their citizens and their manner of living, and explains their various theological preoccupations and other related questions, we almost feel as if we are reading a Baedeker. According to his writings, he had travelled much where few mortals had gone before, and on these journeys had made the acquaintance of a great many angels and devils, together with spirits belonging to an intermediate group who "live between heaven and hell". These and many other things he discussed with Martin Luther. Luther, having arrived in the other world, moved first into much the same sort of house as he had occupied back home in Eisleben, and here he would sit on a throne and declaim his sermons. But in 1757, when his period of transformation in the spirit world had been completed, the house was taken from him, and shortly afterwards, under the influence of Swedenborg and others, he renounced those of his ideas that differed from those of the author. Swedenborg also met the philosopher Melanchton, who spent long periods at his heavenly desk writing, just as he had on earth, that good works did not matter, only faith. But when the new heaven was built, in 1757, he too corrected his original ideas. He now resides in the south-eastern region of heaven, and when he goes for a stroll his footsteps produce the clang of someone treading in iron shoes across a stone pavement.

Swedenborg also discovered that in the other world the Dutch generally did rather well. They ran flourishing businesses that were highly profitable because they were working for the sake of it and not for money. They could be easily identified by the affluence displayed by the way they lived. The Jews, on the other hand, did the dirty jobs, huddled amid stench and squalor; otherwise their main occupation was buying and selling precious stones, and a few of them became extremely rich. From time to time robed angels dressed as Christian converts would seek them out to try and win their souls, but with little success. The English, given their love of independence, of the instinctual life, and of freedom of thought, did relatively well up there. The Germans did much worse, since they "live in separate little states under local despots and, unlike the English and Dutch, enjoy no freedom of speech, spoken or written—and where those freedoms are shackled, so too is thought".

Incidentally, the other world has none of the eternal, impassable borders of Dante's vision. According to Swedenborg, it is simply a state of mind: people are sent to hell or raised up to heaven not by God but by their own mentality, and when they change their spiritual condition they are moved from one place to another accordingly. So how could it be that the denizens of hell, on discovering that their beliefs have been misguided, and that they have been sent there because of their spiritual state, do not instantly change their ways and thus claim their ticket to eternal salvation? The answer, according to Swedenborg, is that hell is not especially unpleasant. Everyone there is comfortable in his or her own way: the inhabitants rather like the revolting smell and feel thoroughly at home. They do occasionally visit heaven, but find it all rather alarming and disconcertingly unfamiliar, and cannot wait to get back to the comforts of the Other Place.

In all this deep philosophising it is the matter-of-factness and surprisingly narrow range of his theological interests that make Swedenborg the belated child of earlier centuries. He has been the subject of some remarkable comparisons, for example with the sort of man whose desires fail to keep pace with the growth in his understanding, like the lecher who hides a whore in his cellar, goes upstairs and has a perfectly sensible conversation with his wife and guests on the subject of virginity, then returns downstairs to give free rein to his passions. But despite these comparisons, Swedenborg's style is in the end somewhat arid and coldly rationalistic. In a strange way what he says rings true, but he lacks a soaring imagination. It could be that he was a great visionary, but a poor poet. He was certainly not Dante. Perhaps he did genuinely see the other world with the eye of the soul, but his vision is much less compelling than that of the great Florentine, who found himself lost 'at the mid-point of our life's journey' in imagination only.

And perhaps that is the secret of his power. Swedenborg is the petty-bourgeois of the supernatural. He stands in the same relation to Dante as the 'blood brotherhood' of the Freemasons does to the Leopard People of West Africa. It would have been no use talking to him about such grandiose matters as the Rose of Heaven or the Worm at the Heart of the World. For him the whole business is really quite simple if approached in a common-sense way. Such is his manner whenever he talks about souls. His souls—this point he cannot stress sufficiently—are no different from the living. They possess everything that humans do; they eat and drink, and live married lives. It is just that they do all this on a spiritual plane, though their spirit status should not be overemphasised. Souls are still human. The secret of Swedenborg's power is that he reduces the spirit world to an everyday level, thus popularising it. Not everyone can pick his or her way through the grim tercets of Dante's vision: not everyone can breathe the alarming air of the world of magic. But with the aid of Swedenborg's guide to the other world we can journey in confidence through the mysteries of heaven and hell, as on a trip to the heavenly Jerusalem organised by Thomas Cook. And of course Swedenborg is the seer whom Cagliostro put to such brilliant use as fodder for his ignorant and simple-minded followers. For his purposes, the great mystics would have been of no use at all. Not one word of the teachings of Jalaluddin Rumi or Meister Eckhart would have been comprehensible either to him or to his disciples.

But we have not dwelt on Swedenborg at such length simply because it was from him that Cagliostro took everything that is intelligible in his theories, as he expounded them; rather it is because we feel that it is precisely through them that we come closest to the essence of the age, to the prevailing mentality and mood that both make it comprehensible and reveal the necklace trial as its most characteristic, dramatic and indeed symbolic event.

The second half of the eighteenth century is described in literary histories as the pre-romantic age. That is to say, it is the period that saw the birth and flowering of the ideas and general sensibility that came to dominate the first half of the following century, the romantic age proper. At this point these developments stood in relation to full-blown romanticism as the child does to the young adult and mature man. The people of the late eighteenth century found themselves living in an old civilisation, one that was approaching its end, a social order that was over-ripe in significant ways, but one whose notions of the world were naive and somewhat childlike. Childlike, and idyllic. No other generation lived at such a distance from tragedy. Beneath their powdered elegance, the earlier decades, those of Louis XV and the rococo, harboured a genuine sense of the tragedy of life, but with the accession of Louis XVI all that seemed to have melted away. People felt that they were standing on the threshold of a new golden age. The leading thinkers of the entire period all stood for optimism. Under Louis XV that optimism had remained a mere triumph of philosophy. Now it became a sense of life. The pre-romantics lived in expectation of some sort of miracle—a miracle that would make everything beautiful and happy, while leaving everything exactly where it had always been.

The people of the pre-romantic age were every bit as rational as those of the baroque and rococo, but—and this is what was new—they also believed in miracles. Or at least, they wanted to. The literature of the time certainly reveals this need for an element of the miraculous. Milton came into fashion, as did the ghost story (though Voltaire naturally would only allow his ghosts onstage in broad daylight), and the mystical, occult and other such movements of the time are evidence that it was not only writers who yearned for that element of the miraculous, but, as it were, life itself.

But this habit of living in the expectation of a miracle is also a widespread attribute of humanity in general; it is a feature of history to which no one age can lay exclusive claim. The early church lived in permanent expectation of miracles, which duly happened. In the year 1000 the whole of humanity waited in quivering excitement for the greatest miracle of all, the end of the world, which didn't. This mentality is never itself the symptom of an age—what signifies is the nature of the expected miracle. The pre-romantics were looking for a pre-romantic one: gentle, idyllic, optimistic and perfectly simple. Which is why Swedenborg is its prophet—Swedenborg who dined in restaurants while the vision waited on him; Swedenborg, who knew in 1757, beyond the flicker of a doubt, that the last judgment was at hand, the new heaven would be built and a new world order come into being—though nothing of course would change, and everyone could carry on with his daily business (if a bourgeois) or simply enjoy the benefits (if an aristocrat).

Each of the actors in our story was waiting for that sort of miracle: Boehmer, that his wonderful bauble would, by some miraculous means, come to encircle some suitably miraculous imperial neck, and that the owner of that neck would pay him 1,600,000 livres with miraculous promptitude. Jeanne de la Motte looked for a miracle to restore her to her ancestral Valois status, and the longer she waited, the less it was likely to happen. Rohan waited for a miracle that would secure the Queen's favour (and indeed favours), and the length of that wait kept him moping about in his fantastical rooms at Saverne. For Cagliostro, who was to enjoy the profits of everyone else's hopes, miracles were his bread and butter. Marie-Antoinette meanwhile drifted from pleasure to pleasure while she waited for the true womanly miracle that would make all pleasure-seeking superfluous, and Louis XVI longed for a miracle-working finance minister who would make the deficit disappear, without the need to grind even more revenue out of the people, or curtail his household expenditure.

And the whole of France was waiting for the greatest miracle of all, the happiness of the people. They knew that a new age was at hand; they earnestly believed that the planned reforms would soon come to fruition. They rather imagined that some celestial monarch, surrounded by his courtiers, would descend between stage clouds while the angels Gluck and Grétry sounded an entrance on their silver-tongued trumpets; the King would raise his sceptre, and everyone in France would be happy. Not in their most fevered dreams did they imagine that, far from descending from above, the new age would burst forth from the underworld, from the Quartier St Antoine, with a Frisian cap on its head. The Lord punished his people's blindness by granting them their wish. A few more years, and the miracle would indeed happen.

After this premonition of tragedy, let us return to the man who represents the burlesque element in our story, the alchemist's Figaro.

In London, Cagliostro not only penetrated the secrets of the Freemasons, he also became involved in a highly complicated lawsuit which turned on a necklace—a foretaste of greater things to come. His defence was that his accusers, from whom he had swindled the necklace, had harassed him, constantly forcing presents on him to get him to name his price for allowing himself to be drawn into the whole shady business. But we must pass quickly over our friend's picaresque adventures, however much they reflect the style of the period (the eighteenth century was the heyday of such adventurers and their escapades), apart from noting that he bamboozled his way with great success across the states of Eastern Europe, via The Hague, Leipzig, Mittau (the capital of the then independent Duchy of Courland), St Petersburg and Warsaw. Anyone who had known Cagliostro and his wife a few years earlier, as pilgrims in Spain or as a starveling couple haunting the inner-city districts of Paris and London, would not have recognised the mysterious Count and Countess they had become.

What a splendid sight it must have been, when the great adventurer arrived in a foreign city, outriders trotting before his four-horse carriage, with footmen clinging to the sides; taking rooms in the most elegant hostelry in town, and promptly inviting his new acquaintances to dinner. In no time at all a little sect would have formed around him, a secret circle of initiates. Among those flocking to his door would be the merely curious and those attracted by his wife's beauty, but the greater part were there for the sage, the prophet, and the great magus.

Cagliostro was now travelling the world as the splendidly aristocratic and splendidly mysterious envoy of the Freemasonry lodges—a man on a cosmic-diplomatic mission. From the enigmatic shadows of his casual utterances one seemed to gather that he had been sent to Europe by Grand Masters dwelling in the depths of the pyramids, to inaugurate the Order's most ancient and uniquely blessed ceremony, the 'Egyptian Rite'. Its highest functionary was none other than the Great Kophta ("What, Your Excellency, you have never heard of the Great Kophta?!"), heir to the secret knowledge of the Prophet Elijah (almost certainly *the* Prophet Elijah) ... and the Great Kophta must, surely, have been one and the same as this Count Cagliostro? These were truly great mysteries, not previously revealed to man, but patience was needed. The time for all these things was at hand, its hour was nigh—you had only to read the scriptures.

Meanwhile the Count was busy healing the sick—with varying results, just like the 'real' doctors, but with a few remarkable successes. He restored the once-unwrinkled faces of elderly ladies, and returned gentlemen of a certain age to their former youthful virility. He saw into the future. At his command spirits appeared in pitchers filled with water. The medium who actually saw these apparitions would be a young boy or a simple virgin, but it was Cagliostro who interpreted them. And he had vast amounts of money. Its source remains a secret to this day.

And so he arrived in Strasbourg.

If we struggle to believe that Cagliostro was the appointed saviour of mankind, but rather suspect that he was driven by somewhat more selfish and less honourable motives—as, sadly, we must conjecture—then we should consider his conduct in Strasbourg his truest work of art, the masterpiece of the genre.

He arrived on 19th September 1780, preceded by his fame as a miraculous healer. A huge crowd lined the banks of the Rhine to await his coming. Everyone had their own interesting story about him. He made his entrance in a carriage drawn by six horses, and his wife's modest, virginal smile enchanted everyone. He wore his hair curled into little bunches; his blue taffeta robe was braided with pure gold and silver and glittered with jewels, both real and false. In his sheer elegance there was something slightly bizarre, a touch too flashy and not quite right, as was the case with his even greater compatriot Casanova. At the side of his hat he sported a tall white feather, an honest detail, since only quack doctors and market criers wore them at the time. For Cagliostro was certainly not the kind of charlatan who mesmerises his worshippers by his aristocratic appearance, his impeccably fine taste in costume and manners. He had no need for that sort of display. He had all the weapons at his command to retain the loyalty of the immediate associates by whom he was really judged. He could remain a mountebank, an organ-grinder, a monkey-tamer, and yet the great and the small prostrated themselves at his feet. A true triumph of the mind.

Nor did he live above his station. In Strasbourg his arrangements were decidedly simple and austere. He took lodgings first with a woman who sold tobacco, then with a canon's wife. The common people adored him, and he in turn treated everyone with the same unvarying courtesy.

In Strasbourg, as in the cities of Eastern Europe, he founded another Egyptian lodge. But here, for the first time, he provided evidence of the sort of good deeds expected of a Freemason. He gave two hundred livres to a poor Italian to get him out of debtors' prison, and followed it up with a full set of clothing when the man was released. He spent whole days visiting the sick, often staying late into the night. He treated the poor of the city without charge, and likewise the rich, who gradually came to seek him out in ever increasing numbers. They tried to press gratuities on him, but he would take nothing. This charlatan was generous, it seemed, to the point of naivety. It took a long time for him to realise that his assistant was diverting large sums into his own pocket, but when he did, he threw him out, and there was a very ugly lawsuit between the two of them.

Dr Mark Haven, quoting reliable witnesses, lists several occasions when Cagliostro's treatment of the sick produced remarkable results. Many of his prescriptions and procedures are recorded. On the whole he knew little more, if not much less, than the official doctors of the time, though he did have one or two special remedies. He made use of the alchemists' *aurum potabile*— 'drinkable gold', a mixture of nitrate, grease and mercury. There was a 'wine of Egypt', reserved mainly for the elderly, and a 'pick-me-up powder' of which he was especially proud. When John Lavater, that rather odd philosopher and childhood friend of Goethe, founded the study of physiognomy and graphology, he called on Cagliostro to ask him what was the basis of his cures. The magus answered with an enigmatic smile: "*In herbis, in verbis, in lapidibus*"—through the magical power of herbs, words and stones—just like the doctors of the middle ages.

Nevertheless, his patients did get better. The obvious explanation, based on everyday experience, is that some of them would have recovered with or without medical intervention. A second reason was pointed out by his contemporary Baronne Oberkirch, whose notes on Cagliostro's dealings with Rohan are extremely valuable. According to the Baronne, "Cagliostro cured only those who had a positive state of mind, or at least those whose imaginations were strong enough to assist the power of the remedy." That is to say, Cagliostro practised what we would now call psychosomatic medicine—he cured his patients through the mind and imagination, directing the healing along an inner path. Like every other charlatan, he must have been a superb psychologist, and there is no doubt that his powers of suggestion were considerable. We should also remember that in past centuries the mentally ill produced many more physical symptoms than they do today. So whoever dealt with the psychic disorder removed the pathological accompaniment at the same time.

His own presence was mesmeric, as the Baronne knew well: "He was not particularly handsome" (Carlyle tells us that he had the broadest nose of anyone in the eighteenth century) "but I never saw a more striking physiognomy. In particular, his glance carried an almost supernatural profundity. It would be impossible to describe the expression in his eyes: at once fire and ice, it drew you in and repelled you; it demanded a response and aroused the most insatiable curiosity."

Gradually, the upper echelons of Strasbourg society gathered round him. Marshall Contades, the Marquis de la Salle, Royal Councillor Béguin, Baron Dampierre, Count Lützelburg, Baron Zucmantel ... their names are not very familiar to us but all were clearly members of the Alsatian nobility. A financier called Sarazin, whom Cagliostro helped to become a father, lived, with his wife, as a close neighbour of Cagliostro for many years, sharing a house for some of that time. Another person healed by the magus was Jeanne de la Motte's patroness, Mme de Boulainvilliers. And all this entirely without charge.

The figure of the miraculous healer is naturally surrounded by countless legends, not all of them favourable. (We can imagine what the established doctors had to say about their unwelcome rival.) One of those stories, although very simple and entirely without foundation, is so delightful we cannot resist telling it.

A nobleman approached Cagliostro to ask for an elixir that would stop his wife being unfaithful. The man was given a little bottle.

"Before you go to bed," he was told, "drink the contents of this phial. If your wife really is unfaithful, by the next morning you will have turned into a cat."

The gentleman went back to Paris, told the story to his wife and drank the liquid in the bottle.

The next day the wife came into her husband's room and saw a large black cat sitting on the pillow.

"Oh my God!" she wailed between her sobs, "I only deceived the poor fellow once, with that awful man next door, who really wasn't worth it, and now I've lost the best man in the world, and I'll never see him again!"

Whereupon the husband crept out from under the bed, and forgave her.

"Yes, yes," I hear you say, my dear, long-suffering reader, "this is all very well, but where's the profit in it? If he doesn't charge the poor, or even the financiers and the aristocracy for his cures, what is he living on? It seems he really did take us all in. He wasn't a charlatan, he was an idiot."

Patience, gentle reader, you really must trust him. Cagliostro was a man of large views. He had no desire to get rich by healing the sick—the occupation of medicine was far beneath him. He was fired by a higher ambition, pursuing nobler game. The whole point of the miracle-doctoring was to bring him to the attention of the one person on whose account he had come to Strasbourg. The true mark of his genius is that he had calculated precisely which *grand seigneur* in all Europe would be the most susceptible to being completely taken in by someone like himself. That person was none other than Cardinal Rohan. Just as Boehmer had calculated that his wonderful necklace must end up around the neck of Marie-Antoinette, so Cagliostro had decided that if anyone would swallow the Great Egyptian mumbo-jumbo, the Great Pyramid moonshine, that person would be Rohan. And he waited—waited most patiently.

He did not have to wait too long. He had been residing in Strasbourg for just two or three months when the Cardinal, suffering from a severe attack of asthma, left Saverne and came into town to consult the miracle doctor. Cagliostro was summoned to the Palace.

He knew the hour had struck. He understood that everything he did now would be of critical importance, that everything would turn on first impressions. He returned the message:

"If my Lord Cardinal is ill, he may come to me and I will heal him. But if he is well, he has no need of me, nor I of him."

Rohan was not accustomed to being addressed in this manner. Cagliostro won the first round, and the Cardinal went to him. The impression Cagliostro had on him is described by his secretary, the Abbé Georgel:

"In his somewhat uncommunicative face I saw such an imposing dignity that I was filled with a kind of religious veneration, and my first words were dictated by pure respect. Our conversation was fairly brief, but it filled me with the most ardent desire to get to know him better."

So Rohan reacted precisely as Cagliostro might have imagined in his most optimistic daydreams. And the miracle he had been waiting for duly followed.

He continued to keep his distance; in fact his behaviour was at times almost hostile. But gradually he softened towards Rohan, and not long afterwards addressed him in these words:

"Your soul is worthy of mine. Your merits are such that I shall share all my secrets with you."

They say that that day was the happiest day in Rohan's life. Poor *grand seigneur*! Fairy godmothers had stood round his cradle to furnish him with everything a man might desire: glory, wealth, a sensitive appreciation of scholarship and art. His life was encompassed by beauty and the calm knowledge of his own superiority. But he was one of those men who burn with a thirst for the eternal that no earthly joy can assuage. Had he not lived at the end of the sceptical eighteenth century he might have found in the Church itself what he looked for elsewhere in vain, and perhaps even become a truly sainted pope. But such was his fate—a false prophet entangled him in a bogus eternity. People in former centuries knew that at the end of the world the Antichrist would appear, doing everything that Christ had done, but that every one of his deeds would be false and his gold would crumble to dust in the hands of his followers. Rohan's age was, in its own small way, the end of the world: its destiny was that of a world approaching its end—the fate of impending revolution.

Before long, the false prophet had moved into the Bishop's Palace and the Cardinal had placed his horse and carriage at his disposal. And soon enough, the two were deep in alchemical experiments. The Cardinal proudly showed Baronne Oberkirch an imposing diamond that Cagliostro had created for him before his very eyes. They even manufactured gold. They predicted, to the precise second, the death of Maria Theresa. They conjured up the souls of women with whom Rohan had once been deeply in love. In his workroom Rohan erected a bust with the subscription: "To the divine Cagliostro, the godlike Cagliostro".

But stop! Is this possible? The cultured Rohan, son of the Age of Reason, believed in the making of gold? He certainly did, and in this respect he was no more credulous than his contemporaries. In truth, the eighteenth century was the heyday of alchemy. Large numbers of professional alchemists lived in the St Marceau quarter of Paris. Some were devilish poor, but others became wealthy through the patronage of people in high places. Casanova himself would cheerfully resort to making gold when things were not going well for him—at around this time he prised a large sum of money out of Prince Biron of Courland with a display of alchemical wizardry. In Hungary during the same period Sándor Báróczi, the guardsman and writer, was experimenting with the Philosopher's Stone. Kazinczy, that most austere of literary critics, read his works with cries of delight, and Kazinczy's uncle, Count József Török, put his entire fortune into alchemical experiments—which was why the Kazinczys lived in such poverty at Széphalom.

Mercantilism, the prevailing economic doctrine of the seventeenth and eighteenth centuries, contributed to the extraordinary rise of the art. Economic thinkers of the time taught—and the nations made their arrangements accordingly—that a country's wealth increased with the amount of silver and gold in its domains. So people did everything they could to raise the price of their exports in the hope of increasing the amount of precious metal coming into the country in exchange for those goods. But the policy actually reduced imports generally, and obstructed the free movement of those metals. No one at the time stopped to consider that if you simply stockpiled your gold and silver, and stifled the flow of imports, thus making it impossible to use your bullion to buy raw materials or other commodities, it was a dead business. Your wealth became purely symbolic. It had no actual currency, and prevented both the state and the people from enjoying the benefits that real wealth would bring.

Nor did they consider that, as the quantity of precious metal increased, its value and purchasing power would be reduced, and the price of goods would rise. Today every child discovers for himself that there is no point in alchemy, because if you really could produce gold in vast quantities it would become worthless.

However, as we have already said, people in those days were unimaginably deficient in their economic reasoning, and unable to foresee the simplest of consequences.

For just this reason, anyone involved in historical research will sometimes feel extremely sceptical not only about historical materialism as such, but about the whole modern approach to the subject, which ascribes such central importance to economic conditions. If people were so little aware of the laws of economic life, then those laws probably had a much smaller influence on their actions than they would today—or, at the very least, the influence would not have been as straightforward and direct. People are swayed not by the real laws of economics but by their economic delusions and superstitions. For that reason it is dangerous to impose modern economic motives on historical periods, and even to believe that wars in those days were fought over raw materials or for reasons of trade.

By the reckoning of his biographer François d'Almeras, between 1780 and 1785 Cagliostro had extracted cash and jewellery from the Cardinal to the value of two to three hundred thousand livres.

Chapter Five

The Bower of Venus

E VERY TYPE OF HOSPITALITY must come to an end, and Jeanne
de Valois and the illustrious Comte her husband could not
live for ever in the fairytàle castle at Saverne. With grieving hearts
they returned to Lunéville. But after Saverne the drabness of life
in a garrison town had even less appeal for them. Jeanne's old
restlessness reasserted itself, La Motte longed for a more comfortable life, and one fine day they turned their backs on the town
and set off to try their luck in Paris.

Luck they certainly needed. Their sole patroness, Mme de
Boulainvilliers, had now died. The Cardinal sent them a few
pieces of gold from time to time, and the pension Mme de
Boulainvilliers had obtained for them was a regular source of
income—but what was that in terms of their pretensions?

Thus began for them that peculiar form of penury that anyone
familiar with the great realist novels of the eighteenth century,
Lesage, Fielding and Smollett, will instantly recognise—endless
quarrels with landlords, with restaurant owners, with pursuing
creditors, and always the sword hanging over their heads that
one day they might be locked up in a debtors' prison.

Nonetheless in 1782 they rented a house in the Rue Neuve, in
St Gilles, among the old palaces of the Marais district.

Under the Valois kings the Marais had been the aristocratic
quarter, and in the present Place des Vosges there still stands
that relic of Paris's most supremely interesting architecture, the
wonderful Place Royale. You step through an archway into an
enclosed square lined with identical houses—it is like diving
beneath the sea into a different world, where time has stood

still. Rohan's palace was also in the Marais, next to that of the Soubises. Nowadays this part of the city is full of immigrants from Eastern Europe, of the poorest and most teeming sort, living in dire congestion and poverty. With city districts it is as with the fashions—they make their way steadily down to the lowest strata of society. The once-proud moustache of the Hungarian nobility is nowadays sported by elderly village carpenters, and the old palace of Henry IV's favourites now accommodates *métèque* families, all tailors and furriers, with eight children. Like everything else, the metropolis is the symbol of constant change.

So how did they make their living, Jeanne and her husband? Partly by their basic quality as fraudsters, their lordly self-confidence. They could always find trusting souls to believe them. One particular line of business that occasionally did very well for them was to buy dress material or something similar on credit, and immediately pawn it. Sometimes they received donations from high-ranking people, in response to their begging letters. They were even supported by loyal old retainers of the Ancien Régime, and were fed for quite some time by the mother of a chambermaid called Jeanne Rosalie.

But we should not think that Jeanne was idle in her penury, or that, like Rohan, she was simply waiting for a miracle to turn her fortunes round. A miracle, yes, but one she intended to bring about herself. Her plan was to recover her ancestral estates (or supposed estates) through royal favour. In this novelettish fantasy she had worked out in great detail how unjustly her illustrious forebears had been stripped of their land. Now was the moment for the King to put everything right. The estates should revert to the royal fisc, then the King, in a kindly gesture, would return them overnight to his distant relatives, the Valois.

The King had after all done far greater things for his followers in this period. All it needed was for someone who had influence in the Court to sponsor her. Patronage has always existed in the world, but in eighteenth-century France there was only one officially recognised and sanctioned way of getting anything done. It was called the royal favour. The royal favour had of course to be earned. But Jeanne had yet to learn that winning it would not be simple.

Apart from her house in Paris she also took a place at Versailles, and she moved constantly between the two venues. Residence at Versailles served partly to make her Parisian creditors, and anyone else to whom she owed money, believe that she was a regular visitor at the Palace, but it also served as a place from which she could watch for any gaps through which she might scuttle into the realm of her heart's desire, the all-powerful world of the Court.

One day Jeanne 'fainted' in the antechamber of Madame Royale, the King's sister the Princess Elisabeth, and when she came to she informed those around her that the reason was that she, the offspring of the Valois, had been destroyed by poverty. The kind-hearted Madame intervened on her behalf and raised another pension for her. But the tiny amount it brought in was of little use to Jeanne.

However, since the fainting idea had worked so well, she tried it again, this time in the antechamber of the Comtesse d'Artois, the King's sister-in-law. It failed completely. There was a third such attempt, even more daring than the first two—in the famous Hall of Mirrors in Versailles, where Marie-Antoinette herself was finally to encounter her—but there was such a throng of people around the Queen that she entirely failed to notice.

Jeanne and her husband tried everything; but there was one step that did not occur to them—to work. In their defence, this was a possibility that would not have occurred to any member of the nobility at the time, not even those very much wiser than themselves. If an aristocrat became bankrupt he looked to the sunshine of royal providence in the same way as, at a later date, the so-called historical classes sought employment with the state or county authority when their lands and fortunes vanished beneath their feet. But when the nobility sank too low to qualify for royal notice, they became fraudsters, trading on the display of rank: the man would become a card-sharper or gigolo, while the woman sold herself. Actual work would have been unthinkable. It would have offended against the ancient order of things, which assigned that role to the middle classes and the peasantry. The concept is difficult to connect with our modern view of the world, but its very absurdity follows directly from the fact that everything in the old order was so fine and wonderful—with everything in its eternally appointed place and moving in fixed circles like the stars. There was no changing your lot in life at will: it was assigned to you forever, by birth. If you fell below your appointed station, you couldn't just swap it for another—you simply plummeted into the void. The aristocrat who settled for the life of confidence trickery rather than work for his living (and besides what work could he do, since by virtue of his rank he had neither craft nor skills?) was effectively keeping a kind of inverted faith with the aristocratic order of things, just as the hypocrite keeps faith with the moral order—if he didn't fundamentally respect morality, he would not pretend to possess it but openly admit his wickedness.

Thus in the eighteenth century, the twilight of the aristocracy, there were a great many fraudsters in France.

All the same, during these years of genteel poverty Jeanne did study for a profession that consorted with her high rank, and even called for a degree of talent. She became a *faiseuse d'affaires*, or, as we would say in Budapest, a lobbyist. It is in the nature of things that business of this type will thrive in the heyday of favour. Like large numbers of her kind, Jeanne was able to persuade middle-class people and tradesmen that she could be useful to them in all sorts of ways through her connections at the Court.

Mercier writes: "For some years now, women have openly played the role of *entremetteuse d'affaires*. They write twenty letters a day, are relentless in their demands, lay siege to ministers, weary the draughtsmen of legislation to death; they have proper offices and keep records, and to get the wheels of fortune turning they find positions for their lovers, their favourites, their husbands and indeed anyone who will pay them."

There certainly were some genuine lobbyists, who produced real results and raised the standing of their trade. But Jeanne was a pseudo-lobbyist. Apart from one royal footman she did not know a single soul at the Court. When she did visit Versailles she shut herself away in an inn to make people believe she was at Court. (It was said that she was not alone on these occasions, but with the hostess's son—the only service that would secure the accommodation.)

For all that, it does appear to have been a profitable line of business. Before very long we find the Rue St Gilles household apparently thriving. It saw a steady procession of guests, and not all of the lowest class. They included: a genuine Comte, who was later forced to resign his officer's rank as a result of the necklace trial; the young lawyer Beugnot, who subsequently left some very interesting observations; Father Loth, a Franciscan, who conducted daily mass for the Countess; and above all, one Réteaux de Villette. Villette was a good-looking nobleman of around thirty, from La Motte's old regiment. His chief qualification was his exquisite, rather effeminate, handwriting. We shall discover soon enough just how important a factor that was.

The household was by now considerable. There were footmen, a cook, a coachman, a jockey, two concierges (a married couple), a chambermaid, a reader (a poor female relation); then Father Loth doubling as major-domo, confessor and drawing-room vicar, in his fine black-lace cassock; a military officer, with whom the Count played a form of draughts called *tric-trac*; a secretary (Réteaux), a family friend (again Réteaux) … what more could one want?

But the freedom from want was an illusion. In fact the only difference now was the greatly increased scale of their debt, and the even greater peril hanging over their heads. Small-scale measures would no longer serve: they needed a master plan, a stroke of genius.

By now we might be thinking that Jeanne had become every bit as obsessed with the Queen as the Cardinal was. Obsession is part of genius. News would naturally have reached her about Her Majesty's intense friendships with the radiantly beautiful Princesse de Lamballe and the Duchesse de Polignac. Perhaps the wonderful woman might take up with her too? For her perverse and twisted nature this was a much more appropriate erotic fantasy than the usual banal notion of the 'wealthy admirer'. To become the King's favourite mistress would be a wonderful thing—one that every Frenchwoman dreamt about then, and continued to do so for over a century, and that Hollywood dreams about still. But to become the Queen's minion would be a hundred times more interesting. Meanwhile her Valois fantasies must have taken on ever more colourful hues. One day the Queen would suddenly discover her. "*Ma chère cousine*," she would say, "I need someone to whom I can open my heart, someone with whom I can be as one human being with another," and, taking her hand, would lead her into the secret, velvet interiors of Le Petit Trianon. In Jeanne's mind the boundary between dreams and reality had long been blurred. Alongside the reality of everyday life, another, more brilliant and surreal reality—the Valois reality—existed for her, as it had ever since her childhood as a beggar. And who could possibly say where the truth began and ended? Thus, by degrees, she persuaded herself that she really was the Queen's confidante. She must have believed it. Had she not, she would not have been able to lie so convincingly. She felt this 'Valois-reality' as an actual something, and it was her duty to find a way to bring it to Paris, and into the Rue St Gilles.

The Queen's intimate friendships had planted ideas in other women's heads before Jeanne's. Earlier, two female fraudsters had put it about that they were royal confidantes. One was

Mme de Cahouet de Villiers (or 'Villers', according to Mme Campan) who with the help of the King's financial *intendant* got her hands on some samples of the Queen's signature, learnt to reproduce them with remarkable fidelity, and swindled an extremely expensive dress from Mme Bertin; she then wrote herself a letter in the Queen's name asking her secretly to borrow 200,000 francs on her behalf, and the *Fermier Général* Beranger had paid out. The deception duly came to light, the woman was incarcerated in the St Pelagia prison, and her husband had to repay the 'royal loan'. In 1782, a second lady claimed that she was a close friend not only of the Queen but also of Mesdames de Lamballe and de Polignac. She signed nothing in the Queen's name, but instead requisitioned goods under a royal seal which the Princesse de Polignac had misappropriated from the Queen's table. Strangest of all, this woman's name was also de la Motte, her husband being a relation of Jeanne's. When she was released from the Bastille, where she too was sent for her various frauds, the two ladies took up the connection.

This latter episode showed Jeanne what she should have realised after the first: that the idea of posing as an intimate of the Queen was not original. She was in the same situation—for a person of genius—as Shakespeare's contemporaries. Like them, Shakespeare had learnt everything he knew, in terms of subject matter, style and method, from those who had gone before—and yet his work stands at the apex of human achievement, towering over all others.

A rather neat saying of Chamfort, who was one of Jeanne's contemporaries, comes to mind: "There is no species of virtue that can raise the social rank of a woman; only vice can accomplish that."

How it all started, no one can say. We cannot be certain at what precise moment the idea struck her, and the artist herself shrouded the circumstances in mystery. We have no idea by what sort of skilful overtures she prepared the way, or even how she broached the subject with the Cardinal. All we can be certain about is the way the plan worked and the unstoppable course it took.

According to the Abbé Georgel it was Rohan who complained to her in confidence about how much the Queen's attitude and behaviour distressed him. "That confidence," the Abbé tells us, "suddenly made her proposed deception easy. It was one that has few parallels in the long annals of human folly."

Jeanne told the Cardinal about her 'intimate friendship' with the Queen. Thereafter, from time to time, as in the strictest confidence, she would show him letters written on white, watermarked paper, with pale borders and the royal lily of France in the left-hand corners, supposedly written by Marie-Antoinette to her *cousine,* Jeanne de Valois.

She must certainly have managed this part with some skill, since the Cardinal finally asked her to put a word in for him with her friend. She quickly brought news that she had spoken about him to the Queen. The Queen had heard her out in silence, but without any show of sympathy. She felt that the situation was hopeless.

Then she appeared with altogether more cheering news of her latest secret trip to Versailles. The Queen was taking her more and more into her confidence, and was slowly starting to reconsider her long-established prejudice against the Cardinal. She was beginning to see through the base intrigues of Comte Mercy-Argenteau, which had always represented Rohan in a bad light, and she had been touched by the magnanimity Rohan had shown over the trouble that had befallen his nephew, the Prince de Guéménée. In short, she was coming round to the view that the Cardinal was a fundamentally decent man. Finally in May, having faithfully promised Rohan that she would do everything she could to advance his interests, Jeanne was able to announce, with a radiant smile, that it would not be long before he was restored to royal favour.

Rohan, the most uncritical child of that most critical age, believed everything. Success increased Jeanne's boldness. She told him to observe the Queen carefully when she passed beside him in the Hall of Mirrors at Versailles, when she would make a sign with her head in his direction. (When I was a child, my father similarly suggested that the Emperor Franz Josef would acknowledge me in Fürdő street.) And Rohan believed that too. When the Queen raised her head, it would be a subtle indication of her increasing friendliness. The gesture was of course intended not for him but for anyone who happened to be standing there.

Then Jeanne took another step forward. She instructed him, in the Queen's name, to write a petition justifying his actions vis-à-vis the accusations made against him. Rohan composed his document with the greatest of care, tearing it up twenty times before finally handing it over.

The reply was swift. "I am most glad," the Queen wrote, "not to have to consider you guilty any longer. I cannot at present grant you the audience you ask for, but I will send you a sign as soon as circumstances permit. Be discreet."

This was the Queen's first letter to Rohan. "Those few words," the Abbé Georgel wrote afterwards, "threw the Cardinal into raptures it would be difficult to describe. Mme de la Motte was from that point onwards his guardian angel, smoothing his path to happiness. From that moment on, she could have whatever she wanted from him."

On her advice, the Cardinal replied expressing his delight. The Queen's next response was followed by a rapid exchange of letters. None has survived, for reasons which will be made clear. But the Abbé Georgel, who saw and read them, affirmed that those written by the Queen showed a clearly discernible progression. The tone becomes increasingly cordial, seeming to promise more and more. They give the impression of Jeanne's well-judged pleadings and Rohan's well-worded letters working their effect, and the Queen's heart steadily softening towards her admirer.

Now the Cardinal sat, in his official residence, the Hôtel de Strasbourg, in almost continuous conference with his advisors,

Cagliostro and the Swiss Baron Planta. The whole Palace was filled with a hopeful, springlike air of expectation. Perhaps nothing was said openly, but everywhere he was met with conspiratorial smiles of congratulation. Those letters were about more than the Queen's general goodwill. She was letting him know personally that she would receive him back into favour as soon as she could summon him openly. And then, in the silence of the night …

Elsewhere too, the days were spent in a fever of excitement. Everywhere the very ground under people's feet seemed to be becoming less certain. Finance Minister Calonne was a kind and intelligent man, but he could do nothing: that terrifying chasm the deficit yawned wider and wider, threatening to swallow everything. Paris sweltered in the appalling, pestilential heat of summer. Far better at such a time to be at Saverne … but Rohan continued to wait in the Hôtel de Strasbourg—to wait, and believe that his star was approaching its zenith.

Finally the longed-for moment arrived. The Queen's message read: "Be in the park at Versailles, tomorrow night, in the Bosquet de Vénus." 'Tomorrow' would be 11th August 1784.

In the Bosquet de Vénus: Venus' Bower … How much promise lay in that name!

The following evening Rohan was in the park. He wore a large black cloak, as agreed, and a broad-brimmed hat pulled down low over his eyes and, thus attired, wandered along the deserted pathways. From time to time he encountered amorous couples out late; sometimes he was startled by the sudden calling of birds. If the romantic drama had then been in existence, we might have thought of him as one of its heroes. But it wasn't. Rohan was a precursor.

He walked until late. The night was very dark. He finally withdrew beside a broad flight of steps. This was the Bower of Venus, so called because there were plans to set up a statue to the goddess there. It was never erected, and the bower was later named the Bosquet de la Reine, in memory of this particular night.

Inside the bower it was particularly dark. Not a single light shone in the windows of the vast palace. The eternal fountains were silent, the trees tossed and whispered to one another, and the statues of classical gods were a ghostly white presence among the bushes.

Footsteps were heard. Three people were approaching: two women and a man. The man Rohan recognised as the Comte de la Motte. One of the women was Jeanne de Valois. The other woman …

The Comte and Comtesse stopped outside, and the woman stepped hesitantly into the bower. Now he recognised her: it was the face … or rather, he seemed to discern the contours … the way she walked … the dress he knew very well: it was the full Gallic cloak recently painted by Mme Vigée-Lebrun in the portrait now hanging in the Salon. Rohan made a deep bow and kissed the hem of her dress. It was not an empty gesture: it was the only way he could express what he was feeling.

The lady murmured something in a low voice; extremely low. But Rohan understood, or thought that he understood, the words:

"You may hope. Let us forget the past." And a rose fell from her hand.

"Monseigneur, down on thy knees," Carlyle shouts at this point to Rohan, from the distance of half-a-century. "Never can red breeches be better wasted." Rohan knelt.

Then a shadow loomed.

"Quick, quick, you must be off!" it hissed, with theatrical huskiness. "Madame and the Comtesse d'Artois are coming."

La Motte stepped into the bower and plucked the Queen away, while Jeanne took the Cardinal by the arm and led him off. Rohan pulled his hat even further down over his eyes. A sweet delirium filled his soul. It did not occur to him to wonder what the King's sister and sister-in-law might be doing in the darkness of the park.

We can inform our gentle readers that the husky theatrical tones were those of Réteaux de Villette, Jeanne's confidant (no doubt in the fullest sense of the word) and the one who had written the Queen's letters, at her dictation, in his exquisite, feminine hand. Later he admitted that there had been an element of *inclination*—seductiveness—in the letters, but he then withdrew the remark and would only concede that the their tone had been *agréable*.

But who was 'the Queen'?

La Motte would often stroll in the garden of the Palais Royal, the residence of the Duc d'Orléans. It was during this period that the building attained the form and outline we see today, but while it was being built the garden remained open to the public. It was here that all sorts of lesser nobility, people like La Motte himself, would take the air—cardsharpers, rumour-mongers, gigolos, the whole aristocratic underworld, whose prince was the palace's owner, Philippe-Égalité. Of course they were not the only people moving about. "There is nowhere like it in the round world," writes Mercier. "You can visit London, Amsterdam, Madrid and Vienna, and see nothing that resembles it. A prisoner could live there and never get bored: it would be years before he even thought about freedom. They call it the capital of Paris. Here you can find everything: a young man of twenty with an income of 50,000 livres might enter this fairy garden and never be able to leave."

Here, under the trees, came all those children of the age whose passion was for free and open talk about the deepest questions of the time—religion, politics, the future of the monarchy, and the great changes impending. This is where public opinion was born. This is where the Revolution was born.

All Europe has at some time or another had much to thank the Palais Royal for. You too, gentle reader, will at some point take a stroll there, or we hope you will. When you do, take a good look at the statue of Camille Desmoulins. He seems to have leapt up into his chair just this instant; his huge head of hair flies in the wind, like the hair of a madman. The very air around him trembles with the excitement of youth—the youth of all mankind.

The Palais Royale was in effect a coffee house. People sat, either beneath the arcades or outside, in the kiosks dotted about the garden, sipping those cunning potions you can still buy in St Mark's Square in Venice, which they so closely resembled. Inside was the Exchange, where the life of commerce pulsed and raged before it was given a palatial building of its own. In the eighteenth century the speculator was still part of a colourful democracy, rubbing shoulders with the gigolo, the oral reporter (that is, gossip columnist) and the streetwalker. It was all very Bohemian, not yet lent a corpulent dignity by wealth. And there were foreigners here too. Foreigners usually end up in the Bohemian district, as a consequence of their own lack of social position. (The English were making trips to Paris for a bit of immorality even then.) In August 1785 five theatres were playing in the Palais Royale: the *Ombres Chinoises*, the *Pygmées Françaises*, the *Vrais Fantoccini Italiens, Les Variétés Amusantes* and Mme de Beaujolais's *Petits Comédiens*.

Beneath the arcades stood a cheerful assembly of jewellers' shops and boutiques selling women's things, in front of which paraded *les filles*, as the French euphemistically termed those young ladies whose careers guaranteed that *filles*—maidens— was the one thing they were not. At the time of our story the Palais Royale was the most famous place not just in Paris but in the whole world, for such maidenly gatherings.

Among the regulars was a young woman called Marie-Nicole Leguay. By day she was a worker in one of the fashion shops where Jeanne had begun her career. In her free time she walked the Palais Royale, and it was there that La Motte first came across her.

He must have been instantly struck by her single interesting feature—her remarkable resemblance to Marie-Antoinette. On this every contemporary source agrees. The portrait still in Funck-Brentano's collection reveals the same round, listless face, the slightly protruding lower lip, the soft features, the tall, fine head of hair. La Motte stood before her as before the Angel of the Lord.

He instantly propositioned her.

Next, he accompanied her to her home, where what passed between them took the same course as it would between many thousands of similar acquaintances made at the Palais Royale that evening. But at first La Motte preserved a deep silence about his real intentions. Some time later he invited the girl back to his house, where the Comtesse received her with a conspicuous display of friendliness. Soon, she even gave her a more suitable name so that she could deal on equal terms in the fashionable quarter. She became the Baronne d'Oliva—the letters deriving from 'Valois', further evidence of Jeanne's strange obsession.

The young woman was completely charmed by the Comtesse, especially when she came to understand whom she was dealing with—the intimate friend of Marie-Antoinette. And since the Baronne d'Oliva was a particularly, indeed infinitely, well-intentioned soul, how could she possibly refuse when the Comtesse asked her one day if she would do her a personal favour, really just a trifle, but it would be doing the Queen a very great service. And of course she could count on the Queen's gratitude. She would get 15,000 livres, and a present, my dear, a personal present, to at least the same value, though what it would be she couldn't yet say. What she would have to do, it was really nothing, just hand over a letter, and a single rose, to a noble gentleman at Versailles.

"It wasn't difficult persuading her," Jeanne admitted later. "She was really stupid."

"O Ixion de Rohan, happiest mortal of this world!" exclaims Carlyle, comparing the Cardinal to the character in Greek mythology who fell in love with Hera, the Queen of the

Skies, and was made by the malicious gods to embrace her in the semblance of a cloud. If ever there were happy days in Rohan's life they must have been those that followed the scene in the bower. What an experience for his soul, with its deep yearning for mysticism and wonder: the park, the dark night, the Queen's appearance out of the gloom—almost like something imagined—the fevered words, the rose let fall to the ground, and the secrecy surrounding everything. Why had the Queen been so nervous? What lay behind that? Perhaps she was ashamed of her feelings that night? ... And indeed perhaps it was better that she did vanish, like an apparition. Had she stayed there a moment longer the truth would have come out— and the Cardinal had had his fill of truth, which had lavished too many of its gifts upon him:

You who are weary of the truth,
Embrace the slippery pearls of dreams.

Jeanne was indeed a kindly villain. Like Faust, and other devils of myth and legend, she gave Rohan what his heart desired. No other mortal could have done more than that.

And she seemed to realise it, because she quickly set about cashing in. On the Queen's behalf she let Rohan know that she would look very kindly on it if he could lend her 50,000 livres: an impoverished relative was in urgent need of assistance, and just at that moment she did not have the ready cash to hand. Rohan was delighted that the Queen had taken him so far into her confidence as to ask him for money. He quickly raised the sum from a moneylender, since he too had no cash to spare at that time ...

Jeanne waited in suspense for the packet to arrive. It was late. Perhaps Rohan after all ... perhaps he was not as gullible as she had thought? Had it all come to nothing—the Baronne, the bower, that memorable night? But behold, it arrived, delivered by Baron Planta. Shrewd as ever, Jeanne now urged Rohan in

107

the Queen's name to return to Saverne for a while, and send her another 50,000 livres from there. The Cardinal duly obeyed.

So—as no doubt many a gypsy had assured Jeanne it would—money came at last to the La Motte household. But Jeanne was not the sort to lack ideas of how to squander it all at the first opportunity. She immediately bought two houses, one back home in Bar-sur-Aube, and a summer holiday home; she paid the Baronne d'Oliva 4,000 livres and promptly threw her out; and she ran up a vast amount of debt.

We believe that this last 50,000 livres, together with the 100,000 francs she had borrowed from Rohan in the Queen's name, was not an end in itself. It was just an experimental balloon, to satisfy her curiosity as to whether the Cardinal really would send her the money for the Queen. The real business, the great and fateful business, was still to come.

Chapter Six

Spirits in Glass Pitchers

WHILE JEANNE WAS DISPLAYING this monumental burst of activity, her great rival for the Cardinal's favour, Cagliostro, had not been sitting on his hands.

In 1781 Rohan had sent him to one of his relatives, the Duc de Soubise, who was ill in Paris. Cagliostro cured him completely, in no time at all. He then spent almost a year in Bordeaux, supposedly at the invitation of the French Foreign Minister the Comte de Vergennes. Here too he was hounded by the local doctors, and he seems also to have become entangled in amorous intrigues: there is no escaping the fact the magus was a child of the times. The sky was darkening over his head, but he extricated himself, just as Swedenborg had done, through a remarkable vision.

He was lying on his bed of illness, surrounded by a handful of his followers. Suddenly he opened his eyes wide, like someone waking from a dream. His face was deathly pale. In a voice trembling with emotion, he revealed what he had seen.

In his vision he was taken by two unknown gentlemen (obviously angels) and led into a vast cave. There, in the darkness, a mighty door swung open and the place was flooded with heavenly light. He stepped into a hall, where supernatural beings in long white robes disported themselves. There were many Freemasons among them, all adherents, naturally, of the Egyptian Rite. He quickly donned the same white robes and took up a sword, in order not to feel out of place. He came before the throne of the Highest Being, whom he thanked most properly for allowing him to experience the delights of the other world while still a mortal. At this point an 'unknown' voice declared: "Behold, you see now what your reward will be, but meanwhile you still have much to do."

This vision was a notable success.

Next he moved to Lyons, the capital of French mysticism. Here, in the sixteenth century, the souls of poets had taken wing and soared to the greatest heights of the arcane world of Platonic ideas. The tendency to the mystical had never deserted the citizens, and there St Martin himself founded the occult Freemasonry Lodge known as the *Chevaliers Bienfaisants*. Cagliostro knew where he needed to be.

In Lyons he made contact with the lodges, gave talks, recruited followers and established another lodge of the Egyptian order, which he modestly named *Sagesse Triomphante*—Wisdom Triumphant. He personally consecrated the site amidst highly festive ceremonies. The foundation document begins with these words:

GLORY, UNITY, WISDOM, CHARITY, PROSPERITY

We, the Great Kophta, founder and Grand Master of the High Egyptian Order both in the east and now part of the west, declare, to all whom it may concern …

The time has come for us to say a few words about what constituted the Egyptian Rite. Cagliostro followed Swedenborg in teaching that man must completely renew himself, both morally and physically.

His prescriptions for moral renewal were not especially difficult to follow. You had to withdraw from the world for forty days, preferably to a pavilion built on the peak of a high mountain, and spend your time there in meditation.

But Cagliostro's followers were far less interested in moral rejuvenation than in its physical counterpart, which involved much more challenging requirements. True, it promised enormous benefits: it would prolong life for several hundred years, bring the body to the condition of an innocent child, and heal every illness. Whoever sought to attain this had to lock himself away in a cell, by the light of the moon, in May, every year for fifty years, and live there for forty days on nothing but a soup made with certain prescribed herbs and boiled twice, otherwise drinking nothing but spring water. On the thirteenth day one of the patient's veins would be slit open and six 'white drops' infused into them. On the thirty-second day the vein was opened again, this time at sunrise. The patient was then wrapped in a sheet and placed on a bed in the open air, where he received the *prima materia*, which God had created to make man immortal, only its use had been forgotten in consequence of original sin. Following this, the patient would actually become worse, but would recover soon after, and be like a completely different person.

Many of Cagliostro's teachings were attempts to discover this cure, but none was ever brought to a conclusion, so we still do not know to this day whether he ever achieved the promised result.

Perhaps he had been taught how to make the elixir of eternal life by that most enigmatic figure of the whole eighteenth century, the Comte de St Germain. Legends of St Germain abound, but there are few reliable facts. He was a real historic personage who for a while enjoyed the confidence of Louis XV. The legends' chief claim is that he was several thousand years old, that he was alive at the time of Christ, and knew the Redeemer personally. On one occasion, in the presence of an acquaintance, he said to his manservant:

"Do you remember, old chap, when we were walking with St Peter beside Lake Genazareth? … "

"Your mind is beginning to wander, sir," the man replied. "You forget that I have only been in your service these last five hundred years."

St Germain was an altogether more elegant kind of magician than Cagliostro. By the latter's time, the end of the century, the whole business had been to some extent democratised. Among the real magi Cagliostro was a Figaro, an impudent barber and footman.

But as far as it is possible to judge from the high-flown meta-physical texts quoted by Haven, and the mass of gossip that has been passed down, there must have been at least some genuine occultism in the Egyptian rite, some communication with the spirit world. It was Swedenborg who, as we have remarked, made that connection so easy and familiar for people of the time. The literary critic Leigh Hunt records of the great English poet and artist William Blake, who was one of Swedenborg's followers, that once, as they strolled beside the Thames, Blake suddenly raised his hat. Leigh Hunt looked around, but saw no one there for Blake to greet.

"Who was that?" he asked, in some alarm.

"No one, just St Paul flying past," Blake replied.

Cagliostro had the same easy and natural relationship with spirits. He would invite them to dinner, lay places for them at the table, and tell his living guests which of the illustrious dead they had the good fortune to be dining with. Sometimes he used mediums, a young boy or an innocent girl (he called these his 'doves'), but his followers had mostly to take his word for it that they were in the presence of the Seven Great Spirits around the Deity's throne: Anael, Michael, Raphael, Gabriel, Uriel, Zobiachel and Anachiel. These last played a central role. The medium would see them in a pitcher filled with water, together, naturally, with candles and the three magical names: Helios, Mene and Tetragammon.

But most miraculous of all was the sheer number of Cagliostro's adherents, and the depth of their belief. Haven quotes the letter of thanks written to Cagliostro by the members of the Wisdom Triumphant lodge:

Sire and Master,

Nothing can match the goodness of your deeds unless it be the happiness they bring us … if you will deign to take us under your wing and bestow on us your continuing protection, your sons will be always grateful, being ever inspired by the proclamation which you in your lofty eminence established among us through the 'dove' who implored you on his own behalf and ours: 'Tell them that I love them, and always will'. We promise, each and everyone, our eternal gratitude, respect and love to you, and crave your blessing to crown the pledge of your obedient, respectful sons and disciples.

Cagliostro achieved this enormous power through his oratory. People would listen enchanted, and believe everything he said. It is a commonplace that the power of a great orator depends not on what he says but on the way he says it. So what was the secret of Cagliostro's performances?

Jeanne's admirer Beugnot once dined at her house when Cagliostro was present, and recorded his impressions in the following words:

"He spoke double Dutch (*baragouin*)—half-French, half-Italian, peppered with words supposedly from Arabic, which he did not bother to translate. He was the only one who spoke, and he managed to touch on twenty different topics in the time. Every few seconds he would ask if we understood what he was saying, and we all nodded. Once he had warmed to a particular subject, he would go into a sort of trance, talking loudly and finishing with large gestures. Then he would suddenly come down from his soapbox and murmur tender compliments and amusing endearments to the lady of the house, calling her his little fawn, his gazelle, his swan and his dove, in short, endowing her with all the softest names of the animal kingdom. And so it went on for the entire meal. I didn't understand very much, only that he talked about heaven, the stars, the Great Arcanum, Memphis, the hierophants, transcendental chemistry, giants, enormous beasts, a city in Central Africa ten times the size of

Paris, and how he had regular correspondents based there—and of course the great ignorance in which we found ourselves in so far as all those fine marvels were concerned, which were known to him without recourse to books."

Beugnot and others confirm that he larded his sentences with bits of Arabic. A German orientalist once addressed him in the language, and he understood not a word. Perhaps his own version was simply mumbo-jumbo. To some extent this might have been forced on him. His command of French was so poor he could not have expressed himself clearly had he wanted to. Another witness said of his performance: "If gibberish (*galimatias*) equals 'sublime', then no one was more sublime than Cagliostro. He would pronounce long words in the middle of his incomprehensible sentences, and the less his audience understood the greater was the miracle he worked on them. They thought him oracular simply because he was obscure. His art consisted of addressing nothing to the understanding and trusting the imagination of the listener to supply a meaning. The truth is always obvious, but only to the wise. The bogus is incomprehensible, which is precisely why it impresses the multitude."

This last witness more or less explains the secret of Cagliostro's power. With these 'Arabic' terms he reduced his listeners to a kind of stupor. The people of the time must have been much as they are today—they might give their assent to wise and intelligent words, but they kept their fervour for those they did not understand. The astonishing power the magician has over the half-educated lies in his ill-formed concepts, his nebulous terminology and high-sounding incomprehensibilities. This is especially true in times of impending social upheaval, when people are looking for miracles. Cagliostro's Arabic words made the benign vision blaze before the devout eyes of his audiences. If he did say anything they could understand, they indulgently heard him out simply for the sake of what they did not.

By 1785, the fatal year of the necklace trial, Cagliostro saw that the time had finally come for him to conquer the capital of the world, and he made his move to Paris. There, he rented a house in the Marais district, as Jeanne had done. The house still stands, on the corner of the Rue St Claude and the Boulevard Beaumarchais. The present writer looked it over, but there is nothing memorable about it.

As we saw in his dealings with Rohan, Cagliostro was a master of the arts of choosing his moment and waiting for the right time. He arrived just as Paris was beginning to feel the need for a miracle doctor. Its citizens, like those of every great city, and the French by their nature, had a permanent hunger for sensation. This was even more true of the eighteenth century, of which that considerable expert Victor du Bled remarked that no other age was ever so bored. In the second half of the century doctors became highly fashionable. Their connection with the flourishing natural sciences steadily raised their social status, and they began to fulfil the role in aristocratic houses once played by the priestly confessor.

In his standard history of medicine, Garrison claims that their social position was even higher than it is today. They wore swords like the nobility, and muffs in winter to protect their fingers, whose sensitive touch was so important in reaching a diagnosis. Voltaire and Rousseau's doctor, Tronchin, was one of the best-known figures of the age. (He was the person who made the then revolutionary discovery that physical activity was not harmful to the constitution.) Also widely celebrated was a M Pomme, who ascribed the *vapeurs*, as nervous disorders were known at the time, to a general dehydration of the central nervous system, and immersed his patients in water. Medical science had become a kind of mania, like everything else at the time. Women threw themselves into it with a passion. The young Comte de Coigny was so keen on his anatomical studies that he kept a cadaver in his luggage to dissect even when travelling. Followers of the Comtesse du Voisenon smuggled a 'news' item into a copy of the *Journal des Sages* announcing that the society of doctors had elected her as their president, and in true eighteenth-century style the Comtesse found this entirely natural. (L V du Bled.)

When Cagliostro arrived in Paris, the previous miracle-doctor, Mesmer, who discovered animal magnetism and produced miraculous forces with his magical buckets, had now gone out of fashion and disappeared from the scene, his pockets bulging with cash. Cagliostro's fame had gone before him, and he arrived in a blaze of publicity. His followers had distributed thousands upon thousands of copies of his portrait, adorned with the inscription:

De l'ami des humains reconnoisez les traits:
Tous ses jours sont marqués par de nouveaux bienfaits;
Il prolonge la vie, il secourt l'indigence.
Le plaisir d'être utile est seul sa récompense.

Acknowledge the virtues of the friend of humanity:
Every one of his days is marked by new acts of goodness.
He prolongs life, succours the needy,
His sole recompense the joy of service.

—It doesn't sound much better in the French—

We can see how much stress Cagliostro placed on his philanthropy. It was far more important in winning people over than his mysticism. It is a truly noble age when the charlatan's first concern is to reassure people that his heart is in the right place.

He immediately found favour through an announcement directed at Parisian taste—he had founded a Freemasonry lodge for women. Its Grand Mistress was Lorenza, and its membership included names of the highest rank: Brienne, Polignac, Brassas, the Comtesse de Choiseul, Mme Genlis and others. The Grand Master and Protector of the Egyptian Rite was the Duc de

Montmorency, its Grand Inspector the *Fermier Général* Laborde, and its treasurer the powerful financier Sainte-James. It can be said without qualification that Cagliostro had arrived.

It is not entirely clear what the women did in their lodges. According to Haven, it was no different from the men. Naturally, the non-initiated were convinced that wild orgies took place, with the ladies' admirers appearing in the form of charitable genies, and that Lorenza taught them that pleasure was everything. What is certain is that they were given pretty little pyramids as presents, and the Seven Spirits, including Zobiachel, duly appeared before them.

But while all this was going on, Cagliostro did not lose sight of the one thing that mattered, his main business: Rohan. He took care to maintain a warm relationship with him, and Rohan almost certainly continued to lavish significant gifts on his guide to all things mystical.

Inevitably, Rohan also sought his advice in the matter of the Queen's favour. Cagliostro had little enthusiasm for Jeanne, because he knew full well that she was fishing in the same pond, but he did not see her as a serious threat. It served his interests that she should keep Rohan's hopes alive, since pessimists are not enamoured of prophets, and his prophesies regularly revealed that the Queen would soon be taking Rohan back into her favour.

La Motte had a little fifteen-year-old relation called Marie-Jeanne de la Tour. It became apparent that this young lady met all Cagliostro's conditions for a perfect 'dove', or medium: an angelic innocence, a highly-strung nature and blue eyes; it was also important that she had been born under Capricorn. Her mother, struggling under the weight of temporary material concerns, and telling herself it would always be advisable to be in the Cardinal's good books, was happy to put the girl at his and Cagliostro's disposal.

Cagliostro received her in the laboratory at the Hôtel de Strasbourg.

"Young lady, it is true that you are innocent?" he asked her directly.

"Of course, sir."

"We shall soon see. Offer up your soul to God, go and stand behind the screen, and concentrate on the thing you would most like to see. If you are innocent, it will appear to you, but if you are not, you will see nothing."

Mlle de la Tour retired behind the screen, while Cagliostro and Rohan remained where they were. Cagliostro drew certain magical signs in the air, and said to the girl:

"Stamp your pretty little foot and tell me—did you see anything?"

"I saw nothing," the girl replied, trusting in the truth.

"Then you are not innocent."

The girl could not bear the suspicion, and quickly called out that she could now see what she wanted to see.

A surviving notebook contains a deposition made to the Court about a second visit.

Marie-Jeanne went with her mother to the Hôtel de Strasbourg, where she was met by the Cardinal and Cagliostro. They gave her a white apron, told her to say a few prayers, and stood her before a table on which a jug of clear water stood between two candles. Cagliostro waved his sword behind a screen and called on the assistance of the Great Kophta and the Archangels Raphael and Michael. Then he asked the girl:

"Tell me, young lady, did you see the Queen in the glass vessel?"

Marie-Jeanne had by now realised what would constitute a suitable response in the eyes of the magician.

"But of course," she replied eagerly ("so that I could get away," she later told the court).

"Young lady, do you see the angels and the little figures" (the so-called *petits bonhommes*) "who are trying to kiss you?"

"No," she replied modestly.

"Make as if you were angry, and stamp your pretty little foot," he said, "to summon the Great Kophta here instantly, and tell the angels to come and embrace you."

"Oh yes, they're here already," the girl replied ("just to get away"), and she gave the *petits bonhommes* a kiss.

Whereupon Rohan fell to his knees and prayed. Then he asked Marie-Jeanne to tell no one about what had taken place.

Three days later the girl returned to the Cardinal's palace. This time they gave her a long white shirt with a "great sun" in the middle and two blue ribbons forming a cross—a costume designed by Cagliostro himself. She was taken into Rohan's bedroom, which was ablaze with candles. Once again there was a glass vessel on a table, filled with water and sur--rounded by stars, *petits bonhommes* and other symbols she had not seen before—Egyptian hieroglyphs representing Isis and the bull Apis. Cagliostro again brandished his sword, and asked:

"Young lady, do you not see a lady inside the jug, dressed in white?"

"Oh, but of course," Marie-Jeanne dutifully replied.

"Tell me, young lady—but think about this carefully, because much depends on what you say next: does that lady dressed in white bear a resemblance to the Queen?"

"Oh yes, very much so."

Rohan raised his head and glanced at the girl, his eyes clouded with happiness.

"Tell me, young lady," the magician went on: "do you not also see a rather older *bonhomme*, also dressed in white, walking in a garden and embracing the Queen?"

"Oh yes, very much," she wisely returned ("just to get away").

"Well then, would you please ask once again for the aid of the Great Kophta, the Archangel Gabriel, and perhaps also Zobiachel."

The girl put her hands together and mumbled something.

"Now pay attention, young lady, and gather up all the strength of your innocent little soul. Do you not see His Eminence the Cardinal, on his knees, with a tobacco box in one hand and a little platter in the other?"

"Oh, yes, of course," she replied. "Now I see it, oh yes: My Lord Cardinal kneeling and holding a tobacco box in one hand and a little platter in the other."

In his excitement Rohan exclaimed: "Incredible! Extraordinary!"

His face, Mlle de la Tour tells us in her deposition, was radiant with happiness and satisfaction. He fell on his knees sobbing, and raised his hands to the heavens.

Poor Rohan! His gestures—throwing himself to the ground, falling on his knees—must have come from his profoundest being, the intense devotion that was the deepest yearning of his heart. Such was his fate, that in all his life he never met anyone who could lead him to where he could fall to his knees with a tranquil heart, before the one true Absolute.

Chapter Seven

The Queen

MARIE-ANTOINETTE, the chief victim of the necklace trial, has probably been more written about than any other woman in world history. Only Mary Stuart—that other Queen Maria to end up on the scaffold—can rival her. The revolutionary years poured out a venomous stream of slander about her; then, with the restoration of the monarchy in the early nineteenth century, she was turned into a sainted royal martyr. More recent writers, in their quest for objectivity, have looked for an answer somewhere between the two. To us it seems she was neither a demon nor a martyr but a woman neither better nor worse than any other woman placed on the throne by fate. Since the portraits by the brothers Goncourt and Stefan Zweig are readily available, and practically everyone has read the latter, there is no need for us to show Marie-Antoinette in *premier plan*, like the other actors in our story. It will be enough to summarise the facts very briefly and then turn the spotlight solely on those areas that are critically important for the historical argument. What we do need to explain is why Rohan should have believed the things he did about her. To answer that we must examine her prodigality, her war on Court etiquette, her friendships with other women and the erotic legend that grew up around her.

Marie-Antoinette was born on 2nd November 1755, the day of the great earthquake in Lisbon. Her mother was Maria Theresa, her father the genial Lotharingian Holy Roman Emperor Francis I. As a young girl she learnt to dance extremely well, to play music and to recite. Taught by the resident poet at the Viennese court, Metastasio, she memorised the libretti of the great operas in Italian. It was an excellent upbringing—for a future diva. In later years she developed an implacable hostility towards any kind of intellectual occupation or difficult reading matter, no matter how much her wise mother urged her in her letters to study seriously. But one can hardly blame her for that. There is no doubt that she was intelligent and witty, perhaps excessively so. When receiving a delegation she would respond with a formal little speech she had earlier composed with great care. This habit infuriated the female members of the royal household, who thought it quite inappropriate for a princess to speak at such length to ordinary people, rather than simply mumble a few incomprehensible words of greeting.

Her fate was decided by the Duc de Choiseul, Louis XV's Foreign Minister. To enable France to turn her full might on England and Prussia, he broke a long tradition of French policy and made an alliance with Austria, her rival of many centuries. The alliance was sealed and underwritten by the marriage of Princess Marie-Antoinette to Louis XV's grandson, the future Louis XVI.

Marie-Antoinette's face and figure have been immortalised in countless contemporary pictures and writings. Mme Vigée-Lebrun alone painted her twenty times.

She was certainly beautiful. A tall, queenly figure, with fine arms and bosom, a full head of ash-blonde hair and a most attractive face—admittedly rather a babyish face, by no means the sort that people nowadays find piquant or very interesting. But the fact is that the women of any particular period do all seem to resemble one other, the way men's handwriting always does. In the eighteenth century women had baby faces, mainly because of their rounded chins. History of course reminds us that these baby-faced duchesses and princesses were cleverer, more passionate and, if necessary, often more vicious than those who came either before or after them. It is only the women of one's own period that one can judge by their looks—and even then the results are completely unpredictable.

But for beauty the raw material, the body, is not enough. It depends on what you do with it. Marie-Antoinette's contemporaries could never praise her smile, her facial expression or her deportment highly enough. Mme Vigée-Lebrun, the painter, said of her afterwards that she had the most elegant walk in the whole of France. That was written after the Queen's death, and may be too generous. We should bear in mind that women were never more versed in the art of deportment than they were then. It was a difficult art and a highly important one, which young ladies studied with great care over many years. Another expert, Count Tilly, who had been one of her pages, disapproved of her eyes and protruding Habsburg lower lip, and thought that her posture could have been more elegant, but even he thought her carriage marvellous. "She had two kinds of walk," he said: "one very decided, rather brisk and extremely aristocratic, and one that was altogether more sinuous, a kind of rocking movement, though that term should not be taken to imply disrespect. No one could curtsey with more grace than she. She could greet ten people with a single dip, while her glance gave proper due to each in turn … in a word, if I am not deceived, a man would instinctively want to lead her to a throne, the way he would offer another woman a chair."

(That curtsey! What would Proust have given to see it!)

Yes, she must have been very beautiful. Perhaps we should be less delighted for her than ashamed of ourselves. Ashamed of our own plebeian century.

These details are offered by way of introduction. We must now move directly on to the subject of the Queen's extravagance.

We have already mentioned that she lived and died for jewellery, and spent vast sums acquiring it. Another of her expensive passions was cards. At the Château de Marly she gambled constantly, always for substantial sums, following royal tradition. The card games here were a form of public ritual, like mealtimes. Any member of the nobility or gentry could attend provided he was properly dressed, and he would be free to play against the nobility seated at the table. The vast octagonal salon was lined with balconies, where the women, who were not admitted to the area below, were seated. The passion for card games in this period was generally ruinous. Both male and female members of the aristocracy who, as we have seen, were often in longstanding financial difficulties despite their vast incomes, would seek to remedy their situation through the gaming table. The stakes were fantastic. The Marquis de Chalabre (the godfather of the card game Kalaber?) lost 840,000 livres at a single sitting, and the next day won almost two million. He later became the banker of the royal casino. At Fontainebleau one epic game of Faro lasted an unbroken thirty-six hours. The King's younger brother the Comte d'Artois was said in 1783 to have lost 14,600,000 over seven years. Nor were these princes above the occasional bit of trickery, and it became necessary to introduce various regulatory measures.

So it is not surprising then, that Marie-Antoinette also played and lost. On one occasion the King paid out 100,000 livres she had forfeited in a single sitting. He was not happy doing it, because he was himself very economical by nature: in fact he was the only Bourbon to be that way. It did him little good. In 1777 Marie's Antoinette's gambling debts amounted to 487,272 livres.

Naturally she also spent unbelievable sums on clothes; probably more than any other queen in history. Her ambition was to be respected and admired not as the Queen but as the prettiest and most elegant woman in France. The pleasure of being a pretty and elegant woman in France has never come cheap— and we can imagine what it meant then, when all her dresses were made from expensive fabrics. According to the eternally well-disposed Mme Campan, the word was that the Queen had bankrupted every woman in the land by the fashions, and the constant changes in fashion, that she dictated.

She was also fond of building—that greatest of royal passions. The King bought St Cloud for her and then made her a gift of Le Petit Trianon, both of which she remodelled to her own taste. Her taste was of course of the very finest, avoiding anything that might be deemed extravagant. The people naturally were convinced that her financial extravagance was unbounded, and when representatives of the *États Généraux* (regional lawyers and state officials) visited Le Petit Trianon in 1789, they came expecting to find the rooms piled high with diamonds, and the twisting columns of sapphires and rubies with which 'everyone knew' the 'Austrian woman' had adorned the grottoes in which she conducted her debaucheries.

But in her own way Marie-Antoinette was thrifty. It was her desire to save money that precipitated the whole necklace affair. We have seen that the King was perfectly happy to buy the fatal jewels for her, but she refused. Had she accepted, she would have been spared the whole painful story of the rest of her life. But her economising zeal was always somehow inappropriate and misplaced. One New Year's Eve, the day on which French children are given presents, she had the latest fashionable toys brought from Paris, and showed them to her children.

"You see," she said, "these are the toys you didn't get, because we prefer to give money to the poor, who are freezing and have no winter coats."

Opinions differ as to whether Marie-Antoinette's extravagance did put as significant a strain on the state coffers as was believed at the time, and whether she really did deserve the name of Mme Deficit. Probably she did not. The sum total of her various extravagances is dwarfed by the running expenditure of the state, especially in relation to the American war. In 1781 the costs incurred by the King, Queen and Royal Princess, together with the King's sister, his aunts and their 'household', amounted to 27,317,000 livres, and they also paid out pensions to the value of twenty-eight million; while treasury expenditure amounted to 283,162,000 livres. So the outgoings of the royal household amounted to just one tenth of the whole. The war alone, including naval and other outgoings, absorbed around a hundred and thirteen million livres.

Then there is the separate issue of whether Marie-Antoinette was especially prodigal. She lived, as the Queen of France, at the very apex of the glitter and pomp so typical of the age. The French people had put up with the free spending of her predecessors without a murmur; she was made to atone for the sins of the centuries. Or perhaps not for their sins, but simply because the times had changed, and the hour had come for the great reckoning.

But for present purposes appearance is much more important than the reality. The common belief was that Marie-Antoinette squandered gold without a moment's thought, and was in permanently dire financial straits. Rohan 'knew' that too, and he believed it—all the more so, because it applied equally to him.

The second great question concerns etiquette. Rohan 'knew' that Marie-Antoinette spurned the ancient protocol of the French court, and lived according to the dictates of her inclinations and caprice. What was the truth in all this?

The life of a court anywhere and in any period is governed by strict conventions. The function of etiquette is to externalise and indirectly express the 'charismatic', specially chosen and divinely ordained nature of royalty, and to instil a sense of religious awe in its subjects. It creates a sense of distance between the ruler and his people, making the king and his entourage seem to them as sacred and unshakeable as the eternal stars that pursue their courses with unvarying regularity. The greater the sense of distance desired by the monarchy, the stricter the protocol. The greatest of all was to be found among the ancient god-kings of the East and the rigid formality associated with them, that lived on in Byzantium. In the West, the most unbending protocol of all was that of the Habsburg court of Spain, reflecting the enormous scale of the empire in its heyday and the eternal preoccupation with heaven and hell that characterised the Catholic world view. It enabled the Spanish to channel their immense personal self-respect into the veneration of the persons of the King and Queen as sacred objects. On one occasion the Queen fell from her horse, her foot caught in the stirrup, and the steed dragged her along with him. A nobleman rushed to her aid, freed her, then leapt onto the horse and galloped away out of the country, knowing that the death penalty awaited him for having dared touch her foot.

Louis XIV seems to have had the Spanish example partly in mind when he created the much gentler, more aesthetic, but no less unbending protocol of his own court. But besides creating a sense of distance, he had other, more practical ends in view. He wanted the aristocrats whom he invited or summoned to Court to have something to do, and something to think about. Everything he personally did was to be made a precedent. In all comparable situations, exactly the same procedures had to be gone through. The majority of his courtiers, it seems, approached the resulting elaborate ceremonial with deadly seriousness. An example is that marvellously talented and inexpressibly dull writer the Duc de Saint-Simon, who meticulously recorded every one of those customs in his monumental tomes, so that posterity would know how to behave.

And Louis XIV had another reason, possibly unconscious. We have mentioned that the unspoken aim of Western culture was to reduce the whole of life to a closed system, like a work of art. The punctilious, undeviating repetition of words and actions imposed by court customs can be seen as analogous to the nightly repetition of dialogue in a play, or movements in a ballet. Etiquette served much the same purpose.

This closed world-system, the triumph of art over the raw material of life, proved no less successful in creating that sense of traditional distance than the Spanish model had done, with its rigid formal attire for men and the great hooped skirts of the ladies (and how uncomfortable their wearers must have been!). But in her early years Marie-Antoinette felt no need for such 'historic' distance. For her these things weren't historic, they were everyday—boring, outdated rubbish.

The capacity of Versailles protocol to produce some strange situations is shown by the famous story of the Queen's shift, as recorded by Mme Campan.

As *Prémière Femme de Chambre* it was her task to hand the Queen her slip. However, if a lady of higher rank happened to be in the room, the honour passed to her. Once, in winter—and the Palace could never have been properly heated—Mme Campan was about to pass the garment to the Queen when in stepped the *Dame d'Honneur*, the person next in rank above her. Seeing the situation, the lady quickly asked Mme de Campan to take off her gloves and lend them to her, as she could not give the Queen her shift without them. But while the gloves were being removed there was a knock at the door, and in stepped the Duchesse d'Orléans. To preserve protocol, the *Dame d'Honneur* followed the rules and returned the gloves to Mme Campan, who curtsied and offered the shift to the Duchesse, whereupon there was yet another knock on the door and in walked the King's sister-in-law, the Comtesse de Provence. The Duchesse returned the dress to Mme Campan, who made a fresh curtsey and offered it to the Comtesse, who apologised and quickly handed it to the Queen, who was by now shivering with cold.

What can also be seen in this story is the way members of the royal family were never left to themselves. They were surrounded by attendants at all times, like the gods and goddesses in baroque paintings. This was true even in the most intimate moments of their lives. We know that the *lever*—when the King got out of bed—was a formal and very public occasion, as was the moment when he put his boots on; and that the members of the royal family gave audience while seated on that discreetly named item of furniture known as the *chaise percée*. The Queen even took her bath in public—in her shift, naturally.

Whenever she passed from one part of the building to the next, four ladies of the court in full formal dress, together with various other flunkeys, had to follow her around in procession. These 'processions' were almost always undertaken in full formal costume.

On certain days, royal mealtimes were a public spectacle. Anyone who turned up could watch. "Once the honest folk," says Mme Campan, "had had a good look at the way the Dauphine drank her soup, they moved on to see how the Princes ate their *bouilli*, and then ran themselves out of breath to behold *Mesdames* polishing off their dessert."

The rule was that only women could wait at the royal table, the *Dame d'Honneur*, kneeling on a little stool, and four ladies *en grand habit*. All these tedious customs were abolished by Marie-Antoinette.

Every book dealing with the Court includes a description of how Marie-Antoinette gave birth to her first child. So many people were milling about the room that she could not breathe, and the King had to haul the windows open with his own hands.

When Marie-Antoinette first arrived at the Court, it was controlled by the most rigidly protocol-minded of the older generation. To counterbalance the situation she found herself obliged to join forces with Louis XV's 'girls'—who had inherited none of the Bourbon magnificence beyond an awareness of protocol and a respect for it, but were otherwise just little old ladies. The *Dame d'Honneur*, the Comtesse de Noailles, she christened 'Mme Etiquette'.

But her greatest horror was Mme de Marsan, who was connected through her husband to the House of Lotharingia (Lorraine) and thus a relation, but who was also one of the Rohan tribe, and the Cardinal's most important patroness.

According to the Goncourts she was like the Bad Fairy in the stories. "She more or less personified the narrow and oppressive morality of the age of Henry IV, and retained something of the character of that infamous Marsan who distinguished himself at the time of the *dragonnades* by the zeal with which he persecuted Huguenots. The Dauphine's easy, rocking walk was in her eyes the saunter of a courtesan; the airy linen dresses she wore were a theatrical costume calculated to seduce. If the Dauphine raised her eyes, Mme de Marsan saw it as the practised glance of a flirt. If her hair was in the slightest bit awry, it was dishevelled ('the hair of a goatherd!' she would complain). If, as was her custom, she spoke in a lively manner, she was talking for the sake of talking when she had nothing to say. If her face lit up during conversation and showed sympathy, Mme de Marsan found it insupportable that she should behave as if she knew everything. If she broke out into happy, childlike laughter, it was simply forced or affected. The old lady was suspicious of everything, and placed an unpleasant construction on all she did. In time Marie-Antoinette took revenge on her, as she did on the Comtesse de Noailles, quite disregarding the fact that Mme de Marsan was the *Gouvernante* to and friend of the King's sisters, which ensured that the least of her actions would be criticised and she would be enmeshed in slander." This was a pattern that would be repeated many times over.

Marie-Antoinette waged war on Mme de Noailles, Mme de Marsan, and even *mesdames* the royal aunts. Primarily it was a battle of the generations, the most instinctive conflict in any society. Perhaps she carried her disdain for formality a little too far the greater to annoy them—an all-too-human trait. But then the two generations grew apart in really significant ways. Those with Mme de Marsan represented the old-style grandeur, the baroque pomp and formality of Louis XIV, which had already been undermined in Louis XV's day by the spirit of rococo. Marie-Antoinette and her entourage were children of that new age, whose sense of beauty depended not on pomp and *grandeur* but on delicacy, grace, wit, the *joli*—charm and prettiness, as critics like Kármány and Kazinczy would say of our own belated Hungarian rococo. The formal severity of the baroque had lost its inner meaning: the age of great passions was over and there was nothing left that needed to be restrained through the imposition of formality. The half-savage courtiers of Louis XIV had had to learn calmness and dignity; the cooler spirits of Louis XVI's needed to display a little vivacity. In her war on protocol, Marie-Antoinette was very much of her time.

This liberation from formality was also, without question, a kind of sexual emancipation—which certainly led Rohan, for one, astray. Wherever she could, the Queen spurned the official court costume and appeared dressed down, in light and comfortable clothing. The ladies were deeply shocked—and frantically imitated her. They queued up for Mlle Bertinel, her official dressmaker. Everyone wanted to be as *déshabillée* as Marie-Antoinette. But the style was not simply more comfortable, it also revealed rather more of the female form.

The Queen organised donkey rides, during which women sometimes fell off, producing a pretty *déshabillée*.

"Send for Mme Etiquette," she cried, " so she can tell us what a queen of France should do when she falls off a donkey." But what people claimed she said was:

"Anyone who wants to take part should come dressed to fall off."

We know from Fragonard's famous painting *Les Hazards Heureux de l'Escarpolette*—The Happy Accidents of the Swing— how much the rococo age valued those gratuitous moments which unexpectedly exposed the normally-concealed charms of women. Mercier tells us that ladies would often receive their guests in the morning while still at their *toilette*, because at those times there would be frequent opportunities for them innocently to reveal parts of the body which the clothes of the time enviously concealed. (But do not think the worst—he means, for example, the arms.)

One by one the ladies of the Court began to follow the Queen's example. They gave up their embroidered costumes, their *talons-rouges* (their red boots, which at one time became so typical that the word was used as a general term for the aristocracy). They began to dress like normal people. One problem was that Parisians could no longer identify them by rank and unpleasant scenes occurred. And here lay a hidden danger. Once a courtier dispensed with protocol, how was he or she different from anyone else?

Even more dangerously, the Queen indulged in that suicidal passion common to every late and over-refined aristocracy: she loved *s'encanailler*, to mix with the common people, though the translated phrase lacks the suggestion of coarseness and vulgarity in the original. She was thrilled when her carriage broke down and she turned up somewhere in a hired carriage, like a common mortal. Her passion for the theatre in particular presented her with a wealth of opportunities to make contact with the populace, in this case people associated with the stage. She was herself an accomplished actress, brought up as such in Schönbrunn, and as Dauphine she would rehearse and present plays with her brothers and sisters-in-law, with her husband as the only member of the audience (he often fell asleep during performances). When she became Queen she had even more such opportunities, and amateur theatricals became the chief diversion at Versailles, this form of amusement incidentally costing 250,000 livres per annum. ("Do I sing well?" the Comte de Provence once asked Mme Vigée-Lebrun, the painter. "Like a prince!" came the reply.) The Queen took an intense interest in everything going on in the theatre and often visited Paris to keep in touch. She befriended the players, supported an actress with the unfortunate name, given her profession, of Mlle Raucourt, and got herself involved in a diplomatic incident with the Venetian Republic over a tightrope walker called Picq. She knew all the gossip, and had she been alive today she would have been the most ardent reader of the theatrical weekly journals.

In 1773 she took part for the first time in an opera ball, and from then on attended them with great enthusiasm. They presented the best opportunities for mingling incognito among her people, the people of Paris, and having direct contact with them, not as subjects but as one human being with another, or rather, as a woman among men. She enjoyed the amusing situations that occurred, the *Jeux de l'amour et du hasard*—The Games of Love and Chance—as Marivaux, one of the most outstanding writers of the rococo period, expresses it in the title of one of his plays: that subtly erotic ambience elicited by simple feminine charm. This naturally gave rise to a great deal of gossip, and to one or two impudent comments from those who recognised her as the Queen and took unpleasant advantage of the situation. Joseph II rebuked his sister severely for these little outings. He worried that they might prove fatal to the French monarchy His anxiety was not unfounded.

The rebellion against protocol also involved the Queen's dressmaker and hairdresser. Mme Campan tells us that Marie-Antoinette would be ceremonially robed in her chamber, in full view of the ladies and other visitors, before briefly thanking them and disappearing into her *cabinet*, where the really important person, her couturier Mlle Bertin, who according to the rules should not have been there, was waiting. But Mlle Bertin did not work for the Queen alone, nor did her hairdresser Leonard, whose job it was to pile up the mighty tower of her coiffure with emblems, portraits and favourite animals—a whole little market town: he attended to every fashionable female head in Paris. Women readers will find this perfectly natural: if the Queen's dressmaker worked only for her, and her hairdresser did only her hair, as protocol required, neither of them would have had sufficient practice or been able to keep up with the fashions.

And—perhaps to overcompensate for feelings of inferiority, as an Austrian vis-à vis the women of Paris—Marie-Antoinette wanted to be absolutely the most fashionable lady in France. But this concern with the *mode* was itself a form of *s'encanailler*.

Elizabeth of England and Mary Stuart were also beautiful queens, but were regal enough to ignore the fashions of the town and be guided instead by those of the Court. This deferential attitude to the 'town' was a sign of the times, the first step towards the downgrading of the monarchy. In this respect Marie-Antoinette was ahead of her own circle—and closer to the Revolution.

But all this applies only to her early years. After the birth of her children the urge to pursue pleasure left her, and she took little interest in fashion. However, her hatred of protocol did not disappear. In fact, it came to a head. At which point she withdrew to Le Petit Trianon.

Le Petit Trianon had been built by Louis XV. This little mansion in the park of Versailles, with its nobly simple outline, had from the very first asserted the spirit of the coming age against its neighbour, the grandiose, marble-clad, pink-coloured Grand Trianon erected by Louis XIV, which stirs up so many painful and humiliating memories for Hungarians. At one time Mme du Barry lived in the newer building, when it was known chiefly for the way the dining table was piled progressively higher from the bottom end so that no one would be embarrassed by the billings and cooings of the King and his mistress. After that, it stood unused for some years. Then in 1774 Marie-Antoinette exerted all her influence to have the banished Duc de Choiseul—whom she had to thank for her becoming Queen of France—recalled to ministerial office, but Louis XVI held out against her, and to make amends he gave her Le Petit Trianon.

"Do you like flowers?" he asked her. "If you do, I have a very pretty bunch waiting for you—Le Petit Trianon."

The Queen set about redesigning both the house and the garden with a passion. It occupied her, and gave her enormous pleasure, for several years. The garden was a particular labour of love. Gardening was a specialist art in the Ancien Régime, reaching its heyday in the eighteenth century, and the park at Le Petit Trianon is a graphic memorial to the major shift in taste that occurred in this period.

Her immediate inspiration was the Anglo-Chinese garden of the Comte de Caraman, though by this time there were already a number of different 'English', that is to say, typically pre-romantic, gardens in the country. People had become bored with mathematically correct creations laid out, in the style of Le Nôtre, like a star—mighty avenues of stiffly erect trees lined with frigid statues of classical gods, with their fixed smiles and disdainful expressions of divine serenity. People were bored with formal fountains and baroque arrogance, bored with the topiarised trees, the geometric figures, the general triumph of art and reason over nature. And the royal family was especially bored with Marly, where, in the vivid phrase of the Goncourts, "The pavilions and gardens were filled with the shades of Louis XIV, his greatness and his tediousness." They were bored, too, with Versailles, where in winter the cold in the predominantly marble and glass rooms was simply intolerable, along with the appalling draught, and the hellish smoke from the old-fashioned, poorly-ventilated fireplaces.

The new fashion, like the whole pre-romantic movement, originated in England. When building, the English nobility began with their gardens. These were to be "like nature itself". Narrow, winding paths led between fresh, grassy meadows, wild groves and woodland traversed by babbling streams, with flowers growing everywhere, just as one imagined them to do, and with birds singing in the trees the way real birds sing—and heard as if for the very first time. And at night the moon shone just like a real moon, and you were once again transfixed by its long-forgotten, silver-blue enchantment.

That was the sort of park that Marie-Antoinette wanted. Her excellent taste protected her from the wilder excesses of the fashion, and her garden in Le Petit Trianon had no professionally constructed ruins or professionally designed grottoes, no Chinese bridges or Swiss log cabins, and only one broken column and one miniature pyramid to evoke the required sentimental melancholy. Along with these pre-romantic accessories we find a single little Belvedere, or lookout tower, where the Queen would take breakfast on summer mornings and from where she could survey the whole of her empire. There was also a *temple d'amour*, a little circular shrine with antique columns: it can be seen in the background of Wertmuller's celebrated painting of the Queen and her children.

It is here that the memory of Marie-Antoinette lives most strongly. As you stroll in the park something catches your throat, some remnant of that pre-romantic melancholy hovers in the air around you. Tongues fall silent, and you stand there secretly hoping for the royal ghost to appear, leading her children by the hand, before vanishing at a bend in the path.

How she loved this place! For a while she was content simply to escape there from Versailles during the day, with only the royal family and her closest confidantes accompanying her. Le Petit Trianon was her happy isle, where protocol was set aside and you did not have to go about in formal dress, and where the prying multitude and the ever-demanding, perpetually scheming nobility could never set foot. Here the family could live out the great dream of the age—"to be human, and to live as ordinary citizens".

Then she began to spend nights there too, with growing frequency. The first occasion was in 1779, on the pretext that she had the measles and needed to isolate herself to avoid passing the disease on to her husband. She arranged for four knights to watch over her in turns: the Duc de Coigny, the Duc de Guines, Count Esterházy and the Baron de Besenval.

"And if the King were ill?" malicious tongues asked. "Which four ladies would watch night and day over him?"

At Le Petit Trianon the Queen did sometimes arrange more formal events. She was much happier bestowing recognition on genuinely talented writers and theatre directors here rather than at Versailles. Here, the guests were genuinely her guests. The grandest occasion of all was the summer evening party, with the invitees strolling among Chinese lanterns, given in honour of the Russian Grand Duke and his wife, with twelve hundred people dining. That was the evening when Rohan spied on her in disguise.

But as time went by the place ceased to fulfil her yearning for the simple life. So inside the park she built the famous *Hameau Rustique*, the model country village and farmstead. It too was the height of fashion. The Duc de Condé also had one, in the park at Chantilly. Marie-Antoinette's consisted of several buildings, the largest of them her own house, where the entire royal family could withdraw from the Court in the afternoon. The King had a billiard room at his disposal, to fend off boredom, and there was a dairy farm, with cows grazing on the turf of the park—from time to time the Queen would milk her two favourite animals herself. There was also a mill, a granary, a poultry yard and a cottage for the gardener. It was a real working farmstead, not just a toy, as the Goncourts assumed.

On the basis of research done by Pierre de Nolhac, the leading authority on the subject, we must set aside the rather charming story that the Queen settled twelve poor families in the village, together with a saintly hermit to tend to their spiritual needs. Similarly discredited is the legend that the royals would occasionally play at village life there, with the King as miller, Marie-Antoinette as the farmer's wife, the Comte d'Artois as gamekeeper, the Duc de Provence as schoolmaster, the Duc de Polignac as magistrate and Cardinal Rohan as curate. It cannot be true, if only for the fact that by the time the village was completed Rohan was already a prisoner in the Bastille.

What is beyond doubt is that in building it Marie-Antoinette was paying homage to the current fashion for folksiness. When, as the new Dauphine, she first arrived in France, at Châlons, actors came from Paris to play Charles Collé's *Une Partie de Chasse de Henri IV* in her honour. The play is about Henri IV, the

French equivalent of our own great King Matthias, who loses his way in the woods during a hunt, comes upon some country folk, does not reveal who he is, and tucks into the village hospitality with hearty appetite. However, when the peasants want to drink to his health he refuses to give his name, whereupon they read him a thorough lecture, just as the grey-haired Peterdi does to Matthias in Vörösmarty's *Szép Ilonka* (The Beautiful Ilonka). At his point his courtiers arrive, reveal who he is, and he marries every girl off to whoever it seems appropriate. Collé's piece is not an isolated instance. Leafing through the volumes of Grimm's *Literary Correspondence* dealing with events in literature and the theatre in the 1780s, we find that a great many plays given in the period had a similar folk theme, celebrating the uncorrupted morals of village people as opposed to the thoroughly corrupt ones of the Court and the city. The convention originated in England, and the French naturally added the sentimental 'back to nature' touch, as in Rousseau's slogan.

That this was how Marie-Antoinette really imagined the virtues of the people is made clear in the letter we quoted earlier, à propos the philanthropic activities of the Freemasons. Amongst other things, she writes: " … there are hidden virtues among these social classes, wise souls who embody Christian virtues to the highest degree, and we should do all we can to reward them." She would have loved to have been the sort of popular, simple, patriarchal ruler in the folk tradition that her ancestors, the princes of Lotharingia, supposedly were. Mme Campan says of them that, if they were short of money they went to church, and when the sermon was over, waved their hats in the air to signify they wanted a word, explained how much they needed, and those of their subjects who were present would immediately club together to donate the required sum. What a fine, pre-romantic dream of the relationship between ruler and people!

From all this it appears that Marie-Antoinette was in her own way just as much a pre-romantic as her admirer Rohan. What the belief in miracles and mysticism were to him, nature, the simple life and a return to the common people were to her. The Queen was bored with her elevated, inhuman role, and yearned for some real connection with a more normal way of life.

In the course of this work we have said many times that the Ancien Régime was brought down not so much by its vices as by its virtues. The crimes, the 'abuses' of Louis XVI's period, were no greater than those of any previous century, and were moreover, steadily diminishing. The difference was in the prevailing morality—in the new philanthropy and cult of all things popular.

When a ruling class starts to show understanding and pity for the lower orders, idealising them in verse, arguing over plans for reform and how to better their lot, it is a fine thing, history tells us, and a sign of genuine nobility. But on the one hand it does very little for those same lower orders, and on the other, it augurs very badly for the ruling class. It is a sign that it has lost its self-belief, lost faith in its own divinely ordained superiority: in short, it has lost its *raison d'être.*

The medieval nobility understood the people far better than their eighteenth-century counterparts, because they lived among them on their estates, and did much more for them in a practical way. But they never talked or spent time thinking about them. They knew that God had ordained that there should be the rulers and the poor, and that when they helped the peasantry they were carrying out God's commandment. It was a debt due to God and to their own souls, but not to the people. And it never occurred to them to *s'encanailler,* to mingle with the multitude; they would not have understood the eighteenth century's strange nostalgia for what lay below them, for roots and origins, simplicity and the Rousseauistic sense of life, which was in fact itself arbitrary and 'cultured'—a form of class suicide. So long as a racial group continues to believe in itself it will keep aloof from every sort of physical intermingling.

The same applies to Marie-Antoinette. It was all very fine, thoroughly human and extremely worthy of her that she should love nature, the people, and the whole romantic ideal that would bring the Revolution to a triumphant head. That she hated stiff Spanish formality and wanted to be just one person among others, was deeply sympathetic in her. But it is not the business of a Queen to be human.

Rather, her duty was to glide through the dazzling, inhumanly magnificent halls of Versailles *in blaser, erdenferner Festlichkeit*—'in pale splendour far removed from earth'—unapproachably aloof from her subjects, her every movement like a formally perfect work of art, and to do, as a beautiful queen, what the King, the man, never could in the same measure, simply by being what she was, to make her millions of subjects feel the superhuman magnificence of royalty: to let them know that in the infinite heights above their heads dwelt powers as fixed as the stars, beings that watched over them by night. That would have been a far greater service to the people. Would it also have been death to her sensitive soul? Every vocation has its martyrs.

Marie-Antoinette did not do that, and the reason was that, like the glittering Court folk around her, she too had lost faith in her calling, in the institution of the monarchy, and with it her own *raison d'être*. The queen who no longer understands what it is to be a queen, who pays homage to the purely personal rather than the radiance of the crown, becomes superfluous. Marie-Antoinette did not fulfil the highest duty of her calling. When viewed *sub specie aeternitatis*, her downfall was not, in the end, undeserved.

The pre-romantic period was the great age of friendship. While the knights of the middle ages enjoyed the kind of brotherhood in arms that expressed itself through sword and deed, and faithfulness in life and death, it was never a matter of 'kindred spirits'. And while intellectual friendships also developed, following examples from the age of classical humanism and involving companionship of the highest order, with long philosophical discussions at dawn, great banquets and fine wine, and the exchange of beautifully phrased letters, it was only in the eighteenth century that the friendship of shared sensibility was born.

In response to the prevailing intellectual aridity of the time, when love had become a sophisticated and devious social game that failed to meet their needs, the women of the late rococo period took refuge in friendship. Female friends were always in each other's company, supporting and comforting one another, and whispering secrets in each other's ears. They would accept an invitation only if their friend was included. The two would walk about the salon arm-in-arm, or sit on the sofa with their arms around each other. They persuaded poets to compose hymns to Friendship, and temples were erected in parks to the same deity. Like everything else in this period, it became a dizzy, theatrical fashion. Women wore each other's hair on their heads, sometimes from a stock taken from a whole collection of friends, or they would have portraits of their favourites worked into their towering coiffures. Hair rings, hair watchstraps, hair chains, hair necklaces, hair bracelets and hair boxes came into fashion, and pictures of girlfriends as angels dangled from bracelets. *"J'ai un sentiment pour elle, elle a un attrait pour moi"*—I have a feeling for her, she has an attraction for me—they would proclaim. (L Goncourt *La Femme au dix-huitième siècle.*)

As a young girl Marie-Antoinette paid full homage to this fashionable mania. The longing for friendship was no doubt intensified by the long years when she had no real relationship with her husband and, finding herself truly alone, really needed someone who could understand her. Her most passionate friendships have been much discussed by historians. The first was with the Princesse de Lamballe, who met such an appalling end in the Revolution. This lady was descended from the houses of Savoy (the old ruling family of France) and Carignan, and was loosely related through her Savoy connections to the wives of the Duc de Provence and the Comte d'Artois, as well as the Queen's sister-in-law. Her husband, the Duc de Penthièvre, the grandson of Louis XIV and Mme de Montespan, had died young. But this lofty status did not shield her from the common disease of courtiers: they all wanted something from the King and Queen, and when they got it, they wanted more. The Princesse, to the great annoyance of her opponents, was made *Surintendante de la Maison de la Reine,* shortly after which their friendship suddenly cooled. She was replaced in the Queen's heart by the young wife of Comte Jules de Polignac—an even more passionate relationship. The Comtesse Jules, as she was known, was relatively poor, but she sincerely loved the Queen, and in the sincerity of her loyal nature allowed herself to be loved in return. But she was a blind instrument in the hands of her relations. Her husband soon became the Duc de Polignac, and within a few years the family had an annual income of 500,000 livres.

The Goncourts tell us that the Queen had a burning need for the Polignacs and the group that formed around them as a party in opposition to the royal aunts and other members of the Court aristocracy, to protect her from being completely isolated and reduced to subservience. But the reverse is also true: by confining her favours to her tiny clique to the exclusion of everyone else, and perhaps too for absenting herself so much from Versailles so that those others would not be able even to speak to her, she drew even more resentment upon herself. By around 1777 the Versailles balls were almost completely depopulated, leaving scarcely eight to ten people to circulate in the vast rooms, to the Queen's great annoyance. She was being boycotted by the offended nobles and left to the company of her friends. That clique of friends was undoubtedly one of the reasons for her unpopularity. Increasingly, the money she set aside for her friends became a source of reproach, and slanderers put an obscene construction on her intense feelings for her lady friend.

The persecution originated in the Court itself. The cause was jealousy. Here, however, we might be permitted to venture a theory of our own, not endorsed by other historians: that it was not the only reason but was exacerbated by feelings aimed at her circle of an even baser kind.

This is of course difficult to prove. Most writers show the Queen's companions as superficial beings, creatures of fashion who lived only for the sterile round of pleasure. The Queen's brother, Joseph II, took precisely that view of them, as is evident from the didactic and reproving tone of his letters to her. But it is possible that he was wrong, and that historians have simply taken over the common prejudice of his contemporaries. The Duc de Polignac, M de Châlons, the Duc de Guines, the Duc and the Comte de Coigny and the rest, were all sensible, intelligent men, and their circle included people of unquestionable intellectuality.

Chief amongst them was the Comte de Vaudreuil. The somewhat taciturn, occasionally demonic, pampered favourite, known to the group as the 'magician', was the Duchesse de Polignac's friend. He was one of the greatest connoisseurs of art in his time, and a powerful patron of writers and painters. It can hardly be fortuitous that the authors he personally helped came also to enjoy the patronage of Marie-Antoinette, who was normally so indifferent towards literature. These were Beaumarchais and Chamfort, the brightest, most cynical and most disillusioned writers of the age—in neither of whom is there the slightest trace of a courtly style, and who would never have achieved official status even under the most liberal system. Vaudreuil must have been the same sort of person himself: he found everything amusing, except when his bad nerves racked him with pain and he was seized with fits of uncontrollable anger, when he lost even his respect for the Queen—as when he once deliberately broke her favourite billiard cue. We should add that he had a rather ugly face, scarred by smallpox, so it was clearly not for his external appearance that he was so much liked. "I know only two men," said one of his contemporaries, a duke, "who know how to speak to a woman: the actor Lekaint, and M de Vaudreuil."

One very popular member of the clique was a parvenu, the Comte d'Adhémar, who had dug up his romantic-sounding name from some old documents and bought permission to use it. He was a modest man, of modest means, but respected in the group because he 'knew everything'. He played the role in the Queen's circle that fell to the abbé elsewhere: he represented the world of books, and had a fine singing voice besides.

The group also included one of the cleverest men of the age, the Duc de Ligne. He was greatly admired by Goethe, and is one of the most notable examples of a genuinely superior man of the world in this period.

Marie-Antoinette, however, was by nature of a sarcastic and critical tendency. Like her brother Joseph II, she was never short of a malicious remark, and the superior tone of her irony and her satirical wit were simply reinforced by her upbringing. Two bad angels struggled for the soul of the young Dauphine: Mme de Marsan, the embodiment of tradition, and the demonic Abbé Vermond, iconoclasm made flesh. Vermond, in particular—a churchman without an ounce of religion in him—exemplified the political morals of the age. He was convinced that at a time when authority and discipline were weakening, a lead should be given by the Church, an organisation that for two thousand years had preserved the secret of holding on to power. Like Thomas Mann's Naphta, he respected its enormous accumulation of authority. "He embodied," in Goncourt's words, "all the ambition and arrogance of the age: the arrogance of thinking himself somebody, and the determination to do everything by himself." Secret, all-powerful influence, without public office or form, was his dream. The role was not entirely different from the one Rohan yearned for, and Marie-Antoinette's attachment to Vermond must certainly have encouraged his hope that one day she would attach herself in the same way to him.

At Schönbrunn Vermond's job had been to teach the young Princess what the French were like. He almost certainly told her that they were a supercilious, hypercritical people who disliked anything that was boring. At Versailles he was constantly pointing out how very much better things were done in Vienna. The formalities, the empty traditions, everything to do with the French past, he treated with the embittered 'philosophical' hostility of a parvenu.

So one can imagine that the group that formed around Marie-Antoinette, of which Vermond was the leader and Vaudreuil the truest representative, was regarded by others as uniformly arrogant. Not perhaps with a strictly intellectual arrogance, nor the arrogance based on greater knowledge and a broader view of the world, but rather the easy assumption of superiority conferred by knowing oneself to be more fashionable, more articulate and more abreast of the times. It was the sort of superiority the citizen of a great metropolis feels towards someone from the country, and the self-consciously 'modern' person towards the people of the past. Lord Chesterfield, the greatest theorist of court life in the eighteenth century, is right when he observes in one of his letters: "It calls for a great deal of intelligence to accept the highest degree of intelligence of other people. The cleverer you are, the more goodwill and courtesy you are called on to display to be forgiven for your superiority. It is not an easy thing!" Marie-Antoinette's entourage, it seems, failed to understand this.

To which we must add that she and her set consisted almost entirely of young men and women, while in the clique opposing them it was the older lords and ladies who dictated the tone. Young people, especially when in a group and with nothing to restrain them from being vengeful, are always mockingly supercilious towards their elders, undoubtedly encouraged to do so by their own wit and intelligence. They find the customs and habits of older people amusing, and wherever they can will exaggerate or even mimic differences between the two groups.

In her circle, the younger members of the Court found themselves ranged against the powerful women, ministers (like Maurepas) of astonishing antiquity, and the King's aunts—all of them religious bigots, political conservatives, people who were hostile to all forms of social change and intellectually dull. It was inevitable that this clique should feel superior in themselves and have little difficulty making other people feel that superiority—and that it would be deeply resented. The feelings of inferiority they imposed on the rest of the Court must have been one of the most important sources of the hatred felt towards Marie-Antoinette.

By the time of the necklace affair, the circle of friends had largely dispersed. Marie-Antoinette now found herself most at ease with foreigners. When anyone remarked on the danger in this, she would solemnly reply:

"You are quite right, but at least they don't ask me for any-thing."

(From the Hungarian point of view, it is interesting to note that among these foreign friends was the already mentioned Count Bálint Esterházy. Born in 1740, he was the grandson of Antal Esterházy, the military general and companion in exile of Ferenc Rákóczi II. His father, József Bálint Esterházy, had left Bulgaria and returned to France, where he served as a soldier, married a Frenchwoman and died young. The present Esterházy was a follower of the Comte de Choiseul, and it was he who took the portrait of her fiancé to Marie-Antoinette at Schönbrunn. Maria Theresa had not been pleased by Esterházy's behaviour in Vienna: he allegedly spent 100,000 forint on another man's wife and became involved in a duel. He was much given to duelling, and continued the practice at Versailles whenever he considered that Marie-Antoinette had favoured someone else over him. Later, when the War Minister proposed down-grading his regiment of hussars, Marie-Antoinette intervened on behalf of her devotee. In 1780 he became a general. He was an intimate friend of the Comte d'Artois. In the Revolution his hussars provided cover for the flight of the royal princes. Esterházy later emigrated, settled in Volhynia, and died there.)

Rohan must have been aware of all these developments at the Court: the Queen's need for intimate friendships and her extreme proneness to taking lively, clever, dominant women into her confidence. Women like Jeanne de la Motte.

When Rohan first became enmeshed in Jeanne's intrigues, he was in truth showing no more credulity than ninety per cent of the population. He believed the Queen was no different from any other young, attractive woman of high birth and did not take the sanctity of marriage very seriously. By this stage a whole erotic myth had grown up around the person of Marie-Antoinette. To some extent it had sprung up independently of any basis in reality, but whether or not any such basis existed, the myth was a necessary one. Every social group has certain collective mental requirements. It needs men it can look up to as objects of hero worship (one of the major driving forces of history) and it needs women who can serve as objects of collective desire. In our time these women are the great screen actresses; in our parents' time they were opera singers, dancers and circus performers. Erotic legends grow up around all female film stars, and publicity agents take great care to foster and sustain them.

In the seventeenth and eighteenth centuries, the heyday of the monarchy, the woman closest to the King, whether his Queen or his mistress, attracted the same level of interest that film stars do nowadays. Their situations were similar in that their lives were played out in the full glare of publicity, and their whole existence was a performance, a role they had to play. The queens of old and the great actresses: figures in the collective consciousness, people to whom everything is attributed that can be dreamt of about a woman.

This phenomenon reached its highest level of importance in the eighteenth century. It was the century, as we are frequently told, of women—the intellectual life of women in salons, women wielding unseen influence, women as members of academies, theatrical productions whose success depended on the power of actresses to charm; in the economic sphere, financiers amassing great fortunes in order to marry their daughters into the aristocracy, and women ruling over whole peoples and empires: Maria Theresa, Catherine the Great, Queen Elisabeth Farnese of Spain, as well as the likes of Mme de Pompadour and Mme du Barry. It was as if some residual matriarchy—the oldest culture of the Mediterranean—was struggling to emerge from the blood and the collective unconscious; as if the time would one day return when, in every tribe, it was the women who possessed wealth and power and the men who 'married out', moving into the wife's extended family, where they became gentle, pampered, more or less superfluous drones. In the nineteenth century, with the age of emancipation, some sort of equilibrium was established, but the twentieth century has seen a reaction, and today we find ourselves once again living in a powerful patriarchy. Even in politics there are similarities with the male-bonded societies of old, with groups of men, to a lesser or greater extent armed, adhering to one another and exercising the power of male strength. What the reasons might be for this alternation between periods of male and female dominance is not yet something science can explain, but it is not inconceivable that they are rooted not in historical processes but in biology.

In the century of women, it was inevitable that these erotic legends should attach themselves to the outstanding female figures of the time, and not just to the likes of Mme de Pompadour and Catherine the Great, who provided plenty of suitable material, but even to the ever-virtuous Maria Theresa, who fulfilled all the duties of a self-effacing monarch, wife and mother. Even today there are countless dreadful stories circulating in this country about the Empress and her Hungarian hussars.

And all this applied even more strongly in France. It was there that women reached the greatest positions of power, and there that this erotic momentum was at its strongest, by virtue of the traditions and nature of the French people.

Nonetheless they still looked to their king to be first and foremost a loving husband, and they respected him as such. Louis XV lost his popularity not on account of his political ineptitude but because of Mme du Barry, and not so much because he had a mistress but because he failed to choose a better one, the sort of woman with whom his more respectable subjects might wish to converse. And it played a large part in Louis XVI's loss of public esteem that people were so dissatisfied with his wife Marie-Antoinette. Besides, it was felt that he did not conduct himself like a true husband, or conform to the national ideal of manliness, in contrast to the gallant Henri IV. This is all characteristically French. With the English, for example, it was only in their most Gallicised period, the reign of Charles II, that they took any interest in their king's mistresses. In the eighteenth century they were so indifferent to the question of whom their monarch was sleeping with that the names never feature in the historical record. This was not a question of morality. The English were at that time a thousand times more moralistic than the French, but even they were not especially perturbed by these royal liaisons: their hatred of their monarchs existed quite independently. No, this was something in the sexual nature of the French, and everything to do with their fundamentally bourgeois attitudes. The basic character of a people does not change, and most of the French were probably no less petty bourgeois under the Ancien Régime than they were later. Their petty bourgeois character is most truly seen in the insatiable delight people took in the gnawing away at the love life of the royals that finally destroyed the life of Marie-Antoinette. Those who condemned her allegedly immoral behaviour were, deep down, embittered by the fact they could not do the same themselves, and found a certain erotic compensation by colouring in the details.

To this we should add the extraordinary tendency to gossip mentioned earlier, which arose from the fact that people no longer believed in the concept of greatness, and had lost that feeling of distance—they loved to see everything in naked, intimate proximity. It was an age of flunkeys.

But all this, you remind me, gentle reader, is just a theory, smoke without fire—what is needed is some sort of basis in fact. So we can no longer avoid closer inspection of the raw material of the myth. Indeed, we are obliged to provide one, lest we give the impression that we are guilty of the same petty bourgeois prurience.

So let us dispose of the most delicate question of all.

Marie-Antoinette was married in 1770, but properly became Louis XVI's wife only in 1777. One morning she told Mme Campan:

"At last I am Queen of France."

The following year her first child was born, the *Madame Royale*, who was christened by Rohan. In 1781 came the Dauphin (who died in 1789), and in 1785 the Prince of Normandy, later Louis XVII, the luckless child inmate of the Temple prison whose fate is lost in the shadow of mystery. "If Marie-Antoinette had known the joys of motherhood earlier," said the excellent Casimir Stryenski, "she would not have taken to seeking a remedy for her idleness and boredom in the pursuit of empty pleasures; she would have had no time to listen to flatterers and self-seeking advisers, and no time to get involved in intrigues. Perhaps then she would have avoided slander, or, at the very least, it would have had no purchase on a life filled with the laughter of children and the tearful joys and pains of child rearing."

Today it is common knowledge what caused that seven-year delay. Stefan Zweig, in his somewhat coarse psychoanalysis, sees it as the foundation of her entire fate. Louis XVI had been born with a certain physical abnormality, which produced no symptoms but which impeded intercourse. After years of hesitation, Joseph II visited France for a heart-to-heart talk with his brother-in-law, and he at last made up his mind to have the necessary minor operation.

So for seven years Marie-Antoinette was a wife and not a wife. A less delicate nervous system than hers would have found those seven years' uncertainty a trial. At all events, they do explain a lot: her yearning for pleasure, her capricious behaviour and the strangely erotic atmosphere that grew up around her—the ambience of a woman whom nothing could satisfy.

In seeking consolation in this way, did Marie-Antoinette behave just as any other Frenchwoman in her situation might have? At all events, her contemporaries tended to see a pattern in her many diversions.

First and foremost of those was the person closest to her, her brother-in-law, the Comte d'Artois. Of Louis XV's three male grandsons only Charles, Comte d'Artois, bore any resemblance to the French kings of old. The future Louis XVI was shy and low-spirited, the Comte de Provence clever, cunning and duplicitous, but Artois was a good-looking, sociable, sunny character, who kept high-born mistresses and ran up appalling levels of debt. Easy-going and sensual, he was a true Bourbon. The melancholy fate in store for him was to become, as Charles X, the very last of the senior Bourbon branch to take the French throne. But the genial young man became an intransigent king. He was the one Bourbon who in his time in exile learnt nothing and forgot nothing, who would have given up the throne rather than make any concession that might diminish his royal status. When, a great many years later, his steadfast supporter Chateaubriand called on the aged ex-King in Prague, he found him just as he had always been: a man who, if he had had his time all over again, would have done exactly what he had done before.

The relationship between the Queen and Artois must have been one of genuine friendship from the start. While Louis XV was still alive, the younger members of the royal family ate together, went everywhere together and entertained one another. Artois even learnt how to rope dance because the Queen admired one particular master of the art. Their fun-loving, pleasure-seeking temperaments brought them close together. She would no doubt have listened eagerly to his revelations about his many amorous experiences, because she was always interested in such stories. Before very long scandal linked their names, and by 1779 an unspeakably obscene poem was going the rounds under the title: *Les amours de Charlot et de Toinette.*

Speculation also strongly linked Marie-Antoinette and a startlingly handsome young courtier called Édouard Dillon. According to the legend, she once said to him, during a Court ball:

"Monsieur Dillon, just put your hand here a moment, and feel how my heart is beating."

To which the King replied, in his phlegmatic way:

"Madame ... Monsieur Dillon will take your word for that."

According to some, Marie-Antoinette bestowed her favours on the not-so-very-young Duc de Coigny (he was aged between forty and fifty). Tilly, who was not ill-disposed to the Queen, was certain of it, as was Lord Holland. According to him, Mme Campan, who presents Marie-Antoinette as a model of sexual probity in her memoirs, was less discreet in her younger days, and did not dissuade Talleyrand from acting as a go-between for the Queen and Coigny. But was Talleyrand a man whose word you would always trust?

It would be tedious to cite every such detail concerning the Queen. But in 1792 a leaflet announced itself with the following title: "A price on their heads. Here follows a list of the names of those with whom the Queen has had illicit relations." The list is a long and varied one. Alongside the aristocrats we also find a guardsman, an official in the Ministry of War and the son of an actor, Guibert. Eventually, the pamphlet becomes bored with its own inventory and summarises it as *toutes les tribades de Paris.* E de Goncourt calls the copy in his possession a *"pamphlet imbécilement enragé"*. It names rather more women than men. The more surprising entries include Jeanne de la Motte, Cardinal

Rohan, Mme de Marsan (whom the Queen hated more than anyone) and M Campan, that excellent lady's pious and devout husband.

There is also one self-volunteered entry, the Duc de Lauzun, the greatest Don Juan in an age of Don Juans and a supreme example of the cynical attitudes that prevailed at the end of the century. To explain why he had abandoned his wife, the charming Amélie de Bouflers, he observed: "Well you see, in the end Mme de Lauzun brought me no more than 150,000 livres a year." "In those words," wrote Sainte Beuve, "you have the whole vanished Ancien Régime and the complete vindication of the Revolution, which in the end, and considering all the other similar outrages, was justified." It was Lauzun who, being at breakfast when they arrived (during the Revolution) to take him off to be executed, remarked:

"With your leave, I'll have another dozen oysters first."

In his memoirs he claims that the Queen was desperately in love with him. She begged him for a heron's feather and thereafter wore it ostentatiously in public; she would not allow him to stray from her presence, and on one occasion, when they were alone together, she threw herself on his breast and, in the refined phraseology of the eighteenth century, offered herself to him. But he declined the honour, because he did not wish to let his mistress, the Duchesse de Czartoriska, down, and his manly soul had no desire to play the dubious role of Queen's favourite. But all the same he allowed her to think that he might nonetheless relent at a later date. In the meantime he went off to the East Indies for a year with the army, and when he returned the Queen kept her distance from him, and the whole court treated him with a derisive coolness.

Lauzun's memoirs became very influential after the restoration, and Mme Campan protested bitterly against his slanders. The heron's feather story was true in that he had bullied her into accepting it from him via the Princesse de Guéménée, but not long afterwards Mme Campan was standing in an adjacent room when she heard the Queen pronounce the words: "Go, sir!" Lauzun left the room dumbfounded, and Marie-Antoinette gave orders that he should never be allowed back. This throws considerable doubt on the veracity of his memoirs. Perhaps they were written not by a successful Don Juan but by a miserable hack.

Rather more serious than all this (not inconsiderable) gossip and conjecture hovering in the air, was the story involving Baron Besenval.

Besenval was a Swiss, a member of the Queen's own inner entourage and the Polignac circle. He was the *naturbursch* of the Court—its raw, straight-talking hillbilly, who expressed his opinions in open, unguarded language but with the courtier's confident belief that he knew just how far he could go.

It happened that Artois and the Prince de Bourbon fell out over some issue, and all the talk at Versailles was that there would be a duel. Marie-Antoinette, who was intensely curious by nature, would peer out through a lorgnette from her bedroom window to see who was walking in the park, and kept asking who had been in the theatre on those evenings when she hadn't been there, calming down only when reassured that "there hadn't been so much as a cat". She was especially curious about the details of the duel and wanted Besenval to explain them. So Campan brought the Baron, in great secrecy, into the upper level of the palace, into a suite of apartments he had never seen before, consisting of an antechamber and a bedroom. The bedroom, in practice, was for the use of the *Dame d'Honneur* when the Queen was ill. Campan let him in and told him to wait for the Queen. And there, inspired by the location, the grizzle-haired Baron fell to his knees before her and offered her his heart.

"Rise, sir," she said. "The King shall be ignorant of an offence which would disgrace you for ever."

And Besenval remained at the Court.

From this story it naturally appears that Besenval was simply another 'volunteer', so much so that his name does not even feature in the extremely long list. His behaviour could be put down to the unbounded stupidity and arrogance of the male sex, which was even more in evidence in this licentious age of pampered knights. To drive a final nail into the gentleman's coffin, Besenval, though an intelligent man and one who knew the Queen well, actually believed that, in spite of his grey hairs, she had invited him into the little room with amorous intent.

We get something of the measure of all this unfounded gossip if we can believe, with the Duc de Ligne, that the basis of the slander was "the Queen's coquettishness, with which she hoped to please everyone", and that "the Queen's supposed flirtatiousness was simply an extreme form of amiability". But even if we also accept the noble, elevated portrait painted by Mme Campan and the nineteenth-century writings that followed her, there remains absolutely no doubt of her feelings for Axel Fersen.

That love, far from destroying the overall charm of Mme Campan's idealised portrait, actually completes and enhances it—the noble passion of a noble mind, the one serious, deep and truly romantic attachment in an age of coldly elegant and frivolous love games.

In the middle of the last century, suitably bowdlerised to fit the prudishness and discretion of the times, Marie-Antoinette's letters to Fersen were published. "That publication," says Stefan Zweig, "totally changed the received image of her as a thoughtless woman. A profoundly dramatic story was laid bare, a story of danger and power played out half in the royal court, half in the shadow of the scaffold—like one of those tear-jerking novels whose plots are so improbable that they can occur only in real life—two people, one of them the Queen of France, the other a minor Scandinavian nobleman, united in passionate love yet compelled by duty and prudence to conceal their secret in the depths, to be separated over and over again, forever yearning for one another across the terrible gulf between their two worlds. And in the background of this tale of two individual fates, a world collapsing, a time of apocalypse … "

The most significant expressions of this great love were enacted only after the main event in our story was over, when the Queen found herself completely isolated following the necklace trial. But its origins went back to a time long before it, and Rohan must have known about them.

Axel Fersen was a nineteen-year-old Swedish count who arrived in Paris in 1774 while on a grand tour of Europe. The Dauphine met him at a ball, in which they were both masked, and the young man discovered only later who it was that he had spoken with at such length. When he returned to Paris in 1778 she greeted him like an old acquaintance. The young man had grown into the most beautiful person in all Europe: tall, slender, blond—like the youthful hero of a Nordic saga. Both outwardly and inwardly he was worlds apart from the likes of Lauzun, the roués, the sort of men most Frenchwomen idolised. Fersen was both shy and proud, pure of soul, reticent and discreet; a sensitive and yet order-loving northerner—almost aridly so. The efforts of the Abbé Vermond and the French Court to turn Marie-Antoinette into a Frenchwoman had not succeeded; instead, the mysterious workings of racial type led this blonde Germanic woman to the fair-haired Nordic man, with his Northern richness of feeling and spiritual purity. While the French courtiers around them seemed to have stepped from the pages of *Les liaisons dangereuses*, these two inhabited the world of the young Werther.

Although they both concealed their feelings with true northern modesty, perhaps even from each other, the gaze of the Court was always on them. The Swedish ambassador Creutz took a certain fatherly pride in telling King Gustav III of his young compatriot's success.

A stanza of Verlaine's comes to mind—it is from the *Fêtes Galantes*, which captures the whimsical mood of the eighteenth century in its most exquisite form:

Ce fut le temps sous de clairs ciels,
(Vous en souvenez-vous, Madame?)
Des baisers superficiels
Et des sentiments à fleur d'âme.

It was a time of cloudless skies,
(My lady, do you recall?)
Of kisses that brushed the surface
And feelings that shook the soul.

And when they could no longer deny what they meant to each other, the wise and sober Fersen thought it better to put an ocean between the two of them, and went off to fight for freedom, as Lafayette's aide-de-camp in America.

But in 1783 he was back.

Did Rohan know of the love that the Queen felt for the Nordic Count? Perhaps not. Fersen was not French. He did not brag about his conquest, and, as a wealthy, independent foreigner, he wanted nothing from her. He was seldom at Court. Probably they met in secret in Le Petit Trianon, or the rustic village. But if Rohan did know about it, it was all the more French of him not to have understood it. He would not have been capable of grasping that, given the nature of their relationship, he could not possibly draw hope from it that the Queen, having given her love to one man, would then bestow it on another; but that, on the contrary, such a love would be truly moral—and the full force of the marriage vow, as well as the Queen's sense of honour, would set a wide gulf between her and any man who was not Axel Fersen.

So far we have spoken of an 'external morality'; there is also the 'inner' morality that Rohan would have been able to understand, and which may well have supported him in his belief.

Appearances certainly suggest that Marie-Antoinette shared the frivolous tastes of her age, including its love of refined and not-so-refined scandal. The eighteenth century had discovered Pompeii and made much use of the motifs of Pompeian art. This was not a chance thing—since the time of Pompeii there had been no period in European culture in which the erotic played such a central role as in the rococo. The novels, plays and paintings of the period are often, by our notions, quite shocking, especially the plays, such as those by Charles Collé, which were performed in the private theatres of the aristocratic houses for the delectation of the noble ladies. It is even possible that Marie-Antoinette acted in these herself. Certainly the conversation in her little circle would not have differed from that in the other salons. People quickly realised that they could say whatever they liked in front of the Queen, and that it delighted her when they did. And perhaps it was no secret to Rohan how much she loved reading dubious literature. In her boudoir were the beautifully bound adventures of *Les amours du Chevalier Faublas* and other such works, which in the prudish centuries that followed could not even be mentioned And perhaps he also knew that the beautifully-bound prayer book she was so busy reading at Mass contained nothing more than a titillating novel.

Above all, people in the eighteenth century thought it rather odd, even vulgar, for married people actually to love each other. Married love had not yet become associated with bourgeois values but with the lower orders. Should it occur in 'good' society, it would be something to hide. Husbands connived at their wives' affairs. In aristocratic circles, according to Mornet, these 'open marriages' were the necessary compromise between arrangements forced on young women and the need to attend to the 'words of the heart'.

There is a well-known story of the Count who opened the door to his wife's room and discovered her in a surprising situation, with a man.

"For God's sake, Madam!" he cried. "How could you be so thoughtless, as to leave your door unlocked! … Imagine if anyone other than myself came in!"

Chamfort's anecdotes show a constant preoccupation with the extent to which jealousy had fallen out of fashion. Someone says to a jealous husband:

"You are jealous? You are very conceited, sir. *N'est pas cocu qui veut*—it is not enough to want to be cuckolded—you have to know how to do it. You need to understand the running of a great house, and be very polite and kind. Who would want to cuckold the sort of person you are at the moment?"

"What a pity that people nowadays have so little respect for cuckolded husbands," says another of his examples. "It used to be an honourable title, now it's just a game—it means nothing."

"One day," Chamfort adds, "Monsieur de Nesle, whose wife was the mistress of the Duc de Soubise, said to her in his presence:

"'Madame, I hear that you've been having an affair with your wig-maker. That sort of thing is extremely bad form.'

"And with the air of a man who has done the right thing, he left the room and Soubise slapped her face."

Another husband said to his wife:

"Madame, I realise that this man has his claims on you, and I have no wish to stop whatever it is that he does with you when I am not here, but I cannot tolerate his demeaning you in my presence. It's an insult to me."

Another man knew that his wife was having affairs left, right and centre, and for that reason exercised his conjugal rights from time to time. One day the lady repelled him with some violence:

"I can't, now. I love Monsieur X."

"What's this? I thought you loved Messieurs Y and Z?"

"That was just a phase. This is true passion."

"Ah, that's different," the husband said, and turned away.

Marmontel, one of the most popular writers of the time, in one of his novellas—*Heartwarming Legends*—makes the following remark:

"Freedom is the soul of love. Without freedom the object of one's choice is no better than a husband." (That is to say, nothing.)

Marmontel also writes:

"You should realise, my friend, that when women transfer their affections elsewhere, they do so out of delicacy and the desire for novelty."

Was the young Queen, the most fashionable woman in France, really any different from the rest of her kind? And would she at some point transfer her affections "out of delicacy and the desire for novelty" to Prince Louis de Rohan? *Qui vivra, verra*—What will be will be—he told himself.

Chapter Eight

How it Happened

T HE AUTHOR, dear reader, experiences an onset of emotion as he comes to the most important moment in our tale. He has done his best to put it off, talking about other things at great length and hoping all the while that some miracle will turn up, that someone else will write it for him. The writer dislikes responsibility, and finds himself on the point of collapse as the great scene approaches. But he can prevaricate no longer. Taking a deep breath, he will try to get it over with as quickly as possible.

A frequent visitor to Jeanne's house, a Monsieur Laporte, happened to know that Boehmer still had the wonderful bauble that no one wanted to buy. One day he remarked casually to Jeanne:

"If you really are on such good terms with the Queen, you should tell her to buy that necklace."

"Have you seen it?" she replied.

"I have. It's a real miracle. The stones alone are worth a fortune, not to mention the work that went into it."

Negotiations began. Monsieur Achet, Laporte's father-in-law and the Public Prosecutor, called on Boehmer and Bassenge to reveal the prospect that lay before them. The jewellers replied that they would gladly give one thousand louis to anyone who could get rid of it for them. Laporte was up to his ears in debt.

On 29th December 1784 Achet and Bassenge took the jewel to Jeanne's house at St Gilles in the Rue Neuve. The box was opened. There, before her eyes, glittering with the lights of a thousand diamonds, lay the long-awaited miracle—the Valois miracle. There lay the accursed treasure of the Nibelungs, finally raised from the depths into the light of day, and now radiating its sinister charm. For a moment she felt quite faint: this was the moment which she had lived for, and relived: the moment that meant that her birth had not been in vain. The inspiration that had so long heaved incoherently inside her soul had found a form. The great plan was born: it brought together two great *idées fixes*, those of Boehmer and the Cardinal, and in so doing fulfilled a third—her own.

The Cardinal, following her instructions, remained at Saverne. But in January he returned to Paris. Baron Planta had brought him a letter from the Queen. "Come quickly," it read. "I wish to entrust you with a secret commission, one that concerns me personally. The Comtesse de la Motte will explain this riddle to you."

At the end of January Jeanne met with the jewellers again, and told them there was a chance they might sell the necklace in the next few days. The purchaser would be a certain nobleman; they would have to be on their guard, because the aristocracy were poor payers. She mentioned no name. The jewellers, intimidated by her high social rank, said they would be presenting her with a rather special gift; they dared not offer her money.

"Thank you, but I shall not accept it," the Valois blood replied. "I'm only doing this to help you."

It was, after all, the age of charitable giving.

On 24th January Jeanne and her husband rose early, and by seven in the morning were at Boehmer's premises in the Rue Vendôme.

"Today will you receive a visit from Cardinal Rohan. He is your buyer. You must not mention me by name."

Soon afterwards Rohan arrived in the shop. He saw the jewel, and did not like it. His refined rococo taste found it gross, barbaric, dated. For a moment he was filled with disappointment.

"But will the Queen like it?" he wondered. "I don't understand this. I thought she liked dainty, airy, *joli* little things. But perhaps not. After all, she isn't French."

Still, the Queen's wish was his command.

The groundwork leading up to this had been as follows: Jeanne, using her tried and trusted method, had told Rohan that the Queen wanted to buy the jewel but was temporarily short of cash. So she wanted to have it on credit, against a bill of exchange, to be paid off by instalments and in secret, without the King knowing. That was why she needed Rohan. She asked that he should not act officially on her behalf but rather pose as the buyer himself. Rohan would be in good standing with the jewellers because of his wealth and good name; she, in turn, would then send him the money. She would explain what she wanted through Jeanne, and by letter if he so wished.

To us the most astonishing thing in all this is that Rohan believed this story. Even considering his habitual naivety, it is surprising. He obviously did not take the Queen's unwillingness to be directly involved in the purchase too seriously, since he actually told the jewellers that he was buying it on her behalf. And when the jewellers questioned his ability to pay, since he was offering her name as security, he showed them the Queen's well-known signature on the letter of agreement. (We shall return to this signature later.) But if there was no reason to conceal her name, then why did she need him in the first place? Perhaps as a guarantor? But that made no sense either. Even he must have seen that, as a third party to the transaction, the Queen would always command far greater credit than he could.

Perhaps he thought that her talk of a 'loan' was simply a matter of courtesy, when really she wanted the jewel as a present from him. But there can be no doubt that Rohan did not feel quite so gallant as to propose buying the jewel himself. He was depending on her to pay for it. That was the one thing he did show any concern about. He had only let himself become involved once she committed herself to payment in writing.

So, however you look at it, his role in the whole business was quite superfluous. If the Queen wanted to purchase the jewellery in secret she did not need him as security, either for his name or his wealth. He was perfectly clear about that. Then why did he think the Queen had turned to him?

Because he was Rohan. We should think back to all that was said about his credulity in Chapter Three, the relevance of which now becomes clear.

And then again, Rohan was not a man of business. In our more financially aware times it is impossible to imagine just how unbusinesslike he was. He must have been thinking something along these lines: "I really don't understand why she needs me to buy this necklace. But then I generally don't understand what happens with money because I have never been without it, as my income is so vast, and I just have to accept that this is precisely the sort of money matter I don't understand, and which it is below a person of my rank to understand."

On 29th January the jewellers called on Rohan at the Hôtel de Strasbourg. They agreed terms: Rohan, acting for the Queen, would pay the 600,000 livres in four half-yearly instalments, the first becoming due on 1st August 1785. Delivery was stipulated for 1st February, as the Queen wanted to have the item by Candlemas.

Rohan put these conditions in writing himself, and passed them on to Jeanne so that she could inform the Queen. Jeanne returned his submission with the reply that the Queen fully understood the terms, sent her gracious thanks, but did not wish to sign her name. At this point, Rohan dug his heels in. It is really rather strange: he was prepared to believe everything in the world, but he absolutely insisted on the Queen's signature. This would be, gentle reader, like having someone send to you, quite out of the blue, to say that the Prime Minister, whom you have never met, has asked you to lend him your winter coat. To which you reply, "But of course, most willingly, only I must have his signature."

Rohan clearly did not do this because he had immediately become suspicious. Not for a moment did he have the slightest doubt that he really was buying the necklace for the Queen.

But it suddenly occurred to him that this was a business matter, so he should act in a businesslike way. He wanted to show that he really was a good businessman, who understood how things were done according to the traditional forms, which must surely be as important in business life as they were in the life of the Court. A document needed a signature—that was the form.

Jeanne was somewhat taken aback. She had provided the fraudulent letters with an easy mind since he was so blinded, but this agreement would pass through the hands of serious men of commerce … But in the end she made the decision that had been forced upon her. She went back to him with the document. Beside every paragraph the Queen had written the word '*approuvé*'—agreed—and, at the end, the name: 'Marie-Antoinette *de France*'.

"Don't show this to anyone," she told the Cardinal.

Then, at the very last moment, something happened which should have saved Rohan, which might have saved Marie-Antoinette, and indeed the French monarchy: Cagliostro returned from Lyons. If he had merely said "take care", the scales might have fallen from the Cardinal's eyes.

On this point, the Abbé Georgel tells us that the night before the jewel arrived there was a great throng in the Cardinal's palace, at which a host of heavenly beings appeared, and advised Rohan that the business he had become involved in would bring him great success, and that he would at last win the Queen's favour, to his own great glory and the inexpressible good of France and all mankind. But the Cardinal—some instinct must have whispered to him that something wasn't quite right—did not enlighten Cagliostro as to what the great business was about, and Cagliostro was unable to warn him.

The next morning Rohan wrote to the jewellers asking for immediate delivery of the necklace. The two men arrived soon afterwards. Rohan took the occasion to remind them that it was the Queen who had purchased the jewel, and he showed them her signature.

Not long afterwards Jeanne also appeared.

"So, what's the problem with the necklace?" she demanded. "The Queen has been waiting for it."

Rohan reassured her—it was there. And at this very last moment, a healthy misgiving crossed his mind. True, it was only a very tiny morsel of misgiving compared to the huge absurdity of the whole. How much, he asked, would the first part-payment be, including interest? Jeanne replied rather grandly that the Queen would take care of that. They agreed that the Cardinal would take the jewel to Versailles that evening.

That evening, the Cardinal's carriage stopped in the Place Dauphine in Versailles, where Jeanne lodged. She was alone. He was received in an ill-lit room with an alcove leading off. In his hands lay the treasure.

Footsteps were heard.

"De par la reine—In the name of the Queen!" someone cried out in the next room. The Cardinal discreetly withdrew into the alcove. A tall, pale man in black entered. Rohan had seen him somewhere before. Where could that have been? Ah, yes, it was the man he had seen in the Bower of Venus, the one who hissed the warning that Madame and the Comtesse d'Artois were approaching. The man gave Jeanne a sheet of paper. She dismissed him, and showed Rohan the letter. The Queen had written to say he should hand over the necklace to the bearer.

We do not know whether Rohan now had a moment's hesitation as he let the cursed Nibelung treasure out of his hand. But he let it go, and it set out on its fateful journey. The pale man in black (Réteaux de Villette) and the jewel disappeared into the night. Shortly afterwards, the Cardinal returned home.

That was how it happened.

A few days later he received a letter edged with blue. Its illustrious writer requested him to take himself off to Saverne and, in the interests of the business just transacted, not to show his face for while. With his usual passivity he obeyed this instruction too. We find him reposing "deep inside" his wonderful mansion, "dozing on down cushions, far inwards," in Carlyle's words, "with soft ministering Hebes, and luxurious appliances, with ranked heyducs, and a *valetaille* innumerable, that shut out the prose world and its discord; thus lies Monseigneur, in enchanted dream." Let us leave him to dream; he still has a little time left for that.

The La Mottes spent rather less time dreaming. They had to solve the difficult question: how could you secretly realise an asset of which there was only one example in the world—an item of jewellery as conspicuous as the sun?

The wisest course would of course have been to hide it in some safe place, and, after a long, long wait, when the storm had blown over, start turning it into cash, very circumspectly, in some completely different part of the world.

But that was not what Jeanne did. She couldn't, because she needed money urgently and she did not have a long, long time. Creditors were pressing her, as, with equal urgency, was the life of greatness, the Valois destiny. Besides, just two days earlier she had not given it a moment's thought—so much is clear from the whole story. If you spent time thinking about the future, you wouldn't be a true adventurer. An adventure is something that happens from one moment to the next; in which there is no yesterday and no tomorrow. Everything else is just petty bourgeois.

So she did the next best thing—she broke the necklace up into its constituent parts to sell individually. Naturally, this reduced their value. The diamonds were separated by a nervous, un-skilled hand and suffered extensive scratching; the mounting was lost, and so was the value of the craftsmanship; all that remained was the raw value of the stones.

Then she eagerly set about selling them.

A few days later Réteaux de Villette was reported by a jeweller whose suspicions were aroused by his having a pocket full of diamonds. Réteaux declared that the stones did not belong to him but had been entrusted to him by a lady of noble birth, and he actually named Jeanne de la Motte. Thus the great project almost foundered at the outset.

However, because of the nature of her profession, Jeanne had been subject to police surveillance for some time. That now proved her good fortune. Thinking she had the diamonds merely in her protection, the police disregarded the report and took no further interest in the matter.

But it taught Jeanne that she would have to be a lot more careful. She gave a large number of the stones to her husband to take to England for sale there. A second lot she kept herself, and a third was entrusted to Réteaux.

In England, La Motte set about his task diligently. His line was that an old family had broken up an item of jewellery in order to raise money on the individual pieces. The English jewellers were made suspicious by the low prices he was asking, but were very familiar with the circumstances of members of the aristocracy experiencing financial difficulties. At all events, they raised the matter with the French Embassy, but the people there had no knowledge of any significant theft involving diamonds. La Motte raised almost £240,000 in ready money, leaving so many stones with the English jewellers that they set them up in framed displays; he also traded nearly £8,000 worth of diamonds for other goods: watches, chains, swords, razors, corkscrews, asparagus spoons, boxes of toothpicks and other useless flummery. The Comte was not a man of business, and can have received barely half of what the diamonds were really worth.

Meanwhile Jeanne too had been busy. She had herself sold about 100,000 livres' worth of diamonds to jewellers in Paris, paid off her debts and gone shopping, paying for everything in diamonds. It troubled her not a whit that she had to tell a few stories about where they had all come from. To prepare the ground for her husband's return awash with money, she told all her acquaintance that he had won a vast sum of money in England on the horses.

He was back on 1st June. The money was there in his hands. And now we turn to you, gentle reader, and ask you to rack your brains and think what you would have done in the couple's place?

You would no doubt consider where you might invest such a sum profitably. Even in Jeanne's time, though the practice was not yet common, you could have bought stocks and shares, annuities and national bonds; you could have purchased land, and, given the general upsurge in, and the great strength of, the economy described earlier, you could, above all, have set up some new industrial enterprise. You could even have bought yourself some well-remunerated state office, such as that of *fermier général*, as a great many financiers were doing.

On the other hand, you could use it to travel to some distant country, where you could buy plantations and slaves ... America was just the place for that.

The La Mottes did nothing of the sort, and we can hardly blame them. They were children of the Ancien Régime, aristocrats of the same breed as Rohan, if not quite so refined in their recent origins. Money-making schemes were every bit as alien to them as they were to the Cardinal. And above all, they were adventurers, people with no yesterdays, and (especially) no tomorrows. They valued life in terms of feeling, and the figure they might cut before it. The whole mighty sum was spent, just as it had come, in the grandiose style appropriate to their station. Jeanne realised the Valois dream, and La Motte went about dressed up like a thrice-compounded pimp.

From his study of police and other contemporary records Funck-Brentano calculated just how much money the couple spent. He lists the number and variety of tailcoats La Motte purchased for himself (they take up an entire page), and he enumerates Jeanne's newly-acquired jewels. We have just space enough for one or two interesting details—her new furniture was hauled from Paris to Bar-sur-Aube, where they set up residence, by forty-two drays. At Bar they kept six coaches and twelve horses. They went about in a grey English carriage emblazoned with the Valois crest and motto: *Rege ab avo sanguinem, nomen et lilia*—I take my blood, my name and the lily from a royal forebear. The coach was drawn by four English stallions ridden by flunkeys, with a negro covered from head to toe in silver standing on the step. They gave soirée after soirée, and their house was permanently full of guests, even when they themselves were away.

Certainly none of us would have behaved in this way. No one living nowadays could possibly be so stupid: the modern way of life is simply unsuited to indulging one's desires with such pomp. But we confess a certain sympathy, indeed, a respect for Jeanne, and for her aristocratic style. She, the offspring of the Valois, had to this point been nothing more than a damp rocket at the great party, her fuse poisonously fulminating and fuming in torment; now the flame had reached the dry tinder and sent up a shower of sparks, scattering flowers and garlands in the sky alongside the stars and all the other glowing rockets. She felt that at last she had found her place in the aristocratic cosmos— and she knew, too, that in due course her fire would fade, and she would plunge back down into the eternal darkness.

Intermezzo

Figaro and Count Haga

T HE READER who is interested only in the story of the necklace can confidently skip this chapter.

The Queen could never for a moment have imagined that
a phantom figure dressed as herself would lure the dream-
locked Cardinal to the edge of the tragic whirlpool. She went
about her royal life totally unsuspecting, and in the summer of
1784 received a visit from, among others, King Gustav III of
Sweden, who was travelling around Europe under the name of
Count Haga.

Ever since she had met Axel Fersen, Marie-Antoinette had
loved everything to do with Sweden. Or perhaps her love of
the Swedes might be traced to an even earlier date—even
before Fersen's time she had had a Swedish protégé, Count
Stedingk. However her initial feelings towards Gustav III were
more likely to have been hostile. She had met him while she
was still the Dauphine, when Gustav, as heir to the throne, was
spending time at the French Court. But he had thought it wiser
to bid for the favour of Mme du Barry and to ignore the young
and powerless Princess—an error that, as we know, she and her
normally indulgent husband found hard to forgive.

But since then, much had changed. News of his father's death
had summoned Gustav back to Stockholm. Before leaving he
obtained full French support for the strange course of action
he was planning. As is well known, Sweden in the eighteenth
century was ruled by an anarchic oligarchy, just as Poland had
been before its collapse. The King wielded rather less power than
the prime minister of a republic: he voted in the state assembly

like any other noble, his privileges amounting to no more than that his vote counted twice. The two factions in the assembly, the Hats and the Caps, were at loggerheads. Between them they were unable to agree on the crucial question of who they should sell the country to, the French, as the Hats wanted, or the Russians, favoured by the Caps. This constitutional anarchy was pushing the country, sooner or later, towards domination by the Tsars, just as had happened to Poland. Both Frederick the Great and Catherine the Great were counting on it.

But France, as Sweden's traditional ally, was not content simply to watch this resurgence of the eastern powers. So Choiseul and Vergennes, the former ambassador to Stockholm who later became Louis XVI's Foreign Minister, encouraged the returning Prince to make a stand. Gustav was made of considerably sterner stuff than his predecessors—he was in fact a nephew of Frederick the Great on his mother's side. And he had the same love of light, and the civilised life—literature, the theatre and public pomp—as any French *grand seigneur* of the time. Ever since the Thirty Years War the Swedish nobility had received an annual subsidy from the French Court, but oligarchical rule meant in practice that this money no longer went into the pockets of the King but was shared among leading members of the nobility. Gustav proposed putting an end to this arrangement and reverting to the historic precedent whereby all the money from France came to the monarch. He received a promise from the French court that if he could put an end to the anarchy, one-and-a-half million livres would be placed in his hand.

For that happy result he had above all to thank one of the strangest episodes of the eighteenth century, the Swedish revolution of 1772. The revolution was unusual in that in this case it was the King who rebelled against his tyrannical subjects. Every detail of this revolt should be taught in that non-existent school in which ambitious young people are instructed in the art of politics. If we read the book by Jacques Le Scène

Desmaisons that appeared in 1781 (and ended up in the bequest of the Palatine Joseph in the University Library in Budapest) we can see the extent to which the King planned and prepared every detail, in the manner of a great—and flamboyant—theatre director.

First, he allowed the Hats and Caps to quarrel for a full year over the drafting of an oath to the King, that is to say, over the best method for tying his power up in knots. Then, when the two parties duly came to heel, he secretly obstructed the distribution of grain, so that the people would go hungry and become dissatisfied. Next, he provoked a small local uprising so that his brother could raise an armed force ostensibly to put this 'rebellion' down. While the government was distracted by this supposed uprising, the real revolution took place miles away, on two fronts. Then he locked all the younger officers up in the palace and would not let them go until he had won them over to his cause.

Throughout all this he gave proof of his remarkable theatrical talent; to the very end he misled everyone around him as regards his intentions, and even allowed the Russian ambassador to think that he was preparing to pay his respects to the Tsarina in the near future. When it came to the final moment, he arrested his senators, occupied all the major strategic locations and toured the capital giving speeches. Everywhere he went the people saluted him as the man who had freed them from the tyranny of the nobles. "This was the king," says Desmaisons, "who had woken that morning as Europe's most politically hamstrung ruler, and within two hours had become a monarch as absolute as the Prussian King in Berlin or the Sultan in Constantinople."

Next, having summoned the Diet, he set up a row of cannons outside the Palace and asked the members of the assembly whether anyone objected to what had taken place. Unsurprisingly, no one did, and the constitution was unanimously amended to ensure that every royal prerogative was returned to the Crown.

All this was done while punctiliously observing the niceties of eighteenth-century decorum. The King personally wrote to the wives and children of the detained senators asking their pardon for having unavoidably kept them as his guests for the duration. At the first opportunity the Diet, now sitting without benefit of cannons, expressed their courteous thanks to the King for depriving the nobility of their excessive privileges and restoring order to Sweden, and ordered a medal to be struck to commemorate the great event.

Considering how little the Swedish Revolution has to do with the story of the Queen's necklace, we have dwelt on it at perhaps inordinate length. We do so partly because we think it an interesting chapter in European history and one that is far too little known, and, more importantly, because it reveals a course of action that arguably was also open to the French monarch. Here was an eighteenth century Swedish King accomplishing with elegance and humanity what, in the late middle ages, Louis XI of France and Henry VII of England had managed with altogether cruder instruments—reinforcing their own power by forging a bond with the people against the ranks of birth and privilege. The idea that something similar might be repeated in these later times entered the head of only one great statesman of the Ancien Régime, Turgot. He alone saw that the royal power should carry out the much-needed reforms itself, in the interests of the people and at the expense of the aristocracy, and that that was probably the only way in which they might have survived, sparing France the Revolution. But Louis XVI was not Gustav III, and Turgot, a proud man and a complete stranger to compromise and strategy, was easily seen off by the intrigues of the Court.

In Sweden, Gustav represented an enlightened absolutism. He did his best to compensate his people for the loss of freedom by improving their welfare, allowing free trade in grain and total freedom of worship (a purely hypothetical freedom in a country with only one denomination), and amending the Poor Law.

Like Frederick the Great, Catherine the Great and many other rulers of the eighteenth century, Gustav considered himself to be French in mind and spirit. He promoted a French-style literary life in Stockholm, and himself wrote plays which Swedish literary historians continue to mention with great respect. But this domestic literary life simply intensified his interest in the Paris equivalent, and was one of the reasons why he yearned for France. The other was that in the end, in the usual melancholy way of these things, the long-awaited golden age never quite materialised under his rule, and Gustav had to look for other sources of revenue. He deliberated whether to sell himself to Russia or to turn again to France. Unable to decide between the two, he eventually travelled to Italy. He shared the late-eighteenth-century passion for relics of classical antiquity, and bought a vast collection of art works to be sent home to adorn the park of the palace he was building at Lille-Haga (Count Haga was the name he used when travelling incognito). The Italians cannot have been too greatly pleased by his standards of generosity, since they composed this epigram about him:

il Conte de Haga
che molto vede e poco paga

Count Haga,
who looks at everything and pays almost nothing.

While thus engaged he received an invitation from the French royal couple. Marie-Antoinette wrote to him personally to say that if he found himself in the vicinity he should look up his old acquaintances at Versailles. The French Court understood the great struggle going on in his mind, and were prepared to make real sacrifices to rescue him from an alliance with Russia.

To avoid unnecessary suspense we can reveal that Count Haga's visit was a complete success. Versailles promised him a substantial subsidy of 1,200,000 livres for six years, in addition to the existing generous support. Of course, payment of the full sum was prevented by subsequent historical events.

But these manoeuvres were not the only reason why Gustav visited Paris. Amongst other things, he was curious about the lady who was so much talked about. His Paris correspondents and diplomats faithfully reported all the current gossip surrounding the Queen, rather like events in a theatre, and these stories interested Gustav not only for political reasons but for personal ones. Like almost every other ruling prince of the century, he too had an exemplary bad marriage. He hated his wife, the royal Danish Princess, and refused to live with her. It was only after 11 years, in 1777, that he could bring himself to take the necessary steps in the interests of the succession, and that great event was undertaken as a ceremonial duty for the sake of the country. There was almost as much gossip in circulation about the Swedish Queen as there was about Marie-Antoinette, and so Gustav must have had a certain professional fellow sympathy for the French royal couple.

But as a rule he did not much enjoy contact with monarchs. Though it may seem strange, he had a sense of inferiority when dealing with the rulers of more powerful countries than his own, for which he overcompensated by behaving too familiarly or too uproariously. Thus he turned up at Versailles unannounced, like an old friend dropping in on a neighbour, and caused considerable distress to the pernickety Louis XVI, who was not attired in the manner in which he received foreign princes.

On one occasion, Mme Campan tells us, Gustav called unexpectedly on Marie-Antoinette just before lunchtime. The Queen sent Mme Campan to enquire whether he had sufficiently dined and, if not, to make the necessary arrangements. The Swedish King modestly replied that anything would do. The lady smiled, because she knew that nothing less than a full meal was ever served, and she found a way to point out the gaffe he had committed: she remembered that, in the world she had grown up in, what people did on such occasions was to scramble a few eggs. The Queen later let him know that this had been done as a lesson to him not to be overfamiliar.

Gustav was much happier dealing with people who were charmed by the fact that, although a king, he treated them in such a kind and informal way. This was especially true of writers and artists. Through his respectful yet unmistakably regal correspondence with the Baron Melchior von Grimm we can trace his passage through the intellectual world of Paris, where we find him mixing with the leading wits of the age. This Grimm was a Frenchman of German origin who wrote perceptive and witty letters to foreign rulers describing literary and artistic events in Paris. The letters, written very much in the manner of the period, show an equal fascination with theories of state economics and the epigrams about actresses quoted in the salons. Their lively shrewdness and rococo lightness of touch make them most enjoyable reading.

Above all, Count Haga frequented the theatre. In his honour the Royal Academy of Music staged some eight or ten operas in three weeks, more than they would normally do in two or three years. The Comédie Française obligingly put on every play he asked to see. This began, apparently, when he arrived unannounced at the theatre after the first act of Beaumarchais's *The Marriage of Figaro* had finished. The audience demanded that they begin again in honour of their distinguished guest. "Whatever that truly French, truly generous and perfectly proper act of attention cost the actors," writes Grimm, "they never performed the piece better or earned greater applause." The other major theatre, the Comédie Italienne (which was Italian only in name, since by then its last remaining Italian actor, the great clown Carlin, was dead) put on *Le Dormeur Éveillé* in his honour, with music by Piccini and libretto by Marmontel, whom Gustav had greatly admired since his youth.

Amongst the most celebrated people in Paris at the time were the Vestris family, famous opera dancers. Count Haga

177

was naturally very curious about them, and when he paid his final visit to the Opera before his departure, Marie-Antoinette sent word on three separate occasions requiring the younger Vestris to appear without fail. But he had returned from a guest appearance in London "with an injured foot", and the doctors "had forbidden him to appear". "It could be that this reply pushed the degree of stupidity or impertinence beyond what was permitted to a dancer," says Grimm. It was enough to persuade the Interior Minister Baron Breteuil to lock the young man up, and, in the heat of revolutionary fever, all Paris took sides for or against him. The older Vestris, the leader of the troop, observed with tears in his eyes:

"*Helás!* this is the first disagreement our house has ever had with the Bourbon family."

(No less pleasing is what Vestris said when he heard that his son had incurred a debt: "Auguste! I want no Rohan-Guéménées in my family!")

Naturally Count Haga, like the whole of Europe and especially the French, was greatly intrigued by the 'Aerostatics', or aeronautical experiments, of the brothers Montgolfier and their followers. The Montgolfiers, as is well known, had realised that warm air rises more readily than cold, so that if we take a strong balloon and fill it with hot air it will rise into the sky. Later they attached a basket underneath the balloon and flew in it. The notion of people flying drove the entire nation into ecstasies of amazement, and the general miracle-hungry mood of the times produced the suitably fairytale name for this—'the conquest of the air'—to the great amusement of those of a more sober disposition.

The strange thing is, how many of those charming fairytales have since come true. For example, Grimm made great fun of the coffee house politicians who had already started to calculate how much more it would cost the state if they had to maintain a fleet of these machines. The time would come, joked Grimm, when people could fly off to China in the evening and be back the next morning. The King's blithe younger brother the Comte de Provence composed an epigram on the subject:

Les Anglais, nation trop fière,
S'arrogent l'empire des mers—
Les Français, nation légère,
S'emparent de celui des airs.

The proud English claim empire over the seas—the French, in their levity, do the same for the skies.

Before the Montgolfiers, a canon named Desforges had designed a gondola fitted out with wings, in which he sat and threw himself off a height, in the hope that it would swim through the air. Apart from some minor damage, no harm was done, but he was very thoroughly bruised.

An almost equal degree of interest was provoked by our own countryman Farkas Kempelen, with his famous chess-playing automaton. In September 1783 Grimm quotes from a book which described the device in detail. The machinery consisted of two parts: a low chest of drawers covered by a chessboard, and the figure of a Turk with a pipe in his mouth, who lifted the pieces and set them up in their correct positions. There was no question of trickery: both the cupboard and the pipe-smoking Turk could be opened up to show the wheels and springs inside, so there was no one hiding there: after a few moves the Turk had to be wound up again. Nowadays it is impossible to believe that it was making the moves by its own volition and playing to win; that in some automatic way it was calculating the moves for itself. No, it was being operated by Kempelen, standing there just a short distance away but too far to be able actually to touch it. In his hand he held a strange device with which he was obviously manoeuvring it from where he stood, but he refused to reveal the secret to anyone.

There were other, more comical, inventions. A watchmaker, for example, caused a great sensation when he conceived the 'flexible wooden shoe', with the aid of which you could walk on water. At first people thought it was a fraud, but when they looked into it, it proved to be nothing of the sort—but nor was it very interesting. The worthy inventor had designed two little rafts, one for the left foot and the other for the right, and that was how you could travel on water. The people of Paris had expected more. It was a time when anything was thought probable. In London, for example, a vast crowd gathered when someone announced that he was going to squeeze himself into an empty wine bottle—and when he declined to do so on the pretext of a temporary indisposition, they smashed up the whole area around the theatre.

During his stay in Paris, Count Haga became involved in a purely private matter, which neither he nor any of the others involved suspected for a moment would feature in world history—this was the marriage of Baron Staël, Secretary to the Swedish legation.

The young Erik Magnus Staël-Holstein was not distinguished for any particular talent, but his good manners and sympathetic exterior had charmed the ladies at the Paris Court, and had even earned the goodwill of Marie-Antoinette, who was already well-disposed towards Swedes. Whatever she and her little circle, in their sophisticated flippancy, thought of the institution of marriage, they enjoyed matchmaking every bit as much as the women of the bourgeoisie, and were therefore much exercised by the question of who should marry the young Germaine Necker, daughter of the great banker and Finance Minister and one of the wealthiest heiresses in France. Since her family were Protestant, the French aristocracy were out of the running, so the plan was that she would be paired off with the handsome Count Alex Fersen. Although his father, one of the leaders of the Hats in Sweden, was extremely keen on the idea, Fersen himself gave it a very cool reception, and Marie-Antoinette felt somehow unable to press him with the required conviction. Nonetheless she stuck with the Swedes, and suggested the girl marry Baron Staël-Holstein instead.

The idea of giving his daughter away to a Scandinavian Baron pleased Necker, who was infinitely vain and a parvenu, but he was unimpressed by Staël-Holstein's position and made it a condition of his consent that the young man should be made Ambassador. Marie-Antoinette asked Gustav to nominate him to replace Creutz, who had gone back home to become Chancellor, but the King, knowing Staël-Holstein's lack of substance, dragged his heels for a considerable time.

The question was clearly much discussed at the garden festivity at the Le Petit Trianon. In due course Gustav did promote Staël, and in 1786 he married Germaine Necker. The marriage was not a particularly successful one: the feckless Baron cost his father-in-law and his wife (who became famous as Mme de Staël) a great deal of money. As Marie-Antoinette and Gustav strolled in the grounds of Le Petit Trianon they cannot for a moment have thought that in time the girl would become Napoleon's feared antagonist, France's 'foremost exile', and one of the best known figures of the romantic age of European literature.

On 5th June 1784 King Gustav attended a meeting of the Académie Française, where he was given an enthusiastic reception and eloquent speeches were read out in his praise. The actual agenda was somewhat less delightful. The new member, M de Montesquieu, eulogised the man he was replacing, Bishop Coetlosquet of Limoges, whose only achievement was to have lived to a ripe old age. Then the Director, M Suard, rose to reply. To inject an element of topicality into the discussion, he gave a spirited defence of the greatest success of the day, Beaumarchais's *Marriage of Figaro*. After that, La Harpe, that arid, sterile critic of his age, read out the second part of his didactic ode on women. According to Grimm, it was received very coldly—if it had to be something instructive, they would much rather have heard the Abbé Delille, La Harpe's chief opponent in the ferocious row between followers of Gluck and Piccini that caused such dreadful civil war among the Immortals. (This was the war between French and Italian music, in which, for some strange reason, the French was represented by the German-born Gluck, Marie-Antoinette's former music teacher, who had grown up with Italian music and was a wonderful example of the international spirit of the age. According to Grimm, Gluck was to music what Corneille had been to the theatre, and Piccini was its Racine. Perhaps it might be argued that Piccini was also what Verdi later became, while Gluck was a forerunner of Wagner. For the 'Italians', all that mattered in opera was the music, while Gluck wanted to subordinate the music to the drama, or rather, argued that it needed both music and text working together to raise the effect above mediocrity.) Finally, the Duc de Nivernois read out some of his simple and informal fairy stories. When the session was over, the King had a few private words with Suard. Grimm believed he knew what they were discussing: Gustav was telling Suard that he did not agree with him about *The Marriage of Figaro*, adding that he wanted to see it again.

From this account one might conclude that this was not one of the more interesting sessions of the Academy, but few of the others can have been much better. Some months later, Grimm tells us, a certain M Gaillard so spectacularly bored his audience with a performance so very unworthy of his immortal name that the Academicians met and decided that something needed to be done. At the following session the Abbé Boismont set about lecturing his listeners, whereupon they whistled like an audience in a theatre. From then on, they decided, fewer invitations would be issued, and only to reliable elements.

But the fact that the same sort of audience went to the Academy as did to the theatre shows that the great institution had lost none of its prestige during these years, and was by no means isolated from the literary life of the day. Earlier, in the middle of the century, far from being a conservative, traditionalist body, it had been a meeting place for revolutionary spirits, entirely under the control of the *philosophes*, the collaborators on the great *Encyclopédie*, at war with the Church and the Sorbonne. Since all the Encyclopedists were also members of the salons, the world of women followed the Academy's elections and proceedings with the greatest of interest. It was genuinely part of the *monde*, of aristocratic society, as were the Comédie Française and the Comédie Italienne.

By the end of the century the Academy had lost none of its relevance, but the original group of *philosophes* were no longer in the vanguard. As with all sects, persecution (imprisonment, the burning of their books and banishment) had simply made them stronger. But although official harassment continued until the end of the century, it had by then become something of a game, final proof of the saying that "the monarchy forbade everything and could prevent nothing". For example, Brissot would be forewarned by the official responsible that his current pamphlet was to be confiscated; the copies would then be seized and sold on the black market by the same official's wife. The Abbé Morelle, imprisoned in the Bastille for his writings, was comforted by his supporters with the thought that he should regard it as a welcome form of publicity. Morelle thought so too, and the calculation proved correct. Even the Church could no longer stand up to the *philosophes* in the decisive way it once had done. Fashionable preachers such as the Academician the Abbé Boismont did not try to refute their teachings—they merely insisted that the God of the Christian religion was rather more likely to inspire benevolent feelings in the human heart than the cold and distant Supreme Being of the *philosophes*. When the Spanish translation of the *Encyclopédie* appeared, its first purchaser was Don Bertram, the Archbishop of Salamanca and Head of the Inquisition.

The Marquis de Condorcet, the man chosen to succeed D'Alembert as leader of the *philosophes*, made his speech of acceptance into the Academy in January 1782. He began: "The eighteenth century has so thoroughly perfected the system of human knowledge that there is no means whereby the new enlightenment could be extinguished, unless some universal catastrophe covered the human race once again in darkness." The *philosophes* had won.

But, year by year, the great generation of the French Enlightenment were dying out. Voltaire went in 1778, after his triumphal return to the Paris from which he had been exiled for so many years. Two months later, his great adversary Rousseau died. In 1780 it was Condillac, in 1784 Diderot. In 1783 it was the leader of the *philosophes*, the director of the *Encyclopédie* and the Permanent Secretary of the Academy, D'Alembert himself.

It happens very rarely in literary history that one great generation is followed by another. The void left by the death of the great Encyclopedists could not be filled by their heirs. D'Alembert's successor at the Academy was the hardworking, many-sided and inconsequential Marmontel, the literary populariser of the *philosophes'* ideas. Its greatest lyric poet was considered to be the Abbé Delille—perhaps because he behaved as a poet was expected to, was permanently distracted and dreamy and "was forever letting himself go at the feet of some pretty girl", as we might colloquially but faithfully translate Grimm's phrase, so expressive as it is of the times. His great rival, as we have mentioned, was the leading critic of the age, La Harpe. La Harpe was a timid conservative who extolled everything from the past and pronounced everything that was antiquated in classical French literature to be 'correct'. He was an outstanding example of the French literary pedant, a proponent of that schoolmasterly deference to the bookish 'rules' that foreigners always find so surprising. La Harpe had been a French tutor to Grand Prince Paul Petrovics, the son of Catherine the Great. When the Grand Prince was in Paris, La Harpe would pay his respects every time the Grand

Prince showed an inclination to receive him. Finally La Harpe announced:

"I have discussed the art of ruling with him on two separate occasions, and I can assure you that I found him most satisfactory." (There were a great many reasons why this could not have been true: Paul I, as he became, was the stupidest and most timid of all the stupid and timid Russian Tsars.)

Although the most severe of critics, La Harpe could not bear to be criticised himself. After the press had savaged his play *Les Brames*, he petitioned the Keeper of the Seal to ban the newspapers from commenting on his new plays before a certain number of performances had taken place, to stop the audiences from staying away—a playwright's dream that has never yet come to pass.

La Harpe was not a great poet, but he was one of the most representative people of his time. There was only one great poet alive in France in this period, and he was certainly not typical of his age, nor had anyone heard of him. This was André Chénier, who was to die young on the revolutionary scaffold. In Chénier the *chrysea phormix Apolonos* was heard again: the golden lute of Apollo, the glory of Ancient Greece. The oldest voice is always the newest, and Chénier is much more modern to our ears than any other poet of his century. We feel instantly at home in his verses. They are the lyre that will sound again in the work of Baudelaire and Verlaine. We cannot refrain from quoting a few lines to show how very fine his voice is, and how little dated. The extract is from an allegorical poem about a queen—perhaps he was thinking of Marie-Antoinette, so the passage is not unconnected with our theme:

Sur la frivolité

Mère du vain caprice et du léger prestige,
La Fantasie ailée autour d'elle voltige …
La déesse jamais ne connut d'autre guide.

Les rêves transparents, troupe vaine et fluide,
D'un vol étincelant caressent ses lambris …
La reine, en cette cour, qu'anime la Folie,
Va, vient, chant, se tait, regarde, écoute, oublie.
Et dans mille cristaux, qui portent son palais,
Rit de voir mille fois étinceler ses traits.

"Frivolity—mother of shallow Caprice and empty Prestige, with winged Fantasy flitting around her, the only guide this goddess has ever known … In this court, so animated by Folly, transparent dreams, fluid and insubstantial, flicker caressingly over the marble panels as the Queen comes and goes, breaks into song, falls silent, stares, listens, forgets … then, seeing her face reflected a thousand times in the thousand mirrors that hang in the palace, erupts into laughter."

While French literature was moving into decline at home, the cult of French wit was reaching its zenith abroad. Count Haga was not an isolated phenomenon—the whole of Europe was just a larger version of him. To be a cultured person was to be like the French. Their language was as much a world language as Latin had once been. The Berlin Academy launched a competition under the heading "The Universality of the French Language". It was won by the youthful, mad and faux-mad (for so he proclaimed himself) 'Count' Rivarol. The motto of his winning entry was: *Tu regere eloquio populus, o Galle, memento*— "Remember, Gaul, that your calling is to rule all Europe by your eloquence."

But at the same time, given its sense of growing internal weakness, and the increasingly ossified nature of its classicism, the country was more receptive to literature from abroad than it had ever been before or has been since. In particular, there was an outpouring across the Channel of English pre-romantic cloud, storm and blackest night. The plaintive, sepulchral tone came strongly into fashion in France. Young's tearful dirges, and the gently mournful departing souls of Ossian, haunted everyone. The Comédie Italienne staged a play called *Le public vengé*, in which the allegoric figure of the National Genius laments:

"Since I was exiled, I have travelled in many lands; there is not one country that does not love my style; everywhere I am sought after—but now I am come home, and behold, I find that everything is given a friendly welcome here except me; here I am the only stranger."

The French had truly broken through the Chinese wall of the neo-classical past, and made the foreign Muses welcome—but those Muses paid a high price in return. They were required to dress up in the formal garb of the French Court.

Bienséance, the rules of decorum instilled by the 'Great' seventeenth century, still held sway, sacrosanct and not to be transgressed. The idea that lay behind them, and the myriad ways in which it was expressed, harmless enough as they might seem to a foreigner, continued to weigh on the delicate sensibility of the French.

Just what this *bienséance* entailed is shown in this graphic example from Taine. A young noblewoman, having arranged a pension for her tutor, the famous dancing master Marcel, ran to him in delight to show him the document. He dashed it to the floor and cried:

"Mademoiselle, is that what you learnt from me? To proffer something in such a way?"

In literature, *bienséance* required a strict avoidance of words not current in aristocratic society, thus excluding all scholarly and other specialist terms, as well as diction favoured by the hoi-polloi and the more effusive poets, and, to maintain a lordly generality, nothing was to be described in excessive detail.

Hence Voltaire decided that, for the famous extended simile from the *Song of Songs*: "His eyes are like doves beside springs of water, bathed in milk", the correspondingly *bienséant* version would read: "*un feu pur est dans ses yeux*"—a pure flame is in his

187

eyes. The example shows how bloodless was the poetry that truly conformed to classical taste. Ducis, who adapted Shakespeare's plays for the French theatre, expunged the fateful handkerchief in *Othello* on the grounds that an object into which, *horribile dictu*, a man blows his nose (the French '*mouchoir*' directly mimics this function), could have no place on the national stage, and Desdemona dropped a bit of ribbon instead—which was considered much more elegant.

Let us stay awhile with Ducis. He led Shakespeare to triumph on the French stage, but what he made of him in the process! The plot of *Hamlet* in his revised version ('*imitée de l'anglais*') runs as follows:

Claudius, is no longer the King but merely the *Premier Prince du Sang* (the King's oldest brother, analogous to the Duc de Provence). He tells his confidant, Polonius, that he wants to step into his late sibling's shoes, but the widow, Gertrude, will not consent to marry him, however politely he asks. Gertrude tells her confidant, Elvire, that, despite having long had an affair with Claudius, her main reason for refusing to marry him is that he incited her to give the poisoned cup to her husband, and she now feels remorse and fears the terrible revenge of her son Hamlet. So she sends for Hamlet's confidant, Norceste, to come and cheer the prince up a little.

But this will not be easy. Hamlet is in a really bad mood. When we first encounter him, we only hear his voice behind the stage. Something is happening to him that only Voltaire among French playwrights could permit himself to show directly—he is seeing a ghost.

"Avaunt, hideous spectre," he calls out from behind a backcloth. "What? Do you not see it? It hovers over my head, it dogs my footsteps—it is killing me."

The ghost behind the backcloth disappears. Hamlet steps out and tells his confidant Norceste that he is in the difficult situation familiar to heroes of all French classical dramas since Corneille—he is torn between love and duty. On the one hand, there is his filial duty to kill the wicked Claudius; on the other, he loves Claudius' daughter Ophelia, who would take it rather badly if he butchered her father.

Earlier, Claudius has explained the cunning political manoeuvres which have won him prestige and the approval of the people; now he informs us that, as a lunatic, Hamlet could forfeit his claim to the throne. Ophelia tells Hamlet that the time has come for him to make her truly his wife, something not previously possible since his father had forbidden it. Hamlet's reply is initially evasive, but he eventually tells her that he cannot marry her because he has to kill her father. Ophelia is not pleased to learn that his passion for revenge is stronger than his love for her. She really had not expected that, and she rebukes him in the following terms:

> *Ah! tu m'as fait frémir. Va, tigre impitoyable,*
> *Conserve, si tu peux ta fureur implacable!*
> *Mon devoir désormais m'est dicté par le tien—*
> *Tu cours venger ton père, et moi, sauver le mien.*

> Ah! you make me shudder. Go, implacable tiger,
> Maintain, if you can, your implacable fury!
> My duty henceforth is dictated by yours:
> You fly to avenge your father, I to save mine.

Thus the full formula of classical French drama is set in motion: on the one hand Hamlet's struggle between love and duty, and on the other, the identical conflict inside Ophelia. Now indeed the shades of Corneille could come to terms with the fact that Shakespeare was being performed on the French stage.

Next, Hamlet produces the urn containing his father's ashes, whereupon his mother confesses all (this is all that is left of their great scene). But, rather than kill her, Hamlet sends her away, since "In my present mood I am capable of anything". Claudius bursts into the palace with his followers, but Hamlet stabs him with a dagger, and Gertrude kills herself, whereupon Hamlet remarks that she "was a human being, and she was royal", and tells us he has to live on in the interests of the people, however difficult things might prove.

Since he was four years old—whether you believe this or not, dear reader—the present writer's single greatest interest has been in history. And yet I have always deeply distrusted the subject as a scholarly discipline. If we could travel in time as we do in space, we would surely have some devilish surprises. When you arrive in a new country for the first time there is usually one outstanding feature that really strikes you, which no one has ever told you about—in France, for example, on every wall you see written in large letters the words '*Défense d' uriner*', followed by the precise date on which the relevant law was promulgated. Surely the same sort of thing would apply if we were to return to the past. And if we did find ourselves back in 1784, perhaps the greatest surprise of all would be that everyone spoke with a lisp. Of course we would not dare assert this as a fact, having no other evidence than a note to the effect by Mercier, who remarks that sooner or later even stage actors will be starting to affect the mannerism in order to please their audiences. So it is at least a possibility, along with a thousand other oddities which contemporaries never mention since they found them entirely natural.

This matter of lisping makes me think that perhaps the biggest of all surprises awaiting our traveller to 1784 would be the phenomena associated with the cult of sensibility—the sentimental emotionalism one sees paraded, for example, in a painting of a pretty lace-maker, with its ostentatious display of good-heartedness and generosity towards the subject, expressed through the colours used for her physical form, her dress and facial expression. A brief glance at some of the pictures of the period will make this immediately clear.

The work of Greuz is not now thought of as being of the first rank. But he was the most popular painter of his time, and even the Academy deferred to this general opinion against their own better judgement. There is just one emotion conjured up in his well-known paintings: this same fashionable good-heartedness. It is not the good-heartedness we find in real life, but in the theatre; and behind it lurks a deep sensuality. To quote the Goncourts' comparison, Greuze portrays his innocent maidens as one might parade a fresh young whore before an old man hoping for rejuvenation.

But the engravings are even more typical. I have two examples before me. One is entitled *The Abolition of Serfdom*, done by Née in 1786. In it, an obvious landowner, his arms held out in a gesture of giving, is hurrying out of the pillared entrance to his mansion towards the distant crowd standing below, whose predominant figure is a man, clearly a peasant, making the same open-handed gesture to the master—not as an offer to take his hand, but to indicate deep gratitude, and to embrace not him (that would be going too far) but the figure of Goodness hovering nearby. His face is ecstatic, raised upwards with a gentle happiness, while the arms of the women kneeling around are held aloft in corresponding gestures. The landlord too is accompanied by a train of followers (in those days no one ever went about alone)—an audience who contemplate the edifying scene with sweet emotion.

The title of the second picture is rather difficult to translate: *L'Agriculture Considerée*—perhaps The Two Sides of Agriculture? It depicts an interior, with a bowl of sugar placed on a table. Once again the landlord greets the simple land-worker with a proffered embrace that seems like an allegorical gesture, while the labourer, who, unlike him, has no wig, makes the same gesture of the hands towards him. The audience here can be found sitting around the table: two ladies wearing enormous hats, and two men in wigs, with somewhat impassive faces—the same figures and gestures of the arms, sentimental and awkward, embracing and not embracing, expressing some mysterious, undefined but overwhelming love. We can be confident that gestures such as these would present themselves on every side to the occupant of our time machine.

The wave of sentimental passion for nature promoted by Rousseau sought out everything that was moving, good and profoundly human in nature. The nobility built themselves village-style houses—*ermitages*—to escape from the noise and bustle of the world, shedding the burdens of convention to spend their time in proximity to solid, upright village folk. We have already seen Marie-Antoinette's little *hameau*. Such cottages were also a response to the mood of the times. In 1782 Grimm noted the same topics recurring, with titles such as *The Land, Gardens, The French Georgics, Nature, Fields,* and, once again, *Nature.* Among the most popular of these poems is the piece by the Abbé Delille on gardens. In it he speaks with scorn of the coldly geometric gardens of the previous age, which were so barely 'natural':

> *Loin donc ces froids jardins, colifichet champêtre,*
> *Insipides réduits, dont l'insipide maître*
> *Vous vante, en s'admirant, ses arbres bien peignés,*
> *Ses petits salons verts, bien tondés, bien soignés.*

> Far from these cold gardens, these rustic baubles,
> These insipid retreats whose insipid owners
> Brag, self-admiringly, of their well-groomed trees,
> Their little green salons, so well cared-for and tended.

Delille goes on to state what it is that he and his contemporaries look for in a garden, and in nature—the human heart.

> *Il est des soins plus doux, un art plus enchanteur,*
> *C'est peu de charmer l'oeil, il faut parler au coeur.*
> *Avez-vous donc connu ces rapports invisibles*

Des corps inanimés et des êtres sensibles?
Avez-vous entendu des eaux, des prés, des bois
La muette eloquence et la secrète voix?

There are sweeter cares, a more enchanting art:
To charm the eye is nothing: you must speak to the heart.
Have you ever known the invisible rapport
Between inanimate things and conscious beings?
Have you listened to the wordless eloquence
Of the waters, the fields and the woods?

Bernadin de Saint Pierre, the author of *Paul et Virginie,* writing in this period found in nature the love of God and a benign and sensitive Providence. In his *Études de la nature*—Studies of Nature—he asserts that volcanoes exist because if Nature did not locate its great chimneys beside the oceans, then oils and fats from plants and animals would coat the surface of the water; that cows have four udders and only one or perhaps two calves at a time because Providence reserves two of the udders for supplying humans with milk, and that fleas are black so that they will stand out against human skin and thus be easier to pick off.

This sentimentality is simply a loftier, more sublime form of hedonism. People want to take pleasure in the soul, in the human heart, in their own sensitivity and in the *fatal présent du ciel*—the fateful gift from Heaven. Above all, they want to enjoy the emotions and the sensitivity that their own goodness, or that of others, inspires in them. The War of American Independence, which the French supported, gave rise to a sort of sentimental patriotism—the enthusiasm was intense. They even shed their blood for the fine, upstanding Americans, for Benjamin Franklin, with his great clumsy shoes that stood for everything simple and natural, for the gentle-souled Quakers, and for the brave and open-hearted pioneers of the virgin forests, who were taming the lands so they could be worked by a peace-loving people.

In the theatre, these sensitive hearts, kindly fathers, chaste maidens, heroic fiancés, faithful lovers and steadfast spouses abound, and virtue is everywhere. Actors praise the virtue of princes to storms of applause, and a minute later the princes sitting in their boxes renew the applause when the same actors praise the virtues of the common people. And the newspapers run columns devoted to *Traits d'humanité* in which heart-warming good deeds are recorded.

Count Haga, whom we have joined on his travels through France, had, as his favourite reading when young, a novel by Marmontel entitled *Bélisaire*. What was it about, this tale that so captivated the heart of the youthful prince? Belisarius, the Byzantine general, has in his old age been the victim of a court intrigue, has gone into exile, and is now a beggar making his way back to his ancestral mansion. Along the way, he comforts all who take pity on him, explaining that they should not be angry with the King—he certainly feels no anger himself—because he had been misled by others, and besides, being exiled was no great hardship, since what mattered was to have a benevolent heart. No one today would be able to read such a tale of good-heartedness and virtue through to the end, but at the time frivolous and worldly young men were bowled over by it, as must have been the case with Count Haga.

All this virtue and good-heartedness was of course principally to be found on the stage and in books. A great many people found it absurd. Amongst them was a Hungarian contemporary, György Alajos Szerdahely, the Jesuit father and Latin poet. *Satirical Verses for our Times* is the title of his poem, "which celebrates nothing so much as the love of one's fellow man":

> *Nullum odium, nulla est dissentio, nulla simultas.*
> *Aurea Saturni tempora Phoebe vehis!*
> *Otia securae ducant mollissima Gentes.*
> *Est sincera fides, regnat amicitia.*

Estne? vel esse potest, qui non loqueretur Amorem?
Cor riget at sermo totus Amore calet.

No hatred or dissension, no quarrelling.
Apollo, you are bringing back the golden age of Saturn!
Secure nations live in sweet tranquillity.
Faith is sincere, and amity rules.
Is there, could there possibly be, anyone, who does not
    speak of love?
Their hearts are cold, yet all their talk is aglow with
    love.

Thus Szerdahely. But we must not be untruthful. The age did love and cultivate charity, and actually practised it. The relevant French word '*bienfaisance*'—doing good—is itself a product of the times. It is significant that in its derivation and morphology it recalls '*bienséance*', meaning 'courtesy'. The two concepts were connected at the time. We know how charitable the royal family could be. The Dauphine would jump down from her carriage and rush to the aid of an injured postillion or a peasant who had been wounded by a stag. The King and the Comte d'Artois would help pull a transport wagon out of the mud. In the severe winter of 1784 the royal couple gave enormous sums to the needy from their personal allowances—the King three million livres and the Queen 200,000. Similar deeds were performed by the Court aristocracy.

Mme de Genlis and the Duc de Lauzun, who was notorious for his cynicism, founded the Order of *Persévérance*—Steadfastness—which soon acquired ninety noble members. To be accepted, one had to solve a riddle, to answer a question on morality and give a talk on one of the virtues. Every knight or lady who uncovered and reported three authenticated acts of virtue received a gold medal. Every knight had a chosen 'brother in arms', and every lady a 'friend of the heart'. And each had their own motto, which hung in the Temple of Honour, at the centre of Lauzun's park.

195

It became the fashion for landowners every year to crown a village girl with garlands if she distinguished herself by her innocence and virtue.

And even the Academy, that austere marketplace of cool scholarship and ethereal art, could not stand aloof from charity. "It appears," says Grimm, "that the example of Christian virtue now has a rival, and Philosophy strives equally to shine in the doing of good deeds, in its charitable institutions and pious foundations." He made this remark in 1782, when announcing the Montyon Prize. The enormously rich Baron Montyon, the Comte de Provence's chancellor, had set up a fund of 12,000 francs with the idea that every year the Academy would reward the man or woman of lowly origins who had performed the most virtuous action in the last twelve months. He also offered a prize to the person who had in the same year written the most morally improving work of literature. It was said, Grimm chuckles, that the lower classes of Paris were so enraged by the way the Academy had begun to exceed its powers that they set up a prize for the best madrigal of the year.

The Montyon medal was first won, in 1783, by a woman called Lespanier, who had spent two years nursing the 'Comte' de Rivarol, during which time she not only received no fee, but sacrificed her own fortune and whatever other funds she could raise on credit, for her patient. The Academy thus made adroit use of the prize to humiliate Rivarol, who only the year before had written a savage critique of the poetry of the celebrated Abbé Delille.

The following year, in the presence of the Prussian Duke Henrik, brother of Frederic the Great, Marmontel gave the prize to another woman who had nursed someone at her own expense, and in 1785 it went to a certain M Poultier, who had refused a legacy of 200,000 livres and persuaded the person planning to leave it to him to bequeath it instead to his natural heirs. M Poultier then gave further evidence of his generosity by making a gift to the value of the medal to a concierge who had done the same as he had some twelve months before (the terms of the foundation allowing it to reward only deeds done in the current year). At the same meeting Marmontel announced that a person of high rank who wished to remain anonymous had donated a gold medal worth 3,000 livres to reward the poem which, in the view of the Academy, most worthily celebrated the self-sacrifice of the Duke of Brunswick, who had died in the river Oder trying to rescue two peasants from drowning.

Taine explains the prevailing *sensibilité* of the second half of the eighteenth century as the result of people looking for some sort of compensation for everything that had been denied them under the cold rationalism and severe neoclassical tastes of the years dominated by the Court. They could no longer bear the spiritual aridity (to which the French mind has a strong tendency, though Taine does not mention this), but the reaction was taken too far, and began to foster sentimentality. "At that moment," writes Taine, "as this particular world approached its end, some degree of fellow-feeling, a softening of the emotions, came into being, and, like the flaming colours and ethereal mists of autumn, dissolved the severity that still lingered in the arid spirit of the age, bathing the elegance of its final moments with the scent of dying roses."

But sentimentality was not a uniquely French phenomenon— it prevailed even more strongly in Germany and England. So it is not possible to see it as simply a reaction against French aridity. On the one hand, that reading does not properly explain why, in France, it took so essentially practical and moral a form, and was so concerned with love of one's fellow man. A more satisfactory account lies in the second, more current, explanation, which argues that since the Enlightenment had undermined the basis of religion, and thus the moral code that depended on it, it became necessary to provide something to guide people through life, and in consequence people discovered social morality, altruism and philanthropy. The transcendent love of one's fellow man was replaced by an immanent sense of fellow-feeling, whose practitioner helps others for the sake not of God, but of man.

However it was, and however amusing the simpler manifestations of that charitable impulse might have been, there is no doubt that the late eighteenth century had discovered for the Western world what can be called social values in the modern sense. Of course it was hardly by chance that the virtue of charity emerged among the privileged classes precisely at a time when the underprivileged were feeling ever more dissatisfied with the social arrangements. The two forces were linked together. The upper classes came to realise that members of the lower orders were human beings too, whereupon the self-esteem and yearning for equality simply increased among the latter, thus preparing the way for the Revolution.

So, in the final analysis, the origins of this cult of sensibility lay in the guilty conscience of the privileged classes. The situation greatly resembles the last half-century of the Russian Tsars. In Russia too the upper strata came to feel a deep 'Slavic' compassion for the lower orders, at precisely the moment when growing industrialism was starting to promote self-respect among the bourgeoisie and a growing resentment among the proletariat. In Russia too, it was the aristocratic writers, Turgenev and Tolstoy, who wrote the finest works expressing pity for the people. So the Tsars too were brought down by their own guilty conscience. It is possible to see similar symptoms in the English literature of the twenties and thirties, perhaps most strongly of all in the later writings of Galsworthy, which deal with the upper bourgeoisie and their troubled consciences, though we have of course yet to see any of the developments anticipated by those particular omens.

This is one side of the coin. There is another. Guilty conscience can manifest itself in other ways.

Mercier not only reveals that everyone in Paris lisped, but also that everyone went about with one shoulder held higher than the other—which gave the citizens a somewhat diabolical appearance.

The young Grimod de la Reynière, the son of an enormously wealthy man, sent out a grotesque invitation to dinner to a motley company of writers, tailors' assistants, actors and doctors. It was bordered in funeral black, and was so unusual that the King had the example that came into his hands framed. On arrival the guests were asked by the porter which Reynière they were calling on—the old man, that bloodsucker of the people, or the young, the protector of widows and orphans. After they had been kept waiting for a quarter-of-an-hour in a darkened room, they were finally shown in to the dining area, which was lit by a thousand candles. In each of its four corners stood an altar-boy swinging a censer.

"Whenever my parents have visitors," the host explained, "there are always three or four who feel the need for purification by incense, so I thought I'd save you the trouble of asking."

This same rather interesting young man was once asked why he hadn't bought himself a seat on the bench (at that time in France you paid to become a judge), and why he remained a simple lawyer.

"Because if I were a judge," he replied, "I might easily find myself in the position of having to hang my father. At least as a lawyer I would be free to defend him."

The situation of the wealthy father and the son rebelling against wealth was often repeated in this sort of grotesque, jocular way in the period. "It is typical of the age," Sainte Beuve would write later, "that what began in frivolity ended in bloodshed." But the underlying and wholly serious fact was that young Grimond de la Reynière had a guilty conscience.

There were those who attempted to silence their pangs of conscience through sensibility and charitable deeds; others simply revelled in their own wickedness the way the first group did in their benevolence. Both responses combined in one man:

the Duc de Lauzun was the most dedicated roué of his time, an inveterate gambler and womaniser, and at the same time the sentimental co-founder of the Order of Steadfastness. Some of the writers, like Marmontel, Florian or Thomas, were so naively *sensible* and idyllic that it is difficult for us to understand how anyone at the time could read anything so false to nature; others were not at all naive—learned, cynical and acerbic—indeed, surprisingly modern. Their work was the sincere expression of a group purged of all self-delusion. And these are the really good writers: Choderlos de Laclos, Chamfort, Beaumarchais.

The rococo impulse sought to distance love from everything that was deep and passionate: it became a matter of charming games. No one ever died, relationships could be lightly broken and everyone was easily consoled. In Laclos's wonderful novel *Les Liaisons dangereuses* the rococo idea of love is pushed to the point of absurdity, perhaps to reveal it in all its danger. Love is shown in this book not as charming but as a pitiless toying with other people's hearts, with the perpetrator revelling in the misery he produces, like a dramatist enjoying the writhings of his own characters. The hero, Valmont, is an *aimable roué*; his coldly superior deceptions are naturally always adored by the ladies (in life just as much as they were in books), and Valmont is unquestionably a forerunner of Richardson's Lovelace, for whom women readers wept for a hundred years. But there is a crucial difference between the two. Lovelace first seduces the middle-class Clarissa but then comes truly to love her, though he refuses to marry her for reasons of aristocratic pride. But Valmont deceives the pure-souled Mme Tourvelt out of simple vanity, according to Taine. And this is still to understate, because Valmont is motivated not only by vanity but by a self-regarding wickedness which is actually satanic. Moreover, Valmont is not the real driver of events, but his cold ex-mistress Mme de Merteuil. She directs his amours simply in order to destroy the lives of the women who become her prey. The novel is a handbook of sexual psychopathology, and is often invoked as an example of mental cruelty.

It is interesting too, how strongly the events in the novel found an echo in aristocratic society. Chamfort referred to it constantly, and the Comte de Tilly speaks of it, and of its harmful influence, at some length in his memoirs. He calls Laclos the genius of wickedness, and says: "His book was one of the waves pouring into the ocean of the French Revolution to cleanse the throne." And yet there is nothing revolutionary about it—it is just a love story, nothing more.

So that was how this society saw itself: so fundamentally wicked that it seemed almost to revel in the artistic perfection of its own wickedness. Tilly thought that the novel helped prepare the way for the Revolution by laying bare the immorality of the aristocracy, whether real or supposed. But he himself is an example of the way the aristocrats themselves delighted in the revelation. It is rather like those American financiers who take pleasure in reading the novelistic indictments of Upton Sinclair, Theodore Dreiser and Sinclair Lewis.

A rather less open hostility to the ruling class is found in the disillusionment and cynicism of Chamfort. The illegitimate son of a nobleman, he was an embittered and defiant *déclassé*. As a young man—when, according to one of his mistresses women would begin by thinking of him as an Adonis but then discover he was a Hercules—he enjoyed the favour of high-born ladies. Later his body and life were blighted by venereal disease, which in those times struck down the dissolute like the workings of an ancient curse. There is scarcely a memoir in which it does not feature.

Chamfort's resentment of the aristocratic world is an unusual and complex phenomenon. Certainly he had no cause for complaint about not being accepted by it. He received two pensions from the King by right, was made secretary to the Duc de Condé, reader to the Duc d'Artois and secretary to Mme Elisabeth. He became an Academician, and lodged with the Comte de Vaudreuil. But his bitterness arose from precisely the fact that he was accepted. As a pampered writer proud of his gifts he refused to play the role of court jester assigned to the intellectual in an aristocratic society. "It is a ridiculous thing to grow old as an actor in a theatrical company in which you count as only half a man." Later he provided the single most celebrated slogan for the Revolution. He is said to be the source of the opening words of the famous pamphlet by Sieyès: "*Qu'est-ce que le Tiers État? Tout. Qu'a-t-il été jusqu'à présent dans l'ordre politique? Rien.*"—What is the Third estate? Everything. What has it ever been in the political order? Nothing. And again: "*Guerre aux châteaux! Paix aux chaumières!*"—War on the chateaux! Peace among the cottages!

Chamfort is the most important forerunner of nineteenth-century pessimism. Schopenhauer learnt much from him. Many of his sayings still in circulation are wrongly attributed to the great German philosopher, who occasionally forgot to mention his sources. But their construction is lighter, altogether more French, than Schopenhauer's, and thus more 'modern'. His aphorisms might have come from the pens of such contemporary French ironists as Paul Morand, Montherlant or Cocteau. With the reader's permission, we shall translate a few of these, since there is no other document that so consistently and concisely expresses the guilty conscience of the years preceding the Revolution.

The poor are the blacks of Europe.

They govern the people the same way as they think. They feel free to utter stupidities the way ministers feel free to commit blunders.

In France they spare the arsonists and punish those who sound the alarm.

Only the history of a free people is worth studying. The history of a people under a tyranny can be nothing more than a collection of anecdotes.

Consider this: for thirty or forty centuries we have struggled to enlighten ourselves, and the result is that the three hundred million people living in the world are the slaves of some thirty tyrants.

Courtiers are like beggars who have grown rich by begging.

Society, and the world at large, are like libraries. At first glance everything seems to be in perfect order, because the books are arranged by size and shape. But in reality everything is chaotic because the books are not grouped by subject, contents or authors.

There are two great orders of society: those who have more dinners than they have appetite, and those who have more appetite than they have dinners.

Life is a sort of illness which is eased every sixteen hours by sleep. But this is just a palliative. The only cure is death.

I have my doubts about wisdom. According to the scriptures it begins with fear of the Lord. I rather think it begins with the fear of mankind.

In some centuries public opinion is the worst opinion.

Society was made necessary by physical disasters and the misfortunes of the human condition. But society merely adds to the calamities of nature: its problems make governments necessary, and governments simply aggravate the misfortune. Such is the history of the human condition.

It was only the failure of the first floodwaters that prevented God from unleashing the second.

And here are a few aphorisms about women and love—

However badly a man may think of a woman, there is always some woman who thinks even worse of her.

Do you know any woman who does not assume, when she sees another paying attention to one of her male friends, that she is taking too much of an interest in him?

It is a very unlucky man who can bear in mind, when he meets a woman close up, what he knew about her from afar.

In our time, the piquancy of secrets has been replaced by the piquancy of scandal.

I remember meeting a man who broke off with an opera singer when he discovered that she was just as insincere as any respectable woman.

Is it my fault that I always prefer women who are loved by others to those who are not loved?

And so we make our way down the social ladder: Laclos, nobleman; Chamfort, *déclassé*; and the third, Beaumarchais, plebeian. Beaumarchais is from the same layer as his own Figaro—the non-privileged person who lives off the privileged: the flunkey. The Revolution, unfortunately, brought this layer above all others to the surface. The future was with Beaumarchais. Figaro was the New Man.

Or perhaps not. Not yet a bourgeois, only a non-aristocrat, Beaumarchais, like Laclos and Chamfort, is the antithesis of the aristocracy.

Here we might mention an episode from Beaumarchais's truly dazzling life, as it is distantly connected with our little history. Its title might well be: *Figaro as Diplomat.*

When Louis XVI acceded to the throne in June 1774, Beaumarchais informed his Chief of Police, a M Sartine, that a pamphlet was being printed in London and Amsterdam that was extremely insulting to the royal couple. He asked for authorisation to travel to the scene to stop the writer, one Angelucci, from publishing. As always in his dealings with Beaumarchais, Louis procrastinated for ages and then, as always, ended by granting permission. The writer received a letter of commission from him which he wore at all times around his neck, hanging from a gold chain in a gold box, out of respect for the King.

His negotiations went well. Angelucci agreed to abandon publication on payment of one thousand four hundred English pounds. Beaumarchais personally saw the pamphlet burnt in London, then the two men travelled to Amsterdam and destroyed the print run there. But what a cunning fellow this Angelucci was! He secretly kept back a copy and took it to Nuremberg, where it was finally printed.

But Figaro was still himself. "I am like a lion," he wrote to Sartine. "True I have no money (author's note—neither do lions), but I have my diamonds. I shall convert everything into cash and continue on my way with fire in my heart. I don't speak German, but I shall travel night and day, and woe to the rascal who has forced me to cover three or four hundred miles when I'd much rather have my feet up. When I catch up with him I shall seize all his papers and murder him, as he deserves, for all the trouble he has caused me."

On 14th August he overtook the scoundrel in a wood in Liechtenstein. Beaumarchais leapt from his coach, grabbed hold of Angelucci, tore the pamphlet from him, plus 35,000 francs, but then gave him back some of the money out of the kindness of his heart. However Angelucci reappeared shortly afterwards, accompanied by another ruffian. Beaumarchais overpowered the two of them but was wounded in the process.

Beaumarchais's rather less imaginative coachman gave a different version of the story. According to him, Beaumarchais got out in the wood to shave himself, leaving the driver to go slowly on ahead. When they met again, his hand was bandaged up. He claimed he had been attacked by robbers, but the driver had the impression that he had simply cut himself while shaving.

In Vienna Beaumarchais was received with considerable suspicion. It transpired that he had not given Angelucci the one thousand four hundred livres, but had promised him an annuity instead. They thought it best to lock the eccentric diplomat up.

He was however subsequently released. He returned to Paris and presented his bill. Louis XVI's government generously, if reluctantly, met his claim for expenses amounting to 72,000 livres. Sartine excused the actions of the Viennese court with the words:

"Look here, old chap, the Empress took it into her head that you were some sort of adventurer."

The suicidally bad conscience of the French ruling class is best seen in connection with Beaumarchais's masterpiece, *The Marriage of Figaro*. Its popularity, together with the outcome of the necklace trial, is regarded as the most notable harbinger of the Revolution.

The King read the play in manuscript and expressed the view that it should not be performed. The Censor was of the same opinion, as were the Keeper of the Seal (the Minister of Justice) and the Chief of Police. This aroused so much popular discontent, Mme Campan relates, that "Never, in all the years preceding the collapse of the monarchy, were the words 'oppression' and 'tyranny' uttered with more passion than at this time." After much wrangling, the play was performed in April 1784. In the leading role was the Comte de Vaudreuil, Marie-Antoinette's intellectual friend and thus an indirect link to the Queen herself. The King's two brothers were present on the opening night. The aristocratic audience received it with wild enthusiasm, whereupon Beaumarchais became even more impudent than ever. To a duke who had asked for a box in the theatre so that his female relatives could see the play masked and incognito, he sent this churlish reply. "I cannot respect, Your Excellency, the sort of woman who is willing to see a play she considers immoral provided that she herself is not seen … "

Not long afterwards Breteuil did lock him up for one of his impertinences—not in the Bastille, which would have been too good for someone like him, but in St Lazare. But by then the time of reckoning was close at hand. The few days Beaumarchais spent in prison produced a far greater outcry than the fate of all of the thousands who, under the three successive Louis, spent years, or their entire lives, without access to trial, in the Bastille, St Lazare and other prisons.

The royal family did their best to placate enraged public opinion and its orchestrator, the mutinous Figaro, by staging *The Barber of Seville* at Trianon with Marie-Antoinette as Rosina. Moreover, which perhaps pleased the great financiers even more, they finally honoured the claim brought against them for 2,150,000 livres.

Meanwhile, night after night at the Comédie Française, Figaro continued to pour his irony and impertinence onto the enthusiastic nobles filling the auditorium.

"No, Count, don't do it!" he roars, when he hears that his master Count Almaviva intends to seduce his bride Suzanna. "Don't even try! Just because you are a *grand seigneur*, do you think that instantly makes you a genius? My, how birth, riches, rank and office make a man proud! But what did you ever do in return for those privileges? You took the trouble to be born, and that was all. Otherwise you're just like anyone else. But I, damn it, when I was just one of the nameless crowd milling around down there, I had to show more learning and wit just to make ends meet than the entire Spanish Empire did in a hundred years; and you want to start something with me? … "

And sitting there in their boxes, Almaviva and all the other counts rejoiced that at last someone had spoken the truth.

Viewed from a distance, Beaumarchais was not the most 'left-wing' of the writers in his time. The Marquis de Condorcet was much more of a revolutionary. In his works he waged war on every kind of social abuse, from forced labour to Negro slavery, and later, when a prisoner of the Revolution, wrote his most resolutely optimistic masterpiece, in which he showed how humanity progresses irresistibly towards freedom and equality … and then took poison. The Abbé Reynal described the behaviour of Europeans in the two Indias, East and West, combining geographical, historical and economic facts with eloquent diatribes against the wars of conquest against the natives. He was introduced to Frederick the Great, and given a ceremonial reception by the Lower House in England; for twenty years his book was a Bible on two continents, and even the young Bonaparte, in his student days, would echo his sayings.

And then "the party of the lost children", as Taine calls them: "Naigeon and Sylvain Maréchal, Mably and Morelly, the fanatics who laid down the binding dogmas and highest duties of atheism, the socialists who proclaimed a common weal in order to exterminate selfishness, and wanted to establish a society in which all who sought to retain their 'contemptible private property' would be declared public enemies, treated as dangerous lunatics and locked away for lifelong solitary confinement."

These people were sometimes imprisoned by the Ancien Régime, sometimes not, but Mably addressed one of his books to the Duke of Parma, and the Poles asked him to write them a constitution.

"The writers and the ruling class waged a bitter war against each other," says Mercier, "but there was never any doubt that the former would emerge victorious."

But the war was not quite as bitter as he suggests. We should not forget that just as the nobility played the role of friends of the people, the writers posed as the upholders of a persecuted but defiant middle-class morality. In reality those who spoke for the Court and the aristocracy were actually in agreement with the writers and the common people: some sort of change was bound to come—in short, revolution. Except that the word 'revolution', as used at the time, did not have its present meaning. The Latin *revolvere* comes from the verb 'to turn' (hence the rotating-barrel 'revolver'), and its early usages all imply a sense of turning, as in '*la révolution des saisons*'—the 'revolving' seasons of the changing year. As we have already said, in that idyllic and optimistic period, with its predisposition to expect miracles, the coming changes were imagined as being entirely peaceful. Never in their wildest dreams did people imagine that when they did arrive they might be for the worse. "Nothing serves better than the history of our Revolution to persuade philosophers and statesmen of the virtues of humility," says Tocqueville. "Never was there an event of such magnitude, or one that was more thoroughly prepared for, over a longer period of time, *that was less foreseen.*"

Count Haga, looking around the city of Paris in 1784, must surely have noticed all the signs, but even he failed to see what was coming. On that negative note I would like to conclude my general survey.

After the Revolution, the often-mentioned La Harpe wrote a little story which better than anything registers the unsuspecting innocence of the years before the Revolution. This account, which we quote word for word in the following, is not a true history, rather a retrospective fiction. But if a prophet, such as Cazotte claimed to be, really had appeared during those years, it might well have been one.

It is as if it all happened yesterday, but in fact we were in the early days of 1788. Some members of the Academy were sitting at table—all noblemen and people of high intellect, since the membership was large and included people from all levels of society: courtiers, high-ranking officials, writers and academics. As usual we had dined extremely well. Over dessert the excellent Malmsey and Rhenish wines had freed up the mood ... Chamfort was reading aloud from his godless and outspoken stories, and the more aristocratic ladies had not yet required the assistance of their fans. There was a flood of jokes against the Church; one came from Voltaire's Pucelle, another from Diderot's philosophical verses. One of the guests told a story that put a sudden stop to the laughter. His hairdresser had said to him, while applying the powder: "You see, sir, I'm just an oppressed starveling, but that doesn't make me any less religious than the next man. It's getting to the point where there could soon be a revolution. It's absolutely essential that all this superstition and fanaticism should make way for philosophy and take some account of reality. But when that day comes, and who those people will be who bring the triumph about ..."

Only one person held aloof from the ensuing uproar of discussion. This was Cazotte, an otherwise congenial if eccentric fellow, sadly given to visionary dreaming. Finally he spoke. In a voice of deadly seriousness he declared:

"Gentlemen, you can be quite sure we will all live to see the great and glorious revolution that people so heartily desire. You know I am something of a prophet, and I repeat, we shall all live to see it."

The guests poured loud mockery on this. Condorcet led the way.

"You, M Condorcet, will end your days on the floor of a dungeon. You will die of poison you have taken to escape the scaffold—poison you will have been forced to keep about you at all times, in the happy days that lie ahead."

There was laughter, and Chamfort sprang to Condorcet's defence. Cazotte told him he would soon know that Eteokles and Polyneikes were brothers, because they were the ones whose appetite was greater than the number of their dinners, and spent a hideous fifteen minutes looking for those whose dinners were insufficient for their appetite. (When the time came, Chamfort opened his veins with twenty-two slashes of a razor.) Next, Vicq-d'Azyr (the Queen's doctor), Nicolai (a leading member of Parlement), Bailly (the astronomer) and Malesherbes, the Minister of Justice, were each addressed in turn. And always with the one refrain—the scaffold.

"This is incredible," people cried out from all sides. "Cazotte has sworn that we'll all be annihilated."

"I haven't sworn … "

"So the Turks, or the Tartars, really are within the gates?"

"Not at all; what I said was that men will be governed by philosophy and reason alone."

"Wonderful," said La Harpe. "And have you no prophesy for me?"

"You will be the greatest miracle of all. You will become a Christian."

"Well, then," laughed Chamfort, "no harm there. So long as we don't perish before La Harpe becomes a Christian, we shall all live for ever."

The Duchesse de Grammont spoke next:

"It's lucky we women won't be part of the revolution. Or rather, I think, we might get involved to some extent, but no one will harm us because of our sex … "

"Your sex, ladies, will not protect you, and it will make no difference whether you involve yourselves or not. They'll deal with you the same as they do with the men. No distinction will be made."

Cazotte was warming to his theme. His words swelled up in waves, like the bars of the scaffold, every one a ghastly prophesy.

"So you see," said the Duchesse de Grammont with a smile, "you won't even grant me the benefit of a confessor."

"No, my lady, there will be no confessor, neither for you, nor for anyone else. The last condemned person to have that privilege … "

He stopped for a moment.

"Well, which happy mortal will have that privilege?"

"It will be his last: that person will be the King of France."

The host instantly rose from the table, and everyone followed his example.

Chapter Nine

The Necklace Explodes

NOW PAY ATTENTION, Reader! "Dramatic scenes, in plenty," promises Carlyle, "will follow of themselves, especially that fourth and final scene, spoken of above as by another author— by Destiny itself."

We recall that Jeanne had told Rohan that the Queen wanted to have the necklace by Candlemas. On the following day, 2nd February 1785, Rohan dispatched a footman, accompanied by an Alsatian officer, to attend the King's public breakfast and note what the Queen was wearing. It seems that Boehmer and Bassenge must also have sent someone, because the day after that they paid an anxious visit to Rohan to ask him what was the matter, that she had not been wearing it. Rohan reassured them, and told them they should rather write and thank the Queen for ridding them of their burdensome treasure. But by this stage the jewellers had irritated her so much that they did not dare go anywhere near her, and preferred to wait for a suitable opportunity. None came, and the months passed. The Queen had of course no idea that Rohan and Boehmer believed that the necklace was in her possession. Jeanne had reassured the interested parties that she would wear it only when she went to Paris. Another time she said it would be worn only when it was fully paid for. Then Rohan had a letter from 'the Queen', saying that he should go back to Saverne for a little while.

At the end of May Jeanne turned up at Saverne, in disguise and dressed as a man (for greater effect) to tell the Cardinal that on his return he would be granted an audience. Once again, Rohan could sleep soundly. "Oh unhappy man!" Carlyle shouts at him at this point. "This is not a world which was made in sleep; which it is safe to sleep and somnambulate in." But Rohan did not wake.

July. The first payment was due on 1st August. Now growing anxious, Rohan asked Jeanne why the Queen was still not wearing the necklace. Because, Jeanne replied, she thought it too expensive. Unless the jewellers dropped their price by 200,000 livres she was going to return it. Boehmer and Bassenge pulled a face, but agreed the discount. This 'real-world' business operation reassured Rohan once again: he felt his feet once more on terra firma. All the same, the jewellers used the occasion, at Rohan's prompting, to write that letter of thanks, which the Cardinal himself polished up into a little masterpiece of decorum.

On 12th July Boehmer went to Paris to give the Queen some jewels she had ordered for the christening of the Duc d'Angoulême, the son of the Comte d'Artois. This was the opportunity he had been waiting for. He handed her the letter, but as fate would have it, at just that moment in came the Finance Minister, Calonne, the most important man at Court. Boehmer made his exit, bowing deeply all the way, to give her time to read the letter and ask for an explanation.

Some while later she did read it, then gave it to Mme Campan to decode, since she was a clever woman and good at solving mysteries. But Mme Campan could make neither head nor tail of a single word. So the Queen burned the letter over a candle, and told Mme Campan that if ever the lunatic returned she should throw him out.

Thus fate spins its web. Since Marie-Antoinette had accepted the letter and said nothing more about it, the jewellers were convinced she did know about the necklace, and nothing would ever drive this notion out of their heads. Unwittingly, but none the less directly, Marie-Antoinette had become involved: she had contributed to deluding the victims.

We are now in the middle of July, and Jeanne is still her calmly superior self. Someone will eventually pay—after all, there are so many rich people in the world. For example that parvenu, the fabulously wealthy financier and Naval Treasurer Baudard de Sainte-James. Sainte-James was a close friend of the Cardinal, a devotee of Cagliostro, and a pillar of his lodge.

"The Queen is experiencing a short-term financial difficulty regarding the first payment," she confided to Rohan. "Perhaps you should turn to Sainte-James—400,000 livres is nothing to him."

The trouble was that others too were thinking of Sainte-James: Boehmer and Bassenge had also asked him to lend them the sum for which they were selling the diamond jewel. Sainte-James scratched his head: he was supposed to lend 400,000 livres so that Boehmer & Co could pay for what they already owned? What sort of business was that? But perhaps he should agree, for the sake of the Queen—he was just the sort of parvenu who doted on titles: it would delight him to do her a favour, in the hope of getting some little medal. So he asked Rohan to bring him a letter, written in the Queen's own hand, asking him, by name, for the money. Rohan went back to Jeanne. But the letter never came.

According to the Abbé Georgel, this was because Réteaux de Villette was not in Paris at the time to forge one. Funck-Brentano prefers to think that Jeanne was unwilling to place a false document in Sainte-James's hand. Aristocrats and Cardinals were one thing, but she could not assume the same credulity in a man of business. So this was not the answer.

Meanwhile time was passing, and now even she began to worry. After all, she too was human. In the inspiration of the very last moment she found a provisional solution: she pawned some of the remaining diamonds and gave the 30,000 livres they raised, together with an appropriate letter, to the Cardinal. Rohan passed the sum on to the jewellers, and asked, in the Queen's name, if he could delay the payment of arrears until

1st October. But that was too much for the jewellers. Sainte-James had told them, they said, that they absolutely had to have the full amount that was due. Only now, it seems, did Jeanne, that glorious mayfly and mistress of the art of living from one day to the next, begin to realise just what danger she was in. Her husband, who had been pottering about in Bar without a care in the world, was summoned to Paris forthwith. And then a great new, and extremely bold, idea occurred to her.

On 3rd August she suddenly informed the jewellers: "You've been taken in. The documents in the Cardinal's possession are forged. But don't worry—he's rich enough. He'll pay."

She made this statement out of conviction. She had very sensibly calculated that that was what must happen. Rohan, as she well knew, had become involved in such a ghastly and complicated intrigue that he would be afraid of the consequences of having presumed that the Queen would enter into an intimate correspondence and arrange a private rendezvous with him in the Versailles Park, and, last but not least, he would dread the general mockery that his appearance in the Venus Bower, and his credulity, would incur. He would surely pay up, and his entire family would pay up, even if it brought the combined Rohans, Guéménées and Soubises crashing down.

But once again fate made a little move of its own. The jewellers did not dare tell the grandee that the signature had been forged. Instead they turned to Marie-Antoinette, and Boehmer scuttled off to Versailles that very day.

Here the story becomes somewhat less clear. Funck-Brentano does not explain why Boehmer should be less afraid of the Queen than he was of the Cardinal. And what business was it of hers at all, if the letter really had been forged? Let us be silent while Mme Campan, who was one of the principal actors, tells us herself:

At Versailles, Boehmer failed to gain access to the Queen, so he rushed off to Mme Campan's summer lodging, where the lady had retired for a few days. She happened to have guests with her, and could see him privately only that evening, in the garden.

"I believe I can recall the dialogue that passed between us word for word. From the moment he began to lay bare his extraordinarily base and dangerous intrigue he was so agitated that his every word is deeply engraved on my memory. And the more clearly I began to see the danger, the more distressing it was, so that I did not even notice when thunder and lightning erupted in the middle of our conversation.

"As soon as we were alone, I asked him:

"'What was the meaning of that letter you gave the Queen last Sunday?'

"'The Queen must know that perfectly well, Madame.'

"'Pardon me; she has instructed me to ask you.'

"'She must have been joking.'

"'I can't see why the Queen would want to joke with you! Even you must be aware that she very rarely wears formal dress nowadays; you yourself have remarked how much the austerity here at the Court is affecting trade. The Queen rather fears you've concocted another of your schemes, and her message is, most decidedly, that she won't be buying any diamonds from you, not even one for twenty louis.'

"'I'm sure she has less need of them than she used to, but then why did she make no mention of the money?'

"'Because you had it some time ago.'

"'Ah, Madame, you are very much mistaken. I am still owed a very great deal.'

"'What do you mean?'

"'I shall have to tell you everything. It seems the Queen has been keeping this a secret from you. She has purchased that large necklace.'

"'The Queen? But she refused it. When the King wanted to give it to her she refused it!'

"'And so? Since then she has had second thoughts.'

215

"'In that case she would have spoken to the King. Besides, I have never seen that necklace among her jewellery.'

"'The fact is, she bought it at Whitsun. I was most surprised to see that she wasn't wearing it.'

"'When did the Queen tell you she had finally decided to buy it?'

"'She has never spoken to me about it in person.'

"'Then who was the go-between?'

"'Cardinal Rohan.'

"'The Queen hasn't spoken a word to him these ten years! I can't see what lies behind your little plot, but one thing seems very clear, my dear Boehmer. Someone has robbed you.'

"'The Queen is simply acting as if His Eminence is in her bad books, but they are getting along all the better for it.'

"'What do you mean? The Queen is only pretending to dislike someone who is such a laughing stock at Court? Royals are more used to treating people as if they approve of them. For four years now she has made it clear she does not want to buy your necklace, or even to have it as a present! And yet she bought it all the same, and is pretending she has forgotten, because she hasn't worn it! You must have gone mad, my poor little Boehmer, and got yourself tangled up in some little scheme. I really tremble for you, and am most displeased with you, on Her Majesty's behalf. Six months ago I asked you what had become of the necklace, and you told me that you had sold it to the Sultan's favourite.'

"'My reply was made according to the Queen's wishes; she left a message by way of the Cardinal that that was what I should say.'

"'So is that how you got your instructions from the Queen?'

"'By letters, bearing her signature. And for some time now my creditors have been demanding to see them.'

"'So you've not received any payment?'

"'Excuse me; I received 30,000 livres, in banknotes when I reduced the price of the necklace. That was the amount the

Queen sent to My Lord Cardinal, and they must certainly have met in secret, because when His Eminence gave it to me he told me that he was present when she took it from the portfolio in the Sèvres Porcelain secretaire in her little boudoir.'

"'This is all lies. But you have made a very grave error. When you accepted your appointment you took an oath of loyalty to the King and Queen, and yet you failed to make the King aware of this very serious matter, even though you were acting without the direct instructions of the Queen.'

"This last expression really shocked the dangerous lunatic— *ce dangereux imbécile*—he asked me what he should do. I advised him to go to Baron Breteuil in his capacity of Royal Jeweller, to tell him everything quite candidly, and trust to his guidance. He replied that he would rather I undertook to tell the Queen what had happened. This I refused to do. It seemed wiser not to get involved in that sort of intrigue."

But a truly brave and loyal soul would have done just that.

If this conversation between Mme Campan and Boehmer really did take place, there are two possibilities. One is that for once Funck-Brentano is wrong, and that Jeanne had not told Boehmer that the letter was forged, so he still believed absolutely that he was dealing with the Queen. The other is that Jeanne did indeed tell him, but that Boehmer took this to mean that the Queen had quite deliberately signed it under a wrong name in case she was found out, calculating that she could then disclaim it. This is a very dark suspicion, though at the time Marie-Antoinette was suspected of even darker things. What gave strength to Boehmer's suspicions was that Marie-Antoinette had not responded to his letter with a single word of acknowledgement or asked to discuss it, so that he had only a tacit understanding that she had received the necklace at all. We have to consider the appalling climate of suspicion that surrounded the Queen. Besides, Boehmer was just another Figaro, and what he assumed about his royal masters was not so very dire.

Meanwhile Jeanne did not remain idle. She gave Réteaux de Villette four thousand livres to make his escape. She did not want him appearing before the police a second time and saying something stupid. Then she urgently summoned the Cardinal. She told him that her enemies were accusing her of committing an indiscretion and bragging about it (which sounds probable enough), so she no longer felt safe in her home, and needed to hide. She begged him to give her refuge in his palace. At eleven that night, accompanied by a chambermaid, she crept through his gates. With this particular chess move she achieved two of her intended aims: first, to reassure the Cardinal once again— would she have gone there if her conscience were not crystal clear? Second, to link her own fate even more closely with his, so that she could hide behind him in case of danger, and to compromise him even more profoundly.

The next day Rohan sent for Boehmer. His partner Bassenge came instead. Bassenge dared venture only one question:

"Does Your Eminence have complete confidence in the person who went between you and the Queen?"

Rohan replied that he had never spoken directly with the Queen, but said he had every bit as much confidence in her as if he had. Finally he agreed to ask Sainte-James to give the jewellers more time. A few days later he actually did meet Sainte-James at a social gathering, and asked him to be patient for a little longer.

After this, on 6th August, Jeanne went back home to Bar. Why did she not make her escape? Why not flee to England? Was the reason, as we rather suspect, her wonderful mayfly insouciance, or was this deliberate cunning? Running away would amount to a full confession, but while she stayed she testified to her innocence and shifted responsibility onto Rohan. Besides, she continued to assume that Rohan and his family would quietly put everything right behind the scenes. Perhaps too she comforted herself with the thought that tomorrow everything would be just the same as it had the day before.

Meanwhile Rohan must have been living through the greatest crisis of his life. The jewellers' doubts must surely have been driving nails into his head. He turned for advice to his master, Cagliostro. Cagliostro knew nothing of the necklace business, as will become clear beyond all doubt in the course of other things. Jeanne obviously had not wanted a second fraudster involved, and had succeeded in persuading Rohan to keep him in the dark. Cagliostro, as we have mentioned, had prophesied a triumphant outcome to the whole undertaking, of whose real nature he was unaware. Which was somewhat careless, for a prophet.

But now Rohan kept it a secret from him no longer. He told him everything, with perfect candour, and showed him the letters. And then something very surprising happened. Cagliostro thought the matter through, and gave Rohan the wisest and most sensible advice anyone could have given in the circumstances. No Apis ram, no Dove, no candles, no Zobiachel. The magician who posed as a man possessed was secretly a shrewd and circumspect individual. It was as if, between two lines of iambic pentameter, a Shakespearean actor were to pull off his wig and declare: "If you please, we will now continue in Hungarian!" Perhaps Cagliostro actually liked Rohan. He certainly had good reason to.

"The Queen could never have signed this letter 'Marie-Antoinette *de France*'," he told him. "You have been duped, without question. You have been the victim of a fraud, and there is only one thing you can do. Throw yourself at the King's feet without delay and confess everything."

There was no doubt that that was what he should have done. The kindly Louis XVI, seeing Rohan's sincere remorse and distress, would clearly make sure the matter was settled quietly and without fuss—and he would do so in his own interest. Once again we find ourselves at a moment in time when everything might still have turned out for the good—and didn't.

It was Rohan's good-heartedness—his eighteenth-century sentimentality and gallantry—that stopped him taking the only appropriate step.

"If I did that," he told Cagliostro, "that woman would be destroyed."

"If you don't want to do it yourself, then a friend could do it for you," the magus replied, discreetly offering his services.

(The scene he proposed was grotesque—Cagliostro before the King, recounting the story of the necklace to the full accompaniment of oriental mumbo-jumbo!)

"No, no, let me think about it a bit longer," said the Cardinal.

This vacillation was his undoing. But how could anyone who had lived such a sheltered life, whose every choice had been made for him by fairy godmothers, come to a quick decision? On the other hand, like Milton's Adam, he was also destroyed by an act of gallantry, protecting the sinful Eve.

This naturally raises the question of whether there was a rather more intimate relationship between Jeanne and the Cardinal. Funck-Brentano, as befits a Frenchman, devotes an entire chapter to the debate. Jeanne did later testify before the court that she had been Rohan's mistress (though he rejected the allegation with considerable dignity). According to Funck-Brentano this 'confession' was meaningless—it was entirely in her interest to appear closely identified with the Cardinal, the better to take advantage of his privileged position. Her confidant Beugnot claimed to have seen some passionate love letters Rohan had written her, but according to Funck-Brentano that too signified nothing, since we know how much she enjoyed composing fictitious billets-doux. Besides, it was part of her nature to be forever making up romantic stories about herself. Against this is the fact that until almost the last minute the Cardinal had been supplying her with pocket money, but this was in the sort of petty amounts that a grandee might casually dole out to a passing beggar, hardly to a mistress. Jeanne asked for and accepted these small sums so that he would not realise that she had meanwhile made herself rich at his expense.

In the last analysis we can never be completely sure what there was between them, but this much is clear: no one could have behaved with greater gallantry or selflessness than Rohan did at the critical moment. If we are to weigh his character in the balance, there is certainly much good to be said of him.

Now to return to Mme Campan. She was a quiet, modest woman, a little grey sparrow among the peacocks, falcons and brilliantly coloured parrots of the Court. She is famous for her memoirs. Everyone who has written about the period and about Marie-Antoinette, including of course ourselves, has gone to her first and foremost for the more intimate details. She is rather like the 'I' in old-fashioned novels who narrates the story but does not directly play a part in it. But now, at this critical juncture, the modest little 'I' detonates the bomb. True, there was nothing else she could have done. So perhaps we might briefly introduce her, as she steps onto the stage.

Jeanne-Louise-Henriette Genet was born in 1752, and went to Versailles at the age of fifteen to become reader to *Mesdames*, the daughters of Louis XV. She was a remarkably cultivated young lady. Louis XV once stopped and asked her:

"Is it true that you speak four or five languages?"

"Only two, Your Highness," the girl replied modestly.

"Quite enough to annoy any husband."

In due course he married her off to the young M Campan, whose extremely learned father was secretary to the Royal Cabinet. She received five thousand livres and was appointed *Première Femme de Chambre*.

Marie-Antoinette had invited Mme Campan to her house in the mock village at Le Petit Trianon, to try out her part as Rosina on her. During the proceedings she casually asked what "this Boehmer" wanted: she knew Mme Campan had sent him but she had refused to see him. So Mme Campan related the full story. Marie-Antoinette became extremely agitated, and immediately sent a message to the man summoning him on some pretext connected with his trade. He duly appeared the next day, 9th August. The Queen questioned him in detail and told him to put everything he knew in writing. According to Mme Campan, the "shameless and dangerous jeweller" simply kept repeating, to whatever was said:

"Madame, this is not the time for play-acting. Would you be so kind as to admit that you have my necklace and to provide me with some assistance, or I shall be utterly bankrupt."

According to Mme Campan, Marie-Antoinette discussed the matter with the Abbé Vermond and Baron Breteuil, both of them sworn enemies of the Cardinal. She also wrote to Joseph II suggesting that he and the King should decide between them what should be done. Mme Campan saw yet another little twist of fate in the fact that Vergennes, that superb diplomat who had saved the country from the danger of so many wars, was not then at Court. He, surely, would have been the person to find a compromise.

In what happened next we see the more passionate side of Marie-Antoinette. She had always hated Rohan, and now the man had made her an object of suspicion and offended her deepest womanly pride by the assumptions he had made. That she might have met him in secret! That she could have asked him for money! No, such things would have been intolerable even to a bourgeoise, and as for this proud daughter of the Habsburgs, the first lady of the age ... No, nothing could be allowed to bring Marie-Antoinette into disrepute. Here she could not be calm and considered: of course she insisted on a punishment that would be exemplary, resounding and spectacular. And, for once, even Louis XVI was moved to anger. He too had been wounded in his most sensitive point: in his capacity as a husband, where his feelings of inferiority were at their strongest.

It is now 15th August, Assumption Day, and Versailles has gathered to celebrate.

For centuries the day has been used to commemorate the moment when Louis XIII placed his crown and the monarchy under the protection of the Virgin. A huge crowd has come from Paris, some on horseback, some by carriage, some in those communal coaches known because of their rounded shape as *pots de chambre*.

In the morning a council of ministers meets in the King's Cabinet Room. Present are the royal couple, Baron Breteuil and the Keeper of the Seal (that is to say, Minister for Justice) Miromesnil. Breteuil reads out the jewellers' memorandum. Miromesnil, his voice quavering with echoes of the fairy godmothers, advises restraint and caution—they should think of the Rohan family. But Breteuil insists on the need to make an example. Hot-blooded and violent by nature, he is the sort of man who sees something in everyone that requires to be disciplined and brought to heel. His moral indignation provides a fine cover for his long-standing resentment of Rohan: he too has been insulted by the man, in Vienna. But Louis XVI leans towards Miromesnil's view. He tells Breteuil to call the Cardinal in.

Rohan is present in the Palace, along with the rest of the aristocracy. As Grand Almoner he is waiting to take the celebratory mass. Summoned, he enters in full priestly regalia, a scarlet silk cassock with white English-lace sleeves.

"Mon cousin," the King begins. "So what is all this about a diamond necklace you bought for the Queen?"

Rohan turns pale.

"Sire, I know now that I was duped, but I have deceived no one."

"If that is the case, *mon cousin*, then you have nothing to fear. Nonetheless you must explain what happened."

The King's voice is gentle enough, but what is the King to Rohan? There sits Marie-Antoinette—to him nothing less than the embodiment of pride, anger and loathing. His knees start to shake; he is on the verge of fainting. The King notices this, and tells him to make a full statement in writing. He is left to himself.

In such a state of mind he finds it difficult to find the right words. Nonetheless he puts a few lines together: there is nothing for it now but to point the finger at the one who really is guilty, Jeanne de la Motte. The royal couple and the Ministers return. They want to know where are the documents signed in the Queen's name. And they repeat what Cagliostro said: how could a prominent member of the Court possibly think that the Queen would sign herself 'Marie-Antoinette *de France*'? Only a flunkey would have believed that. Rohan replies that he will hand the letters over to the King and pay for the necklace. The King declares that, considering the circumstances, he will have to order his arrest and detention.

"I consider it necessary for the Queen's good name," he adds.

Rohan implores the King not to shame him before such a large number of people, and bring such disgrace on his family.

The King appears to be swayed by these words, but at this moment the Queen erupts. Her voice is loud and agitated, and as she is speaking she bursts into tears. She rounds on Rohan:

"How could you possibly imagine that I would write you a letter, when for nine years I haven't been on speaking terms with you?"

Her words decide the matter.

Meanwhile, packed into the rooms outside, the magnificent courtiers are growing restless. The Mass should have begun long ago. People sense that something is in the air: there is an anxious murmuring—the crowd is breaking up into little groups—a sense of gathering storm. Finally Rohan emerges through the glass door, deathly pale. He is followed by Breteuil, whose face is flushed with pleasure at his great and unexpected revenge. In loud tones he calls out to the Captain of the Guard, the Duc de Villeroi:

"Arrest the Cardinal!"

Rohan now has to make his way along the endless succession of halls—to left and right, behind him and in front of him, the astonished French aristocracy, their individual features dissolving into one enormous face before his blurred eyes, the endless rows of mirrors seeming to spin as the sunlight crashes and roars down on him through the huge windows. And underfoot, grinding and crackling like shattered glass, the Ancien Régime itself.

The formal reception is due to be held further on, in the Hall of Mirrors, where a hundred years later the names of Teutonic Caesars will be loudly proclaimed and the sacred *gloire* of France humbled in the dust; there too, another fifty years on, will be signed the Treaty of Versailles, bringing peace with the Germans. Anyone can enter the Hall of Mirrors, and now it is crammed with people who have come at dawn for the celebrations. They look on in shocked amazement as the Duc de Villeroi hands the Cardinal—the illustrious prince of the Church, in his radiant ceremonial finery—over to Second Lieutenant of the Guard Jouffroy. In the long peaceful years of the previous two Louis such sights were seldom seen in Paris, Now even these superficial, garrulous and generally irreligious people are silenced by the nameless horror of it.

By some miracle Rohan has so far remained calm. In fact he is the only calm and controlled person in the whole vast multitude. In these moments of crisis and disaster, the resounding footsteps of his countless noble forebears are entering his soul, while those with no thousand-year legacy to speak of have lost their heads. Now, very calmly, he asks Jouffroy for permission to scribble a few words on a bit of paper which he rests on the scarlet rectangle of his Cardinal's hat. He gives it to his attendant, says something to him in German, and the man rushes off. Then he is led away to a suite of apartments.

The following day he is taken to the Hôtel de Strasbourg where his papers are confiscated in his presence and the building closed off. But the red portfolio in which the "Queen's letters" once lay amongst his private papers has vanished. The day before, the same attendant had galloped at breakneck speed back to Paris, to announce: "All is lost; they have arrested the Cardinal!"—before handing the slip of paper to the Abbé Georgel, and promptly collapsing. Georgel, however, did not collapse. He carried out the instruction he had received in the note and destroyed the correspondence.

On 17th August, chaperoned by Beugnot, Jeanne was a guest at Clairvaux, the famous convent named in memory of St Bernát. She was given a most gracious welcome by the Abbot, who knew that she was on particularly good terms with the Grand Almoner. They were just sitting down to dinner, having waited patiently for the Abbé Maury to arrive. (Maury was a famous pulpit orator who became Mirabeau's great rival. It was after one of his sermon's that Louis XVI remarked: "What a pity he didn't say something about religion; then he really would have covered everything.") Maury was due to give the special sermon in honour of St Bernát, but as he had not appeared, they sat down to eat without him.

At that moment he burst in, in great excitement.

"What? Haven't you heard? Where have you been living? Prince Rohan, the Cardinal, has been arrested. Something to do with diamonds, apparently … "

Suddenly Jeanne felt unwell.

She went out, ordered her carriage to be made ready, and she and Beugnot left the abbey. By the time they were sitting in the coach she had regained her composure.

"This whole business is Cagliostro's doing," she told her astonished companion.

Then she lapsed into a deep silence. His advice that she fly to England before it was too late was met with scorn. She had already worked out her battle plan: how to shift the blame for the whole affair onto Cagliostro.

She was arrested at four the next morning. The amiable police made no objection when the Comte de la Motte, who had otherwise conducted himself very calmly, tore the glittering jewels off his wife and thoughtfully put them aside against better times.

Rivarol, that witty and whimsical commentator, wrote: "M de Breteuil plucked the Cardinal out of Mme de la Motte's clutches and dashed him against the Queen's brow, where he certainly left his mark." It is a grotesque image, but an expressive one.

Chapter Ten

The Bastille, the Parlement and the King

To M de Launay,
I write to request that you receive my cousin the Cardinal Rohan into
my fortress known as the Bastille, and hold him there pending my
further instructions, for which I beg thanks for your assistance.
Louis, Baron Breteuil
Versailles, 16th August 1785

Such was the tenor of the royal arrest warrant, the *lettre de cachet* on whose authority, on the evening of 16th August, the Commander of the Bastille (the same de Launay who died when the building was stormed in 1789), and the Comte d'Agoult, Captain of the Guard, escorted Rohan by coach into the prison. He had spent the day at home, and had been seen in the great window of his salon playing with his pet ape: perhaps they were taking their leave of one another.

At dawn on 18th August, on the authority of a second *lettre de cachet*, Jeanne de la Motte was also detained. The summons served on her husband failed to reach him. He had in fact set out for Paris with the idea of defending his wife, but had second thoughts along the way, and took himself off to London instead.

The modern visitor to the Bastille finds only the spot where the old building stood, the circular *Place* with the lofty memorial column at its centre. The historic building was destroyed on that memorable *Quatorze Juillet* which has since become the National Day, since it marks the beginning of freedom not just for the French but for people all over the world.

The Bastille was originally a circular fortress. Later, when no longer used to defend the city, it became a prison, playing much the same role as the Tower in London. It was so hated that it came to be seen as the physical symbol of tyranny, thanks above all to the *lettres de cachet*, whose victims were for the most part imprisoned there—but not only there: every region had its own equivalent, where people were locked away in hospitals, madhouses and solitary cells.

The *lettre de cachet*, as we have noted, was a warrant for arrest. Its significance lay in that the King himself issued it, without needing to give any reason. The detained person did not appear before any court. He remained in prison until the King saw fit to set him free. "The Bastille," wrote a contemporary, "is a place in which anyone, without regard to age, sex or social rank, might find himself, without having any idea why he is there, how long he might remain, or how he will ever get out."

Everyone at the time knew that the police had special agents from whom, for large sums of money, one could buy *lettres de cachet* already prepared—you had only to fill in the name— and furthermore, that both in the Bastille and others of His Majesty's prisons large numbers of people would languish for the rest of their miserable days simply because they had been arrested on the basis of one of these documents and then forgotten about. In 1784, a M Latude was released after thirty-five years in prison. He had been locked away for planning an attack (involving a time bomb) on one of the Pompadours. And Malesherbes mentions one unfortunate who had gone blind, had been let out with no one to care for him, and promptly begged to be allowed back into the prison. The Bastille was not a comfortable place. Malesherbes once told Prime Minister Maurepas that he ought to show Louis XVI around it.

"I never have," was the reply. "If I did, he'd never send anyone there again."

In recent decades the intellectual life of France has been largely dominated by writers and historians of the royalist persuasion, who, partly by astute reasoning and partly through the sheer mass of data they have assembled, have established that the Ancien Régime was for the most part innocent of those crimes that the Revolution, and libertarian writers of the nineteenth century, ascribed to it. Among those prepared to judge on the basis of facts is Frantz Funck-Brentano, and it was he who went through the entire body of documents relating to the Bastille and came to the surprising conclusion that the *lettre de cachet* was generally not the cruel weapon of a tyrannical monarchy, but on the contrary, an outstandingly useful institution for the rest of society.

Its great advantage was that it enabled the prosecuting authorities to make rapid progress in situations where the slow and cumbersome nature of criminal proceedings might otherwise drag matters out for years. It could also be used to invoke the power of the monarchy to intervene in situations which did not fall within its normal jurisdiction. These were almost always family cases.

Lettres de cachet were often used by parents against their own children; for example, if the son were an impulsive and incorrigible gambler, he could be taught discipline by showing him that he might spend the rest of his life being arrested and charged—thus preserving the family from shame. Funck-Brentano generally saw the device as a way of defending traditional French family life. His idea was that the world order of the Ancien Régime was based on the power of, and respect for, the family, and that the main cause of its collapse was that that respect was undermined by the influence of eighteenth century philosophy. If, for example, an young aristocrat wished to marry a bourgeois girl and thus dishonour his family, there was a simple solution. On the basis of a *lettre de cachet* the young man or the girl would be locked away and kept a prisoner until there was a change of attitude. Events of that kind naturally did not cause much of a stir, unlike those occasions when a writer such as Voltaire or Beaumarchais was imprisoned for showing too much self-assurance in the eyes of his betters. But such examples, at least according to Funck-Brentano, were very isolated.

While we have every respect for Funck-Brentano, and the present work has so much to thank him for, and although we would not for a moment dare question the accuracy of his information, from a moral point of view we cannot agree with him. We give greater credence to the worthy Cagliostro, another of those who were unjustly imprisoned in the Bastille, who, following his release, declared in a pamphlet he wrote in England entitled *Letter to the French People:*

"You, the French people, have everything you need for happiness: a fertile land and a gentle climate; good hearts and a enchanting *joie de vivre*; you have both genius and grace, no equals in the art of pleasing, and no masters in the others. All you lack, my friends, is this one trifle: the right to sleep soundly in your beds while you remain innocent."

Be that as it may, the French Revolution greatly enlarged our sense of the worth of the individual. However much we might try, few of us nowadays would consider it an offence that cried out to heaven if a young aristocrat wanted to marry a girl from the middle class, and as for any shame that might bring on the family name, we would simply mutter *"tant pis"*—so much the worse for the family name. While we are no stranger to historical relativism, and agree that every age must be judged by its own standards, we also take the view that under every sky (since it is always the same sky) freedom is better than servitude. And since it was the very first thing they did, it seems clear that the people of Paris felt they really had to demolish the Bastille, and none of the reasoning and statistics of the Funck-Brentanos of the time have ever persuaded them that they were not right to do so.

So, one by one, all the principal actors in our story are gathering in the Bastille. Jeanne arrived on 20th August, Cagliostro and his wife three days later, on the basis of a deposition she had made. Jeanne still felt she had nothing to fear. Very soon, using her juggler-and-monkey tricks, she had worked out a complete system of lies; Cagliostro would be shown to be capable of anything.

But it was to no avail. The truth was beginning to come out, and its instrument was none other than the good Father Loth, the Franciscan monk who acted as Jeanne's chaplain and major domo. He had set his sights on the office of Preacher to the King, and was angling for an opportunity to speak in his presence one Whitsuntide. He had poured his heart out to Jeanne, and she had promised to have a word on his behalf with Rohan, who as Grand Almoner was head of the spiritual branch of the royal household. Rohan told Loth to show him the speech he would give, then passed it on to his deputy, the Abbé Georgel, who thought it simply inadequate. So Rohan, at Jeanne's request, gave Loth a better one, so that he might perform more tolerably before the King.

It is possible that Father Loth had been serving the interests of the royal household all along; or perhaps he felt a stronger debt of gratitude to Rohan than he did to his patroness. But it was enough to make him call on the Abbé Georgel after the Cardinal had been arrested. Georgel was to Rohan what Mme Campan was to Marie-Antoinette, the indispensable confidant of French classic drama (we saw how Ducis felt he had to supply even Hamlet with one)—the person who listens to everything, but does nothing in his or her own right. Georgel plays the same role of reliable witness as Mme Campan, and he too has a moment when he both listens and acts, turning Loth's disclosure to his master's advantage.

Father Loth had compared Réteaux de Villette's handwriting to that in the letters signed by "Marie-Antoinette *de France*", and lo and behold, they were the same. He revealed that before she fled the house Jeanne had burnt the letters she claimed to have received from Rohan. He recalled the occasion when they took d'Oliva to Versailles; it had struck him then how closely she resembled Marie-Antoinette. He now suspected that the Comtesse had tricked a lot of money out of the Cardinal, and perhaps the necklace with it.

In his *Memoirs*, Georgel clearly sees Jeanne in the role of the Devil. But she is not the only one he blames for destroying Rohan: delicately and obliquely, he also accuses the Queen. His grounds for this are that when she received the letter from Boehmer she did not immediately insist that she knew nothing about it, or deny that she had ordered it or even received it. Georgel claims that she kept silent in order to implicate the hated Rohan even more deeply. Reading between the lines, he felt that the possibility could not be ruled out that Jeanne de la Motte was indeed working on her instructions, or at least, that she deceived the Cardinal with the Queen's full knowledge.

"When I questioned Bassenge in Basle in 1797," Georgel writes, "he did not deny but in fact formally acknowledged that statements he made during the trial, like the evidence submitted by Boehmer, sounded very much as if dictated by Breteuil, and that, if the two of them had not actually followed his orders blindly, they had, at the very least, been forced to remain silent about matters he did not want them to mention. After that revelation, how can one possibly exonerate Her Majesty of a degree of culpable connivance—which sits very ill with her own standards and her social rank? The dishonourable actions of the woman La Motte, abusing the Queen's name in order to carry out her monumental theft with greater audacity and impunity, ought to have outraged any royal person. How could anyone not be shocked by it? If the Queen had acted on her initial feelings of insulted honour, it would almost certainly have prompted the jewellers to tread more carefully. But even if we accept that she did want to take revenge on the Cardinal and be rid of him, the fact remains that what had already happened, and what she already knew, were more than enough to force him to resign his position at the Court and return to his diocese. No one would have been able to challenge the justice of her actions;

the Grand Almoner would have been properly humiliated for his credulity; the house of Rohan would have been disgraced, with no grounds for complaint against her; there would have been no scandal, no Bastille and no criminal proceedings. And that is what Marie-Antoinette clearly might have done, had she followed her own line of thinking. But she listened instead to two men who persuaded her to act quite differently." The two men Georgel refers to, the Abbé Vermond and Baron Breteuil, were the Cardinal's sworn enemies.

Like Georgel, Mme Campan also went on to write her memoirs. She makes it clear that she does convict the Queen of a certain complicity, in that, when she received the jeweller's letter and failed to understand a word of it, she gave it no further thought. But it also appears from Campan's book that the Queen and her entourage were every bit as suspicious—without justification—of the Cardinal as his people were of her. Marie-Antoinette was convinced that Rohan had used her name in the forged letters to defraud Boehmer and Bassenge of the necklace, in order to repair his notorious financial position. Her phobia about Rohan was such that it even made her fear that he and his co-conspirators might have hidden the necklace in her bedroom with the intention of 'finding' it at a suitable moment and laying a false charge, the way people did in medieval legends. But however it was, if we knew nothing else about this episode, the Grand Almoner's opinion of the Queen, and her opinion of him, constitutes the most frequently discussed topic in connection with the last days of the French monarchy.

From her prison Jeanne managed to send word to Nicole d'Oliva that she had been arrested on the basis of an evil slander, and that, because of the episode in the Bower of Venus, the same danger threatened her if she did not leave forthwith. The girl set off at once for Brussels with her current beau, Toussaint de Beausire. The Paris police quickly discovered her address and informed the French legation in that city. D'Oliva and her suitor were arrested and imprisoned. But their extradition was not a simple matter. Amongst the ancient privileges of the land of Brabant was one waiving the obligation to return refugees except in cases where they themselves requested it. So the police sent their wiliest operator, a man called Quidor, who quickly persuaded d'Oliva that it would be in her own interests to apply for extradition. Which is what happened; whereupon the French government, which revealed its economising tendency on the most surprising occasions, paid her full travel expenses, then locked them both up in the Bastille.

A few months later they were followed by Réteaux de Villette. Réteaux had fled to Geneva, had been arrested there and then extradited. The situation regarding La Motte was rather more complicated. He had gone to England, but even in those days the English were punctilious about such matters. They would not send refugees back for any reason; moreover, the French government was not especially popular in London at the time.

Since there was so little hope that the English authorities would return him, the Paris police decided on abduction. Their efforts in this direction read like a true-life detective story—it seems there are eternal truths even for crime writers. La Motte was living in Edinburgh as the paying guest of the family of an elderly Italian language teacher called Benevent Dacosta. He reckoned that this arrangement would attract the least attention to himself, since people would take him for a member of the family. But Dacosta was not just a language teacher. He was also a man of business, and the French ambassador to London, the Comte d'Adhémar, persuaded him to hand La Motte over for ten thousand guineas. He felt rather bad about doing it, he wrote, but poverty dictated his actions.

The plan involved two police officers travelling to Newcastle, where they were to meet Dacosta and La Motte. Two more officers, one of them the wily Quidor, would be waiting for them in a port called South Shields. French ships regularly called in there for coal, so their boat would not attract any particular notice. There, Dacosta was to betray La Motte. They would pour a soporific into his wine and carry him onto the boat while he was asleep—the classic formula.

The French police proceeded in a very circumspect and low-spirited sort of way. They knew that if the English collared them they would be hanged without mercy.

But the plan failed. First, because La Motte became suspicious and refused to go to South Shields. Secondly, because the agents were unable to find a suitable house in the port, and even if they had found one, Dacosta had insufficient money to pay the rent. Thirdly, and principally, because the Italian took fright. He feared that the scheme would fail and he would be hanged. Instead he revealed the whole plan to La Motte. La Motte, whose sunny disposition we have already observed, was not in the slightest bit angry, and helped his good friend spend the one thousand guineas he had had as an advance from the French.

Rohan, however, remained a prisoner in the Bastille. He could have had no complaint on grounds of comfort. The largest suite in the staff officers' building was placed at his disposal. He took three footmen in with him, and was given a daily allowance of a hundred and twenty francs. (Should that be multiplied by ten?) He dined in princely style, and could receive any visitor he chose. He gave banquets for twenty people, with oysters and champagne. Because of the extraordinarily large number of his visitors the drawbridge was, most exceptionally, left down all day. Every afternoon he took his walk around the tower terrace, in his brown overcoat, with a large hat drawn down over his eyes, to the delight of the vast crowd of Parisians gathered below. In the city the only topic of conversation was the trial, and interest in it was just as strong abroad.

The King, following the rules, began by appointing Breteuil, as his Paris Minister, and Thiroux de Crosne, the Chief of Police, as examining judges. But Rohan rejected the first as a personal enemy, and the second as being of too low a social rank to question him. Vergennes, the Interior Minister, and Castries, Minister for the Navy, were brought in. The Cardinal gave his evidence coolly, shrewdly, and in strict accordance with the truth.

Jeanne's hearing was somewhat stormier. She sat on the *sellette* (the prisoner's bench, or rather stool) day after day for months, directly facing each witness. If they attacked her defences in one place, she would plug the gap in the wink of an eye with some impromptu remark that introduced three or four random new points; above all, she made fine use of that perennial woman's weapon, hysteria. This Rohan, who had called her to account, how much money did he have? She hurled it in his face that he had been her lover. To Baron Planta, who had brought separate charges against her, she replied that he was only saying what he did because he had attempted violence on her, and got the worst of it. Father Loth she accused of living a riotous life, especially for a monk, and of procuring women for La Motte. She gave lurid details of Nicole d'Oliva's moral life. She screamed at Cagliostro that he called her his "lamb" and was always billing and cooing, raising his eyes to the heavens, pronouncing great sayings, calling on God to witness, and pouring out his Italian and so-called Arabic jargon. There was no stopping her. The moment she opened her mouth a filthy and obscene atmosphere poured out and clouded the entire hearing.

Jeanne's methods of defence always bring to mind that fearful scene when a pack of dogs have driven a cat into a corner. Realising that it cannot run up the wall, it suddenly turns on its attackers, seems to become twice the size it was before, hisses and makes the terrifying sound of a time bomb about to explode. If we were to erect a statue symbolising courage, it would have to depict a cat in this situation.

Carlyle, however, questions Jeanne's courage. "Had Dame de Lamotte a certain greatness of character; at least, a strength of transcendent daring, amounting to the bastard-heroic? Great, indubitably great, is her dramaturgic and histrionic talent;

but as for the rest, one must answer, with reluctance, No. Mrs Facing-both-ways is a 'spark of vehement life', but the farthest in the world from a brave woman ... Her grand quality is to be reckoned negative: the 'untameableness' as of a fly; the 'wax-cloth dress' from which so much ran down like water."

The housefly image is apt. But is the housefly not brave? We are not saying that Jeanne's hysterical courage has any moral worth—but that she showed courage, indeed great courage, we would not venture to question. Carlyle himself says of her elsewhere: "O worthy ... to have been Pope Joan thyself, in the old days;" and surely it took a devilish amount of courage for anyone to become a female Pope?

Louis XVI offered Rohan the choice of being tried either by himself, under royal jurisdiction, or by Parlement. In a letter, co-signed by members of his family, which made clear how much they identified with him, Rohan chose to go before Parlement. The letter was finely calculated, and indeed somewhat defiant:

Sire,

I had hoped, given the opportunity of a proper hearing, to be able to provide sufficient evidence to persuade Your Highness that I have been the victim of an intrigue. In that situation I could wish for no other jury than your own sense of justice and goodness. But since your refusal of a direct meeting between us deprives me of that hope, I accept with the most respectful gratitude Your Highness' permission to establish my innocence through legal process.

This in fact meant: 'If you accept the fact that I am innocent, I should be willing to submit myself to your sentence; but if not, Parlement must decide between us.'

Rohan well understood the nature of his choice. The Parlement was the King's greatest enemy. By giving way to Marie-Antoinette's womanish anger and insisting, in contrast to Rohan's openness, on having him arrested in an atmosphere of great scandal, Louis had committed his first major blunder.

And now he made another, a hundred times greater and this time quite irreparable—he allowed those hostile to him to adjudicate the matter, so that, if they chose, they could pass judgement both on it and on the King.

Our Nordic friend Count Haga would certainly not have done that. Referring to the necklace trial, the Swedish King wrote to his confidant, Count C F Scheffer, as follows:

"I should have advised him, had I been asked, not to give such great éclat to this affair, which does not really concern the Queen, but which, if it does come to trial, might require a lot of uncomfortable explaining. We monarchs, though just as likely to be tripped up as the rest of humanity, have the advantage that we are not held to account for mistakes involving small amounts of money, and are generally trusted. But once we attempt to excuse ourselves, then we appear to acknowledge the possibility of blame on that side, something that would never occur to the common people of their own accord." He felt that the necklace affair would damage the universal respect for the institution of the monarchy, and he was right.

Apart from the incompetence he showed, should we really blame the King for allowing the matter to pass into other hands and submitting it to the Parlement? It is possible to assume that he did this under the Queen's influence. It is very interesting what Napoleon said in connection with this to a confidant on St Helena, where he had plenty of time to reflect.

"The Queen was innocent, and in order to give maximum publicity to her innocence, she wanted the Parlement to pass judgement on the case. The result was that everyone considered her guilty, and that undermined trust in the Royal Court."

As is well known, the Paris Parlement of the day was neither a legislative body nor a house of representatives but the highest court of law. It was the Parlement not just of Paris but also of several other large provincial cities. Its members were paid for their services, like all judicial officers in the kingdom. Thus they had for many centuries been drawn from the wealthy upper bourgeoisie. One of the most important developments in French society was that the power of the King became entrenched at a very early date, and in consequence the bourgeoisie did not evolve into an urban patriciate ambitious for self-government, as in Italy, Germany and Flanders. Instead, they served the King, and in that service made their way as lawyers and state officials.

The most high-ranking section of the upper bourgeoisie consisted of those who held the administration of justice in their hands. A great many of them had attained nobility, the collective term for them being the *noblesse de robe*—the *robe* here signifying the judge's gown.

Some were extremely rich, with palaces in the cities and mansions in the countryside, and lived like the true nobility, who were distinguished from them by the term *noblesse d'épée*— nobility of the sword. Some even came to rival the blue-blood aristocrats in the matter of debt. Their incomes were generally very considerable. M d'Aligre, the leader of the Paris Parlement who presided over the necklace trial, was worth 700,000 livres a year. But while there were those who displayed all the vices of privilege, the greater part were extremely respectable, almost puritanically solemn and plain-living people, exhibiting the true bourgeois mentality: sobriety, integrity and unquestionable probity.

By the eighteenth century all the institutions of the monarchy were to some extent dated or obsolete, and everywhere riddled with corruption, the justice system not excluded. Those who wanted reforms naturally played that up. They complained that judges were often too young, inexperienced, ill-educated, and susceptible to undue influence. Legal costs were intolerably high, secretaries had to be paid vast sums to expedite the astonishingly slow procedures, as did the *huissiers*, to deliver sentences already pronounced. The criminal justice arrangements were outmoded, cruel and inhumane. France, like Italy, was coming under the influence of the teachings of Beccaria, who urged radical changes to the system. He also demanded reform of the prisons. In 1782 the horrific For l'Évêque prison, whose inmates had to stand in water during years of high rainfall, was closed and the Hôtel de la Force built, where every prisoner had his own bed, and—to contemporary eyes—the whole place appeared astonishingly clean and comfortable.

The monarchy had tried on many occasions to reform the criminal system, but their intentions were always frustrated by the stubborn resistance of the Parlement. It was one of the most conservative bodies in all history. Every new law, and almost every other new development, was seen as an affront to its ancient rights and privileges. It is quite extraordinary the way it objected to everything: to the *petite poste,* by which private individuals delivered letters and packages; to the planting of potatoes, and even to the use of emetics. Above all, it opposed reform. In the eighteenth century, every right-thinking proposal for change made by a monarch foundered because of its opposition.

These abuses of power did nothing to harm its popularity. Neither the die-hard conservatives nor Voltaire, Diderot and the entire reformist camp of acerbic-minded philosophers ever attacked it. It never lost its popularity, because its members were eminent, belligerent and fearless, and were seen by the people as the representatives of the very idea of freedom.

Their ideal, since the start of the century, had been the British constitution, but by the time of Louis XVI their political theories had moved on. It was now accepted that every aspect of power, and all legal process, derived ultimately from the person of the King, but there was nonetheless a need for some sort of mediator between the monarch and his people to supervise the enactment of the laws he handed down: and that role fell to the Parlement.

In reality it had exercised this supervisory function for centuries, by virtue of the fact that its duty was to 'register' bills promulgated by the King—without such registration, bills could not become law. If the Parlement saw fit, it could block them. Naturally France was for this reason never an 'absolute' monarchy, since the King could not flatly impose his will against its members' wishes. If the latter dragged their feet for too long and formally remonstrated with the King, he could call a *lit de justice* in his palace, at which he simply informed the relevant authorities that the bill was now in force. But this was very much a two-edged sword. It poisoned relations between the King and the Parlement, and with the passing of time the latter body became identified with protest, resisting everything, including the most welcome and necessary social reforms, since the very notion of 'reform' had come to be associated with 'tyranny'.

It obstructed generally welcome measures because it felt that any increase in popular contentment resulting from initiatives handed down from above would at best treat the symptoms of the malaise rather than the malaise itself, or indeed, would exacerbate it by reinforcing the power of absolutism. And in these struggles the people, or at least the 'Third Estate' (the collective citizenry) stood not on the side of those reforms that would improve the lot of the people as a whole, but with the conservatives, the old reactionary Parlement, because they felt that freedom was more important than mere prosperity. Paradoxically enough, this conservatism did indeed represent a kind of freedom, as it had once before in the Roman Senate, against the 'progressive' dictatorship of Julius Caesar.

Under Louis XV the Parlement had waged war above all on the clergy. Its members mostly shared the mental outlook of the Jansenists. That grim tendency has very much the same sort of place in French history as Puritanism, the nonconformist movement, has in England, with its prohibition on worldly pomp and beauty in the church.

The Parlement's long war against the clergy reveals the sociological roots of its animosity. As we have mentioned, by virtue of its upper-middle-class elements it represented the bourgeoisie as against the Church, the nobility and the Court.

A century-and-a-half before the French Revolution, the same social stratum in England had fought in Cromwell's revolution and then, at the end of the seventeenth century, in the 'Glorious' (and thoroughly bourgeois) Revolution, to create the British constitution. The citizenry no longer languished behind the nobility in terms of wealth and culture, and began to question why it was inappropriate for them to benefit from the laws and the higher life generally, as did the privileged few.

Such was the Parlement on whom the responsibility fell to decide Rohan's case. Now we can understand why one of its most influential councillors, Fréteau de St Juste, rubbed his hands in glee when he heard that it was to come before it, and cried:

"What a stroke of luck! A swindling cardinal and the Queen embroiled in a fraud case! All that mud on the cross and the sceptre! What a triumph for the ideals of freedom! And how it will raise the importance of the Parlement!"

Now that we have introduced the Parlement, we must bring in the other side, the King. In all honesty we should have preferred to introduce him at the start, centre stage, along with the other dramatis personae. The only reason we did not was that the queue of people waiting to come on was rather lengthy, and we feared we might weary the reader who is interested in the 'action'. But the fact that we were able to leave the King until now means that he is already established as a character. "The principal reason for the downfall of the French monarchy," we read in Lavisse's great Standard History of France, "was the failure of the King."

Louis XVI was a very different person from the French Kings, the endless line of the Capet dynasty, who preceded and followed him. In some respects, both morally and as an individual, he was unlike any of them. The Kings of France owed their popularity to the fact that they shared the character traits of their people. For the most part they saw living as an art form: they loved women, food and drink; they relished brave, brief, triumphant adventures; they hated boredom, work and anything that went on too long, and they always wanted to be in the thick of things. That was true both of the grandest of them—Francis I and Henry IV—and of the gloomiest—Henry III, Louis XV and, after the Revolution, Charles X. But wise or cunning, they also produced kings worthy of the Age of Reason, such as Philippe-Auguste and, again after the Revolution, Louis XVIII. The most exceptional were both wise and chivalrous, like St Louis and Louis XIV. But our Louis was neither wise nor chivalrous. It was his brothers who inherited the royal qualities. The Comte de Provence was shrewd and cunning, while the Duc d'Artois had the adventurous traits. In his younger days it tormented the King that his brothers were so much more successful than he was, and when on one occasion a speaker praised his intellect, he ungraciously interrupted him:

"You are mistaken: I am not the clever one; that is my brother, the Comte de Provence."

He possessed none of the characteristic traits of a French king. He was more like a German or some other northern prince. Which is not really all that surprising. The leading members of the French royal family had always found wives among the ruling houses of neighbouring countries, so there was far more foreign than French blood in his veins. His ancestor Louis XIV was married to Maria Theresa, the Infanta of Spain; his son, the 'Great Dauphin', to a Bavarian princess; his son, the Duc de Bourgogne, to the Princess of Savoy; his son, Louis XV, to the Polish Princess Maria Leszczynska, and his son, the Dauphin, to Louis XVI's mother, the Saxon Princess Maria Josepha. So even if we consider only the interbreeding that had taken place since Louis XIV, Louis XVI had scarcely any French blood at all, not to mention the fact that Louis XIV's mother had not been French, and so on and on. Viewed in this way, Louis XVI's queen, the Austrian princess Marie-Antoinette, comes across as much more typically French in her character; which again should hardly surprise us, since she was Habsburg only on her mother's side. On her father's she sprang from the effectively French house of Lotharingia, or Lorraine, so that there was considerably more Gallic blood in her than in that scion of the Bourbons, her husband.

Naturally, until science sheds rather more light than at present on the secrets of heredity, this is all just a game. The King was unquestionably French, made so by the whole atmosphere and tradition, by upbringing and destiny, and no one in their wildest dreams would have called his Frenchness into question. But what is also beyond question is that there is every good reason why, in his external appearance, his physical movements, his gestures and temperament, he might have resembled one of his German or Polish ancestors.

Joseph II said of his brother-in-law that he was like primal matter before the proclamation *Fiat lux*. He classified him with those people whose minds are ruled by their bodies. This was shown by his favourite diversions: spending his free time in wood and metal workshops, or playing billiards. Had he not been born to be King, he would have been a conscientious, respectable, and no doubt perfectly contented craftsman.

But his real passion was for hunting—the sport of kings—which he pursued with even greater dedication than his forebears, clearly because only through frenzied activity and vigorous movement of the body could he work off his excess physical energy. It was the only time, it could be said, when he lost his timidity and clumsiness, found himself in his element, and emerged as a man. "His gentleness and altruism notwithstanding," says Boiteaux, "he hardened, and would deal ruthlessly with people if anything got in the way of his freedom to exercise his royal prerogative of hunting, like some old Germanic tribal chief. If a peasant strayed into the royal forest he would be in a rage for the rest of the day. The roads would be closed and all work would stop in the fields for miles around."

On these occasions he would even dispute the prize with his brother the Duc de Provence, and often did. The numbers were huge: in the fourteen years of his reign he took part in thirty-five fox, a hundred and four boar, one thousand two hundred and seven stag and two hundred and sixty six deer hunts.

As is well known, almost the only thing he ever noted in his diary, apart from where he attended mass, was the outcome of these expeditions. Even in the stormiest days of the Revolution, if he had done neither he would simply enter '*rien*' (nothing). One cannot be sure whether this should be taken as yet another sign of his mental hebetude; the diary was his personal secret, in which he wrote only what touched on his most personal life. Hunting and religion—these were the two areas in which his soul felt truly at home. Alongside the painstaking craftsman, there was a medieval lord of the manor inside him.

But also a minor civil servant, and an accountant. He kept a meticulous accounts book. In it he wrote what he spent his pocket money on, carefully totting up the receipts, his gains and losses at cards, and even what he paid his 'royal secretary' (for duties he carried out himself). He notes that he gave twelve thousand livres to the Queen, a figure that recurs frequently. But he also records that he spent three livres on bathwater; thirty-six on shoes; one livre, eighteen sols on a leg of mutton; twelve sols on a bottle of red wine; three livres on a dozen fresh herrings ... What is really mystifying about these notes is that there were eight cobblers in the royal household who submitted large bills every year, while the *bouche du roi*, the 'King's mouth', as the royal kitchen was known, spent several thousand livres on his victuals every day. But then nothing is more impenetrable than the finances of the Ancien Régime. Apparently even Louis occasionally found them confusing. In 1782 he writes in his accounts book that some sort of error must have crept in, since he finds an item in the same notebook which he had completely overlooked, and he has to start the whole reckoning again from the beginning. The sum he had failed to notice was 42,377 livres ...

This is the outer aspect of the man who is ruled by his body. However active he is, he remains fat. This is true even in his youth, and thereafter he puts weight on 'in the twinkling of an eye'. His gaucheness is clearly a version of the fat little boy's withdrawn and embarrassed shyness. Otherwise his obesity is not a pathological symptom; there is no need to think about mysterious glandular problems. In one respect he had a great deal in common with his ancestor Louis XIV: he too ate a huge amount.

The public dinners at which he sat with the Queen (though Marie-Antoinette absolutely refused to touch food in front of an audience) consisted of fifty courses: four soups, two large *entrées*—beef and cabbage, tenderloin veal spit-roasted; sixteen *entrées*—giblets of turkey *au consommé*, sweetbreads *en papillotte*, suckling pig, roast mutton chop, calf's head, and so forth; four *hors d'œuvres*—forequarters of veal, fillet of rabbit, cold young turkey cock, leg of veal. Then six baked dishes, two intermediary *entremets* and sixteen small *entremets*—vegetables, eggs, milk dishes; next, the dessert—grapes, pomegranates, pears, bitter oranges and so forth; and last of all, four hundred chestnuts and forty-eight slices of bread and butter. It seems unlikely that he ate all of these, but it is said that he set about doing so with a will.

He was not just fat: he was slovenly. While he was still the Dauphin, the Neapolitan ambassador described him to Queen Maria Carolina as "*selvaggio e rozzo, a segno che sembra nato ed educato in un bosco*"—like a wild man of the woods. Mme Campan, who was truly well-disposed towards him, later wrote: "His features were noble enough, and expressive of a certain melancholy; his deportment was clumsy and lacked distinction; his person was worse than neglected; his hair, though tended by a skilled barber, was always unkempt, because he took no care of it. His voice was not particularly harsh, but nor was it pleasant: when he became excited in conversation, it became sharp and high-pitched."

Along with this physical makeup went a certain boorishness. Louis had a tendency to brawling. Even after he was married he came to blows with his brother the Comte de Provence over some trifle, in the presence of their two wives. He loved crude jokes, if only to make a stand against the over-refinement of the Court. When Benjamin Franklin visited Paris it became the fashionable thing to sing the praises of the hero of American freedom and inventor of the lightning conductor, and women wore medallions bearing the inscription:

Eripuit caelo fulmen sceptrumque tyrannis

Lightning burst from the sky and dashed the sceptre from the tyrant's grasp.

So the King had a chamber pot made in Sèvres carrying the same quotation, and sent it to the Duchesse Diane de Polignac, one of Franklin's enthusiastic admirers.

Otherwise, his mental and moral attitudes were inherited from his father (the Dauphin, the son of Louis XV, who died young). The Dauphin had lived his exemplary married life, with the 'gloomy Pepa', as Louis XV called his daughter-in-law, in scorned and scornful isolation in his father's frivolous and sinful Court, and, like so many sons, had made it his business to oppose everything his father did, to expiate his sins. He was deeply religious, immersed himself in serious studies, and gave much thought to how he might make the French people happy.

Louis XVI also enjoyed serious study. He read English readily and well (he was especially fond of Milton) and concerned himself above all with history and geography, the true subject matter of kings. But literature held little interest for him, and this was a great pity. It was a major deficiency in a French king at a time when his people read feverishly and unceasingly, and acquired their ideas about the world through the medium of the printed word.

He was deeply religious. That was how he had been raised, first by his father and then by the man entrusted with his upbringing, the Duc de Vauguyon—about whose own piety there is little to be said. But his own nature inclined him that way too, and his religion gave a deeper colouring to his innate good-heartedness and the love he felt for his people. His faith was the secret, immeasurable source of inner strength that enabled him—a man who in life was so shy and self-effacing—in his hours of trial and affliction to face death like a hero and a martyr: a death that retrospectively ennobled the memory of all he had done before.

He lived in Puritan simplicity. He loathed the pomp of the Court, and his first act after mounting the throne was to incur the bitterness of the aristocracy by trimming the royal household. Amongst its members was a class of persons known as the *menus plaisirs,* the 'little diversions', whose honour and duty it was to attend to the monarch's pleasure. No sooner had he been crowned than their *intendant* La Ferté presented himself to the King, who asked him:

"Who on earth are you?"

"I am the person in charge of the 'little diversions', sire."

"Well, my little diversion is to take a stroll in the park," the King replied.

But the greatest of his virtues, and what might indeed be considered his dominant characteristic, was his goodness of heart. This was a king who spontaneously and sincerely loved his people. This sincerity shines through his remark: "*Il n'y a que Monsieur Turgot et moi qui aimons le peuple.*"—It is only Monsieur Turgot and I who love the people.

Gentle and humane, he had a horror of cruelty and bloodshed. He was prone to tears and full of sensibility, as was the entire age, but in his case it came from the heart. When Chamfort's neoclassic drama *Mustafa and Zéangir* was staged in the royal theatre—a play that celebrates sibling love—he shed a fountain of tears. He actually loved his own brothers and sisters, which, in the circumstances, and considering their own cooler feelings for him, was rather remarkable.

I could continue to enumerate his virtues, and that might seem well worth doing in view of all that has been said about his weaknesses. But there really is no need. In recent decades royalist historians have reiterated to the point of tedium what a kind and noble soul he was.

We must also consider how very different a king was from an ordinary mortal. From the moment of his birth, he was raised in so rarified and sheltered a world that it must necessarily have weakened his grasp of reality. He could never become familiar with the common people and the difficult raw material of their daily lives. For this reason—because they were an unknown quantity—he was every bit as uncomfortable meeting commoners as his grandfather, Louis XV, had been. The reason why he failed to recognise the danger hanging over his throne, and made no effort to counter it, is, quite clearly, that he was a king. In the clear sunny sky depicted on the ceiling of his throne room he never noticed the gathering storm clouds …

However, contrary to what I have just argued, we have also to recognise that the rulers of old lived in much greater proximity to life and to their people than those of today. Or more precisely, the people of those days lived in greater proximity to their rulers. They could enter their great halls, stroll in their parks and shout abuse at them with impunity. Louis XVI probably knew much more about his people and their moods than the leaders of society today. Somehow, both monarch and people were cut from the same cloth. The social gulf between them was confined to the external world, not the inner one. The King was more akin in spirit to his serf than the director of a modern business is to his office-boy; and more able to strike the right note when they spoke to one another.

The sad thing is that it should be necessary at all to draw attention to Louis' virtues, as opposed to his shortcomings. Those virtues did almost as much to pave the way for the Revolution as did the sins of his predecessors. As Sainte-Beuve expressed it, rather more elegantly: "Louis XVI's spiritual virtues ran far beyond what was required for the role of king. It was his very kindness and humanity that drove him unremittingly towards the role of sacrificial victim, and, as he stumbled from one act of weakness to another, the only way in which he would ever attain greatness was through martyrdom." And so this kind-hearted, saintly king proved to have been of the least possible use to the institution he represented at that precise moment in history. Had he possessed the easy-going, sanguine, rococo spirit of Gustav III of Sweden, he might have come up with some stratagem to protect, or at least prolong, its existence. But at that precise moment only a king with the mind of a Machiavelli could have measured up to the situation. Instead, they had Louis XVI, the humane, indulgent soul who loved his people and shed bitter tears over their fate.

"On that final day," Sainte-Beuve continues, "Marie-Antoinette poured out her heart, urging him to die like a king, like a true descendant of Louis XIV. But he had resolved rather to die like a Christian, as his forebear St Louis had done." It was the fate of the French monarchy that this Louis had more in him of his sainted ancestor than of Louis XIV.

The Verdict

THE HEARING LASTED FOR MONTHS. The arrests of d'Oliva and Réteaux changed everything. Once d'Oliva had confessed to her appearance in the Venus Bower, and Réteaux that he had written the letters from 'the Queen', Jeanne's lies collapsed one after another. On 12th April she was brought face to face with Réteaux and d'Oliva and finally compelled to admit to the Venus Bower charade. The confession was torn from her between a thousand screams and convulsions; her superior manner vanished, and she fainted. A warder took her in his arms and carried her back to her cell. But the moment she recovered herself she bit him in the neck, whereupon he simply let her fall.

With the collapse of her scheme to blame everything on Cagliostro, she concocted a fresh one intended to make Rohan the sole villain and herself merely the blind instrument who had had no idea what she was involved in. When that became untenable, she tried another experiment: taking refuge in secrecy—"the sort of secret," she claimed, that "she could reveal to no one, not even to the head of the royal household in strictest confidence." And finally, when that too proved ineffectual, she began to feign madness. She smashed everything in her room, and refused to eat or to go down to the hearing. When the warders entered her cell, she would be found lying on the bed stark naked.

Cagliostro however found himself in top form on several occasions during the trial. He castigated Jeanne roundly, making her so angry that she grabbed a candle-holder, pulled it towards her and inflicted a burn on herself. When Réteaux was brought before him, he unleashed a powerful moral lecture—if we can believe him, he "talked until his lungs could no longer bear it". Réteaux broke down completely, and the judges thanked Cagliostro warmly.

But by the time he had recovered his normal self the strength had gone out of him, and so it seems had the Ram Apis, and even Zobiachel, and, like all the other accused, he suffered something of a collapse. His Italian temperament made him far less able than his French counterparts to withstand the loneliness, and stress, of imprisonment. It seems that he, the great mystic, commanded the fewest sources of inner strength, which rather confirms the bogus nature of his grand spiritual claims. He needed constant supervision, as it was feared that he might kill himself.

Rohan bore his own ordeal with quiet, sombre dignity. When his case came before the Parlement and he ceased to be the prisoner of the King, he lost the right to maintain a great household and receive visitors. Only his doctors were allowed to see him (he was suffering from inflamed kidneys), and it was they who took his letters, written in invisible ink, to his lawyer. He became increasingly exhausted, and began to lose heart. He was deeply anxious about his friends and allies, Planta and Cagliostro. He even required his lawyer to take an oath that he would always address Cagliostro as Comte, as it pained him so much when people did not. But deep in his heart lay the real concern, which troubled him even more strongly than his own fate and that of his friends—his grief for the Queen. "Write and tell me," he begged his lawyer, "whether it is true that she is still so upset."

It was customary at the time for lawyers involved in cases of unusual public interest to print and circulate their memoirs, or rather their own accounts of what happened. The first to do this had been Beaumarchais himself. Now the public were waiting in a fever of excitement for 'memoirs' of the necklace trial, which of course duly appeared, with huge success. The version put out by Jeanne's lawyer Doillot saw ten thousand copies instantly snapped up from his home address, and another five thousand distributed through booksellers. This Doillot was an elderly gentleman who had not been in practice very long. Jeanne had completely turned the old fellow's head. He believed everything she told him, and faithfully recorded her fantastic tales in his memoir. Which of course only served to make it even more of a success.

Cagliostro's lawyer, the young M Thilorier, was very aware that this was his great chance to make a name for himself. The basic text was written for him, in Italian, by the magus himself, and he then worked it up, with considerable literary flair, to suit the taste of the time. Grimm and other experts declared that had it been a novel, they would have considered it wonderfully interesting and skilfully wrought. In this work can be found the more fanciful stories about Cagliostro's youth already quoted. As for the actual legal issues, Thilorier was in a very easy situation, as Cagliostro was able to prove his alibi, having arrived in Paris, from some way away, the day after Rohan first talked to the jewellers.

Nicole d'Oliva's lawyer, the equally youthful Maître Blondel, produced a lyrical little masterpiece, a gem of *sensibilité*, and the age lapped it up. It tapped the same vein of sentimentality we find in *Manon Lescaut* and the later *La Dame aux Camélias*. People were shocked by Nicole's innocence, for who could be more innocent than an innocent courtesan?

Blondel's work ran to twenty thousand copies. Scarcely less popular were the minor personages, Planta, Réteaux, Mme Cagliostro and others who had been more or less incidentally caught up in the case. But the greatest expectations of all were aroused by the memoirs of the Cardinal's lawyer, Maître Target. Target was an Academician, and the pride of the legal profession. Finally, on 16th May, the long-awaited work appeared. It proved a huge disappointment to the public. Target wrote with wonderful scholarly, indeed Ciceronian, eloquence, but he described nothing but the truth, with not a jot of poetry or fantasy in it.

Alongside the memoirs came the flood of pamphlets. Their authors, whose livelihoods depended on the popular hunger for sensation, naturally had no wish to miss out on the boom. Everyone had some new detail to add. They were able to reveal that Rohan and d'Oliva had spent the night together after the scene in the Bower, Rohan in the belief that he held the Queen in his arms. They reported that La Motte was now in Turkey, where he had been circumcised and made a Pasha. The more gruesome and shameless the pamphlet, the more certain it was of success. In this burgeoning tide of filth, Cagliostro became immensely popular. But as for the Queen …

Of these pamphlets Carlyle writes:

"The mind stops in dismay: curiosity breaks of it, whether this vortex of deception should ever close while delirium becomes general and the human tongue incomprehensible jargon, like the squalling of jays and magpies."

Images and caricatures of the dramatis personae poured into circulation. The publishers were not overly scrupulous. The face of St Vincent's wife (he was the President of the Parlement) was circulated over Jeanne's name, while the Duc de Montbazon stood in for La Motte.

How could the government possibly tolerate all this? Was there no censorship yet in the world? Well, of course there was, and extremely strict provisions regulated the presses. But those provisions were every bit as toothless and impotent as every other function of the Ancien Régime. Any pamphleteer caught in the act would have his work burnt and would be severely punished, but such people were never caught, nor were their distributors. The police had good reason not to arrest them, since it was rumoured that the very worst of these productions was the work of no less a person than the Finance Minister, Calonne, while other pamphleteers enjoyed the protection of the Duc d'Orléans and operated under his direction.

We have already related one colourful tale involving the tracking down of pamphlets by Beaumarchais. Perhaps even more instructive is the tale of police inspector Goupil. Shortly after Louis XVI took the throne, Goupil announced that he had discovered a secret press near Yverdun that was about to print something that was deeply scurrilous about the King, and even more so about the Queen. He had managed to procure one or two examples, but to secure the rest he would need a great deal of money. He was given thirty thousand louis, and shortly afterwards produced both the manuscript and all the copies that had been run off. For these he was given another thousand louis. But at this point another policeman, prompted by envy, revealed that the author of the pamphlet was none other than Goupil himself. Ten years earlier, he had been a prisoner in the Bicêtre, and his wife had been in the Salpêtrière. On her release she had managed to delude Rohan into believing that she could act as a mediator on his behalf with the Queen. (Was that such a very widespread fashion among the women of this period?)

These pamphleteers were repulsive little nobodies, and their productions give pleasure now only to bibliographers and collectors, but their importance was considerable. They played a far greater role in bringing about the Revolution than the truly great writers. It was they who served public opinion, both feeding and directing it. At the time there was no daily press in the modern understanding of the term. In the turbulent years before 1789 one had to look elsewhere for material to supply the ever-chattering and gossip-hungry people of Paris. Hence the pamphlets. They existed in immense variety. There were the 'little books' (*libelle*, source of the modern English 'libel'), and there were handbills and leaflets carrying pictures and verses. The eighteenth century was extremely fond of the verse form (even for textbooks), so naturally slander too could be versified. There are many such poems written about Marie-Antoinette, each more appalling than the last.

But all the while the shadow of the Bastille hung over the pamphleteer. Any day the little scene might take place which Mercier euphemistically calls the 'delivery of the *exempt*', with the police officer sidling up beside you and fluting softly in your ear:

"There must surely be some mistake, Monsieur, but I am instructed, Monsieur, to order your detention, Monsieur. In the name of the King, Monsieur."

"The victim might want to howl," says Mercier, "but the *exempt* is delivered so very meekly! If you had a pistol you would do better to fire it into the air rather than at him. Better to bow low, and enter into a exchange of politenesses with the man. You could pile up the mutual compliments until nothing stood between you and your rival in courtesy but iron bars."

One can hardly wonder that the people who directed public opinion felt such venomous resentment towards the prevailing system.

The power of popular sentiment derived from the sociable disposition of the French character and the extroverted, outward-looking nature of French society. "Most foreigners," wrote Necker, the great banker, who was himself of foreign origin, "have not the slightest conception of the importance of public opinion in France. They find it hard to understand that such an invisible form of power could exist. Without financial resources, official protection or a standing army, it imposes its laws on the city, the Court and even the Royal Palace." Necker was absolutely right: foreigners do not understand it. Even Wahl, the modern German scholar who is the greatest expert in every aspect of the years leading up to the Revolution, fails to grasp the French mentality. In his book he reproaches Necker, and all those who were in power in the final years of the Ancien Régime, for placing so much emphasis on public opinion. He cannot understand how it could be that while the King could nominate ministers, public opinion could bring them down, and he would certainly have found Chamfort's remark incomprehensible: "Everyone hates a fishwife, but none of us will accost one when she makes her way through the market hall." It seems that in Germany either the fishwives hold their tongues, or the self-confidence of the bourgeoisie is so unshakeable that they pay them no attention.

The extent to which the power of popular sentiment had grown is wonderfully seen in this well-known anecdote:

Louis XVI once asked the elderly Richelieu, who had lived through three reigns, what had been the difference between them.

"Sire," the Marshal replied, "in Louis XIV's day no one dared utter a word; when Louis XV was on the throne, they spoke in whispers; under Your Highness they shout at the top of their voices."

And now public opinion began to influence the necklace trial. Initially, people were against Rohan. He had brought this on himself long before, by his worldly behaviour and general voluptuousness so unbefitting a man of the cloth; the word now was that he kept a harem, consisting of all the women featuring in the case. Everyone 'knew' that Jeanne, d'Oliva and Mme Cagliostro were his mistresses. Much play was made of his position of Grand Almoner, and caricatures showed him collecting alms to pay off his debts. The age of Voltaire, with its underlying contempt for the clergy, wallowed in this slander.

But then the mood changed. He soon came to be seen as the pitiable victim of 'despotism' and signs of sympathy for him began to appear. The ladies, who, as we have seen, liked to express their opinions through their coiffures, now started to sport red and yellow ribbons on their heads: red above and yellow below, to signify "the Cardinal lying on straw", that is to say, in a dungeon. These women, as a contemporary noted, were eternally grateful to the gallant Rohan for taking care, even in his hour of crisis, to burn the love letters which would have compromised so many fine ladies.

This reversal of public opinion strongly affected the Parlement, which, proud as it was of the independent spirit displayed by its judges with regard to the supreme power in the land, was prepared to make any number of compromises to preserve its popularity, and was by no means independent-minded where its public standing was concerned.

The change in the public mood was so rapid and so complete that one has to assume a degree of orchestration from above. This originated at the highest level, from government ministers and Versailles. Marie-Antoinette had lost her popularity with the public long before, but her real enemies remained those at Court. It was only there that anyone had a real interest in her emerging from the trial in disgrace. First of all, there were the Rohan clan, Mme de Marsan, Mme de Brionne and all the fairy godmothers, who had always despised the young Queen for her attack on protocol. But she had even more powerful foes, such as Calonne, the Finance Minister, who had never forgiven her for opposing his appointment; and there was the powerful family of the late Prime Minister Maurepas, who were still furious that she had wanted the banished Choiseul to be put in charge.

And, in the background, there lurked even loftier enemies: the two royal princes, counting on the demise of Louis XVI to bring one of them to the throne. One was the Comte de Provence, that witty and cunning free spirit; the other was the Duc d'Orléans, Philippe-Égalité, who flirted with revolution, and who, as the elder son, was waiting for the throne to become vacant. There is something rather eerie about the fact that at the time of our story there were three people living at Versailles who would attain the French crown through the beheading of Louis XVI: the Comte de Provence, later Louis XVIII; the Comte d'Artois, as Charles X and the twelve-year-old Duc de Chartres, the son of Philippe-Égalité, who became Louis-Philippe, the Citizen King. And there was a fourth, the infant Duc de Normandie, who after his father's death became the legitimate King of France, Louis XVII, but never ascended to the throne. His story was lost during the Revolution in circumstances of insoluble mystery. One thinks of Macbeth when the witch conjured up the 'horrible sight' of the line of future Kings of Scotland, not one of whom carried his own features.

Representatives of the Church also met and drew up a statement of protest, asking the King to allow Rohan to be tried under their jurisdiction, as the Parlement was not an appropriate body to arraign a prince of the Church. Even the Pope protested, though when he understood the more intimate details of the case he backed off. People sang this satirical song:

Mais le Pape, moins honnête
Pourrait dire a ce nigaud:
Prince, à qui n'a point de tête,
Il ne faut point de chapeau!

A man with no head has no need of a Cardinal's hat!

But at the same time the rabble 'knew' that Marie-Antoinette certainly had the necklace and was simply denying the fact.

Mme Cagliostro, whose complete innocence became clear in the course of the trial, was duly freed. She was the first of Rohan's entourage to leave the Bastille. It now became apparent for the first time just how far popular feeling had shifted towards Rohan and away from the Queen. Mme Cagliostro was enthusiastically fêted, was received in the highest places, and three hundred people signed the visitors' book at her home on a single day.

Another sympathetic female prisoner in the Bastille also had a happy result: the comely Nicole d'Oliva gave birth to a healthy boy, who was christened Jean-Baptiste Toussaint, his natural father Toussaint de Beausire having had no hesitation in acknowledging him.

At last the *Procureur Général*, Joly de Fleury, completed his indictment. He read it out on 30th May. It invited the jury to agree that the documents signed 'Marie-Antoinette *de France*' were fraudulent; that the Comte de la Motte *in absentia* and Réteaux de Villette should be sentenced to the galleys for life; that the Comtesse de la Motte should be birched, branded with a hot iron and imprisoned for life in the Salpêtrière. Rohan was to be given eight days to confess before the Grand chambre that he had recklessly given credence to the meeting in the Venus Bower, and that he had contributed to the deception of the jewellers; and should therefore express his full repentance, and ask pardon of the King and Queen; in addition he should resign all his official positions, give alms to the poor, and keep away from the royal residence for the rest of his life.

De Fleury's indictment acquitted the Cardinal of fraud, but found him guilty on the higher charge that he had insulted the Queen's honour by the assumptions he had made. Considered objectively, this was entirely justified, and the punishment imposed not especially severe.

But those who were determined both to humiliate the Queen in every possible way and to undermine the King, did not think so. When Joly de Fleury had finished reading out his statement, M Séguier, the *Avocat Général*, who stood above Fleury in rank, rose to speak. He protested vehemently, demanding that the Cardinal be acquitted on all counts. His raised tones were hardly in keeping with the dignity of the occasion; it was like a foretaste of the embittered rantings soon to be heard in the courts of the Revolution.

"You, who already have one foot in the grave," he roared, "want to heap the ashes of shame upon this man, and to bring that shame upon the Parlement itself."

"Your anger, sir, is not surprising," replied Fleury. "People like you, who are so deeply sunk in debauchery, have no choice but to take the Cardinal's side."

"It's is true that I know a few 'girls'," retorted Séguier, "and in fact my coach does sometimes wait at their door. But that's entirely my business. No one could say of me that I basely sold my opinions to those in power."

His meaning was that Fleury was in the pay of the Court. The accusation shocked him so much that he couldn't speak.

Such were the circumstances in which the hearing began. Réteaux did not deny that he had written the letters in question, but, he pleaded, he had done so with good intentions, since he and everyone knew that the Queen would never have signed herself 'Marie-Antoinette *de France*'.

Jeanne responded to the judges' questions with indomitable courage. Rohan and the Queen had certainly corresponded: she had personally seen some two hundred letters written between them. In hers, the Queen used the intimate '*tu*' form with him, and most of them involved arranging rendez-vous. And they really had met.

This assertion deeply offended the judges, even those who were passionately against the Queen. They were aristocrats, and they felt that enough was enough. Jeanne curtseyed with a saucy, mocking smile, and left the room.

The Cardinal was next. He was very pale, utterly exhausted: a broken man. Observing that he could barely stand, the court gave him permission to sit, not on the bench for the accused but on a seat reserved for their own use. When his submission was over and he was about to leave, they gave him a standing ovation.

Next should have been the turn of Nicole d'Oliva, but she had asked to be excused for a short while as she was suckling her child. The judges were men of sensibility, and readily gave her permission. Finally she did appear, and won everyone's hearts. Her winsome innocence and charming disarray put them in mind of a popular painting by Greuze, *The Broken Jug*. Some had tears in their eyes. They did not trouble her for very long; everyone took her innocence for granted. Decidedly she was their favourite.

Then Cagliostro stepped up. He too was an instant success. Even the way he wore his hair, with locks dangling in little plaits down to his shoulders, gave them something to smile at. To the standard opening question about who he was and where he was from, he replied in his most metallic tones:

"I am a noble traveller."

That put an end to any solemnity in the proceedings. There were no further questions, as he held forth about himself, happy in the knowledge that at last he had an audience. The sophisticated, acerbic judges found him a breath of fresh air, a kind of southern bumpkin, an especially amusing market-hall barker, or an organ-grinder with his monkey. At the end they even congratulated him, which Cagliostro naturally took as his due.

When the prisoners left the Palais that evening to return to the Bastille by coach, a huge crowd was waiting to cheer Rohan and Cagliostro. The Cardinal was less than comfortable with this reception, but Cagliostro was in his element, gesticulating, shouting and throwing his hat into the throng, where (he claimed) people fought for it in their thousands.

On 31st May, at six in the morning, the Parlement sat in judgment. Despite the early hour, there for all to behold stood those late sleepers and late risers, the assembled aristocracy of France. Since five am nineteen members of the Rohan family and the related house of Lotharingia (Lorraine), including Mme de Marsan, Mme de Brionne, the Duc Ferdinand de Rohan (the Archbishop of Cambrai), the Duc de Montbazon and others, had been standing at the gate of the Grand'chambre in full mourning garb. It was like that scene in the Spanish *Romanzero* when the sons of Count Lara process before the King after their father's honour has been impugned. Everything about the scene was charged with a sense of ancient aristocratic feudal—and Spanish—grandeur. Mme de Brionne, the most formidable of the fairy godmothers, had already called on the leader of the Parlement at dawn and upbraided him furiously, as only these formidable old ladies can, hurling it in his face that he had sold himself to the Court. ("How proud people are of their own independence when they betray that of others for money!") When the judges filed past, the nineteen Rohans and Lorraines met them with a profound and sombre silence. The judges, even those who were of noble birth, were all from families far younger than the two Illustrious Houses, and were deeply moved.

Jeanne de la Motte's fate was the first to be decided. In flat, unvarying tones her crimes were read out. When the time came to determine the sentence, two Councillors, one of them Robert de St Vincent, a passionate opponent of the monarchy, called for execution. This was just a manoeuvre. Had the discussion really got on to the death penalty, the clerical members of the Parlement would have been obliged to withdraw. It was a way of ensuring that thirteen of them would stay out of the debate, since, with two exceptions, they would have taken a stand against Rohan as a disgrace to his religious order. And so the two Councillors now demanded the ultimate penalty for Jeanne: "to be taken from this place and put to death". The actual form her punishment would take, we shall see.

The Comte de la Motte was sentenced to the galleys for life. Réteaux got off extremely lightly, with lifelong banishment from the kingdom. D'Oliva and Cagliostro were acquitted, but on differing terms. D'Oliva was deemed *hors de cour*—dismissed from the court—while Cagliostro was acquitted on all counts. The first of these acquittals was less absolute than the second, having a certain implication of disgrace attached to it.

All these decisions had been handed down in a relatively routine manner. Now the real business began—deciding what to do about Rohan.

The discussion lasted seventeen hours, and the result was announced only at ten pm. Those who were sworn enemies of the Court, Fréteau de St Just and Robert de St Vincent, had made powerful speeches in Rohan's defence. The outcome was that everyone voted for his acquittal, but they could not agree on the precise manner of it. Twenty-six speakers voted for outright acquittal, while twenty-two wanted simply to discharge him *hors de cour*. In the end there was a majority decision—Cardinal Rohan was completely cleared on all charges, with no shadow of infamy attaching to his name.

Paris received the verdict with widespread rejoicing. The Parlement's popularity had increased yet again, and everywhere people drank to its health and the Cardinal's. The fishwives, those proud representatives and symbols of the people, stood waiting for him in the courtyard with bunches of roses and jasmine, and clasped him to their bosoms with joy.

The next day he and Cagliostro left the prison. Later Cagliostro painted this moving picture of his return home:

"I left the Bastille towards eleven-thirty in the evening. The night was dark, and the quarter where I live was relatively abandoned. So, great was my surprise when I was suddenly greeted by some eight or ten thousand people. They had broken down the gate to my house. The courtyard, the staircase, the rooms—everywhere was packed. I took my wife in my arms. My heart could not endure the many feelings that contended for mastery within me. My knees were shaking. I fell unconscious to the floor. My wife shrieked and fainted. My friends gathered around me. They were trembling, not knowing whether this most beautiful moment of our lives was also its last, and the loud rejoicing turned into a grim silence. But I recovered myself. Tears poured from my eyes, and at last, as if in death, I clasped her to my bosom … but here I must leave off. Oh you privileged beings, on whom Heaven has bestowed the rare and melancholy gifts of ardent souls and sensitive hearts, only you could understand; only you could know what such an exquisite moment of happiness might mean after ten months of suffering!"

But let us intrude no further on the happy couple. We should rather consider how a somewhat more important, and much less happy couple, the King and Queen, received the news. The Queen's sense of humiliation and grief was boundless. She had trusted that in the end the law would unequivocally condemn those who had brought scandal upon her, and the very opposite had happened. She could not understand how it was possible. She knew of no precedent for such a thing in all the annals of royalty. When her Habsburg relations had been on the Spanish throne, anyone who chanced simply to touch the Queen's foot could expect the death sentence, but here someone could lay sacrilegious hands on her good name, her womanly honour … and the highest court in the land would find him not guilty. It was incomprehensible. She had no way of knowing that this incident no longer belonged in the annals of royalty but was the first hunting cry of the Revolution.

"So there you are," writes Funck-Brentano: "The King entrusts the defence of the Queen's honour to a court of law which is independent of him and is generally hostile to him. During the course of the trial the Finance Minister, the Minister of Justice and the King's Librarian, Le Noir, all of them therefore in his confidence, are more or less openly manoeuvring to have Rohan acquitted. And no one is the least bit surprised. Is there any government today that would allow the freedom people enjoyed at that time?" This hypocritical sophistry, which insists that people were never so free as under the Ancien Régime, is the extraordinary conclusion, typical in its *mauvaise foi*, of French royalist writers. Funck-Brentano must surely have been just as aware as we are that what happened was not a sign of freedom but of impotence. Such events did not occur in the last days of the Ancien Régime because there was no tyranny, but because that tyranny had become weak. And an enfeebled tyranny is even more odious than a violent one. The situation cried out for the cleansing storm of 1789.

Louis XVI, incidentally, hastened to crown the two blunders he had made over the trial with a third. The one wise thing he could have done in the circumstances would have been to behave as if nothing had happened; a true king would never have admitted that his subjects had so upset him. Instead Louis gave free reign to his resentment, and set out to punish the pardoned Rohan as much as he could without risking a furore. The Grand Almoner was forced to resign his position and leave Paris within three days, to return to the Chaise-Dieu, the cloister where he had been a monk. Cagliostro was given eight days to leave Paris and three weeks to be out of France.

Naturally, the fairy godmothers could not acquiesce in this. Mme de Marsan called on the King and reminded him for the umpteenth time that she had nursed him as an infant and brought him up, and she implored him to send Rohan into exile somewhere else, as the climate at Chaise-Dieu would be so bad for his knees; and she threatened never to set foot in the Court again. But now that there was no need for it, Louis was obdurate. However this time he did not push the matter too far. He did eventually agree that Rohan could base himself at Marmoutiers, in the beautiful Loire valley.

And now we come to the final scene, in which Jeanne de Valois de la Motte undergoes her appropriate punishment. When she learnt that the Cardinal had been acquitted, Jeanne had one of her usual fits and began to rage. A soul filled with malicious fury finds its own misfortunes much easier to live with than the good fortune of others. She could not bear the fact that the Cardinal, who had always been so good and so chivalrous to her, should have escaped from the danger that she had brought on his head.

On 21st June 1786, she was woken by her warders at five in the morning. Thinking it must be something to do with another court hearing, she refused to get up. Finally, after much delay, she decided she would and went out into the courtyard. There she was seized by four powerful executioners assisted by two footmen, and bundled along to the foot of the stairs. She kicked out and bit, and the usual deluge of never-ending curses poured from her mouth. She was forced to her knees and made to listen while the sentence was read out. When she heard that she was to be birched, she shrieked:

"You will shed the royal blood of the Valois!"

Her screams filled the whole palace.

"How can you bear to let these people shed the blood of your kings?"

Even at this early hour, the commotion drew an audience of some two or three hundred people. They watched while her clothes were ripped from her as she fought with her hands, her feet and her teeth, and was beaten over the shoulders with a birch.

Then she tore herself free and flung herself about on the stone floor in a hysterical fit. She pulled up her skirt and thrust herself forward obscenely, to express her defiant, diabolical feelings about the world. At that moment everything else fell away from her—that pose was the most sincere gesture she ever made.

The executioner managed to brand her with only one of the Vs (for *voleuse*, 'thief'). When he tried to apply the second, as she thrashed about in agony, the scorching iron slipped onto her breast. She leapt up and bit the shoulder of one of the executioners through his clothing, drawing blood. Then she collapsed.

Later she was moved to the Salpêtrière hospital, which also served as a prison. There she was made to wear prison uniform, and the gold ring was removed from her ear. A doctor offered her twelve livres for it. Jeanne, who up to that point been sunk in taciturn silence, suddenly came to herself:

"What? Twelve livres? The gold alone is worth more than that!"

She was not going to be cheated.

Shortly afterwards the second part of the sentence was carried out. At Bar-sur-Aube all the La Motte possessions, both fixed and personal, were sold off on behalf of the Treasury.

In its days of greatness the French monarchy would surely have found a way of removing Jeanne from the land of the living without the publicity attached to locking her up in the Salpêtrière. No true governing power could have tolerated the restless, malcontent nature of such a creature. In this too, the Ancien Régime was simply weak.

And so it happened that, in time, and with the help of a kindly nun, Jeanne quietly and effortlessly slipped out of prison. The nun is said to have shouted this pleasantly ambiguous piece of advice after her:

"*Adieu, Madame, prenez garde de vous faire remarquer.*"—Farewell, Madame, and try not to draw attention to yourself.

She went to London, where her husband was waiting for her. And there she lived, perhaps on money left over from the sale of the diamonds, or perhaps secretly helped by the King's enemies—possibly the Duc d'Orleans himself; but above all, she lived by her writing. Neither she nor Réteaux de Villette allowed the popular sympathy for her cause to go untapped, and both of them poured out a stream of pamphlets and memoirs.

Jeanne's literary imagination, unlike the practical imagination revealed in her intrigues and machinations, was not of the first rank. Her literary fantasies are those of a hysterical parlour maid who concocts interminable fictions to the discredit of her employers. It seems that the Valois blood did not predominate after all; she too belonged rather to the house of Figaro.

The most notable of these masterworks appeared in London in 1788, entitled: *Mémoirs justificatifs de la Comtesse de la Motte, écrits par elle-même.* According to this testimony, the affair between Rohan and Marie-Antoinette began back in Vienna. Their relationship finally ended when the Princess left him for a German officer, whereupon Rohan, wounded in his manly pride, committed various indiscretions and brought her wrath down upon himself. He hoped he might win her heart again when she came to Paris, but now the Comte d'Artois had come between them.

The instant Marie-Antoinette met Jeanne she took her to her heart and gave her ten thousand livres, as friendship is strengthened by such little gifts. Out of pure kindness Jeanne mediated between them on Rohan's behalf, but he had another, far more powerful, patron, the Emperor Joseph II, who thought it in the Austrian interest to demand that his friend Rohan should be made Prime Minister of France. (Here she neatly worked in the greatest of all the accusations levelled at Marie-Antoinette, that she served the interests of a foreign power.) Marie-Antoinette did not really like Rohan, but she blindly obeyed her brother and so made her peace with him, and their passion flared up again. The expression is of course colourful rather than precise, since both were merely feigning, Marie-Antoinette for political reasons (the Austrian cause) and Rohan from ambition. Rohan was at the time both morally and physically a broken man, who needed to take Cagliostro's magic pills with him to the assignations; and on the way—oh masterstroke of the parlour maid's imagination!—he would call in on his young mistress at Passy to "get his head up … "

Then she comes to the letters. She had not kept all two hundred of them, only some thirty or so—copies—supposedly made at the time. They are indeed love letters, but not very entertaining. Here, all the same, is a brief example—a graphic illustration of just what the French were capable of believing about their royalty:

16th August 1784

Yesterday someone made a rather nosy and suspicious remark, and that has prevented my coming to T… [Trianon] today, but it will not make me deprive myself of the sight of my darling slave. The minister (the King) *is going at eleven to hunt at R … [Rambouillet]; he may be home later, but more probably only in the morning; I hope to compensate myself for his absence by taking revenge for the boredom I have endured these past two days …*

... Since you will play the leading role in my plan, it is essential that there should be perfect understanding between us à propos this subject, as there was last Friday on the s ... [sofa]. *You will smile at the comparison, but since it is appropriate, and since I want to give you proof that it is this evening while we are talking about serious things, you must dress as a messenger, with a parcel in your hand, and walk up and down between the columns of the chapel at eleven; I will send the Comtesse who will lead you up a hidden staircase to a room where you will find the object of your heart's desire.*

The time has come for us to say a few words about Marie-Antoinette's dire and ever-increasing unpopularity, that shift in sentiment which played such a significant part in the outbreak of the Revolution.

When she arrived in Paris with her new husband in 1773 she was given a rapturous reception by the people. As she stood on the balcony of the Hôtel de Ville, that fine old cavalier Maréchal Brissac said to her:

"*Voila, Madame*—two thousand admirers stand before you."

And it was no exaggeration. The French passionately admired the beautiful little princess who had brought a touch of youth to the ageing Bourbon Court. She sensed this, and was happy in the knowledge of it. At around this time she wrote to her mother:

"As we withdrew, we waved to the people and they were so delighted. How happy is our situation when we can win the friendship of an entire people so cheaply!" This did not mean that she would not have been prepared to pay a great deal for it.

But as the years passed and the impatiently-awaited Dauphin failed to appear, her popularity began to wane. When a son was born to the Duc d'Artois, the fishwives pouring into Versailles demanded to know why she was not following the example. But when the Dauphin did finally arrive, the enthusiasm was not what it would once have been, at the start of the reign. Without ever noticing it, Marie-Antoinette had lost the people's love.

By degrees she came to be held responsible for everything the public disliked. Even the King's refusal to be vaccinated was laid at her door. People knew that the Queen was all-powerful—so she must have been to blame for whatever happened or failed to happen. But seen from this distance, Marie-Antoinette was not all-powerful. Her greatest wish in the field of politics, that Choiseul should be recalled from exile, was never fulfilled. Instead, despite her every protest, Calonne was made *Contrôleur Général* (Finance Minister), and it was as a result of his profligacy, his ineffective and doomed financial policies, that people turned against Marie-Antoinette and ridiculed her as *Madame Déficit*.

When, in March 1785, Marie-Antoinette attended the thanksgiving service held in Notre Dame for the birth of her second son, the Duc de Normandie, she was received by the crowd in icy silence. She returned to Versailles in tears.

"*Mais que leur ai-je donc fait?*"—But what have I done to them?—she asked her companions, in bewilderment.

For a year now, ever since the affair of the necklace, she had been so passionately hated by all sections of society that the kindly old Duc de Penthièvre advised the King to lock her up in the nunnery at Val-de-Grâce in the interests of public order.

Mais que leur ai-je donc fait? What had given rise to such bottomless hatred?

According to the brothers Goncourt, it originated in the Court, from where it was skilfully fostered, and made its way out into an ever-widening sphere. We have already discussed why the majority of courtiers so disliked her: the more elderly, because she was young and so much at ease with younger people; the zealots, for the general gaiety of her life; the 'old French' party, because she stood for the Austrian connection; those who did not belong to the Polignac circle, because they felt themselves slighted; and everyone else, because the witty superiority of her entourage diminished their self-esteem.

History provides many examples of courtiers taking to a new queen with less than total enthusiasm, but it is unusual for them to foment such powerful and far-reaching intrigues against one; and it is quite without parallel for them to involve the common people. This itself was a sign of the times. But it is more than that. Not only does it suggest that public opinion had become a factor in a purely internal palace revolution; it also shows the extent to which the Court had lost its political instinct. Its chief source of strength was now to make common cause against the authority of the King with his greatest enemy, the mob. That alone would have been enough to bring down judgement on the leading section in society. Had the power of the aristocracy not been ended by the Revolution, it would have collapsed of its own accord, precisely because it had lost its most fundamental instinct, its whole raison d'être, which derived from the same instinct that brought it to leadership in the first place: its capacity to survive.

If we were to ask a sober-minded French citizen of the time what his complaint against the Queen was, he would no doubt have summarised it under three headings: her extravagance, her immoral life and her lack of patriotism. The first charge—whether founded or not—we have explored elsewhere. The second we touched on in the discussion of the vast number of lovers she was imagined to have. And of course, after the necklace trial, this particular accusation was greatly reinforced by the influence of the literary productions of Jeanne de la Motte and the pamphleteers.

By this stage there was nothing the Queen could do to stop those Parisians with filthy minds and the souls of *concierges* instantly 'seeing through' her schemes for debauchery. If the Queen was so fond of spending her summer evenings out on the terraces overlooking the park at Versailles, it was perfectly clear what she got up to in the dark ... Thus it rapidly got abroad that she and her intimate circle—Coigny, Vaudreuil, Besenval and the rest—had ordered costumes representing wild animals, and "after dressing up as harts and hinds, had strayed through the park, giving themselves up to the pleasures of harts and hinds". That could only speak for itself. According to others, Marie-Antoinette would wander through the Versailles gardens dressed as an Amazon, offering herself to anyone—man or woman—she came upon. One young man in particular, an official from the War Ministry, a real Adonis, had caught her eye, but Artois became jealous, the young man vanished without trace shortly afterwards, and his family never saw him again. And so on, and on, and on …

Popular opinion demeaned and besmirched her gaiety of spirit, her love of a beautiful and freer-flowing life, her desire for friendship, and the innocent flirtatiousness by which she sought to please everyone: in short, *les plus belles vertus de sa jeunesse*—the loveliest qualities of her youth—as the brothers Goncourt put it. But even if the Queen were not a Vestal Virgin, did that really deserve such moral outrage from the not-so-puritanical French? "It was a strange kind of censoriousness," the brothers exclaim, and they are right to do so, "that even in the so-called century of women the Queen was to be forgiven nothing that expressed real femininity." French historians of this most frivolous of periods seem to tolerate everyone else's peccadilloes as something to be expected, and find them perfectly natural—so why not those of their queens?

The answer to this question becomes clear when we confront the third of these accusations. The French did not dislike Marie-Antoinette because she was immoral. On the contrary, they found her immoral, and piled the decaying products of their basest fantasies on her, *because* they did not like her … And the chief reason why they disliked her, it seems to us, can only have been that she wasn't French.

The Queen, it cannot be denied, was bound by a thousand ties, emotional and political, to the house of her birth and the powerful family from which she had come. Sanguine by nature, it never occurred to her for a moment that the interests of the two allies, Austria and France, might not always exactly coincide. Public opinion, which had never felt much enthusiasm for the Austrians (the French had always passionately hated any alliance with them) exaggerated her links with that country, spoke of the millions of livres she sent back to her brother, and took great delight in passing on stories by word of mouth, such as the following:

When Joseph II of Austria ordered the closure of the Schelde corridor, Marie-Antoinette defended him with all her might before the French Court, and told the Foreign Minister Vergennes:

"All you ever think about the Emperor is that he is my brother."

To which he replied:

"I do always bear it in mind. But before all else I have to consider that Monsieur the Dauphin is your son."

France was a closed society, in which outsiders had no place. There has never been a European country in which foreigners were shown less sympathy. A foreign-born queen, tainted with foreign interests, could never be popular, and when the hostility towards her reached its peak, the very worst term of abuse they could find for her was *L'Autrichienne*: 'that Austrian woman'.

This fact can perhaps only be fully understood, and felt on the skin, by people from outside the country. If someone in Hungary remarks that "You're not Hungarian", it is of course not exactly flattery, but nor is it necessarily an insult. It could be a simple statement of fact. If an Englishman happens not to be pure English, and has Scots or Welsh blood in his veins, he will be openly proud of it. But if someone in France tells you, "You are not French!" it denotes something lacking, some fundamental moral deficiency. You probably go around at night with a false beard stealing small change from the caps of blind beggars, are furthermore physically deformed, and carry Lord knows what weapons concealed beneath your garments; in short, you are a subhuman creature, though rather less likeable than an animal.

As can be imagined, this powerful French xenophobia may well have been the basis of Marie-Antoinette's unpopularity.

However, as we have said, Marie-Antoinette was neither a demon, as the Revolution painted her, nor the angel portrayed by the counter-revolution. Perhaps Stefan Zweig is right: the real problem was that she was simply mediocre. Her final martyrdom is very touching, but there really is nothing in her life to make us think of her with particular veneration or emotion. As we take our leave of her, we should quote, in their original beauty, the words of Lamartine, in which he characterises her as follows:

Favorite charmante et dangereuse d'une monarchie vieillie, plutôt que d'une monarchie nouvelle, elle n'eut le prestige de l'ancienne royauté, le respect; ni le prestige du nouveau règne: la popularité. Elle ne sut que charmer, égarer, et mourir.

The charming and dangerous favourite of an ageing monarchy, rather than the queen of a new one, she lacked the prestige of old royalty, the respect due to it; and she also lacked the prestige accorded to a new reign—popularity. All she knew was how to charm, to lose her way, and to die.

Epilogue

COMING TO THE END OF OUR STORY and reading through what we have written, we are somewhat alarmed to find that however much we have tried to paint a full and many-sided picture of the age, we have still not really succeeded in placing sufficient emphasis on what Talleyrand called 'the sweetness of life'. The reader might well be left with the impression that the final hours of the Ancien Régime were careworn and oppressive, a 'moral wasteland', a time of drought before the storm, and he would perhaps be glad not to have lived then. Which would be quite wrong. To have been alive then must have been to experience one of the most delightful of European centuries.

Huizinga notes in another connection that 'chronicles', that is, works of history written as literature, almost always paint a rather dark picture of our period, because they find its grievances so vivid. Anyone who wants to learn about the brightness, beauty and happiness of a particular age has to turn to the record left by artists. And if we follow the great Dutchman's advice and compare the painters of various centuries from the 'eudaemonic' point of view, would we find any other age whose canvases reflect the sweetness of life with the same intensity as that marvellous line of artists from Watteau to Fragonard?

The painters of eighteenth-century France are not much in fashion nowadays—indeed it is almost in bad taste to mention Boucher, the great master of the mid-century, in the presence of those in the know. And this is perfectly natural. They marked the end of one great period, and after them something quite different began. Far be it from us to argue with those who are

279

better qualified, but all the same we cannot help feeling that the time will come when these painters will once again be of interest. Our concern is not with their relative greatness, but with that sense of the sweetness of life reflected in their pictures.

Watteau and Fragonard … according to the Goncourts they are the only poets of the eighteenth century. The verse writers suffer from the dry rationalism of the period, while these two great artists proclaim what in other ages is the subject matter of poets: the world of dream, fable, intoxication and nostalgia.

Watteau lived at the very start of the century. The great representative of our own period is Fragonard, the delegate from the flower fields of Grasse in perennially happy Provence. With a kind of dreamlike intensity, his works conjure up in our souls the eternal myth of the great woodlands: mighty trees, tiny human and animal figures; the trees bent in sorrow, the men and women depicted beneath them existing in a kind of superhuman joy that almost succeeds in making their baby faces seem serious—a joy that, like music, is almost painful. What makes the paintings of Watteau and Fragonard so special is that they seem to depict scenes from an old novel—very beautiful, subtly erotic, and tinged with melancholy—scenes from some wonderful mythological story such as Psyche and Eros. The viewer is seized by a rich, complex yearning, an intense longing to know their secret, their unspoken mystery, a desire to return to the woodland world that is sweeter than anything in this life, and, finally, the desire for something—one knows not what—that great and inexpressible nostalgia which truly creative art awakens in the soul.

And then it begins to dawn on one: this age was as beautiful as the most finely-worked lace, as a piece of Sèvres porcelain with its timeless charm and fragile delicacy; as the noble oozings of the Tokai grape, full and rich with sweetness; as the autumn air in Hungary, when the reddening leaves are scented with the inexpressible sweetness of death.

Only poetry can express this—nothing else. Verlaine's lines, from the *Fêtes Galantes*.

Clair de Lune

Votre âme est un pays choisi
Que vont charmant masques et bergamasques
Jouant du luth et dansant et quasi
Tristes sous leur déguisements fantastiques.
Tout en chantant sur le mode mineur
L'amour vainqueur et la vie opportune,
Ils n'ont pas l'air de croire à leur bonheur
Et leur chanson se mêle au clair de lune,
Au calme clair de lune triste et beau,
Qui fait rêver les oiseaux dans les arbres
Et sangloter d'extase les jets d'eau,
Les grand jets d'eau sveltes parmi les marbres.

Your soul is a landscape set apart
For charming masques and rustic dances,
Where lovers step and strum their lutes, but seem
Melancholy beneath their fanciful disguises—

Where, even as they sing, in minor key,
Of love victorious and life's sweet moments,
They seem not to believe in their own happiness,
And their song drifts away in the moonlight—

The calm moonlight, here so sad and beautiful,
That makes the birds dream among the branches,
And jets of water sob with ecstasy
In the tall, slim fountains between the statues.

The necklace trial took place in 1786. Three years later the Revolution broke out.

The revolution was of course 'carried out' spontaneously by the people, as an uprising, a devastating volcanic eruption—or more precisely it was the work of the street people of Paris, the dark mob from the St Antoine quarter, the workers who in consequence of a blundering Anglo-French trade agreement were made temporarily unemployed, and who, because of the equally blundering politics of superstition, could not for the time being buy bread; and this was followed on a wider scale by the whole nation, as a people oppressed by local village taxes and emboldened by the example of Paris took revenge for the way they had been ground down over the centuries.

But it would be pushing at an open door to argue that the populace did not rush off into revolution all by itself, but went there because they were led into it; that they were merely an instrument wielded by their superiors; or that, like Victor Hugo's famous loose cannon, the uprising went on to destroy the very people who set it off. The revolutionaries, as everyone knows, called one another *citoyens*—citizens—and the essence of and influence behind the revolution was neither popular nor proletarian but bourgeois. It was the middle-class-dominated Third Estate that put an end to the power of the privileged.

The causes of the Revolution are no longer in question. It was not so much that the populace were destitute as that the bourgeoisie were increasingly prosperous. The peasantry certainly had their sufferings, but that had been the case for centuries, and by Louis XVI's time people were at last beginning to think that it might be necessary to assist them. Moreover, the situation of the agrarian workers was not uniformly bleak. The notorious abuses of the landowners were not everywhere equally oppressive. Wahl draws attention to the fact that around this time the peasantry were turning woods on the great estates over to arable land without asking permission of the squirearchy and without resistance from them. The institution of serfdom, which the peoples of Central and Eastern Europe had suffered for so long, was by now confined to the easternmost provinces. Louis XVI had freed his own serfs, and his example had been spontaneously followed by many aristocrats. The remainder were given their freedom wherever there was enough money in the Treasury to compensate landowners.

And in fact, where things were at their worst, the people did not revolt. It was Tocqueville who noted that the most mutinous estates, for example the relatively affluent Île de France, were those that had suffered least from the old institutions, while those that had endured the most—in Brittany and the Loire estuary—became the powder keg of the counter-revolution.

The nobility were of course rich, at least in theory, since aristocratic privileges had never been as strong as they became immediately before they were terminated. But in practice this group was also struggling, since the obligation to maintain a style of living was proving ever more expensive, and many great families were going bankrupt.

On the other hand the bourgeoisie, in reality if not in theory, were doing rather better. They had been fostered and enriched by the great economic upswing we discussed at the beginning of this book, and they grew wealthy on the luxurious habits of the aristocracy, not just of France but also beyond its borders.

We are not primarily thinking here of the petit bourgeois craftsmen and shopkeepers. In Louis XVI's reign, such families would all come together to eat in the kitchen in winter because they could not imagine the luxury of lighting fires in two rooms in the house at the same time. And for people at this level there was one traditional attitude that had not yet been eroded by the Enlightenment—Louis XVI was not alone in his religiosity. It was from a section of the bourgeoisie, in fact if not officially the leading sector, from the *noblesse de robe*, the lawyers, and the financially and intellectually pre-eminent, that the revolutionary discontent originated.

For a hundred years the higher bourgeoisie and the intelligentsia had felt aggrieved by the fact that while the real power lay in their hands, all the grandeur and distinction that should accompany it remained with the nobility. And the arrogance of the nobility increased as their real power declined. In the second half of the century they attempted to seize power again: not only were the most senior positions in both the army and the law restricted to members of noble families, but they sought on the basis of obsolete documents to enforce their former landowning rights over a peasantry that had long been liberated. The attempt failed miserably: the expropriation of the army and the law took place on paper only, simply because the leading bourgeois families had long before bought their way into the nobility. But that futile attempt, together with the steady ennoblement of the bourgeoisie, simply deepened the rift between the old privileged class and the new leaders of society. The intellectuals and the wealthy, says Rivarol—that grandfather of all right-wing ideologists since—found the arrogance of the aristocracy insupportable, and for that reason many of them purchased rank for themselves; but this simply produced a new form of misery. They had been ennobled, but they were not nobility. "The King's subjects were cured of their bourgeois condition as from scrofula—it left its mark."

The indignity of finding themselves not quite noble was felt most strongly by those leading intellectuals who were invited into the salons of those aristocrats who so much enjoyed their wit. They stayed as guests in country manors and were showered with all sorts of gifts and distinctions, and yet—in most cases no doubt unintentionally—they were still not accepted as equals. Of all forms of pride, that of the writer is the greatest and the most aggressive, and this pride was constantly being trampled on by the privileged, by their very acts of kindness and goodwill. The best examples of this are Beaumarchais and Chamfort.

"Your Excellency," Chamfort said to someone. "I know very well what I ought to know, but I also know that it is much easier for you to patronise me than to treat me as an equal."

There could be no better expression of a writer's prickly self-regard. There is an echo of this in our period in what happened to a certain Abbé Rousseau. He, like Abélard before him, fell in love with one of his aristocratic pupils, and "finding no way to resolve the conflict of feelings between nobility and low birth", as he wrote in his farewell letter, he dined at the Palais Royal and then shot himself in the heart.

Between Wealth and Intellect, observes Spengler, there was an unspoken pact of mutual resistance to, and contempt for, the common enemy, Blood. Intellect provided the justification for what Wealth brought about by brute omnipotence—the destruction of privilege and the dethronement of irrational, arbitrary selection on the basis of birth, in the interests of rational selection on the basis of talent and wealth. "Who would have believed," says the same Rivarol, "that it was not the level of debt, or the *lettres de cachet*, or any other of the abuses of power—not even the *intendants*—that provoked revenge, nor was it the interminable tardiness of the justice system that so enraged the nation, but the privileges of the nobility; as is confirmed by the fact that it was the bourgeoisie, the writers, the financiers and all those who envied them, who stirred up the little people in the capital and the peasantry in their villages."

Chamfort complained that he could never afford to keep a coach under the Ancien Régime, when his weak constitution made it absolutely necessary for him to have one. But he later remarked:

"I only continued to believe in the Revolution while there were so many coaches they knocked people over in the streets."

"In 1782," Sainte Beuve explains, "everyone wanted their own carriage, but because they couldn't all have one, they demanded in 1792 that nobody should."

But that brings to mind the much-maligned Hegel's always valid lesson: "The *Weltgeist* uses human selfishness, envy and other passions as the moving force that drives humanity towards its goal, the unacknowledged but ultimate goal of history—freedom". And that remains true even if we don't believe in the great German *Weltgeist*.

When the besieged fortress finally fell, two different processes came to an end: the attackers had seized and occupied it, but the besieged, whether willingly or unwillingly, had already consented to its being taken. And when the monarchy was brought down in the Revolution, that event also had two sides. The Third Estate and the people demolished the ancient edifice, but the nobility and the monarchy allowed them to do so. And this second element is perhaps just as important as the first. The French aristocracy and the monarchy itself, in very large measure, contributed to the making of the Revolution. This is the key to our symbolic narrative, and its true meaning.

In the second half of the eighteenth century, as we have said, that great if gradual shift of sensibility came about to which we assign the all-embracing term 'pre-romantic'. But in the France of Louis XVI there were signs of another shift in taste which it would be difficult to link with pre-romantic sentimentality and restlessness. At first glance it would seem to be an omen of a very different kind.

From Mercier we know, for example, that by this time the *petit-maîtres* were no more. These were people who flittered like butterflies from box to box in the theatre, peeped out through gaps in the stage curtain, clung to the necks of actresses in the passageways, and stood around in the foyer or leant over to assess the legs of ladies stepping into their carriages. Gone too were the *bureaux d'esprit*, salons presided over by blue-stockings where only very clever remarks could be uttered and the ladies had no other ambition than to be learned. The place of the *petit-maîtres* was taken by the *élégants*. The word is still in use today and its meaning is little changed.

The *élégant* no longer drops the names of his aristocratic friends and high-born mistresses. He speaks of his solitude, in which he busies himself with chemistry, but generally he says little. A barely discernible smile of mockery sits on his lips; his face wears a distant, dreamy look; he seldom stays long, leaving early and without fuss. But the women are even more advanced: the only words they utter are '*délicieux*' and '*étonnant*', spoken with a studied simplicity and indifference. In a man they admire *délicatesse*. Mere eloquence is out and the 'art of conversation' is in. Very little wine is taken, only water. Parisians speak much more softly than provincials. They keep themselves trim, and should they by chance begin to put on weight, drink vinegar.

The new style expresses itself in *déshabillé* rather than formal dress. Men now carry walking sticks rather than swords. Questions of honour are less of a concern than in previous generations, and duelling is much rarer. Where once people flaunted their vast wealth, they now boast of being on the verge of bankruptcy. Black clothing is now the fashion, and the extraordinary pomp and splendour of the court of Louis XV is steadily being pushed out.

After all this, even had Mme de Campan had not written her memoirs, we would still have guessed: "This Anglomania had reached such a pitch that Paris was now indistinguishable from London. The French, formerly imitated by the whole of Europe, were now become a nation of imitators ... Since the trade agreements concluded under the peace treaty of 1783 not only carriages, but everything from ribbons to common earthenware were of English manufacture." Young men wore tails and discussed the constitution, the upper house, the lower house, the balance of power and Magna Carta.

And what was the meaning of all these trifles? The end.

However bombastic that may sound, it really was the end—the end of aristocratic culture. Its ideal, *savoir vivre*, the art of living, had reached its zenith in the Court of Louis XV and the Paris of his time, and been unable to develop any further. People had by then become so distinguished, so refined and so perfect that now the great baroque expressions of that distinction, its classical pomp and dignity, had to be renounced. It was followed by charm and nuance, in that age of the art of delicate little things, the rococo. And then, by the closing years of the reign of Louis XVI, even that was too highly-coloured, too loud; and gave way in turn to the mode for softly-spoken conversation and silence: in a word, 'Anglomania'.

But those who saw this Anglomania as mere imitation failed to notice the social significance of its roots. By this stage the English, having concluded an alliance of the aristocracy and the upper bourgeoisie, and taken, by way of the slow but steady transformation begun in 1688, to the upper-middle-class way of life, had become as we have seen (or imagined) them ever since. Earlier, they had been the noisiest people in the world, as evidenced by the uproar and garrulousness of Elizabethan drama. In imitating the English, the French nobility was taking its cue not from another aristocracy but from a quite different section of society, the upper bourgeoisie. This was the moment when aristocratic culture over-reached itself.

In his writings on the sociology of power Max Weber asserts that every historical regime that is not rationally based rests on a hidden principle which he terms 'charisma'—a kind of divine power or grace which one person is regarded by his fellows as possessing, and by reason of which he is obeyed. Such power depends on direct personal contact and thus cannot survive long—usually only until the death of the charismatic individual. To consolidate and perpetuate this power, the charisma must be 'routinised', institutionalised by substituting symbolic acts for the real thing. The early Carolingian kings, for example, still exercised such charismatic power over their people, while later French monarchs were merely invested with symbols of that sacred power by the act of coronation and anointment with holy oil. The allegiance paid by their subjects was no longer to some irresistible force emanating from the royal person, but to the institution of kingship as a surviving sanction against non-obedience.

The special 'chosen' nature of the charismatic individual's power extends to his entourage, and so the concept of a nobility comes into being. In time, this nobility also becomes a mere institution, its power deriving not from itself but from the law that sanctions it.

In our earthly existence, everything living in time must obey time. Through time, everything wears out and ebbs away. Palaces fall into ruin, and the silk and velvet of formal dress fade. But ideas wear out too—"after many a summer dies the swan"—and with the passing of so many centuries the force of charisma also becomes attenuated. There were many 'reasons' for the demise of the French Monarchy, but if we take a longer view, from the sort of distance at which the details start to dissolve into one another, then perhaps this might emerge as the one fundamental reason that gathers all those details into one single causation. The charisma faded, people no longer felt the specially chosen nature of the King and his entourage, and neither the King himself or his nobility felt it either.

Very few people die of pure senility. Even very old people generally fall victim to illness or accident, but usually these are the sort of illnesses and accidents that in their younger days they would easily have survived. In the final analysis, one might say that time had simply finished with them. And so it was with the Ancien Régime.

The aristocracy, partly as the result of its own prolonged inactivity, and partly under the influence of intellectual trends, had, as we have already noted, lost its sense of vocation. It no longer believed in itself. Its desire was simply to *s'encanailler,* and this above all showed its bad conscience. Perhaps that might explain the significance of what Wahl considered one of the most important causes of the Revolution: that eighteenth-century France produced no great men of action. There were none, because the social arrangements were such that men of this type could emerge only from the old aristocratic families, but the loss of a sense of vocation among those families also meant the loss of their whole *raison d'être*—to produce leaders for the country.

But it was the singular misfortune of the monarchy that the last two kings before the Revolution, Louis XV and even more importantly Louis XVI, suffered from that same bad conscience. The latter's kindly heart was filled with fine intentions, and his ministers with plans for reform. He was the first king in many decades who sincerely, from the goodness of his heart, wanted to help his people. That proved fatal. As Tocqueville once again observes in his great work: "Only real genius can rescue a prince who sets out to ease the lot of his people after a long period of oppression." Such a course can lead only to even greater oppression—or to surrendering power altogether.

Tocqueville also suspected, but it was Wahl who showed with his mass of incontrovertible facts, that the Revolution broke out not because the Monarchy was especially tyrannical but because the last French kings were not tyrannical enough. They introduced arbitrary measures, but lacked the strength to see them through. There were no revolutions in other countries where abuses were far worse but where royal power remained strong, and perhaps one might have been averted in France too. That is of course a rather lazy expression—the casual and playful use of the historical 'might have'. And yet there are so many moments in the approach to the Revolution when one feels that it might indeed have been avoided if only Louis XVI had behaved differently.

The highly symbolic episode we have narrated was just one of those moments. Contemporaries saw the necklace trial as an example of absolutist royal and ministerial behaviour that cried out to the heavens, but now that the details have been clarified we can see it rather as the King's incompetence that did so. Even the revolutionary Condorcet recognised this: while the people imagined themselves to be groaning under tyrannical oppression, properly speaking they were the victims of a headless anarchy.

We urge you, dear reader, not to misunderstand us. It is far from our intention to mourn for the French Monarchy in the manner of modern French historians, nor is it to grieve, like Wahl, that they did not deploy the most powerful weapons at their command. In some strange and indefinable way, we do believe, amongst all the other forces at work in history there are also moral ones, and that in the great deeds of nations the struggle between Good and Evil will go on for ever. Louis XVI's good-heartedness and weakness arose from a bad conscience, and the French King's conscience certainly had reason to be bad. Because neither the lace-frilly, sweetly-autumnal beauty of the *Régime*, nor the King's always heartfelt good intentions (themselves a reflection of the prevailing sensibility and the habit of living in the constant expectation of miracles)—ever quite amounted to the salt-sweet spring gale that was really needed. And what came after Louis XVI … we do not of course forget the horrific aspects of the Terror, but nonetheless, the glowing twilight of those years … permit me, reader, once again, for the last time, to give you the words of Tocqueville:

" … it was an age of youthful enthusiasm, of noble and sincere feelings, and for all its blunders it will live for ever in the memory of mankind and serve to shock people out of their reverie whenever they seek to destroy or enslave their fellow men."

In Carlyle's words, "The diamond necklace vanished through the horn gate of dreams"; but its fame spread throughout Europe. None of the events that occurred in the decades leading up to the Revolution received press coverage, but contemporaries instinctively felt its fatal significance.

And even here, in far-away Hungary, at that time so desperately cut off from the mainstream of world events, it haunted people's imagination. This is shown by the fact that a Jesuit father and neo-Latin poet, György Alajos Szerdahely, celebrated it in verses written in his fine Jesuit-humanist manner, mentioning each of the mythological personages who came to grief through the necklace.

DE MONILI FAMIGERATO, QUOD IN GALLIA MAGNAM LITEM, IN EUROPA EXPECTATIONEM CONCITAVIT ANNO MDCCLXXXV. ET VI

Quae Furia est? Certe illa fuit; fortasse Megaera
Quae Stygio retulit tale Monile specu?
Parcite Francigenae dirum adfectare Monile!
Thebaidem Statii Patria vestra legat.
Harmonie, et Semele, Iocasta, nocensque Eriphyle,
Atque alii interitu vos monuere suo.
Fatale est; et quisquis adhuc mortalis habebat,
Morte, vel infami labe Monile luit.
Lemnius huic varias pestes, laetumque venenum
Miscuit, et propriis hostibus ipse dedit.
Frustra ago. Romano vestitus murice Princeps
Heu! domino semper triste Monile petit.
Quid tibi femineo cum cultu et merce Sacerdos?
Femineum nescis sic recubare malum.
Infelix, quicunque putat se posse placere,
Dum sibi feminea credulitate placet.
Vos damna et poenas emitis? La Motthe feroces
Ad furias salvus triste Monile tulit.

Concerning the infamous necklace, the subject of a trial in France, which aroused great interest in Europe in 1785 and 1786.

Which Fury was that? For certain it was one; perhaps
    Megaera
Bringing the necklace back from the Stygian cave?
Beware, children of France, that dire necklace!
Let your countrymen study the Thebeiad of Statius.
Harmony and Semele, Jocasta and the mischievous
    Eriphyle
And others shall warn you of the ruin it brings.

It is fatal; and whatever mortal has so far possessed it
Has paid for it by death or deep shame.
With various plagues and deadly poison Apollo
Has infused it, and gives it to his very own enemies.
I speak in vain. A prince dressed in the purple of Rome
Pursues, alas! the unhappy necklace.
Oh priest, what have you to do with female adornments
    and hire?
You should know to beware of feminine malice.
Unhappy the man who thinks he can please
While pleasing himself with womanish credulity.
Will you purchase condemnation and imprisonment? It
    was La Motte
Who, himself unharmed, took the unhappy necklace to
    the wild Furies.

But the strongest literary response to the trial came from the greatest writers of the age, the giants of German classicism. Goethe, as we have already mentioned, visited Cagliostro's family in Palermo and wrote a play about it called *Der Gross-Kophta*. The play does not rank among the best of his great Weimar productions, but on the other hand it is certainly not his weakest. The principals have no names, only titles. Some are slightly reduced in rank. The Queen is a mere duchess, the Cardinal a *domherr*. True, Cagliostro remains a count, and the La Mottes are a marquis and marquise. The play, clearly for stage reasons, has a happy ending: a *Ritter* (knight) who is in love with the character corresponding to d'Oliva discovers the intrigue just in time, and the guilty parties receive their due punishment immediately after the truth is revealed about the scene in the Venus Bower. In the play the *Graf*, or Cagliostro, represents the comic element, and is a highly entertaining figure, a fine example of Goethe's humour and gaiety.

Schiller, also under the influence of the event, wrote a great and sadly unfinished ghost story, *Die Geisterseher*—The Man

Who Sees Ghosts. And while we are with Schiller, we cannot resist mentioning our hypothesis, difficult as it is to prove, that the necklace trial may also have inspired one of the truly great creations of world literature, his *Don Carlos*. We know of course that Schiller wrote the play on the basis of a conversation with an author called Saint-Real, and that Lessing's *Nathan der Weise* encouraged him to stress the yearning for freedom; but if we study or even just glance through *Don Carlos* with the necklace trial in mind, we find interesting similarities of mood and atmosphere. The play begins *in medias res*: Don Carlos has long been languishing in despair of ever speaking face to face with the Queen. Someone goes between them and helps him to a meeting. Like Marie-Antoinette, the Queen is the unhappy and protesting prisoner of protocol.

In what follows, the entire action turns on letters that are stolen, handed over, recovered, and fall into the wrong hands, and you can find yourself quite lost among the huge number of documents (analogous to Marie-Antoinette's letters to Rohan, Rohan's to Jeanne, and the whole fog of mystery about this correspondence that Jeanne spreads around herself). Then there is the King's secret and tragic suffering as he sits in solitude on the throne brooding over his wife's fidelity—could Schiller have been thinking of Louis XVI? Chronology seems to confirm our theory. Schiller took a long time writing the play. One act was finished in 1785, and the completed work appeared in 1787, so it was composed precisely during the period of the necklace trial. That Schiller always followed, and indeed took the greatest interest in, the more sensational French criminal trials, is well known.

But now, as is proper, we must say some brief closing words about the subsequent fate of our dramatis personae—brief, because their later careers are of little real significance. The royal party are of course excepted: after the conclusion of our immediate narrative, they really did step into the centre stage of history, as their portion of suffering and martyrdom increased. The reader doubtless knows their story; so we will speak only of the others.

Jeanne de la Motte escaped to England in 1787. For a short while she lived off the éclat of the necklace trial, her malicious memoirs and supposed persecution. Thereafter she sank into the London underworld, fell into dreadful poverty, and in 1791, perhaps in one of her hysterical fits, threw herself out of a window and died. Her husband lived on. Little is known of his fate, but it could hardly be much to his credit. He ended his days in 1831, in a beggars' hospital in Paris. The cursed Nibelung treasure had not brought him luck, or even wealth—but rather the "death or deep shame" predicted in Szerdahely's verses.

Prince Rohan spent two years of banishment in his former cloister, then was allowed to return to Strasbourg just as the Revolution broke out. As a prelate he was also a member of the *États Généraux*. He was later charged with counter-revolutionary practices, but never appeared before any court. From 1793 onwards he lived in his Ettenheim diocese as a Prince of the Holy Roman Empire, one of his many titles. When in year nine of the Republic the Pope signed a Concordium with the new French state which gave the Assembly the right to appoint bishops, Rohan resigned his office and returned to his chateau, where he lived in retirement until his death in 1803, a proud, taciturn and forgotten relic of the Ancien Régime.

As a consequence of the sensational trial, Nicole d'Oliva's market value soared. Aristocratic young suitors competed for her favour. Its first recipient, if only out of gratitude, was her clever young lawyer Blondel. Later, from a wide field, she chose Toussaint de Beausire, the father of her child. Carlyle records that he became a well-known informer and played a significant role in the Revolution.

Mme Campan served her mistress with touching and heroic loyalty. Following the Queen's death, she founded a girls' school in St Germain-en-Laye, after which Napoleon put her in charge of an academy for young ladies at Écouen. It is an irony of fate that Mme Campan, who had the good fortune to live through the Revolution, the end of the monarchy and finally the return of the Bourbons to the throne, was eventually dismissed from her post by her former employers. At which point she wrote her superb memoirs, to set the record straight about the Queen. She died in 1822.

For Cagliostro and his wife, fate still had years of trouble in store. The trial proved a tragic turning point in the magician's life; thereafter his road led downwards. His weeping disciples followed the Great Kophta to Boulogne, where he set sail and crossed the Channel. In London his luck ran out. Nothing he started went well for him.

Business matters took him back to France for a short while. He brought an action against de Launay, the Governor of the Bastille, and Chenon, the police inspector who had sealed off his home while he was in prison. He sued them for some 150,000 livres for cash and jewellery stolen from it through their negligence, and a further 50,000 livres in compensation for ill-treatment. Unfortunately, as he acknowledged in his notebook, all his possessions had been recovered without loss, and he had on numerous occasions declared that he had been very satisfied with the way he had been treated in prison. He did not win his case.

In London he made an attempt to renew his miracle-doctoring, but somehow the locals proved less susceptible to his cures. He tried to get in touch with his former students of the occult, and picked up the threads of his Freemasonry, but the sensible English simply made fun of the absurd, exaggerated gestures of the Italian.

And then to top it all he made a formidable enemy, in the person of Théveneau de Morande. Morande was a member of the lowest underworld of French journalists and pamphleteers based in London. But by this time he was no longer producing pamphlets. He had no need to—the poacher had turned gamekeeper. The well-paid spy of the French King, he edited the *Courrier de l'Europe*, a French-language paper printed in London as a source of information for the French government about British public opinion.

Cagliostro became Théveneau's favourite theme. He could attack whoever he chose and the French government loved it: it is quite possible that his attempt to discredit Cagliostro was carried out on instructions from Paris. The journalist brought a detective-like zeal and thoroughness to his inquiry into Cagliostro's former doings, especially those in London, and including his disgraceful little court cases. No detail was spared. Amongst other things, scorn was poured on his claim that his relations the Arab sheikhs controlled the numbers of marauding lions and tigers by raising pigs on fodder laced with arsenic (the gradually increased doses would permeate their flesh without harming them, but would be strong enough to kill any wild animal that devoured them).

Cagliostro replied to all this with rather surprising wit. He disdainfully (and wisely) ignored references to his minor, more squalid, misdemeanours, and wrote instead that he had so much enjoyed M de Morande's French style that he would like to meet him personally, and to that end was inviting him to breakfast on 9th November. He would like Monsieur the editor to bring the wine and other provisions, while he, Cagliostro, would provide the meat, a suckling piglet he had reared according to his method. Morande would be entrusted with killing and preparing the pig and would be free to eat whichever part he found most to his taste. "The next day four things would be possible. Either both of us would be dead, or neither of us; or I would be dead and not you; or you would be dead but not I. The first three results would be a win for you, the fourth a win for me. But I will lay 5,000 guineas that you would be dead the next day and I would be hale and hearty."

Morande backed away from this. For all he knew, he said to himself, Cagliostro might be right. With typical eighteenth-century credulity, he considered that such a wily (and fat!) rascal might well be immune to poison. So he suggested that perhaps either a dog or a cat should try the pig instead of himself. To that Cagliostro replied with biting scorn:

297

"You propose that a meat-eating animal should stand in for you at the breakfast. It would certainly represent you well. What other carnivore so aptly reflects what you are among men?"

To his shame, Théveneau de Morande withdrew, but Cagliostro's victory was a Pyrrhic one. As a result of what they had learnt during the dispute, his followers mobbed him and tried to strangle him. He rapidly decided to leave London. He went off with his wife's diamonds, leaving her behind without a penny. In revenge she spread it abroad that Théveneau de Morande had been right on all counts.

Once again Cagliostro travelled around Europe, but this was a very different journey from the one he had made in his heyday. Everywhere his infamy went before him, and poverty was his constant companion. He was driven out of Switzerland; then the Austrians expelled him from Trient, where he had met a well-disposed archbishop who in time might well have become a second Rohan to him.

Meanwhile his wife joined him. The lovely Lorenza was now desperately homesick. After so many years of restless wandering she longed to be back with her family in Rome, where she dreamt of a quiet, simple married life. Perhaps she hoped that one day Cagliostro would become a respectable citizen, give up his visionary dreams and perhaps even get himself a job. Her weary, ageing, persecuted husband finally gave in to her wishes—gave in, and stepped into the jaws of the wolf.

Cagliostro, it seems, if only from force of habit, made contact with the local Freemasons. Even here, at the very heart of the hostile city, they maintained a presence. Their number was small, but even so they had to take their vow of secrecy most seriously, for fear of falling into the hands of the Holy Inquisition.

But in fact the Inquisition had been following the noble traveller's every step, and in 1789, once they had gathered enough evidence against him, he was arrested and locked up in the Castel Sant'Angelo—compared to which the Bastille was a seaside resort.

The Inquisitors were delighted to have caught such a well-known Freemason because they intended to make an example of him. Moreover, they had acquired an undue sense of his importance as the result of his ceaseless bragging. He had written to his friends abroad urging them that if he were ever arrested they should engage in a world-wide action of Freemasons to besiege the Castel Sant'Angelo. The Inquisition believed that this amounted to a serious plot.

He made regular appearances before their court, but to the very end he hoped they would release him. He did not think of himself as a great criminal. He had always spoken of God and encouraged religious feelings among his followers. Though he seems to have been well versed in theology, he entirely failed to understand the hair-raising nature of the heresy he was proclaiming.

So at first he took it all quite calmly, full of good faith that there was no truer son of the Church than himself. He even asked if he might have a personal word with the Pope to persuade him of this. It still took him a while to see that his teachings were heretical. At that point he declared that he was fully repentant, he would return to the true faith, and when they freed him he would convert a million adherents of the Egyptian Rite as a favour to the Church.

The court's main interest lay in whether or not, in the course of his occult practices, he had ever had dealings with Satan. It was just his fate that at this point his 'baby angel', the ever-unreliable Lorenza, who could never grasp the importance of anything, betrayed him in a momentary fit of exasperation. She told them that most of the time the mediums had been told what to say in answer to his questions; however, on more than one occasion, Satan had indeed appeared.

Sentence was finally passed in April 1791. The court stopped short of handing him over to the secular arm, which would have meant the death penalty, but as a dangerous heretic and Satanist he was given life imprisonment.

It was probably only at this point that it began to dawn on him that everything was lost. The gates of the world had finally closed against him, and he would remain a miserable inmate of the Castel Sant'Angelo until his death—he who had always lived amid uproar and popular acclaim, in exhilarating escapades and the theatrical limelight, with the added perpetual frisson of proximity to the supernatural. He was still only forty-five.

No portrait of a true adventurer would be complete without mention of a daring attempt to escape. Cagliostro told the prison governor that he wanted to confess his sins and show proper remorse. A Capuchin monk was sent to him, delighted to think he would be receiving the sincere repentance of a famous heretic. In his confession Cagliostro went so far as to invite the monk to join in his flagellation. The Capuchin agreed to the request, unbuckled his waist-cord and struck him a few blows across the shoulder. Then Cagliostro suddenly wrenched the cord from his hands, pulled it round his neck and began to strangle him. But fate had decreed that this monk was not the senile, gaunt ascetic he had been banking on but a strapping son of the peasantry, who threw the flabby magician off and summoned help. The plan went up in smoke.

One night, not long afterwards, the Papal authorities took him to a faraway fortress somewhere behind God's back in the Duchy of Urbino. Here his path reached its eternal end. He is thought to have died some time in 1795.

We must not forget Count Haga. He may not be central to our story, but it is instructive to note how everything went so well for this for this relaxed and easy-going monarch, while for Louis XVI it all went so wrong. Slowly but steadily he dismantled all the remaining constitutional power of the nobility, established a flourishing royal dictatorship with the support of the Third Estate, and forced the privileged classes completely into the background. Meanwhile his country prospered. He fought heroically against Russian numerical superiority before signing the Treaty of Värälä in 1790, none of whose terms was humiliating to Sweden, and a year later concluded a pact with Catherine the Great. The Tsarina guaranteed him 300,000 roubles annually, which he now thoroughly needed, having lost his French subsidy with the Revolution. On 16th March 1792 he fell victim to a conspiracy of nobles: a Captain Anckarström shot him from behind, at a masked ball. Where else should a great rococo prince have died?

And now only one of the actors remains, the non-human, demonic principal, the necklace itself. Or rather, not the actual necklace but its ghost, the debt that lingered after it.

The ever-gallant Cardinal fully intended to reimburse the jewellers, despite the fact that they had lied in their evidence against him during the trial. He offered them the annual revenue of 200,000 livres from his richest diocese, St Vaast, to pay off the debt by instalments. They rejected this, because if he died early the money would remain forever unpaid. They consented only when the King decreed that the revenues from St Vaast would continue to go to them even after his death until the cost of the necklace had been fully met.

But then the Revolution intervened, and the assets and revenues of the diocese were confiscated. Boehmer turned to the National Assembly and claimed payment from the Treasury. The Treasury did not pay. The huge social changes taking place had left the two men bankrupt; Boehmer died, and his wife married his business partner, Bassenge. But the suit continued.

In 1860 the heirs of a M Deville, one of the creditors of the Boehmer estate, sued Prince Rohan-Rochefort, a successor to the Rohan heirs, for the sum of two million francs, including interest. In 1863 the Civil Court gave its judgment, rejecting the claim. In 1864 the Imperial Curia ratified the decision, and subsequently turned down an appeal made in 1867. With that the trial came to an end.

But to this day the necklace has not been paid for.

Antal Szerb's English readers might be surprised that a writer they know only as a novelist should, at the height of his powers, have turned his attention to history. They might equally feel that not all the explanations he offers for this change of direction tell the full story. When he informs us that "since the age of four, whether you believe this or not, dear reader, his single greatest interest has been in history", we must believe him, and the remark certainly rings true when placed against certain passages in Journey by Moonlight. But such enthusiasms rarely lead to full scholarly studies on this scale. There must be more to it than this.

In his foreword he offers other suggestions. First, he ascribes the shift to "the times we live in", and this does seem to make sense, those times being 1941-42, when history, in a rather more pressing form, had begun to show an interest in him, or rather, in his once-irrelevant Jewish descent. So when he adds that the first duty of any historian is to describe the past of his own country, it would seem reasonable to expect a book about wartime, oppression, or indeed the Hungarian past. Ah, but you see, he continues, there are two periods—the Italian Renaissance and the French Revolution—that were so seminal they can be thought of as part of the common European inheritance; the latter of course being the more pertinent to his own times. True again. But perhaps more telling is the subsequent remark that, with the world closing in on him, the past had become, as he puts it, "my home, or rather my country of refuge".

The significance of all this becomes clear if for the Italian Renaissance we read high European civilisation, and for France the birth of human freedom. By 1941 both were staring into the abyss. To go on writing this book amidst the degradation all around him was—as it had been with the defiantly insouciant novel (*Oliver VII*) he had just finished—to make a very clear statement—a celebration of those values that mattered to him most. And with his own identity as a Hungarian, and indeed as a human being, under attack, it was also an affirmation of his deepest sense of himself.

This might also explain why he poured into it not only the vast mass of material he had gathered over the years, in the great libraries of Paris "now closed to me for the indeterminate future", but also the full range of his literary experience—as poet, essayist, reviewer, literary historian and novelist. That experience was central to his sense of who he was, and was determined to remain. The resulting many-sidedness makes it a highly personal document, and is the source of its great strength and charm.

For some readers, however, that might also make a problem. Serious historical arguments, based on political, social, constitutional and economic data, are not usually presented in such an apparently freewheeling manner, with the lightness and gaiety, the irrepressible playfulness, that characterise this book. Could anyone having so much fun really be serious?

The objection was a familiar one. It had been applied to his work many times before, not least to his (still used, and still highly regarded) histories of Hungarian and World Literature; and he deals with it directly:

"People in this country expect scholarly works to be un-readable; from which they are led, quite logically, to the erroneous conclusion that anything that is readable cannot therefore be scholarly. A great many critics have reproved the relaxed, often slightly mocking, tone of my books, insisting that I cannot possibly respect literature if I talk about it in such a cheerfully familiar way." But he remains unrepentant. His way is "to speak as one human being to another, looking to find kindred spirits and good company".

His notion of 'good company' means treating the reader like an old friend, a congenial companion with whom he is sharing a relaxed conversation, without the slightest pressure in the world. Thus he defers the decisive 'action' to Chapter Five, turns aside for two further chapters, revisits it briefly, then regales us with an *Intermezzo* that sets off in the general direction of Sweden before returning, very gently, by way of a great many other curiosities. Topics covered elsewhere in the writing include a history of the changing fashions in clothing, manners, music, theatre and landscape gardening. These 'digressions' occupy a significant part of the book.

Naturally, they draw directly on Szerb's experience as an essayist, cultural critic and literary historian. But the fiction has also left its mark. Despite his claim that the work "eschews every kind of novelistic embellishment and amplification", once he warms to his theme old habits get the better of him, and the result is some of the finest and most memorable writing of all. The ever-shifting, ever-mimetic and playfully ironic style gives the character portraits an intense immediacy, while leaving us in no doubt about what the author really thinks.

Szerb's hallmark as a novelist was the manner he described as 'neo-frivolous'—the insistence on exploring the weightiest of themes through the slightest of materials: for example his use, in *The Pendragon Legend*, of multiple parodies of English minor fiction of the 1930s to explore the nature of the self. This deceptive frivolity is nowhere more in evidence in *The Queen's Necklace* than in that constant flow of amusing and apparently inconsequential diversions. Analytic historian turns cicerone, becomes a wonderfully informed guide, philosopher and friend as he shows us round the age. It is one that, for all its problems, he knows intimately, and loves.

But these digressions always serve a purpose. On the simplest level, they flesh out the broader picture he is painting of the period, including the mood and atmosphere of the time, and the attitudes of the various social groups he is interested in.

And they are more than mere background. They gather up, not quite 'causes', but a whole range of contributing elements, small tributaries of the gathering river of political revolution. Such matters as taste in the fine and applied arts are not incidental but expressive of underlying truths about any age, and few historians would nowadays contest that. But even the lesser titbits and jollier asides play their part in illustrating, or widening, some specific argument. A simple example is the bizarre anecdote about the rich man's son who offers purifying incense to those visiting his father's house, which looks like a mere squib until the writer locks it into his thesis about the bad conscience of the ruling classes and its role in the catastrophe.

The catastrophe itself, however, remains forever just around the corner, and that stopping point is another clue to his purposes. While his narrative necessarily glances back to the reign of Louis XIV, when so many of the moods and mechanisms leading to revolution were unwittingly put in place, the forward gaze is halted three years before the event itself. Unlike most accounts of this period, we get no demagoguery, no Robespierre, no tumbrils, no guillotine. The reader, he tells us, already knows about all that.

Such an attitude might also reflect a sensitive person's unwillingness to face up to the savagery, the gratuitous cruelty and carnage that ensued—especially as these had so dramatically resurfaced in the immediate world around him. On the other hand, what Szerb does give us spares us none of the greed, folly, cynicism and selfishness that mark every human age. But in the end, they too are not his final concern. There are dimensions of experience that interest him beyond the world of politics and the mechanics of social change.

And so we get the Epilogue, with its quite unexpected stress on what Talleyrand called "the sweetness of life". "The reader might well be left with the impression that the final hours of the Ancien Régime were care-worn and oppressive, a 'moral wasteland', a time of drought before the storm, and he would perhaps be glad not to have lived then. Which would be quite wrong. To have been alive then must have been to experience one of the most delightful of European centuries."

There follows yet another 'digression', about the (then as now) somewhat unfashionable paintings of Watteau and Fragonard, and it too confirms, if we ever doubted it, what an intensely personal document the book is; what a naked expression of the writer's own mind and sensibility. We are back in Mihály's world of *Journey by Moonlight*.

> *With a kind of dreamlike intensity, (these) works conjure up in our souls the eternal myth of the great woodlands: mighty trees, tiny human and animal figures; the trees bent in sorrow, the men and women depicted beneath them existing in a kind of superhuman joy that almost succeeds in making their baby faces seem serious: a joy that, like music, is almost painful ... The viewer is filled with a rich, complex yearning, an intense desire to know their secret, their unspoken mystery, a desire to return to the woodland world that is sweeter than anything in this life; and finally, the desire for something—one knows not what—that great and inexpressible nostalgia which truly creative art awakens in the soul.*

At which point the real Antal Szerb steps forward.

> *And then it begins to dawn on one: this age was as beautiful as the most finely worked lace; as a piece of Sèvres porcelain with its timeless charm and fragile delicacy; as the noble oozings of the Tokai grape, full and rich with sweetness; as the autumn air in Hungary, when the reddening leaves are scented with the inexpressible sweetness of death.*

The Queen's Necklace bristles with such unexpected moments. Its blend of the orthodox and the eccentric, the objective and the intensely personal, the formal and the seemingly irresponsible, results in a work that, he concedes, 'is somewhat experimental, and I am naturally curious to see how it will be received by the public'. Its immediate reception took the form of an instant and total ban; but with time, and in spite of its disconcerting charm and readableness, it has come to take its place in his native Hungary along with his great scholarly works, the histories of Hungarian and World Literature. One can only hope that in the anglophone world, where Szerb is known only as a novelist, albeit a fine and subtle one, it will both broaden and deepen our understanding of this highly original writer.

LEN RIX 2009

Other Antal Szerb titles published by

PUSHKIN PRESS

Journey by Moonlight
Translated by Len Rix

The Pendragon Legend
Translated by Len Rix

Oliver VII
Translated by Len Rix

"*The Queen's Necklace* is a wonderful book, both
thoughtful and blasting, and another revelation of
Szerb's light-footed erudition."
Ali Smith

"Szerb belongs with the master novelists of the
twentieth century."
Paul Bailey *The Independent*

"Szerb is a master novelist, a comedian whose
powers transcend time and language, and a playful,
sophisticated intellect."
Nicholas Lezard *The Guardian*

www.pushkinpress.com